"Weaves ... a breathless ... and delightful voices, and she's developed considerable skill at blending the gritty and the supernatural."
—*Publishers Weekly* (starred review)

"A thrilling and darkly erotic tale of betrayal, passion and redemption that will ensnare the senses with lush prose and a deadly vision of the Fae that conjures fairy tales of old."
—Caitlin Kittredge, bestselling author of *The Mirrored Shard*

"A mind-bending blast into a darkness that enfolds and ensnares you from the first page . . . Pure magic from the word go."
—*Bitten by Books*

"Steamy urban fantasy . . . Magical [and] fast-paced."
—*RT Book Reviews*

"Hayes's debut and series opener exemplifies erotic urban fantasy at its most visceral, illuminating the splendor and squalor of life on the edge. Fans of Laurell K. Hamilton's Merry Gentry novels and Caitlin Kittredge's Nocturne City books will enjoy this tale of sex, violence and the supernatural."
—*Library Journal*

"Readers will thoroughly enjoy this entertaining tale of forbidden love. Erica Hayes has a great future ahead of her as a bestselling author."
—*Genre Go Round Reviews*

"Hot, spicy and well-rounded . . . Awesome . . . I'm waiting for the next round!"
—*Tynga's Reviews*

"Fast-paced . . . and smoothly written, with plenty of action, danger and conflict. Hayes continues to seduce me with her addicting, dark and cruel erotic urban fantasy that appeals to the darker side of our nature."
—*Smexy Books*

PRAISE FOR THE NOVELS OF

ERICA HAYES

rich, sensual imagery and dark eroticism into
thriller plot . . . Hayes's characters have distinc-
ful voices . . .

Berkley Sensation titles by Erica Hayes

REVELATION
REDEMPTION

REDEMPTION

A NOVEL OF THE SEVEN SIGNS

ERICA HAYES

BERKLEY SENSATION, NEW YORK

THE BERKLEY PUBLISHING GROUP
Published by the Penguin Group
Penguin Group (USA) Inc.
375 Hudson Street, New York, New York 10014, USA

USA / Canada / UK / Ireland / Australia / New Zealand / India / South Africa / China

Penguin Books Ltd., Registered Offices: 80 Strand, London WC2R 0RL, England
For more information about the Penguin Group visit penguin.com

REDEMPTION

A Berkley Sensation Book / published by arrangement with the author

Copyright © 2013 by Erica Hayes.
All rights reserved. No part of this book may be reproduced, scanned, or distributed in any
printed or electronic form without permission. Please do not participate in or encourage piracy
of copyrighted materials in violation of the author's rights. Purchase only authorized editions.

Berkley Sensation Books are published by The Berkley Publishing Group.
BERKLEY SENSATION® is a registered trademark of Penguin Group (USA) Inc.
The "B" design is a trademark of Penguin Group (USA) Inc.

For information, address: The Berkley Publishing Group,
a division of Penguin Group (USA) Inc.,
375 Hudson Street, New York, New York 10014.

ISBN: 978-0-425-25838-5

PUBLISHING HISTORY
Berkley Sensation mass-market paperback edition / March 2013

PRINTED IN THE UNITED STATES OF AMERICA

10 9 8 7 6 5 4 3 2 1

Cover art by Kris Keller.
Cover design by Rita Frangie.
Interior text design by Kristin del Rosario.

This is a work of fiction. Names, characters, places, and incidents either are the product
of the author's imagination or are used fictitiously, and any resemblance to actual persons,
living or dead, business establishments, events, or locales is entirely coincidental.
The publisher does not have any control over and does not assume any responsibility for
author or third-party websites or their content.

If you purchased this book without a cover, you should be aware that this book is
stolen property. It was reported as "unsold and destroyed" to the publisher, and neither
the author nor the publisher has received any payment for this "stripped book."

EARNING   PEARSON

CHAPTER 1

And the third angel poured out his vial upon the rivers
and fountains of waters; and they became blood . . .

—REVELATION 16:4

Japheth gazed into the hot moonlit sky, and prayed. *Lord, let
me kill every last vampire in Babylon.*

Starting with this lot.

Six of them, soaked in blood, creeping from steamy shadows. Streetlamps flickered, burning their crazed eyes crimson.
One had dreadlocks. Another wore a cheap suit. One had
pink-dyed hair and pierced eyebrows. They snarled with long
sickle teeth, and clawed the air with bitten hands.

"Charming." Dashiel flashed his blue-flaming sword, two-
handed, and flared his dark wings for balance. His silver
armor glowed, angry. "It's *Night of the Living Junkies*. Did
you bring popcorn?"

"If they kill us, we'll be just as dead." Japheth's golden
feathers prickled, a warrior's instinct. His spell-sharpened
gaze snapped left and right, his senses itching for scents, alive
for the tiniest rustle. Distances, heights, relative strength. Tra-
jectory plotted, bing-badda-boom.

Killing demonspawn was what he was made for. And every
dead vampire took him one step closer to heaven.

He conjured his sword and dived full length. The sky-lit
blade burned cold in his hand. The creatures spat hell-stung

curses, slashing at him with ragged nails. Japheth somersaulted over them, a flurry of gold. *Snick!* A head flew, spraying crimson. *Splat!* Another. He sprang a backflip, slicing a third creature apart at the waist.

He landed with a crunch on the bloody sidewalk and surveyed the carnage. Dashiel had already head-sliced two more. Their corpses leaked red puddles on the concrete. The last vampire screeched, insane with hunger, and hurtled for Japheth's throat.

Its teeth scraped his shoulder. Its breath stank of dead flesh. Japheth ignored the sting, the burning hellcurse. He flashed his sword away, grabbed the creature's neck in both hands, and twisted.

Snap! Its head flopped. He tossed the corpse aside, and sizzled the blood from his breastplate with a hissing heavenspell. "Four for me, two for you. Getting slow, old man?"

"Bite me, baby face." Dashiel vanished his sword, a blue flash, and wiped blood from his eyes. "Jesus. Last month shambling corpses, this month hungry metrosexuals with bad teeth. What gives?"

"You know what." Japheth flexed scorched palms. Already the wounds were healing. Angelflesh on demon always burned. He didn't mind the pain. It meant he was doing heaven's work.

And since he'd been Tainted—since Michael tore his soul from his body and banished him to this dirty, decadent earth, neither damned nor saved—he couldn't afford to sin. Not if he ever wanted back into heaven.

"You really think these blood-munching idiots are another vial?" Dashiel laughed. "Isn't it meant to be rivers of blood this time? These days everything's a fucking sign. The wind blows the wrong way across Times Square and suddenly it's the end of the world—"

" *'They have shed the blood of saints and prophets, so you have given them blood to drink, for they deserve it,' "* quoted Japheth ironically. "It's in the Book, right next to the rivers of blood. You really should read more, Dash. It's kind of important."

"I must be the prophet, then." Dash grinned. "Because sure as hell's a shithole, I ain't no saint."

"Isn't that the truth." Japheth hoisted a severed head to the light. Even dead, the thing's hair sizzled in his fist. The corrupted stink assaulted him, that unmistakable mix of charcoal, rotting meat and shit. Moonlight glinted a gleeful hellcurse in its empty eyes. *Give me your soul, angel,* it seemed to cackle silently. *Die screaming. The world's ours now.*

Not on my watch, scumbreath. He poked a stinging finger into its mouth. Its jaw gaped, blood and broken teeth. Sure was crowded in there. Curved canines and incisors, unnaturally long, with sharp serrated points. This thing wasn't human, not anymore. "Look, it's a new variant. Three rows of teeth. Brutal."

Dash peered closer, wrinkling his nose. "Okay, that's ugly. The curse must be mutating. Spreading, too. There's more of 'em every week. Slimy shitballs are crawling from here to SoHo."

Japheth tossed the reeking head away. "Well, whatever it is, we can still kill 'em. I call that good news."

"You've got a one-track sense of fun, you know that?"

Japheth grinned, feral. "Whatever gets you through the night."

"Bloodthirsty bastard." Dashiel cracked his neck bones, tense, and flexed his glittery brown wings. "Fucking hellspawn. There goes my quiet evening."

Japheth could hear Dash's heartbeat, strong and swift, sparkling with heaven's glory. Dash had issues with glory. Until he did something about it—likely, he'd find some willing woman and take it out on her—he'd have sweet-fire poison pumping in his veins, a raging headache, the hard-on from hell.

Japheth preferred to fight himself into exhaustion. It was safer that way . . . but he suppressed a dark twinge of envy. "Yeah, right. When's the last time you spent the night alone?"

"When's the last time you didn't?"

Japheth smiled brightly. "Screw you."

"Tricky, with the size of the stick up your ass."

"Yet somehow you manage." Japheth wiggled his little finger, smirking.

Dash snorted, shaking his dark head. "You know, I get your whole sinless, warrior-for-god, let-me-back-into-heaven kick? But it wouldn't kill you to relax once in a while."

"You sure about that?" Lust was a sin, even for a Tainted angel. He'd never win redemption that way. And besides, all that meaningless carnal pleasure was . . . sordid. Self-indulgent. His heart wasn't in it. He had better outlets for heaven's holy wrath than getting hot and breathless with a beautiful stranger.

Like slaughtering hellspawn. Killing was a sin, too. That was in the Book. But not when the monsters had already sold their souls to hell. That was mercy, or heaven-sweet vengeance. Either way, it was good.

He flexed fervent wings. He didn't want to talk, or play heartless sex games. He just wanted to coat himself with demon-cursed blood, score a few more dead hellspawn for heaven. "Relax, yes. Sludge my wits with some dirty crap cooked up in a toilet bowl in Queens, and make a slut of myself with some woman I don't care about? I'll skip it, if it's all the same to you."

"Who said anything about sluts?" said Dash innocently. "Chicks dig that silent-warrior vibe of yours. Lots of them are perfectly nice girls—"

"Which is why they're better off never knowing me."

Dash tilted his gaze skywards. "He's a killer, not a lover. I'm sorry, did I miss the chapter where it says 'thou shalt be a frosty-assed son of a bitch'?"

"Yeah. It's right under the part where it says 'go forth and screw yourself into damnation.' I think you stopped there."

"Okay, fine, I give up," Dash grumbled. "Your loss." He rolled tight shoulders, and the golden snakecharm around his neck glinted in evil red moonlight. "This vampire thing is getting worse. I'll run it by Mike, see what he wants to do."

Japheth sweated, like he always did when he thought of Michael, who alone had the power to return him to heaven.

Once, he and the icy archangel had been close. Now? Not so much. "Because that worked so well last time," he replied tightly. "We barely got out of the first two signs alive."

Dash shrugged. "Above my pay scale, brother. Stopping this Apocalypse is Mike's circus. Let him be ringmaster."

"You're gonna trust him? After he ordered me to kill you?" Sometimes, Michael tested him, to see how far he'd fallen. He still remembered how close he'd come, the fire licking his blade, the horrid compulsion to kill racing in his blood . . .

"Still alive, ain't I?" Dash waved a careless hand. "Spit it or swallow it, Mike still owns our soulless asses. Does it piss me off? Every damn day. But what am I gonna do, get another job? Oh, wait, opportunities in the private sector for 'kick-ass angel of death with no soul' seem to have dried right up." He dragged his long dark hair from its curled iron clip and refastened it. "So screw it," he announced happily. "Let's get drunk. You coming, or is that a daft question?"

"To a bar, with you and your hard-on? Let me think."

"Suit yourself." Dash clapped him on the shoulder, a gesture that never failed to irritate. "Happy killing. Watch out for the Angel Slayer."

Some jerk-off in the West Village was killing angels. Almost a dozen in the past few weeks. Stabbing them through the heart with a demonblade and pissing off into the night like a mincing coward.

Hungry lightning crackled around Japheth's sword grip. Bring it on. Just let the bastard try it. "Yeah. Right. The Angel Slayer better watch out for me."

"Atta boy." Dash winked, and flashed out.

Alone in the moonlight, Japheth ruffled clotted golden feathers. Thick summer heat slicked his skin. Flames flickered in an upstairs window. Shadows leapt. Smoke curled, gritty in his mouth. Gunfire cracked, and in the distance, a woman screamed.

He whispered an ancient prayer, and glory sparkled into his blood like frosty flame. His breath quickened as the rush hit him hard. His eyes watered. His muscles tightened, shuddered. Yeah. Pleasure, hunger, sweet desire—it was no contest.

His heavenly gifts hadn't been taken from him, not in all these long years of being Tainted. But he knew the glory could desert him at any moment.

Better use it while it lasts.

He crouched, one hand braced on the pavement. His nerves glittered on a fighting edge, his senses razor sharp. No time to lose. Somewhere, demons plotted destruction. The Angel Slayer lurked in shadow. The street still reeked of hell-cursed vampire blood.

And Japheth of the Tainted was just in the mood for more.

CHAPTER 2

"Don't squeal, godscum. Just die."

Rose Harley twisted her demon-spelled knife deeper into the angel's heart. Blood gushed, and her skin blistered with holy wrath.

How she loathed the self-righteous stench of heaven.

She drove the knife in harder. Angry red hellsparks crackled from her blade. The angel choked, his eyes blank, and stopped thrashing. Blood soaked his jeans, his shirt, his prissy white feathers.

Dead. Skewered on demonsteel. Meat for the rats.

Rose ripped her knife free, sick but satisfied. Just as her demon master ordered. This was the fourth angel she'd lured to his end this week. They were easy targets. Stupid things weren't even smart enough to come to the Village in full armor.

Killing them wasn't a nice job. But when you were a demon's slave, you did as you were told.

The angel's corpse slumped to the pavement, face-first, a pile of limbs and stained feathers. At the smell of his cooling flesh, Rose's guts rumbled. Her fangs pressed at her lips, demanding that she feed. But angels' blood was poison to a vampire. She'd have to wait.

She yanked a bloodstained white feather from his wing and stuck it into her braid with the others. Her hair singed in protest, but only weakly. The dead angel's glory was already fading. Idiot flyboys. Always so superior, with their false tales of salvation.

Oh, their God was real, all right. That wasn't the issue. It was the *love* and *forgiveness* part she had a problem with. She'd seen precious little of those, and now, apparently, God was flushing the world down the john like an unwanted stash, and everyone who wasn't in his club was going to hell. The Apocalypse was happening. The End was now. It was too damn late to be saved.

So much for love and forgiveness. Rose slipped her knife away in its thigh holster and stalked away into the dark.

In her vampire night sight, the street glittered like it was encrusted with evil rubies. Dark doorways jewel-edged, barred windows glinting, neon signs flashing broken. A damp fragrant vine brushed her face as she turned the corner. Deserted, shadows dancing like ghosts. Firelight flickered, crackling an eerie melody, and heat hung thick and gritty. Like half of the West Village, the place was burning.

Her sturdy boot heels clunked on the broken sidewalk. She didn't bother to mask the sound. Sure, she was being hunted. She'd refused allegiance to the West Village vampire coven master—what a whackjob he was, with his barbed-wire piercings and sadistic pleasure games. His bloodthirsty ways made her retch, and saying *no* to him had made her fair game for his most devoted minions.

So yeah, Rose was a wanted woman among the creatures of darkness. But the night was hers, too, humming in her blood, licking her muscles to tingling strength.

Bad luck for any dumb-ass vampire who tried to jump her.

She wiped bloody hands on her jeans, wincing as the burns on her palms scraped raw. Angel on demonspawn always burned. No matter. It'd heal overnight, slowly but still faster than a human. There were a few upsides, if you could call them that, to being tricked into servitude by a demon. Hell possessed vast power, and now it was at her fingertips. All she had to do was surrender to the dark.

She flexed her strong thighs. All those hard years of dance rehearsal—in her previous life, and how long ago that seemed—had made her flexible, agile, stronger than she looked. Now, she was lethal. She was Chosen, the first rank of vampires, made not by fleeting infection from another vampire, but by the demon Prince of Thirst himself.

She was condemned forever. One step from hell. But sometimes, it felt damn good to be powerful.

The hour was growing late. Time to find a place to hole up. Again her belly growled, an unwelcome reminder of what she needed. Demon-haunted moonlight cast reddish shadows across silent brick apartments. Smoke drifted, the crackle of flames from an upstairs window. A cat scampered across her path, twitching its black tail.

She searched the sky warily for dawn's pale tinge. Nothing yet. Sunlight didn't burn her, or any Count Dracula shit like that. But it itched, deep inside where the demon's curse coiled and muttered like a hungry slug. Morning would sting her eyes, make her achy and weak, like a flu. And it'd only get worse, each day she lived with the curse.

She used to love the sunrise. Now, it just made her cringe and hide. One more thing lost, among so many . . .

On Greenwich Avenue, lamps cast bright halos over empty shops and cafés. Village Square lay deserted, eerie, lit orange by a burning pile of garbage. She crossed over to Ninth Street. No sensible human walked abroad at night in the West Village, not since the vampires moved in. But the neighborhood rustled and murmured, unseen, every sound distinct in Rose's preternatural ears. Late-night traffic from Sixth Avenue, thumping car stereos, a siren's distant wail. Whispers from locked apartments, sobbing, sighs of despair or pleasure. Stinging sweat, pain's bright static, the hot poison tang of a kiss.

Terrifying, when she'd first been made, the cacophony of human existence. Now, her rich senses exhilarated her. Was it wrong, to enjoy that part of it, when so much else about her vampire life was revolting?

Sweat trickled in her hair, and she swiped it away. Sultry summer closed in around her, the sickly stench of blood and angel sweat still strong . . . and her stomach still grumbled, demanding. Speaking of revolting . . . she needed to feed.

Her throat tightened, reluctant. Killing angels was one thing, those princes of bullshit and false promises. They deserved it. Once, she'd thought it possible that their God cared about her. Now, she knew it was just another lie.

But feeding on people was another thing entirely. She'd have to crunch her jagged teeth on flesh, feel that awful liquid fire splashing into her mouth, down her throat, the horrid salty tang of human terror . . .

She shivered. The first time she'd fed, weeks ago, she'd choked it right back up, disgusted. She was clumsy, newly made, and the guy had died, of course, just a skinny kid wearing eyeliner and bruises, desperate for cash. He hadn't deserved the dumb, lonely death of prey . . .

But it wasn't the boy's tears that sickened her the most. Not even her guilty flush of excitement.

It was the banality. So easy, to drain his life away. Such a stupid, fleeting gift. Fire had thundered in her veins, triumph, exultation. Her first kill.

Actually, no. Her second . . .

Horrible images raped her, stark and flash-lit like a crime-scene tableaux. The night she was made, a ravenous fever-drenched nightmare. Twisted wet sheets on the bed, a gore-streaked teddy bear, a wet blond hank torn out by the roots . . .

Rose swallowed, sweating. That night, the demon prince's curse had made her a monster. He'd tricked her. She'd discovered his true purpose too late. Surely, that counted for something? She'd screamed aloud to heaven, begging for absolution. Just one mistake. One little mistake, and now Bridie was gone forever. Brown-eyed Bridie, six years old, who liked apple cakes and hide-and-seek. Who called her Auntie Rosie, and had mostly (but not altogether) stopped asking when Mommy was coming home.

But silence had greeted Rose's prayer.

Silence, and dark eternity as a demon's slave. Never be free. Never enjoy the sun. Never sate this terrible thirst . . .

Defiance burned like poison in Rose's hell-cursed heart.

She'd pleaded for forgiveness, and been denied. Praying was useless. There were no second chances. Heaven had abandoned her.

So she'd become the Angel Slayer, her demon master's lethal weapon. The online news feeds followed her exploits with ghoulish fascination. Her tally had reached twelve. She wore the bloodstained feathers in her hair to prove it. And it wasn't like she'd had a choice. Her demon master demanded tribute, and the trail of heavenly bodies amused him. If she killed enough, then maybe he'd let her stay out of hell.

Her own personal, nightmarish hell. Where a little murdered girl lived, full of hatred and black vengeance . . .

Her ears pricked.

Footsteps. Just around the corner. Sure, and almost silent.

She paused, beyond the streetlamp's dim halo. Listened harder. Light breathing, the spritz of male sweat . . . and blood.

Fresh, coppery, delicious, disgusting blood.

Her mouth watered in spite of her reluctance. Prey. A human, abroad late at night in the Village, alone . . .

Then, the dry stink of altar smoke made her gag. Ew. How had she missed it? Feathers zapping electric, bright steel like salt, the ozone tang of heavenspells.

Angel.

But this one smelled different.

She inhaled deeper. Mmm. Sweeter, somehow. Fresher, the reek of heaven worn thin. Almost . . . human.

Her fangs crunched out, famished, and she forced them back in. Drinking angel blood was like swallowing acid. She'd tried it in ignorance, when she first slew an angel, and it blistered her mouth raw. A demon's curse and an angel's glory didn't mix.

But *this* angel's glory sure smelled good.

The footsteps whispered closer. Rose murmured a poisoned wish, and around her, the darkness thickened. Warm magical shadows wrapped her body, caressing her. She crouched, thighs tingling. Two in one night. All the better to please her master. She'd stab this prince of bullshit through his lying heart and watch him die.

And tomorrow, she'd hunt down another. And another. And more, until her demon prince was contented and her thirst for retribution was satisfied—yet she knew with hell-black certainty that no matter how many she killed, it'd never be enough.

Before the curse, like any ignorant beast, she'd pondered the meaning of life. Whether she had a higher purpose. If there really was a God.

Now, she knew.

Her sins would never be forgiven. Her life meant less than nothing. This bleak existence of desolation and disgusting things was no more than she deserved for what she'd done to Bridie. And her purpose was to kill every lying, self-righteous asshole of an angel she could find.

Because God was real, all right. And It loathed her.

Japheth paused, feathers twitching.

There it was again. The faint reek of demon corruption . . . but with the added coppery stench of stale human blood.

Vampires. Maybe the Angel Slayer.

Cold satisfaction tingled his tongue. The shadowy vigilante had killed eleven, that they knew of, and Michael was pissed. Everyone was pissed, even the Tainted Host. Word was, the Slayer must be a higher-level demon, maybe even a new prince.

Japheth blotted sweat from his eyes with one forearm. Demon, hell. Sure, the Slayer was inhumanly strong and swift. But it wasn't a demon's style. Demons were like terrorists. They gloated. Wanted everyone to know who was responsible for their dirty deeds. They valued infamy over safety, a twisted breed of courage.

This craven Slayer, now, just stabbed you in the heart and flitted off into the dark. Japheth's mouth soured. A killer with no principles, just random malice. Worse: a coward.

Yeah, the Angel Slayer was definitely on Japheth's list.

But a few more vampires? They'd do sweetly, too.

He inhaled, relishing the power flooding his body. Since he'd been cast to earth, black rage frosted inside him, a monster who hungered to devour every hot, sweet, aching thing it couldn't have . . . and only the blood of the damned could satisfy it.

Only killing hellspawn sprang the glory alive. A hot sweet rush, better than sex or uneasy chemical oblivion. It reminded him there was a heaven, and that one day he'd go back there . . .

Keep it frosty, angel. Michael's advice, from some ancient battlefield before Japheth fell. *Save your hard-on for the enemy. They're sure as shit saving theirs for us.*

But it was more than that. Japheth was Tainted, banished to earth with his soul held to ransom. Just one stumble away from hell. If he screwed up again, he'd never be redeemed.

And unlike Dashiel, Japheth hadn't given up on redemption. To bask in heaven's liquid golden sunlight again, away from the ugly temptation of earthly things . . .

Japheth sniffed, tasting rich summer air. The dirty scent was thickening. Silently, he lighted upwards, and drifted around the corner.

Fragrant leaves brushed his face. Red neon letters crackled, casting a hellish glow. Sweat slicked his golden hair. He floated into the shadows, searching with his magical angel-sight for the telltale auras of living souls . . . and then his nerves wrenched at the sound of a woman sobbing.

There. His sharp gaze pinpointed her. Crouched against the wall, hugging her knees in tight. Bloodstained jeans, tangled dark hair in a braid. He couldn't see her face, but she was long legged, lithe, with a glimpse of smooth skin showing where her t-shirt rode up over her hip.

Japheth stared, his heartbeat quickening. So . . . delicate. Vulnerable. And smeared in blood, both vampire and human. Had she been attacked? Live or die, it was lose-lose. A bloodsucker's bite drove them mad, boiled their minds in screaming nightmares until they starved, or bled to death from self-inflicted wounds . . . or else they mastered the curse, and lived on as vampires.

He should kill her now, while she was still herself.

"Get away!" The woman scrambled back, hugging those long legs tighter in an effort to make herself small. She was sniffling. Trying not to cry.

Japheth bit back a bad word. He'd seen countless humans suffer at demon hands over the centuries. His indignation was blunted, the sorrow dulled. But the idea of some sniggering hellshit wiping its foul sticky fingers on this woman . . . Cold rage made his head ache. He had a job to do. Flash his knife, and slit her pretty throat . . .

The vampire behind him chuckled.

He whirled, and grabbed the slavering monster by the neck.

Crunch! He held the thing at arm's length, fingers digging in. Just a young man, tiny fangs dripping, demon-spelled hunger lighting his eyes.

Close call. He'd lost concentration. Curse her.

The boy squirmed. "Don't kill me, I didn't do nothin' . . ."

Japheth's palm sizzled. He squeezed harder. He didn't mind pain. Pain was manageable. It reminded him what was important. "Tell me something I don't know about the Angel Slayer. You've got five seconds."

"Don't know nothin'!" Blood trickled down the boy's chin. Only a few days made, still mad with thirst. *Three . . . Four . . .*

"I ain't never seen—ugh!"

Five. Japheth flashed his sword left-handed, and stabbed the vampire through the heart. Blue flames exploded, and the body withered to a pile of stinking ash. He vanished the sword, and his burned hand healed with a swift blue sparkle.

He was a man of his word, after all. Lying was a sin. And he didn't remember it written anywhere that a promise to hellspawn didn't count. Since Michael had cast him down—the memory still stung raw, deep in his empty heart—that was the story of his life: *Better safe than screwed.*

Speaking of which . . .

That female still huddled against the wall. He could smell her terror, bitter and sharp like lemon. It bristled his feathers. What was she thinking, hanging around the West Village at night? Everyone knew the vampire coven ruled these streets. And now she was doomed . . .

But his fingers clenched, unwilling to strike. Damnation was a b—well, it was unfair, when it wasn't your fault. When you caught it like a disease. Unlike the Chosen—who'd all submitted gleefully to the demon prince's tricks, how else did you swallow a demon's blood from the source?—she likely didn't deserve the place she was going.

But he didn't know for sure she was infected. And he couldn't just leave her here, covered in blood like shark bait. "I'll take you home," he offered coldly. "It isn't safe here."

She just sobbed, hiding her face.

He crouched, impatient, wings flaring aglow. "Don't be afraid. I won't hurt you . . ."

The woman looked up, and Japheth's voice died, strangled by the sudden hitch in his throat.

Heaven's sweet grace, she was lovely.

He swallowed, painful. Hot dark eyes, bottomless, framed in long curling lashes. Exquisite heart-shaped face, bruised with bloody tears. A pretty dark freckle graced her left cheek. And that mouth . . . he'd be haunted tonight by visions of those full, cherry-ripe lips. He wanted to taste them, drink the soft honeyed heat of her kiss . . .

He coughed. Yeah, well, he wanted a lot of things. Wanting and doing weren't the same. Like he'd remember how to kiss a woman in the first place.

But his skin tingled, hot and glittery, and blood rushed to all the awkward places. He shifted, aching. Lord, he was flushing. She'd see what he was thinking, laugh at him for it. "Umm . . . are you okay? You've got blood . . ."

"Yeah." Low voice, a husky promise of pleasure. She wiped her face, and laughed shakily. "They attacked me, but I ran away . . . God, I'm so embarrassed. I don't usually lose my cool like this. You must think I'm such a flake." She licked her bloody bottom lip, and turned her haunting gaze up to him.

Japheth stared, transfixed. The tip of her soft pink tongue was the most hypnotic thing he'd ever laid eyes on. *Hell, no. Don't go there* . . . but too late. He'd already imagined her warm dark flavor, the softness inside her mouth, that naughty tongue teasing his. Those swelling cherry lips, sliding over his cock, drowning him in her sweet heat . . .

He clenched shaking fists, willing this ugly desire to fade. He didn't know her. She was wounded, bleeding, frightened.

Thinking about . . . those things with her was very uncool.
Heaven, forgive me . . .

She inhaled, and the tiny catch in her breath quivered his
feathers stiff.

And for the first time in centuries, his ice-walled resolve
melted.

In a flash—how did it happen?—he was on his knees. The
wall at her back grazed his palms. Her breasts swelled against
his metal-clad chest. She gasped, rich with excitement, and hot
blood pounded in his head and he wrapped his fingers in that
sinful dark hair and gave himself up to her kiss.

Oh, Lord. She tasted of flames and blood, so good he
groaned. For one precious, shocking moment, her lips molded
to his, delicious, alive . . .

And then his mouth caught fire.

Pain flashed, accusing. Burnt skin soured his tongue. Her
hair sizzled his fingers with telltale wrath. And a hot demon-
spelled blade pressed sweet agony against the thudding pulse
in his throat.

Vampire!

Ash rained like snow, the broken remnants of demon
magic. Too late, hellcurse's foul stink sickened him. He'd been
holding his breath, he realized distantly. Hadn't smelled it.
Too fixated on sinful pleasures to see the evil glimmer in her
eyes. But now, her scent was unmistakable.

No accidental vampire, this scheming seductress. She was
Chosen. Hell's whore. The demon's willing slave.

She laughed, and her sharp fangs crunched out. "Bleeding
Christ. You're all so *stupid*."

Japheth's mind stumbled, dizzy. His heart still pounded,
his blood still screaming with toxic need. Should've known
his irrational lust for her wasn't real. She'd spelled him with
her evil magic, and he'd fallen for it spectacularly.

But that didn't change the ugly truth. The beautiful bitch
was hellspawn. And he'd kissed her.

CHAPTER 3

Rose laughed. The dumb shock in this angel's eyes was better than sex. She could still taste him, coffee and chili and delicious *what-the-fuck-just-happened*? She licked scorched lips. Mmm. So innocent, this golden-winged altar boy.

Different from the others, who'd taken what she offered with furtive delight. Angels had the morals of rats, only worse, because they lied about it. But this one had kissed her wildly, his passion uncontrollable. Almost like he'd never kissed a woman before . . .

Whatever. His innocence only made her revenge on heaven sweeter. Her demon prince would be pleased. She gritted her teeth, and thrust her knife in for the kill.

But her steel met empty air.

He'd already swept up on golden wings. *Shit. Too slow.* She'd gloated too long, and now he'd gotten away.

She sprang to the balls of her feet, brandishing her knife.

The angel crouched, glittering wings backswept. One hand outstretched for balance, the other leveling his sky-fire sword at her. He wore dark leather pants and a silver angel's cuirass that sparked with electric blue rage. Blood spotted his feathers, slicked in his sweaty golden hair. A dark and angry warrior, primed for battle. His gaze stabbed her, poisoned with malice, frigid and greener than hatred.

"Angel Slayer," he hissed. Barely audible, quivering . . . but not the passionate, reckless head rush of thirty seconds ago. Frosty, lethal rage, calculated to the last inch for the kill.

Jesus. Rose thought *she* had issues.

But her pulse raced, lacing her blood with heady fight or flight. She'd lost the surprise advantage that had helped her make her previous kills. And the bastard was strong, agile. Big, too, those glistening muscles packed with power. She'd need all her wiles to win . . .

"Very good," she mocked, circling to get better range. "What's the matter, angel? Can't fight properly with a hard-on?"

"I always fight with a hard-on, whore." An ice-spiked laugh. His accent was elusive, mixed. "Maybe slitting your throat will get me off. Whaddaya say?"

"Have at me, then, sucker, you're cutting into my feeding time—umph!"

Sizzling blue fire scythed past her nose. She swayed, dizzy. She'd ducked his blade by an inch. Fuck, he was fast.

But so was she. She dived into a handspring and rolled to her feet. He was already there and kicked her legs from under her.

Her flesh tingled. Fighting was dancing, but with sharp objects. She whiplashed, and jumped, aiming a backhanded slash at his face. He thrust up a wing to block her strike, and grabbed her wrist, flinging her off her feet.

Her skull cracked on the pavement. Groggy, she fought, but he straddled her, pinning her shoulders with his knees.

Wildly, Rose kicked, but connected only with a cushion of feathers. He slammed her wrist into the concrete. Skin sizzled on bare skin. Her knife dropped from numb fingers, and smoothly he aimed his burning blue sword point at her throat. "Don't talk and fight. It makes you careless."

Fuck! She wanted to scream in frustration. That had been way too easy. She'd been too confident.

He was good, she'd give him that. He was breathing hard, and she couldn't help noticing the bastard filled out his silver chest plate admirably. Blood stained his golden hair, and the big muscles in his arms gleamed with sweat. His shining feathers quivered taut with rage. His thighs strained inches from her nose—strong, hard-packed thighs, not one wasted curve—and as her gaze traveled upwards, treacherous heat rose in her belly. He hadn't been bullshitting about the hard-on. She could smell him, heady, more chili espresso than angelstink, with a musky lash of hot male flesh. An impressive hunk of powerful masculine beauty.

And what a *stupid* fucking thing to be dwelling on, when he was about to send her screaming to hell.

Rose thrashed, and spat curses that blistered his fingers. She threw a spell, hellsmoke stinging, but he deflected it easily now that he was on his guard, and ash exploded, raining harmlessly. His blade singed her neck. Her wrist sizzled where he crushed it. She didn't care. "Spare me your preaching, god-scum. I don't want to be saved."

"Oh, I won't preach to you, bloodsucker." His gaze glittered, icy. Impossibly green, this angel's eyes. "I wouldn't waste my time. You're already damned."

For a moment, she quailed. She didn't want it to be true. She'd made a mistake, let herself be seduced. What happened to Bridie was an accident. She hadn't wanted this stinking, disgusting life. The blood, the slaughter, a demon prince's dirty urges, the endless threat of eternity in hell if she didn't comply . . .

But too late. She'd crossed that bridge. Bridie was dead. No going back.

And this angel's precious heaven didn't care.

"Fine." She tried to cover the crack in her voice with sass. "Then fuck your God, and fuck you." And she spat, right into the angel's face.

It hit his bloodstained cheek, and sizzled to steam, and she waited for the burning thrust of steel into her throat.

But he just stared, his handsome mouth trembling, and in a sweet-smelling blue flash, he vanished.

* * *

Japheth hit the ground in some dirty Babylon alleyway and cursed. Windows shattered, and the evil words carved acid welts into his tongue. He rarely cursed. Bad words were self-indulgent. They lacked restraint.

But . . . *fuck*.

Angry red fireworks burst from his wings. Her scent still sparkled his feathers. Her kiss still burned his mouth with sweet hellflame, the hot delight of her lips parting under his . . .

Moonlight glared in his eyes, accusing. He wanted to howl his frustration to the sky. He slammed his fist into a brick wall, cracking a dozen bones. Pain was good. Pain was penance.

Tonight, it only felt dirty.

He gritted his teeth. Curse that demon's slut. He'd over-powered her no problem. She'd been a fool to take him on, he was half again her size and could fly. He'd every chance to slit the evil seductress's throat, to paint the ground crimson with her blood and send her howling to hell where she belonged.

But he couldn't.

Couldn't ram the blade home.

He yanked his hair, hard enough to bleed. If only he just wanted her.

Oh, yeah, this was way worse than simple lust. No matter that her sultry dark eyes hypnotized him. That he'd not touched a woman like that in centuries, that the lithe play of her athletic body under his made him shudder with poisonous desires long forgotten. If it were just a hard-on, he could atone.

But for a fateful instant, when she lay at his mercy with his sword's edge thirsting for her blood, he'd felt *sorry* for her.

Deep in her bottomless eyes, beneath all the rage and vit-riol, he'd seen guilt. Self-loathing. Bitter longing for for-giveness.

His hand healed, a swift crunch of bones. He wanted to smash it again, punish himself bloody. A demon's wicked slave would never be forgiven. She'd made her choice open-eyed. Too late to pretend she was sorry for it now.

He closed his eyes, and retreated into his icy darkness, let-ting it enfold him, encase his heart like armor, pushing earthly temptations to a safe distance . . . and the glitter in his wings faded. His skin cooled, his heartbeat slowing. Detached, remote. Untouchable.

He opened his eyes. The red-stained moonlight glinted on glass windows, gloated over his skin, like demon voices cackling softly from the darkness . . . but frost settled in his veins, and he flexed cold fingers, satisfied.

Yeah, he'd messed up. No getting out of that. Lust, he could atone for. Pitiful and disgusting, but a simple sin. He'd make penance, maybe stop eating for a few weeks. Work himself to exhaustion on the battlefield, chalk up a few hundred dead vampires for heaven.

But compassion for hellspawn? Holy mother of mercy, he was lucky he hadn't gotten himself killed on the spot . . . and then, he'd *let her go*. The Angel Slayer. And a Chosen. A demon's willing slave . . .

His ringtone shredded his thoughts. He yanked the phone from his pocket, flushing. "Yeah, Dash. What?"

"You still alive? Was expecting you ages ago," Dashiel shouted, whiskey-rough over party noise and vapid electric trance music.

"Very funny. Do I sound like I need to get drunk and laid right now?"

"Sound like you could use both to me."

Japheth sighed. He always walked right into that one. "Yeah, piss off, wiseass."

"Always glad to help. You coming down here or what?"

"So I can watch you pick up girls? What an education."

Dash laughed. "C'mon, man, it's a brave new world since the Apocalypse went public. Chicks dig us. How can I disappoint them?"

"How, indeed," Japheth said sardonically. "I love being famous. Guys picking fights, teenage girls putting my photo on the internet. I'd rather peel my eyeballs with a toothpick."

"Right. You just miss the old days, where they all fainted and groveled."

"Now that you mention it? Yeah." Japheth raked his bloody hair, itching. "What do you want, Dash? You're interrupting my slaying here."

"Ariel's back in town." Dash named another of the Tainted, a bad-ass warrior with a fiery temper to match. "The ugly bastard asked after you, fuck knows why. Maybe he wants to restart your little heaven-screwed-me-and-I'm-pissed-about-it club."

Japheth halted in mid hang up. Ariel had been sent by Michael to hunt for the remaining vials of wrath, hidden away centuries ago by their nameless guardian angels and lost. All very well to slaughter the demon princes once the wrath was already spilled. Better to recover the vials while they were still full, put a stop to the whole demon-cursed business. "Does that mean he found one?"

"You'll have to ask him. Tight-lipped son of a jackal. Hey, you sound a little edgy. Is something going on?"

Japheth gritted his teeth, for once wishing he had a lie handy. Dash was uncanny at seeing through him. "Like what?"

"You tell me. Everything okay?"

Yeah. I just practically raped a hell-cursed vampire bitch. Everything's peachy. "Why wouldn't it be?"

"Hell, I don't know. Because you're not giving me a straight answer?"

"Don't start."

"I'm not starting. Just calling it like I see it." Mercifully, Dash let it go. "So are you coming, or what? The gang's all here."

"With that rotten excuse for music? You're kidding."

"Dude, this is genuine nineties retro. Better than that wailing opera-house crap you listen to. C'mon, just one drink. Ariel's buying."

Japheth sighed. He knew how this would go. The smell of unaccustomed alcohol sickening him, kids offering him drugs, losers picking fights, those gushing social-media girls . . .

But his skin still glittered, his body still warm with shock and ugly desire. Maybe, it'd take his mind off *her.*

He snapped his blood-crusted feathers tight, willing the sparks to fade. "One drink, Dash. Five minutes, no more. And if you spike my tonic water again? I'll kick your brown-feathered ass to purgatory."

"There's no such thing as purgatory, kid. People made that up."

"Don't think that'll stop me."

Rose banged her skull into the broken sidewalk and strangled a scream.

Screw that wiseass angel. He'd provoked her into weakness. Seen the despair flash over her face. And then he'd had the nerve to take *pity* on her.

She leapt up, raking her hair back. Her hell-spelled knife lay in the dust. Red demonflame flickered sullenly over the bronzed blade. She slammed it back into its sheath, so hard it nearly tore the buckles from her thigh.

She'd thought him beautiful. For one hormone-drunk moment, she'd wanted him to touch her in something other than fighting rage.

Sweet Satan, how humiliating.

Frantically, she scrubbed bloodstained hands on her jeans. But his innocent scent lingered, maddening. Why couldn't she get it off? Angels were just monsters in pretty packages. She'd entertained their lies once, and look where it had gotten her. Even her demon prince had the class to admit he was a treacherous asshole when you called him on it. That angel had consigned her to hell—and had the *arrogance* to act like he felt sorry for her.

She kicked the pavement, raising furious dust. This wasn't how it was supposed to work. To be the Angel Slayer—to satisfy her demon master—she had to be sure. Confident she was right. Not flirting on the edge of doubt. *I'm one filthy bloodsucker you'll regret leaving alive, godscum. Because I'm gonna hunt you down . . .*

"Rose."

She whirled, her hand flashing to her knife. Too late, hell's stormy scent curled in her nostrils. Her blood groaned, slithering with shared hunger, and inside her, like a hot slug, the curse stretched and sighed in contentment.

Her demon prince smiled.

Rose cursed under her breath, and forced her hand to relax.

That ethereal whisper, so cold yet warm on her shoulder. Slick rosy lips, dark eyes flashing with unholy fire. Fluvium, Prince of Thirst. Creator and master of the Babylon vampire covens.

And she was totally, helplessly, irrevocably his slave.

Sick fever crawled up her spine. Her voice trembled. "Damn it, Fluvium, you scared the shit out of me. Why can't you just walk up and say 'hi' like a normal person?"

"Sweet Rose, I'm disappointed you'd say such a thing." Fluvium shoved hands in pockets, his embroidered black coat flaring around his knees. Freakish face, ethereal, his bones impossibly sharp and fine. Tonight, his perfect chin was artfully unshaven, and a shiny golden ring pierced one earlobe. He wore a ruffled white shirt, black trousers and tall boots, a glistening violet scarf, and his deliciously dark hair—just a midnight purple shadow belying his inhuman nature—tousled at his collar beneath a raven-feathered, three-cornered hat.

Fluvium liked outlandish costumes. He even wore a cutlass, hooked into his belt, the bare curved steel glittering. Where the hell had he gotten a cutlass? He looked like a lunatic pirate, complete with fucked-up grin and that out-of-focus possessed gleam in his eyes.

Still as lethally, disgustingly attractive as the night they'd met.

Thinking about it still made her want to vomit. She'd just danced her first ever opening night on Broadway— Broadway!—and she was celebrating, still dizzy from the lights, the crowd, the adrenaline. The man who'd caught her eye through the smoke in a lantern-lit bar in Chelsea wore a velvet-soft leather jacket, jeans in cowboy boots, a smile that licked her sex from across the room. He'd danced a passionate rumba with her, intoxicating, the feel of his body a rich delight. She'd swooned, drowning in his hot ashen scent . . .

Rose's cheeks burned. She'd thought herself so streetwise, a girl from the projects who'd seen it all. Fit, trained in self-defense, pepper spray in her purse. Besides, she'd dated— ahem, read *slept with*, she didn't have time for real dating, not with stage rehearsals and shows until late, and looking after Bridie since Mommy had sold one baggie too many and earned

herself ten-to-twelve in the state pen—she'd *dated* guys who
were a lot less classy. Just warm bodies, staving off loneliness.
But this man had style, charm, a hint of sexy threat that
tempted her breathless.

Surrender, he'd whispered later, in his firelit bedroom on
Fifth Avenue, the scent of sultry summer blossoms drifting
through the open French doors. A beautiful body, lean and
muscular, his skin adorned with strange markings, that sexy
violet-tinted hair sifting silken heat over her thighs. He wore
a threaded necklace of teeth around his neck. Polished human
teeth, clinking against her chest as he kissed her. Not real, of
course. How could they be real?

Surrender to me. Just a sex game, right? The way he held
her down drove her wild. How his mouth tortured her breasts,
her back arching into his caress. His tattooed fingers crushing her wrists, the shattering force as he speared into her, filling
her, dragging her screaming to completion. Nothing ever felt
this good . . . and then . . .

In the moonlit street, Rose forced a smile. Her nipples hurt.
She wanted to cover them, deny her horrid hunger. But still her
curse responded to him, yearning for his dark glory . . .

She coughed. "I'm tired, master. What do you want?"

"To discuss your debt, of course." Fluvium kissed her hand
with lips slick like hellfever. His spiked ring scratched her
palm and sucked up the blood like a living creature. "The
moon's nearly full. You know what that means."

Rose shuddered. Fluvium's demonic powers waxed with
the moon. And this month, he had some big scheme plotted, a
grand catastrophe he'd conspired and giggled over with his
little demon friend, the sly crimson-haired one called Zuul.

Zuul—ugh!—Zuul was as creepy as Fluvium, in his way.
He liked pain, which made him Fluvium's new best buddy.
She'd heard the two of them, howling and groaning in the
dark. Sometimes Zuul played evil hide-and-seek games with
the coven vampires, games that ended in rivers of blood.

Whatever they had planned for that full moon? Not good.

She resisted a shiver. "My debt? We're square, aren't we?
I've been working."

"I can see that, you sexy bitch." Fluvium sniffed the new angel's feather knotted into her hair. "Mmm. Is that for me? My beautiful consort. Say you love me."

The bitter ashen taunt on his breath sickened her. Unwilled, she recalled that wild golden angel, how he'd tasted her, drank her in, hungered for her touch . . . She faked a smile. "Umm . . ."

"Marry me, Rose. We'll be so happy." Fluvium tilted her chin up, and swept her into a kiss.

Ugh. Hot, slick, talented, so disgusting she retched. His lips bore down, bloodstained and hungry and so vile . . . She gagged, and broke away.

She staggered, panting. She'd refused her demon prince. Not a good survival strategy. He was her master. He could kill her, torture her, take her powers away on a whim. Send her to hell, where Bridie waited for her . . .

But Fluvium just clicked his tongue, gloating. "That's no way to treat your future husband. Isn't there meant to be sub-mission involved in this wedding business? I'm afraid I shall have to beat you, wife."

"Why me?" She backed away, her nerves crawling. "You must have a thousand minions. Why do you want me?"

He smiled, devilish. "Give yourself some credit. You fuck like a goddess. Best tits I've seen this century, *and* you can do the splits. You hate me more than the others, too. I love a good fight. Screaming Jesus, my dick's getting hard just thinking about it—"

"You're disgusting!" The words burst out before she could stop them. She knew he liked to do this. Provoke her, punish her, make her beg for forgiveness. But the memory of what he'd done to her—what she'd done to Bridie because of him— clogged her guts with hot-sick guilt.

Angry smoke curled from Fluvium's fingernails. "Are you displeasing me, Rose? You know what happens if you dis-please me. Caliban's already told me you're being uncooper-ative."

Rose shuddered. Caliban was master of the West Village vampire coven, a Chosen maniac who believed that wallowing in blood was his destiny. He'd invited her to play his sickening games. She'd refused. It hadn't ended well. Caliban's Chosen favorites had been hunting her ever since.

She shrugged bravely. "I don't like his style."

"You'll like what I tell you to like. Do I need to remind you who your master is?"

"Go ahead," she snapped, defiant. God, she was so sick of his games. "Hell can't be worse than five more minutes in your company—ugh!"

He vanished and snapped back in a puff of stinking smoke, inches away. He yanked her against him, and she struggled but he was too strong.

"Oh, it can. You know it can." He stroked her cheek, possessive. His knucklebone bracelet clattered against her face. His ashen scent nauseated her, the silky fabric of his coat, warm and horrid on her skin. "Hell's become quite . . . inventive, with Azaroth in charge. Imagine when Satan returns and brings it all to earth. Shall I describe the torment, Rose? Shall I try it out on you?"

His breath crawled down her throat, a smoky devil hungry to take her. She choked, but his spell had already taken hold, and agony flayed her skin raw.

She struggled, helpless. Dimly, she heard Fluvium laughing.

Images drowned her, poisoned quicksand that dragged her down, down into the stifling dark . . . Bridie screaming, a mess of blood . . . Thirst, howling like a beast, demanding more, harder, again and forever, blood, always the blood, rich and delicious, feeding the shrieking emptiness in her soul, only the hole was bottomless, an endless, ravenous void that could never be satisfied . . .

"No!" Her scream ripped her ears. Before Fluvium, she hadn't truly believed in heaven or hell. But now, she knew they were terrifyingly real. Hell haunted her nightmares, smoking, burning, raw with howls and the stink of excruciated flesh. She'd scream and thrash and beg them to stop, but they never would. They'd never let her out. She'd never be forgiven . . .

Her legs went to water. God, she was sobbing in Fluvium's arms. "No, please, I can't, not that. Not again . . ."

"Then you'll have to try harder to please me." Fluvium branded her lips with another kiss. "Say you'll try harder, Rose."

Disgust scorched her throat raw. But she swallowed the bile, and made herself say it. "Yes."

"Yes . . . ?"

"Yes, master. I'll try." Yes, she loathed Fluvium to his hell-cursed bones. But she feared hell more.

"Good." He released her, and gave a smug grin. "Then tell me about tonight."

"Huh?"

"The angel." Impatience smoked black from his fingertips.

"Oh. Yeah, I got another one. Stabbed him right through the heart—"

"Not that one." His tone slicked cold. "The other one."

"What other one?"

The demon's claws dug like needles into her wrist. "Don't lie. I can smell his filth on you. What happened?"

"Nothing." The lie sounded false, even to her. "I just . . . he got away."

"Mmm-hmm. And did he have a name, this angel-who-got-away?"

"I didn't ask—"

"You didn't ask. But you kissed him, didn't you?"

"Of course not—"

"Don't bother," he snarled in her face. "I can taste it on your heaven-reeking breath. Did you spread your legs for him? Suck his stinking cock?"

"What? No!" Her cheeks burned.

"Is my queen an angel's whore, now? Do you know what I do to unfaithful queens?"

"It wasn't like that!" But her belly heated. That angel's mouth alive on hers, his rich coffee-spice scent, muscles and hot male skin and luscious golden hair . . . "It was an accident, okay? I didn't mean it. He . . . he tricked me."

"Ah, the truth at last," he mocked, and traced a smoking fingertip over the crimson stains on her t-shirt. "His blood?"

She nodded, sick.

Fluvium pressed his palm to the stain and hissed a few sibilant words. Red light glimmered. Evil smoke stung her eyes, and a symbol flashed in the air like virtual neon. A twisted blue lightning bolt, crackling with heavenly energy. An angel's sigil.

Fluvium's eyes lit. "Japheth! We meet again, you sorry sack of sin." His snarling devilmagic struck like a flaming red serpent. The blue sigil writhed, glittering in pain, and dissolved with an unholy scarlet flash.

Rose blinked, dizzy. "Who?"

"Your lover-boy angel. One of the Tainted Host, Michael's naughty little pets. I'd quite forgotten he existed. Ooh, this is gonna be *fun*!"

Golden Boy was *Tainted*?

Rose's blood salted, indignant. Of course. That explained his faded heaven scent . . . But the godscum was halfway to the abyss himself, and he'd had the nerve to tell her *she* was damned?

The lying bastard. If she ever saw him again, she'd make him sorry . . . But unwilled, she remembered how he'd tasted—fresh, his passion bright and unsullied, innocent . . .

Fluvium patted her head. "Now that's what I like. Some healthy rage! Wouldn't want my Slayer going soft." He tweaked her nose, then abruptly his smile died, and he shoved her away.

She stumbled, then righted herself, tugging her clothes straight. Never mind this Japheth's so-called innocence. He'd humiliated her. "I'll kill him, I promise," she insisted.

"No, you won't." Fluvium's whisper sliced cold.

"Come again?"

"The Demon King's coming. I need something special." He giggled, insane. "A gift."

She shivered. She'd never met the Demon King. Azaroth, second to Satan himself, caretaker in hell while the boss was sidelined. Mastermind of this perverted demonic Apocalypse. Part of her still couldn't believe all this stuff—Satan, hell, the end of the world—was real. But Fluvium spoke of Azaroth with fulsome reverence, and Zuul's pointy face paled at the mention of his name.

Azaroth, Lord of Emptiness and Despair. He didn't sound easily pleased . . .

"So I'll get you a dead angel," she offered, but her heart

sank. "This Japheth, or whatever his name is. I can hack off his wings for a trophy, if you want. Your king will get off on that, won't he?"

"I like the way you think." Malice twinkled in Fluvium's eyes. "But what's better than a dead angel? A *damned* one."

Her blood chilled. Not just dead and bleeding. Damned. His soul in torment forever. She knew what that was like . . .

But excitement flashed, too. He was just another superior, deceitful angel, peddling salvation where there was only death and torment. He deserved his own medicine, didn't he? And she'd seen the desire in his gaze. She could lead him there *willingly*. Just a few little tricks and he'd be hers.

Fluvium would reward her. She'd stay out of hell. And she'd have her vengeance on that skinny, dying God.

Fluvium smirked, delighted. "I see the idea pleases you."

"Oh, sure." Her mind raced. She could do it. This Japheth wanted her. She'd seen his gaze linger over her body, forbidden passion melting those frosty green eyes. His kiss, a sensual explosion, his body's visceral reaction when he'd pinned her down. Repulsive . . . but it turned her on, too. A hot, gorgeous, straining hard-on of an angel.

Oh, yes, he wanted her all right. She shivered illicitly. What would it be like to touch him? Tempt him, flames of perdition wrapping her skin, drawing him ever closer to the edge . . .

"That's my girl." Fluvium sliced a sharp fingernail over her bottom lip. Coppery blood welled. He licked at it, and she squirmed in his embrace, disgusted . . . but fever swelled inside her, aching her stomach hollow. "Fight him, fuck him"—he nipped her lip hungrily—"I really don't care. Just give him my blood, and he'll be mine forever."

She wanted to scrub his filth from her skin, spit it out like spoiled milk . . . but inside her, the curse yearned for him. "Umm . . . what will you give me in return?"

Another kiss, salty and hateful. "I'll let you live, of course."

"Is that all?" Demon deals were dangerous. She should pay attention. She had to extract his promise to save her from hell, or it'd all be for nothing . . . But his monstrous curse rippled deep, devouring her reason. Thirst dizzied her. She needed his blood, that dark liquid ecstasy, burning through her, making her strong . . .

She groaned, opening for his rich flavor, letting him take her . . .

He bit her tongue, and spat the blood back into her mouth. "Don't get cocky. You already refused me. I should flay you raw. Stake you out in the sun to starve, hmm?"

He hurled her away, and she hit the pavement, bones jarring. Groggy, she tried to raise her head. Fluvium snapped his fingers, and ash rained over her, little burning motes of hellfire that drilled into her skin and smoked like napalm.

Rose yelled, and writhed on the ground in agony. She knew he enjoyed her pain. But she couldn't stop screaming.

Fluvium leered down at her, his black coat swirling on foul ashen breeze. "Bring me Japheth's soul, by full moon—that's two nights from now, so no wriggling out of it—and you get one more month on this earth. Fail me, and I promise you, by the time I'm done, you'll be begging for hell. Are we clear?"

Defiance twisted her muscles tight. God, she wanted to sink her teeth into his face, thrust her demon-spelled knife deep into his heart . . .

But hell awaited her if she defied him. And no matter how she loathed this vampire life—human skin foul on her tongue, flesh crunching in her teeth, blood thick and disgusting on her lips—hell was infinitely, excruciatingly worse.

Because hell was where Bridie lived. And Bridie would never forgive her.

"Are we crystal, Rose?" Fluvium's magical compulsion impaled her, opening her up, shoving deep like an unwelcome lover. "Or must I remind you who your master is?"

"I promise!" The scream flayed her throat bloody. But the humiliation hurt worse, a rusty brand in her misbegotten soul. "I promise, master . . ."

Fluvium sniffed, and vanished.

Abruptly, the pain ceased. Ash rained like gritty snowflakes, the remnants of his magic. Rose's pockmarked skin hissed and healed, and she stumbled to her feet, disoriented. *Screw him.*

But she knew what she had to do. Seduce this Tainted angel. Relish her revenge. Stay out of hell. Everybody wins.

Her lost conscience twanged. Killing an angel? An easy mark. But condemning another person to eternal damnation . . .

She brushed the qualm away, desperate. *Fuck it.* The vampire hunger still screamed in her blood. She needed strength. First, she'd feed. Find some unsuspecting human, drink what she needed to survive, let them wander off dizzy and disoriented.

And then, she'd hunt this Japheth down, and make him hers. Lure him into her warm dark lair and rip his innocent ass to shreds.

Determined, Rose stretched like a cat. She wrapped her fingers around her knife's hilt, working up courage. The demon-spelled silver cooled her palm, comforting, and she exulted, lifting her face to the greedy moon.

The bloodstained light spilled over her, energizing. She was a powerful seductress, a dark and splendid creature of the night. God hated her. Might as well take as many of heaven's slaves down with her as she could.

And bringing this one down—this handsome golden liar, with his fuck-you-hellspawn attitude and haughty emerald eyes—would be a doubly sweet pleasure.

CHAPTER 4

Japheth shouldered through the glossy nightclub crowd. The scent of sweat and chemical-drenched sex hung in a damp cloud. Dancers jostled him, lithe flesh exposed, leather and latex and perfumed rainbow hair. Electric music screeched and pounded. Nineties retro, Dash called it. Japheth called it a headache.

But at least it was emotionless, this empty electric throb. Real music was dangerous. He remembered watching in tears on the edge of his musty velvet seat as Mozart conducted *Don Giovanni* in Prague, the composer wan with latent illness but still transported to some eerie surrogate heaven by his creation. Years later, hidden behind a curtain in an ornate palazzo above San Marco, he'd listened transfixed to Signor Paganini playing Vivaldi, alone and heartrending, spilling out his tortured soul to the uncaring darkness. No devil inside him, Japheth had confirmed later for his masters. Just talent and misery, an unearthly gift in an all-too-earthly body.

Lately, he'd just avoided it. He'd played the piano, years ago, an excellent way to sharpen discipline and hone his fine motor skills. He'd spent hours repeating exercises, perfecting scales, learning Bach inventions and Beethoven sonatas by heart. But the music played tricks in his empty soulspace, moved him to laughter or tears or violent passion. He got too emotionally involved. Better to let it be.

A woman stumbled into him on too-high heels. Her raspberry vodka splashed his chest. She giggled, pleasantly tipsy. "Fuck. I'm so sorry . . ." Her eyes glazed over, a dazzled double-take. "Oh. Umm . . . wow. I really am sorry. Can I get you another . . . ?"

"It's okay." Japheth forced a quick, cold smile. He'd put on his human disguise, which meant his wings vanished, and his glittering colors faded to a more acceptable human level. But he was still bigger than everyone else. Blonder, eyes brighter, skin more luminous. And he hadn't bothered to flash home first to rinse his hair or change out of his bloodstained armor.

Still stood out like a dog's balls, in fact. He'd set off the metal detector at the entrance, and the security guys had waved him through anyway. His warrior's hackles lifted. Morons. Like he wouldn't kill them all in an eye blink if the war demanded it . . . but in Babylon at the End of Days, *angel* was right up there with *rock star* or *celebrity chef.* He could do anything, go anywhere.

Have anyone.

And this woman gazed up at him, raptly fascinated. Japheth shifted, awkward, trying not to glow or smell nice or whatever the trick was. Dash was right: girls liked angels. Some of the boys, too. If you wanted attention, Babylon in mid-Apocalypse was your own little private heaven.

Japheth didn't want attention. He just wanted to kill demons, and go home.

The woman—a girl, in truth—fidgeted, twirling a brown curl with one purple nail. She had long coltish legs and a skirt that barely covered her butt. She flirted at him through thick sparkly lashes, and sipped on her straw. "Listen, can I make it up to you? You wanna dance?"

Japheth sighed coldly. He could hear her heartbeat fluttering, swift like a bird's. Smell her scent, alcohol and feminine perfume, her skin's warm musky flavor. *Easy game,* Dashiel or Trillium or any of the others would say. Dash would flirt, of course, make her feel like a princess with his rough-edged charm. Trill would drag her to the dance floor, make her breathless and promptly forget her for the next one. Ariel would whisper something hot and filthy in her ear and coax her away for a quick screw against the bathroom door.

Japheth just walked away.

Her indignation stung the air bitter. He kept walking, sidling around the crowded dance floor towards the stairs. Pleasantries were pointless. Talking gave them the wrong idea. He'd no wish to be cruel. Just cold.

Are you insane? That quiet devil's whisper in his heart. *She's nice. What's wrong with you? Can't stay alone forever, Jae. It's not normal.*

Frosty, he ignored that demon voice. He'd had centuries of practice at ignoring it . . .

Unbidden, the memory of that sexy vampire's kiss throbbed in his blood, arousing him swiftly. He flushed, sweating. Dirty. Deceitful. Delicious, her hot mouth an evil delight. For an instant, before it scorched him, he'd tasted her tongue, bold and hungry, laced with sweet female pleasure . . .

You wanted her. The sly voice caressed his skin taut. *You still do. And she wanted you. Don't deny it.*

"Just you watch me." Above, a glass mezzanine flashed blue and green, the floor pierced by swirling lasers. Even immersed in intoxicated humanity, he could smell Dashiel, fresh earth and rain. He dodged a pair of kissing girls and headed for the spiral stairs.

A boy in a zipped black vinyl shirt stumbled on the transparent steps, distracted by Japheth's sweet scent. Japheth picked him up, pushed him on his way. At the top, a glass bar curled around the back wall. Bottles of colored spirits gleamed on the shelves. He smelled yeasty beer, sweat, the faint medicinal twinge of opium. Heroin, most likely, or its latest demon-ashed variant, *hellcry.*

Japheth's nose wrinkled. He'd chased the dragon, a time or two, in his younger days when Michael still ruffled his hair and forgave his transgressions with a smile. Even with his stiff angelic resistance to human drugs, the opium pipe made him sleepy and reflective.

But these modern concoctions? Evil stuff. It scoured their minds black and hollow. Made them perfect demon bait.

He drifted to the bar, following his nose. A skinny white boy, picking scabs from his arms, his dull eyes rolling. Japheth grabbed his chin, caught his gaze. "You should stop using."

The boy laughed, spilling his beer onto his t-shirt. "Hey, man, fuck you, okay?"

"Die all you want, I don't give a damn. But space out on that stuff, and you're fair game for demons."

"What*ever*." The kid shook him off. "Fuckin' angels. Screw your bible-thumpin' shit."

Japheth sighed, impatient. They didn't get it. They never did. "Wanna see hell, kid? Let me show you." He slammed his palm into the boy's clammy forehead and whispered a charm.

Blue light flashed. The kid stumbled backwards and screamed.

He was still screaming when Japheth walked away.

He leaned his elbows on the warm glass bar. Bass throbbed, a desperate, off-beat rhythm that unsettled him. The barboy flicked a pierced eyebrow. "What'll it be?"

"Tonic on ice, no lime." Lime was an extravagance, useless for anything but the pleasure of that citrus tang. Useless pleasures were dangerous.

The barboy filled a tall glass. His tight black t-shirt said DANCE LIKE THERE'S NO TOMORROW, and below his shaven hairline, a tattoo read 666. Japheth dug in his pocket, but the boy waved him away. "On the house, *Señor Ángel*. The world's ending."

"Not while I'm still standing, kid. Have a little faith." He tossed the boy a twenty, and walked away, swallowing half the drink in a chilly gulp. Cold, bitter. Acceptable. He needed the hydration, and the quinine would enrich his blood, strengthen his resistance to demon poisons.

After tonight's ugly games? He'd take all the help he could get.

The glass floor flashed, scattering blue and green and pink like broken prisms. A glint of red-gold caught Japheth's eye. Trillium, laughing like a hyena at rude jokes with a bunch of young guys dressed like drug dealers in sharp shirts and bling. Trill's wild orange hair glistened with that eerie angel gleam, and he draped one muscled arm around his choice for the night, a handsome kid with startling blue eyes.

Trill saw Japheth and waved, whiskey and cigarette in hand. Japheth waved back, shaking his head in mock disgust. Trill indulged in everything Japheth denied himself, and more. But that was okay. Trill was a kick-ass demon slayer, never shirking on a job or pulling the hangover card when there was work to be done.

Whatever gets you through the night.

He didn't see Iria or Jadzia, the ladies in their Tainted gang, but it was nearly dawn. Iria had likely left already, with some arrogant, seen-it-all alpha male she could bring to his knees. And lately Jadzia had been absent, preoccupied with her own affairs.

But here was Dashiel, perched on a steel stool, bathed in liquid green light. Dark brown hair caught back in a curled iron clip, powerful warrior's body in jeans and a white shirt, golden snake charm at his throat. He hadn't bothered to conceal himself, and his wings spread out behind him, luxuriant brown feathers shot through with laser green and blue.

Dashiel spotted him, and grinned. "Nice vision spell. Was that your good deed for the day?"

Japheth dragged up a stool. "Is this yours? Pardon me, miss, don't let me interrupt."

The girl astride Dash's lap giggled, dyed-blond pigtails bouncing. "No problem, handsome. Join us, if you want."

Dash stroked her thighs. "Don't let those bedroom eyes fool you, darlin'. Under that smoking-hot, fuck-me-senseless exterior, Golden Boy here has a heart of pure ice."

Japheth sipped his tonic, and gave a cool half smile. A cute Tokyo Lolita, frilly white skirt and stockings, but her painted eyes showed keen womanhood. Her lacy white top sported a red love heart. Dash always chose the tiny ones, so much so the others teased him about fetishes and cracked midget jokes.

Fetish, hell. He'd watched Dash enough times—dirty, sure, but watching was what Japheth had instead of doing, and it steeled his powers of resistance—and he'd never once seen the big bastard really lose control. Saving it for the right woman? Not likely. Something else was going on there.

Japheth cracked his neck, but the ache didn't ease. "Where's Ariel?"

Dash's girl downed a tequila shooter, and Dash fed her the lemon wedge, watching the juice drip down her chin. "He's around. Something about urgent business . . ."

"And I'm all done." Ariel shoved Japheth's shoulder, knocking him off his stool. Big, feline, sharp eyes blacker than midnight above a violently hawkish nose. He wore dark trousers and a crisp shirt, elegant, no doubt worth a mint, but even high fashion sense couldn't civilize this rude bastard. Half playboy prince, half hot-blooded thrill killer. "J.J., you frigid little asswipe," Ariel said. "How's tricks?"

"Trickier than you, by the looks. You've got a wet patch on your pants." Japheth flashed a grin and resumed his seat. For all his desert-sheikh pretensions, Ariel was uncouth and opinionated. Honest. It was refreshing.

Dash cocked a sly brow. "Quick work."

Ariel adjusted himself, wincing. His cinnamon-dark hair was tousled and damp, his dusky Arabian skin flushed warm. "We skipped the talking. Saves time."

"Who's in a hurry?" Dash eased his girl closer, squeezing her thighs lightly. She arched into him, eyes glowing.

Ariel snorted, contemptuous, and gulped half his G and T. "Me, usually. Warm and willing is all I ask. What's the point in taking all night? It only makes them think you give a shit."

"Thoughtful of you." Japheth sipped his tonic. Ariel was Tainted for rebellion. He'd seen the unconditional love Himself lavished on the monkeys—Michael's word, that—and hadn't contained his bitterness. Still couldn't. His rageful black eyes belied that. Beyond his benefit and pleasure, he'd no interest in humans.

"Yeah," Ariel said, sharp with sarcasm. "Whatever."

His casual cruelty was enviable. But Japheth didn't have it in him. Better just to keep his distance.

Whatever gets you through the night.

"So," he ventured. "Vials, Guardians, all that. What's the story?"

Ariel shrugged. "As you'd expect. Took me a month to hunt

just one of those Guardian pricks down. Locked up tighter than a frog's asshole."

"So where was he?"

"She," Ariel corrected, grinning. "Holed up in this moldy stone monastery on some mountain plateau in Bhutan. Bunch of psycho warrior monks praying for enlightenment, or some such. Keeping her satisfied, more like. Nice work if you can get it." He ruffled his dark hair, gold rings glinting. A trio of teenage girls in tiny skirts and halters gawked at him, and he winked back. "Demonspawn everywhere, though. They're under siege. Corpses piled knee-high, throat slitting and screams, that kinda thing. Fun and games."

"So why doesn't she just flash out, and get her enlightened butt down here?" Dash tipped up the bottle, gulping pale tequila neat. The worm bobbed in the bottle as he swallowed. It took a lot to get an angel drunk. "The world's ending. Doesn't she watch CNN?"

"No cable, no broadband. The monks don't allow electricity. Bitch doesn't even have a phone." Ariel grinned maniacally at the girls, and let loose a stealthy flash of angelspell. They stumbled, disoriented. One fainted, and crumpled to the floor. He laughed. "And, the whole place is wrapped in some shady-ass demon spellwork. No flashing in or out. You can't even fly without pinging their shit-stinking radar. I had to *walk*." He drained his drink, crunching the ice. "Can you imagine that? My feet still hurt."

"And?" Japheth's nerves whetted. If even one vial was safe, the demon Apocalypse was done. They could all go home . . . Better still, he could go slaughter some vampires. A dark-eyed, raven-haired vampire vixen, by choice . . .

"And, nothing," said Ariel. "My orders said 'find,' not 'rescue.' You know how it works. The holy crew gets the glory. I'm just the Tainted buttboy—"

"And a mighty fine buttboy you make." Smooth, icy, lethal like a crystalline blade.

Japheth jerked from his stool, chilly with distaste. Too late, he caught the sparkling blue reflection on the floor. Inhaled that familiar sugar-ice scent . . .

Oh, crap.

CHAPTER 5

Sparkling wings the color of a deep glacier. Eyes so blue and cold, it hurt to look. Ice-blond hair glittering razor keen. Impossibly perfect. Perfectly impossible.

For a treacherous moment, the world stopped spinning.

"Hey, babe." Michael grinned, brutally charming, and tweaked a stray lock from Japheth's cheek.

Japheth averted his face, and shot Dash a poisonous glare. "You didn't say *he* was here."

"Wanted you to show up, didn't I?" Dash shrugged, but his dark eyes fired a warning shot. He knew firsthand the hold Michael had over Japheth. The murderous things Michael had coaxed him to do . . .

Did Dash want them to kiss and make up? That'd be a snowy night in the hellpit. Disgusted, Japheth flashed out to his empty apartment.

He didn't get there.

Dirty pavement slapped beneath his boots. Moonlight watered his eyes, green foliage, a high concrete gutter, rainbow-sprayed brick walls. The alley behind the club.

Michael regarded him coldly, arms folded. His icy wings

shed a crisp sapphire halo, tarnishing his black leather jacket with midnight blue. "Don't run. It never works."

Japheth's hidden wings crackled taut, a burst of angry static, and his human disguise snapped like glass. Golden light erupted. His fists clenched, itching to punch the archangel's arrogant face in. He'd done it, too, last time they'd met. Broke every bone in his hand.

But Michael owned him. Held his Tainted soul to ransom, halfway between heaven and hell. If he wanted redemption . . .

"What do you want, Michael?" *Misha.* He'd almost said the nickname, like toxic sugar on his tongue. Force of habit.

But bad habits could be broken.

A smile, silky with malice. "What, no sweet talk? Here I was thinking you'd missed me."

"Not for a heartbeat. Out with it, I don't have all night."

Michael ruffled diamond-sparkling hair with one wing. "Well, if we must talk business: I have a job for you."

Japheth shrugged, but his nerves scraped a ragged edge. His mistake with that vampire seductress had unsettled him. Surely his guilt was obvious. "Ariel can carve out your Vial Guardian. I'm busy." And he prepared to flash out.

Michael gripped his wrist, stony. "Not that. I'll take care of that personally."

Japheth yanked free, striding a few steps away. "Getting your hands dirty? Spare me. You're just trying to weasel back into Gabriel's good graces."

"None of your damn business." Michael's eyes stormed, black discontent.

Japheth laughed, savage. "That really sticks in your throat, doesn't it? Beholden to big brother's rules? You messed up the last demon vial, and Gabriel's pissed at you. Good thing for you Lune and his girlfriend saved your butt—"

"And yours," reminded Michael coldly. "I haven't forgotten you disobeyed me. I wanted Dashiel dead. Seems he's still here."

Heaven, he wanted to crush that beautiful face to blood and bone . . . But wrath was a sin. He gritted cold teeth. "I told you, I won't betray my friends. You want him dead? Go do it yourself."

Angry white sparks showered from Michael's wings. "Don't test me. I could kick your rebellious ass straight to hell right now and no one in heaven would blink. Fuck, maybe I'll do it just for fun."

Japheth flashed, snapping right into Michael's face. "Do it, then," he challenged hotly. "Cast me down. You don't need me. Plenty of other suckers to stroke your massive ego." He flushed. That came out wrong. Damn it.

A satisfied smile. "Thanks for the offer, babe. But my massive ego aside, I really do have a job for you. You interested, or are we going to flirt all night?"

Japheth edged away. "Say on."

Idly, Michael flicked a dirty fleck from one feather. "This Prince of Thirst. Demonscum stinking out the West Village. Ringing any bells?"

Oh, yeah, it sure did. Sweet ladyflesh, sultry vampire eyes, a kiss that burned in more ways than one . . . Japheth coughed. "What about him?"

"His name is Fluvium. Manic little asshole with a costume fetish. I believe you've met?"

Michael knew damn well they'd met. A snowy seventh-century battlefield, dim with fog, rotten with the fearful stink of death and the Dark Ages. A golden era for demons, who preyed on ignorance, fear, isolation. Entire villages succumbed to curses and plagues, driven mad with hunger or rage, willing disciples for the demons' ugly desires. The people—illiterate, short-lived, lied to by greedy monks—simply didn't know any better.

Not heaven's finest hour.

But that day, they'd won a stirring victory, Michael and Japheth and the heavenly host. His last battle before he fell. They'd hunted down the snake-hearted demon in charge, and Japheth had sliced his laughing head from his neck, thrust fiery angelsteel through his heart and watched him crumble to ash. Fluvium—just a sniveling minion with a sharp-toothed blade then, jostling to get noticed by his masters—Fluvium had gotten away. But not before he'd soaked the ground with poisoned angels' blood.

The screams still resonated in Japheth's nightmares. Fluvium didn't just enjoy killing. He liked it to hurt.

Japheth nodded, cautious. "Sure. I remember. Didn't know he was a prince."

"Yeah, well, they promote any mad motherfucker with a grudge these days. Word is he and Azaroth are tight." A slick smile. "Pity you didn't waste him when you had the chance."

Japheth ignored that one. He'd killed so many that day, crimson rivers had soaked deep into the melting snow. Glory had burned his blood alive like never before. He'd lived by the sea in heaven then, deep blue water to the horizon, salty air, the musical squawk of gulls. Simple but comfortable.

He'd even had a friend, a pretty copper-winged warrior who'd teased him, sparred with him, watched his back. Back then, friends were uncomplicated. Innocent. It never occurred to him to want more from her. When carnal desires tempted him, he killed hellspawn. When that didn't suffice, he chose strangers, and got it over with quickly. Humans, or angels he barely knew.

Or sultry archangels with ice-blue eyes. That was a mistake he'd never gotten over.

But that night, he and she lay on the beach, flushed with celebration and laughter. Drunk on wine and the waves' hypnotic crash, heaven's enormous stars spinning fire bright overhead. He'd gazed across at her, those dusky wings scattered with sand. Her laughing gaze met his, twinkling. Subtly, his heart quickened. His skin tingled alive. All the air sucked from his lungs, replaced with her soft sweet scent, her laugh, the silky slide of her hair . . .

Impulsively, he'd leaned over, and kissed her.

Just a gentle kiss, done in a second or two. But the surprised sweetness on her lips thrilled him like nothing else.

He laughed. She wrinkled her pretty nose at him, affection brimming in her eyes. Secret warmth stole into his heart. And they lay, fingers and wingtips entwined, gazing at the shimmering stars.

The next dawn, Michael cast had him down. No warning. No explanation. Just dirt thudding into his back, wing bones cracking, fiery angelsteel aimed at his throat. *I know what you are, Japheth of the Tainted.* Michael's razor-blue hair sliced Japheth's cheek bloody. *I know what you're doing. Think you can hide from me? Think again.*

In the alley, reddish moonbeams savaged Japheth's eyes. She'd loathed him, once he fell. Held him in contempt. Seen him at last for what he really was . . .

What was he, then? He'd been all confusion. It wasn't as if Michael cared what he did, who he saw. But whatever he'd done, he surely must have deserved it . . .

"Hello?" Michael snapped bright fingers, inches from Japheth's eyes. "Still with me?"

"Uh. Yeah. Fluvium. What about him?"

"His head. On a spike. Preferably with an expression of excruciating agony frozen on his face."

Japheth's wings glittered, eager. Demon slaughter. Excellent. And if he put an end to a certain crafty bloodsucking whore while he was at it? Purged her from his darkest fantasies, carved those evil memories from his flesh? Even better. "Okay. I can do that. What do I get?"

"Excuse me?"

"I think I mentioned we're not friends anymore. I work for you, fine. What's it worth to you?"

Michael considered, an amused diamond glint in his eyes. "Depends what you want."

"You know what I want." Japheth shrugged coolly, but his heart skipped. "That's one of Azaroth's demon princes you want dead. Won't be easy. I bring you his head, I want my soul back. And I want to be free of *you*. Deal?"

A crafty smile. "Well, well. Look who grew some balls. You know I like that."

"Believe it or not, Michael, for once in my life, I don't give a damn what you like. Yes or no?"

Michael measured him with a stare, ice-blue, all his amusement faded. "I want the demon prince dead. I want the vial, empty or not. And . . ." He leaned closer, enveloping Japheth in hot glitter-sweet silence. The city's sounds faded, mere distant echoes, but Michael's whisper zinged like crystal. "I want your promise that when the questions start from upstairs—

and they'll come, I assure you—you'll keep your mouth shut. About this. About the vials. About everything."

"You want me to lie to Gabriel." Not a conniver like Michael. A holy man, with tough morals and tougher justice. A pure, unsullied archangel, who'd surely skip the Tainted part and hurl Japheth straight into the pit . . .

But his blood sparkled warm. Redemption. His soul returned to him. A way back into heaven . . .

Michael wrinkled his nose, affectionate. "Bless your sweet little heart. Gabe will never know."

He didn't like that indigo gleam in Michael's eyes. "And what exactly will I be covering up?"

A glassy laugh. "You know it doesn't work like that. Relax. Think I'm gonna rat on you? There's more at stake than your cute golden ass, believe me."

Japheth hesitated. He wouldn't put it past Michael to betray him to cover the lie, once he'd gotten what he wanted . . .

Michael folded massive arms. "Your soul, for a lie and a murder. On any other day, you'd be headed the other way. It's a good deal, Jae. Yes or no?"

Ancient longing for home ached in his bones. Where everything made sense, and the last fourteen hundred years of guilt and sorrow faded into a bad dream . . .

Fierce conviction frosted his heart. Killing demons wasn't a sin. As for the lie . . . well, it wasn't lying unless he knew the truth. Michael's real plans didn't matter a damn to him. Better not to know.

His soul, for a killing and an innocent shrug when Gabriel asked what was going on. Worth it?

Absolutely.

"You got it," he whispered, and flashed out.

CHAPTER 6

Michael stretched glacial wings, and laughed.

Snotty little fucker had finally grown a pair.

He could live with that. Hell, maybe he'd even make good on his promise, when the time came. He'd missed the little bastard, so help him.

Michael raised his gaze to heaven, calling on his servant. Unlike the Tainted, his closest heavenly host could use a mental link to communicate. It was quicker, and saved messing about with cell phones. "Esther, get your feathery butt down here."

A second later, Esther flashed in, coppery wings aflutter. She bowed, fulsome, her smooth brown ponytail flipping over her shoulder.

Michael sighed. His new minion was prissy, but hot. She'd totally rock fishnets, or one of those tight rubber dresses. "Always with the suit and heels? You look like a fucking accountant."

It was a sharp suit, he had to admit, silken gray and meticulously shaped. Her dark-skinned face was calm. Observant. Showing proper deference, her gaze downcast a few inches from his face. She clasped her hands behind her, waiting. "As you say, Seraph."

Probably, she'd say that to whatever he asked. One day, he'd test it. *Bring me the moon, Esther,* or *I'd like a mammoth-tusk burger with a side of dodo fries,* or *me and these chainsaw-wielding painwraiths are going to gangbang you three at a time now, Esther, is that okay?*

"Get down to the West Village," he ordered. "Make sure Japheth does the right thing. I don't want him holding out on me."

"Yes, Seraph." Another bow. Not a fleck of dust on her feathers. The perfect corporate minion.

Michael sighed. At least she was obedient. If he said it, she did it. But Jesus fucking Christ on a barbecue, heaven bred them timid these days. Back in the day, His messengers had fire in the blood. On the other hand, Esther was a chiseler to the core. Cunning, desperate to get ahead, and quite evidently stomped on anyone who got in her way. Including old friends like Japheth. Handy.

"Don't let him smell you," he warned. "He's Tainted, not stupid. And Esther?"

"Yes, Seraph?"

"If he screws up, kill him."

Her expression shadowed, but swiftly cleared. "As you say, Seraph." She fidgeted, clicking rose-painted fingernails. "Gabriel . . ."

"What about him?"

"He's asking questions. About you. That Manhattan virus thing last month, he's . . . curious."

Michael scowled, and the sidewalk groaned, the brick wall beside him cracking. Ever since the first vial set off a zombie plague in Babylon—which Michael had let carry on, just to see what the demon's plan was—Gabriel had been in a bitch of a mood. "Don't tell him anything. Hear me? Not a damn thing."

"But, Seraph—"

Michael backhanded her. Her jawbone crunched, satisfying, and she stumbled to her knees. "Listen to me, you little greaser. Gabriel is nothing. He's a fucking bean counter. For five thousand years, I've killed and bled and stained my soul rotten for heaven's sake. What did Gabriel ever do, besides kick a pair of horny monkeys in fig leaves out of the garden?"

Yet Gabriel was set above him. Gabriel would always be above him.

Well, screw *that* for a shitty idea.

Esther spat blood. Her broken jaw healed with a blue flash. Baleful glitter coiled in her copper-brown feathers. At last, defiance. It just made her look petulant. "Seraph—"

"Not a damn thing, that's what." Michael raked his hair, vicious. Soon, when this was over, he and Gabriel would have words. Yes indeedy, they would. "So don't give me crap about questions. Just do as I say, when I say. And if I say 'fuck Gabriel,' you say, 'how hard?'" Now there was an image he'd keep for later. "Understand?"

"Yes, Seraph." Still on her knees, Esther kept her head down. Dirt and blood smeared her suit. Her fragile body trembled. It didn't turn him on. It just made him wish he had Japheth back. Frost-fire defiance, challenging smile, spectacular ass. What a fucking waste.

Michael shoved Esther with one foot. "Get up. You're a good minion, Esther. Don't make me kill you. Just do as I say, and it'll all be giggles."

"As you say, Seraph."

"As I say. Now get out of my sight, before I forget my manners and hurt you."

"Yes, Seraph." Hastily, Esther flashed out.

Michael cracked his knuckles, pleased. This twisted Apocalypse was a pain in the ass, sure. Stopping demons from overrunning the world was probably a good thing, and if Michael ever got his hands on Azaroth, there'd be demon entrails from here to Jerusalem before he was through.

But what was the hurry, with power still for the taking? Vials brimming with wrath to be had? Sure, the Book said that angels were supposed to spill the seven vials, set off the chain of signs that led to the End. Whatever. Demons, angels, the result would be the same: Satan, sprung from his shackles, roaming the earth.

Where Michael could eviscerate the selfish little motherfucker, like he should have done the first time.

And who'd stepped in his way, hmm? Which smug, silverassed brown-noser had stolen Michael's glory? Counseled mercy? Whispered to Himself of eternal bondage and torment, when all Michael wanted was bloody vengeance?

Fucking Gabriel, that's who. And no one—not even Gabriel—stole Michael's glory and died smiling.

He flexed hungry muscles, itching. The final battle? Bring that bad boy on. This time, Michael would get his way. Lucifer—the prick's angelic name still hacked blunt razors into his nerves—Satan would die screaming on Michael's sword. Ultimate glory.

Even if it meant a few billion monkeys died. There were too many of the greasy little bastards anyway. You only had to sniff their filthy polluted air, or sip their foul poison-laced water to know that. Hell, this was the Apocalypse, not a garden party.

But first, he had to keep up appearances with Gabriel. Otherwise, the job of stopping the demons would be taken away from him—and who did Gabe think would take over? When did Gabe last hold a sword, or feel the burning splash of demon blood on his face?

Michael laughed, brittle. Tempting, to let the stupid bastard try.

No, he had to keep control of the war effort. Make sure Azaroth and his scum-licking friends played ball . . . without getting his own hands too dirty.

And that was what the Tainted Host were for. Heavenly angels like Esther might be fine for honest soldier work like killing, fighting and punishing disobedient servants, but they were worthless in matters like this. Bound by heaven's rules, strict codes of behavior forbidding useful things like cheating and lying and fucking your enemy over. But the Tainted? Their souls were his. Everything to lose, no choice but to obey.

And so far, it'd worked. Ariel had done Michael's bidding with typical kick-ass efficiency. Vial number four was within reach . . .

But Ariel was too rebellious to keep his mouth shut, and possessed irritating loyalty to Dashiel that Michael had never quite thrashed out of him. He scowled. Dashiel, too bloody noble for his own good. If anyone would dare betray Michael's plans to Gabriel . . .

No. That would never do. Besides, Ariel was too lethal a warrior to waste. Michael needed someone more . . . pliable, who wouldn't ask too many questions.

Someone expendable.

He flipped out his phone, and called. No answer. He called again, impatient. Voice mail. *Hi, this is Jadzia. Leave a message. Or not.*

Where the hell was the stupid girl? "Jaz, darling," he said smoothly, "when you've got a moment." He ended the call, wondering if he should take someone else. He didn't have all day . . .

"Can't find your Tainted slave girl? You should keep that bitch on a leash."

Michael tore his sword from the ether and stabbed for the demon's throat.

Zuul grinned, lifting skinny hands in surrender. He backed up against the broken bricks, crimson hair falling over his studded leather armor. "Ooh, careful what you skewer, big guy. A demon could get the wrong idea."

"How long have you been skulking there?" Michael's sword point pricked Zuul's neck, above his spiked dog collar. The skin sizzled, smoking, but the fetish-y bastard just giggled. Zuul was a demon of pain. He liked torturing himself— or better still, he liked Michael torturing him. He'd spent months in a thrall cage in Michael's basement, humiliating himself.

Such fraternizations with demons were forbidden, of course, on pain of damnation, but Michael had never been one for rules. Still, Gabriel would roast his ass over a slow fire.

Michael snorted. He'd like to see the crusty old bastard try.

Zuul's hell-black eyes glinted, wicked and utterly insane. "Saw you bickering with your boyfriend, if that's what you mean. Or, should I say, *ex*-boyfriend. Did Blondie dump you for a chick again? Dude, it is so *humiliating* when that happens—"

"Shall I gut you now, or are you planning to say something interesting?"

"Just popping in to see how you're doing. Heard you're in trouble with big brother. So sad."

"You filthy snotbag, you're breaking my heart." He should kill this grotty demonslime. Slit his throat and bathe in his stinking blood . . . but Zuul amused him, and sometimes told tales on Azaroth. Ambitious, this skinny kid with pain-thirsty eyes. If the reward was tempting enough, he'd do anything. Too valuable to kill.

"Don't be like that. I'm just the messenger. Azaroth said to say . . ." Zuul frowned. "What was it again? Something about ramming a hell-spiced pitchfork up your ass? No, wait, my mistake . . ."

"Five seconds, shitball." But a smile quirked Michael's lips. Gutsy little prick.

"Okay, fine, don't get your dick in a twist." Zuul folded his arms, lounging, careless of the blade. "It's about this fourth vial. In Bhutan? Azaroth said to say he's sending his favorite new prince to fetch it. The Prince of Fire, I'm told, some frothing lunatic named Luuceat. Should be a nice bloody time for you."

Luu-ce-at. *Ch* for the *c*, like the Latin for *shine*. One of Azaroth's psychopathic cronies, no doubt. The Demon King liked to promote the insane ones. He wanted maximum chaos.

Michael licked eager lips. Chaos, there'd surely be. This plague was gonna be good. *And the fourth angel poured out his vial upon the sun, and power was given to him to scorch men with fire . . .*

"Oh, there'll be blood," he agreed silkily, shifting his blade crosswise so it sliced under Zuul's chin. Crimson oozed, steaming. "Shall I demonstrate on you?"

"Baby, please." Zuul rolled his eyes in mock ecstasy, enjoying himself. "Like you give a feathered fuck about that vial, Mikey."

"Excuse me?"

"I'm a pain demon, not a bloody idiot. You let us get away with that last one, didn't you? Using your Tainted fuck buddies instead of the heavenly host? If you'd squared things with Gabriel, you could've waltzed in with the entire holy crew and flattened Vorvian and Quuzaat any time you wanted."

"Now you're just stroking my ego." Michael's fingers tightened around his flaming sword grip.

"Kind of difficult to stop the Apocalypse when the vials are already empty, isn't it? That's Fluvium down in the West Village, in case you hadn't noticed. He of the sawtooth blades and the body-part jewelry?"

"So?"

"So, Vorvian and Quuzaat were sane compared to this freak show, and you send Blondie? Anyone would think you were on our side."

"Don't underestimate him." A mistake he'd made, once. He laughed, poisonous, and in the street, trees wilted. "Japheth has flayed more demons alive than you've had jerk-off parties. I've seen him cut down a host of hell's aristos single-handed."

"And then you Tainted him for it, didn't you?" Zuul giggled. "Spare me, lover boy. He drinks tonic water, for fuck's sake. You could at least *pretend* you're trying to win—"

"How about painting the ground with your guts? Convincing enough?"

Zuul chuckled. "Just looks guilty to me."

Michael flung Zuul to the ground, a savage crunch of bone. Zuul howled, his bleeding face alight with bliss. "Azaroth never sent you." Michael kicked him, and he doubled over, groaning. "The cringing worm wouldn't show his hand to me. Why, Zuul? What's in it for you?"

Zuul laughed, coughing up blood. "You're the archangel," he gasped, struggling to his knees. "You figure it out."

Michael cursed, blistering ice-blue fire, and flashed out.

Zuul sprawled bleeding on the rough pavement, and laughed until his guts tore.

Satan's hairy balls, tormenting Michael was fun. His cracked skull felt so damn good he groaned, hot and hard. Zuul was a pain demon. Pain nourished him, gave him life, and Michael was never shy about doling out agony.

For a while, he'd been in Michael's thrall. He still missed the beatings, the bloody power games. Michael had an insatiable appetite for sex and violence, preferably at the same time. Zuul squirmed at the memory . . . but the handsome archangel was just an amusing trick. His true master of torment still awaited him. Satan, lurking in the pit, ready to burst out and excruciate the world. Oh, yes.

Too soon, his skull bones shifted, and healed, a stinging curl of hellsmoke. He stumbled up, his vision a pleasant blur. Maybe he'd visit one of his favorite underground torture clubs—enough of them in Babylon, what with the End of Days craze—and get the living crap beaten out of himself . . .

"Zuul."

His guts watered with cold sweet dread. He shivered, his blood cooling rapidly. Nothing like a visit from the Demon King to wilt a perfectly good hard-on.

"My king." He bowed, trembling, though he saw no one. Satan was the Lord of Torment, promising eternities of ecstatic agony. But Azaroth, Lord of Emptiness and Despair, was . . . something else. Zuul gibbered, terrified. Oblivion. No sensation, no pain, no feeling at all. Just numbness, and darkness, and eternal silence . . .

He groveled on the cracked sidewalk. "Forgive me, my king. I swear I meant no treason. Michael, he . . ."

Icy breeze caressed his crimson hair, corking his throat with frigid black silence. "Don't be afraid, Zuul. You've done well."

His lungs convulsed. He couldn't breathe. Azaroth would throttle him right here . . . He choked, forcing up black acid that ate at his lips. "Thank you, my king," he gasped. "I won't forget your mercy—"

"A wise vow." Sweet amusement, stroking his cheek like an icy claw. "Don't worry about Michael. He flirts ever closer with darkness. Necessary, Zuul. All part of my plan."

"It is?" Excitement warmed his chilled blood. He'd impressed the king with his mayhem during the zombie plague. Azaroth had promised reward . . .

"Naturally. Michael defeated Satan once. I won't let him do it again." Wind swirled, furious, and shiny ice crackled up the brick wall. "Michael's power makes them mighty. I want them weak and running for their lives. Michael must fall, Zuul, and you're going to make it happen."

Ohhh . . . Dark lust scorched Zuul's flesh, and with an abrupt, heated groan, he spilled himself, aching. Sweet Satan's blood. He wanted to laugh, dance, rake at his skin until it bled under his nails. Michael, so long his master, soon to be hell's slave . . .

"My king," he panted, shuddering still. "I . . . I don't know what to say. I won't fail you!"

"Oh, I know you won't." Agony spiked Zuul's skull, knocking him almost senseless with delight. "Luuceat and Fluvium have their rewards. But the fifth vial is still unclaimed. Win Michael for me, and it's yours."

Zuul licked bleeding lips, scarcely believing his luck. He'd lure Michael to the dark side if he had to chew the archangel's deceitful heart out. And then he, Zuul—imagine it!—would be a prince of hell. Slaves aplenty, minions waiting to do his bidding. Second only to Azaroth himself. Satan would surely reward him most excruciatingly . . .

But Michael was . . . well, Michael was a fucking god. A powerful spellworker, twice Zuul's size, the finest warrior heaven ever spawned. Tricking him wouldn't be easy.

Not without inside help.

Zuul's mind twisted, devious. Michael's heavenly angels— that frigid bitch Esther, for instance—were sycophants and cock lickers, bound to Michael by ambition and terror. Trying to turn them traitor would lead only to blood and screaming, all very enjoyable, but getting Zuul nowhere. The Tainted Host, now . . .

He recalled Japheth, that golden-feathered princess, seething with defiant rage, and hot inspiration spiked his skin. Michael and Japheth, already at odds for centuries. So set them against each other. Feed the fire of discontent. Pick a fight or two, shatter a few illusions . . .

He felt like laughing. Besides, last time they'd met, Japheth had crushed Zuul's skull. Without asking. Presumptuous little asshole. Nothing like revenge on ice to spice things up. "I will obey, my king—"

"Fail me, and I'll swallow you." A sweep of frigid wind sent him reeling. Azaroth was gone.

Evil delight shivered Zuul's bones. He bowed deeply to the empty silence, just in case. "Thank you, my king."

* * *

Six thousand miles away, on a deserted midnight beach, Jadzia's phone chimed.

Michael again.

The screen glared, a dazzling blue accusation. Jadzia hovered her finger over the glass . . . and tapped Reject. The ring tone cut off.

She slipped the phone away, uneasy breeze ruffling her creamy feathers. Three times tonight, her archangel had called. Three times she'd ignored it. Waves whispered over her bare feet, tiny bubbles frothing on the sand. Her wings shed a soft white halo. Frangipani sweetened the salty air and, across the broad beach, shadowy palm trees lined the shore. Gossamer clouds misted over the moon, and huge tropical stars sparkled, broken diamonds on black satin sky.

Sultry breeze played with her loose blond hair, toyed with her flimsy skirt. She shivered, feathers prickling despite the heat. She felt weird, out of armor and leather battle trousers. She should be in Babylon, fighting demons with Dashiel and the rest of the Tainted Host.

Instead, here she stood. On a beach, in Tahiti. With perfume on. Wearing a dress, for heaven's sake.

Her friend Iria would laugh. But Iria was world-weary, cynical, nine hundred years Tainted with a string of sexual conquests to match. Jadzia, on the other hand . . .

She flushed, her halo shimmering brighter. She knew almost nothing about men. Except that they didn't want her, not really. Not since she'd been Tainted. She was a toy to be used, a distraction at best. So she used them back. Took what she could while it lasted, and moved on. Tried not to get attached.

But Shax was different. Weeks ago, they'd met by chance, in a burned-out Babylon office block amid battle's fiery chaos. Since then, she'd thought of him day and night, giddy like a lovesick girl. They'd spent enchanting hours, stolen in secret. He made her think. He made her laugh. They'd climbed the Great Pyramid at midnight, strolled in a fragrant Paris evening, swum in sunlit waters off the sparkling Mediterranean coast.

Mercy, how he haunted her. In her daydreams, he stalked her, invisible, a burning breath on her shoulder, a ghostly caress in her hair, a sweet touch of unseen lips. But at night, she dreamed of him, soaked in fever and nightmarish desire . . .

"My princess." Hot velvet darkness, the dizzying scent of ash and thunder. His burning body caressed her back, his fingers featherlight on her shoulders, his soft kiss teased her hair . . .

"Shax." Jadzia fought dizzy wits, unbalanced. Oh, to lean back, inhale, let him consume her . . . She edged away, her pulse racing. "I thought you weren't coming."

"Miss the sight of you? Never." Shax captured her hand, twirling her about like a dancer. Her warm silken skirts whispered over her thighs, and suddenly she didn't feel ridiculous, but powerful, feminine, desirable . . . and he was hot, deadly, male. He pulled her into his arms, crimson-flame eyes alight. "Gorgeous," he murmured.

Her stomach fluttered. No, *he* was gorgeous. Perfect face, luminous like moonshine. His hair caressed her bare shoulder, blue-black and so soft it might dissolve. Sweet hellsparks danced over her skin. They didn't burn, like they should. But something surely did, deep inside her, sinful and darkly delicious . . .

"I hope you've not waited long." He stroked her chin, one long finger. Wiry muscles, tight under black studded leather armor that smelled of flames. *Demon armor. My enemy* . . . "Sometimes my duties keep me. I'm sorry."

She swallowed, dry. Shax worked for Azaroth, the Demon King. He'd been fighting in Babylon, most like. Killing her friends. Spreading his master's evil like a plague. "I didn't mean . . . that is, I . . ."

"Don't be afraid." His crimson eyes glinted, drinking her platinum glow hungrily. "No one can see us. It's just you and me."

That's what I'm afraid of . . . But her voice withered, sucked away by his heat, his hard body, his hair's ashen fragrance . . .

His mouth hunted hers, and swiftly made the kill. Sweet hellfire. He tasted of storms and blood. His lips, gentle yet hungry on hers, leading her on, inviting her to open for him, yearn against him. Her breasts ached against his chest. Her hands sought his body, his hair, his burning skin beneath the leather. His muscles played under her palms, taut, so smooth . . .

"Jadzia." God, she loved how he whispered her name. How he kissed her, so hot and soulful, just the way she liked. Desire dizzied her. "My moonlight princess. So beautiful it hurts. How I've missed you."

He slid teasing fingers into her feathers, stroking deep. She trembled. "Shax . . ."

"Mmm?" He nuzzled her throat, sharp teeth stinging, and it oozed straight to her sex. She shuddered, unconscionably alive. She'd resisted him until now, pulling away like a nervous teenager before she lost control. But she wanted more than his kiss. Much more.

Oh, lord. She groaned, lost. She wanted to climb him. Open her legs, fold them around him, suck his tongue into her mouth. "We can't . . ."

"We *must*." A sweet flicker of tongue burned her ear. "We belong together. My stunning angel."

His pretty words melted her. It was foolish. She didn't care. He made her feel . . . desirable. Special. Not just another conquest. He actually wanted *her* . . .

Just a demon's lies. Kill him right now. Slit his throat and be done.

Her nipples poked at her thin dress. She wanted him so badly her head ached. But the threat of hellfire scorched her raw, deep in the dark bleeding void where her soul once lived . . .

She fluttered away, her heart pounding. Warm waves splashed her toes, sinking into the sand. "I . . . I can't. Not tonight. Michael called. I've gotta go. I'm sorry."

"Ah." Shax's crimson gaze glittered. He tucked shy hands behind his back with a rueful smile. "I understand. Michael. Charming fellow. No doubt it's about his vials. I hear there's one in Bhutan?"

Jadzia coughed, grateful for the change of subject . . . but she couldn't rip her gaze from Shax. Ghostly flames licked his midnight hair, a faint cascade of fire. His plum-red lips still shone from kissing her. Her skin still craved his lost heat. So easy, to slip into the darkness . . .

But her feathers stung in confusion. Bhutan? She hadn't checked her voice mail, didn't know what Michael wanted. Who was Shax, that he knew so much? "How did you . . . ?"

"I pay attention, that's all." Shax's crimson gaze licked over her, hungry. "The demon's called Luuceat. The Prince of Fire, now, I'm told. The King rewards his favorite subjects, and the one thing they all want is a vial."

And what about you, Shax? What do you want? "But . . . we killed the first two princes."

An amused flicker of eyebrow. "Indeed."

"Not much of a reward if you're dead. Aren't they afraid?"

"Possibly. But they crave power more. Prince Luuceat has an explosive temper. He likes things to burn. If he brings that vial to Babylon . . ." He cleared his throat, and smiled, mild yet terrifying. "Well. Perhaps I've already said too much."

Urgency itched at her. "Why would he bring the vial to Babylon? What's going on?"

An elegant shrug. "Because that's where Azaroth wants the final battle. He's in charge. No one asks those questions. Just be careful in Bhutan, Jadzia. Michael breaks his toys."

And you don't?

Jadzia's thoughts whirled, crazy. Again—just like in Babylon, when he'd helped her defeat the Prince of Blood—Shax was warning her of danger. But why?

He smiled again, dark and secret. His ashen scent caressed her. Illicit heat sank deeper, so good she wanted to groan, unfold, let it take her . . .

Despair sweetened her need. Surely this couldn't be real. He was seducing her. Preying on her aching loneliness. *That's what demons do, girl.* Iria's experienced voice clanged in her skull. *They're so damn reasonable. They chip away at your convictions. They caress you until you expose your weaknesses, and then they skewer you. Don't let him coax you into darkness . . .*

Their gazes locked. Silence stretched tighter, tearing.

"Well," Shax said eventually. His sigh was sweet, disappointed. He turned. "I'll leave you be."

Jadzia's heart contracted, a swift stab of pain. "Wait."

He halted. His shadows flickered on the sand, the rushing water.

End it, Jadzia. While you still can . . . She inhaled, crisp sea air and courage. "When can I see you again?"

He vanished, and suddenly he surrounded her, folding her in his arms. Glittering ash tingled into her skin. He inhaled, an inch away, thieving her breath. "Let it be soon. My world is parched without you. Kiss me, my princess, or I'll die of thirst."

His mouth claimed hers once more. God, he was so perfect. Their bodies molded together like long-lost parts of a whole. His ashen flavor made her drunk. His touch lit fireworks in her blood, not hellfire but storm-drenched desire. She could feel it, the way his cock pressed hard and angry against her. Her legs rinsed to water. She melted against him, yearning, alive like she'd never been. *I can't resist this. You win. I surrender . . .*

A tiny laugh, sparkling into her mouth. "I know," Shax whispered, and dissolved to smoke.

CHAPTER 7

Japheth stole down the narrow firelit street, sword in hand. The moon glared between looming buildings, a fat red fireball, only one night from full. It poured eerie shadows through the trees, licked down the walls, dripped on the barred windows like blood.

Broken glass littered the sidewalk, the remnants of some protest or riot. The charred shell of a car still flickered with orange flames. A starving dog rooted through garbage, bloody foam coating its jaws. Rat bites oozed corruption on its skin. Somewhere, a baby cried.

His nose twitched, hunting rotten hellflesh. Elusive, this Fluvium. He didn't keep just a single nest, where he could be besieged and slaughtered. No, he flitted ghostlike through the West Village streets, spreading his curse like a poisoned shadow.

And no one was talking. Already tonight, seven vampires had perished on Japheth's sword, and before they'd died, he'd demanded everything they knew about their demon master. And he'd gotten nothing.

Not a damn thing. Just cackles, spitting vitriol, fear. One had dirtied himself, the stain spreading on his jeans before

Japheth skewered him in disgust. All terrified to their putrid bones of hell.

Coldly, Japheth pushed damp hair from his eyes. They'd made their choice. They'd given up, succumbed to the hunger. It was too late for them. They deserved what was coming.

But he still hadn't found *her*.

His ears twitched. He spun, searching . . . Nothing. Just leaves, rustling in some non-existent breeze. Surely he'd heard footsteps, smelled some faint sweetness that tingled his tongue . . .

He gritted cold teeth, sweating in his silver armor. Last night, he'd fled home in pale pre-dawn, tried to scrub his mind of Michael's taunts and get some rest. But he'd spent a restless few hours, fevered and comfortless, dreaming of *her*.

The vampire bitch, dark eyes flashing, her spicy female scent torturing him. Her mouth warm and delicious on his, her hair spilling over his hands. Muscles straining, hot hard flesh, pinning her beneath him, fighting for her wrists, spreading her taut thighs and pushing into her, pounding within her, rage and passion and unslakable thirst and . . .

Well, yeah. That.

He'd woken in a burning sweat before they'd finished. It still felt like someone had kicked him in the balls. But he preferred aching balls to the alternative.

Normal male lust was one thing. Wanting to make love to . . . He squirmed, mortified. Wanting to *fuck* some dirty hellspawn . . . Even a vicious workout and a stinging cold shower had barely calmed him down.

If twitching feathers and a stone-hard dick could pass for *calm*. He was still thinking about her. Still imagining how she'd feel. Her devilmagic might be dissolved, but he still struggled under her spell. And only her screaming death on his sword could break him free . . .

"Looking for someone, angel?"

That honey-blood voice quivered his feathers taut.

She grinned, mocking. Leaning against the redbrick wall beneath a rusted fire escape, steeped in magical shadow and hot vampire stink.

He stared, dumb. Tall for a girl, only a head shorter than

he. Long legs, encased in blue jeans and black army boots. Her short black t-shirt stretched over full breasts, flashing that tempting skin above a silver belt buckle. Her bare arms shone, muscular but womanly. Sexy dimples in her cheeks, perfectly shaped for cupping in his palms.

The bloody feathers of slain angels, gold and white and red, stuck through the thick dark braid she tossed over her shoulder. A few wisps escaped to play around her face in the summer-night breeze. He wanted to trace their path with his fingertips, cheekbone to chin to cherry-ripe lips . . .

"Matter of fact, I am," he said tightly. "Your sniveling master. Fluvium, is it? Prince of Thirst? Tell me where he is and I might kill you quickly."

She laughed, fangs glinting. Sharp, lethal like a tigress's. "You've come to kill Fluvium? Good luck with that." She lolled on one foot, eyeing him speculatively, sizing up her prey. "Japheth, right? Of the Tainted Host? Cute name, for a hamster."

Sweet lord, his name in her mouth sounded . . . dirty. He swallowed, rough. "How'd you know that?"

"I know my enemy." She licked ripe lips.

"Yeah?" he said coldly. "Well, I don't want to know you, whore. I don't care what your name is—"

"Rose Harley," she cut in swiftly, with a wicked grin. "Whoops. Too late. Sorry about that. You like it anonymous, don't you? So you can pretend they're not people when you damn them to eternal torment?"

His grip spasmed around his sword. Sweet heaven, he wanted to stab her. Fill her with burning steel. Twist it, thrust it deeper, make her moan . . . "You don't need me to damn you. You made your choice. Tell me where Fluvium's hiding, and I'll put you out of your misery."

She laughed again, and strolled towards him, hands in pockets. "You sure could learn a thing or two from demons about making deals. Like, I dunno. Offering me something I actually want?"

Her knife still lay sheathed, in her thigh holster. Unafraid, was she? Grudging admiration tingled under his skin, and he crackled it off. Nothing admirable about a demon minion's attitude. "So you do know where he's hiding, then."

"And what if I do?" She draped her gaze over his silver-clad chest, his bare arms, his glowing blue sword . . . Her scrutiny flushed treacherous heat right to the top of his head. He could smell her, blood and corruption, yes, but underneath, the hot salty musk of female flesh . . .

Surely, she was his nemesis. Sent to tempt him into falling. Well, he wouldn't give in. Not when he was so close to redemption.

But his heart pumped hard, and unwilled, his body jerked, muscles rippling.

She caught her bottom lip in her teeth, a playful smile that made him think dirty thoughts. "Suppose I could tell you where he is, angel," she crooned. "What would you give me?"

He wanted to back away, put distance between them. But he wouldn't give her the satisfaction. "A painless death?"

She pouted. "Not what I had in mind."

"I can make it hurt, if you'd rather." His left hand twitched, the one with the Tainted sigil burned into the palm. Oh, yes, he certainly could. Drag his blessed hands over her, burn her with sweet heavenflash until she writhed. Glide his blade slowly under her skin, peel away the layers, expose the hot trembling flesh beneath and torture it until she . . .

"Now you're just teasing." She inched closer, a sultry invitation. "How about . . . a kiss?"

He laughed. "Don't make me puke."

But her cursed ripe scent maddened him. How dare a vampire smell so . . . sensual? She wouldn't smell half so nice dead . . .

"Oh, I dunno. You seemed to enjoy it last time." Lazily, she twirled her braid in one deft finger. Her short fingernails were painted black.

"You spelled me last time." He stared at them, dizzy. Damn, that was hot. How would those sexy nails feel? Teasing him, her fingers wrapping around his cock, trailing sweet fire, her ripe red lips . . .

"Are you sure?" A husky laugh that made him tremble.

"C'mon, angel. You're already Tainted. What's it matter? Just one little kiss. It'll feel so good—ah!"

He grabbed her belt buckle and yanked her hips against him.

Strong, yet soft and female. She gasped, and it stabbed right to his balls. His thumb sizzled on her belly, inside her jeans. He didn't care. The wicked sensation felt so good. Almost as good as her body pressing against him, her hell-curse burning him, matching the ugly fire inside. His hard cock jutted against her belly, only a few layers of rough fabric between them. Those luscious breasts almost—not quite—brushed his silver-clad chest. God, a man could live a thousand years and never see breasts as sweet as hers. Her nipples made tiny quivering peaks against her t-shirt, begging for his tongue . . .

Sweet fucking Jesus. He growled, deep in his chest, a long-forgotten animal sound of need. "You want me, vampire?"

She laughed, her eyes dark. "You asshole. Hell, yes, I want you."

"Then come get me."

She pressed closer, almost purring, and desire dizzied him. Blood gleamed crimson on her lips. God, he wanted to kiss them. He could almost taste her, feel her slick heat, her tongue alive in his mouth, those magnificent breasts crushing ripe in his hands . . .

He slammed his left palm against her forehead, and murmured a breathless charm to heaven.

Blue light flashed. Flesh sizzled, the stink of unholy smoke. And she howled, rich with thwarted fury, and stumbled backwards.

CHAPTER 8

Damn it.

Rose staggered. Pain chewed between her eyes, a rabid disease. Her forehead sizzled, his Tainted spell eating her flesh almost to the bone. But the acid sting to her ego was worse.

The bastard tricked her. Let her think she'd won. A triumphant kiss, the cursed blood already on her lips. Slide her tongue into his mouth, let the hot crimson fluid flow, and it'd all be over. So easy, to push him over the edge.

But she hadn't.

Instead, the hunger raged like fever inside her. Her nipples stung. Her mouth hurt, fangs straining for blood. Deep in her belly, she starved for him. Hot angry release, the rough ground scraping her raw, his flesh driven so deep inside her it hurt. Bruises, biting, fists yanking her hair . . .

He'd tricked her. Violated her. And she'd fallen for it like a drunken skydiver.

His spell dizzied her, sickening. She grabbed her knife and rounded on him, unsteady. "You lying bastard. What have you done?"

Japheth grinned, savage. Green frost glittered in his eyes. "Enjoying it, demonslut? It's a Tainted angel's mark."

"What's that mean?" Frantic, she swiped her forehead with the back of her hand. Moisture smeared, a weeping burn. Already the pain subsided, the fiery sensation fading. Didn't make it any less humiliating.

The damn angel was still breathing hard, too. His muscles still gleamed with sweat, his big body quivering, the evidence of his arousal staring her in the face.

Ditto on the humiliating.

"It means you're mine." He flashed his sword away, laughing coldly at her expression. "Not like that, idiot. Maybe if you were human, I could save you. But you're still a demon's slave, if that makes you feel better."

Strange fever still wracked her, making her sweat. A peculiar smell radiated from her body that made her queasy. She wanted to rake her nails down his handsome face. "Then what? What have you *done*?"

"It means you're under my protection. All those friends you thought you had? Your stinking vampire coven, or whatever you call it? They aren't your friends anymore." He shrugged, casual, but feral amusement tweaked his lips. Charmingly roguish smile, when he wanted. Bastard. "To them, you smell of angel now. You smell of me."

"Screw you." Not very eloquent. But it was all she could think of. A madwoman's laughter bubbled in her throat. The night Bridie died, she'd screamed her heart out for one scrap of heaven's attention. Now, she was marked by an angel, and it'd kill her.

"Hell, you probably even taste of me. They'll attack you on sight. Hunt you down like the traitor you are."

"You're lying, asshole." But her throat tightened. What if he wasn't? Caliban's Chosen were already gunning for her. With the rest of the coven hunting her, too, there'd be nowhere to hide. Never mind what Fluvium would do to her, if she came back with an angel's sigil burned into her forehead. Never mind the hell that awaited her if she couldn't do his bidding.

Fight him, fuck him, I really don't care. Fluvium's words slithered back, fanged with malice.

But he did care. Her demon was a jealous god. And his vengeance would be terrible.

Japheth shrugged. "I never lie. Not even to hellspawn. Face it, I'm the only friend you've got."

She wanted to flee. To run, and keep on running until she died. But instead, she laughed, and stalked up to him, threatening her blade at his eyeballs. "What, are you offering me *protection*? Forgive me if I spit it back in your face—ugh!"

She hit the ground flat on her face, beneath a sweep of golden feathers.

And two slobbering vampires leapt screaming from the rusted fire escape, and landed square on the spot where she'd stood.

Rose and Japheth rolled, and thudded against the gritty gutter. Great. Now the big bastard lay on top of her, shielding her with gleaming golden wings. She fought to see her attackers. A guy and a girl, skinny and undernourished. Their hungry eyes glittered, fledgling fangs drooling. Their clothes were torn, their skin ragged with fang marks. They'd bitten each other, in a doomed effort to sate their hunger.

A clumsy ambush by any standards. She'd been too preoccupied with this damn angel to notice them coming.

Japheth grinned down at her, breathless. "Told you so."

"Gallant prick, aren't you?" Her heart pounded. He was surprisingly supple, all that bulging muscle lighter than she'd expected. And . . . oh, yeah. She squirmed, a hot ache swelling inside. Did he ever not have a hard-on?

Was he easing it against her? Feeling her? Jesus, it sure felt that way. Her breasts ached. She wanted to open her thighs, wrap her leg around him, put that hot hard pressure to use where it'd feel good . . .

The vampires moaned in mindless hunger, and advanced. Rose struggled to keep her thoughts in line. They hadn't attacked him, jumping in to defend her as she'd expected.

They'd attacked *her*.

Her head ached. Something was strange. Japheth's steely fingers, crushing her wrist. His feathers curling in her hair . . .

Shit on a stick. He's not burning me.

Her head swam. No sizzling skin or melting flesh. He'd marked her, all right. And those bloodsuckers were crouching for the kill . . .

"Get off me," Rose snapped. "We kill 'em, then I kick your golden ass. Deal?"

A blinding smile. "Try it."

And he leapt off her, a golden-blue whoosh of wings and heavenflame, and flung her to her feet.

She came out stabbing, whirling to keep balanced, swinging her blade in a wide arc.

The vampire girl leapt backwards, her eyes afire with unholy hatred. She'd chewed her own hands bloody, trying to quench her thirst. "Come here, heavenbitch," she snarled. "Let me eat you."

"You're not my type," said Rose coolly, and dived for the girl's legs. Her shoulder connected, a sick crunch of bone. The girl tumbled on top of her. A swift hack of her knife across that pale bitten throat, and it was done. She pushed the corpse away, disgusted. Stupid girl.

Behind her, flesh ripped, wet. She spun on her toes, ready to fight.

Japheth dropped the vampire boy's dripping head. Cursed blood sizzled on his fingers, but he just flexed them, watching them heal. He caught his breath, muscles cording in his arms. His wings danced with ruby sparkles, the shimmering shadow of glory.

She stared, transfixed. He got off on this. He liked the blood, the rush, the slice of steel in flesh . . . and like a sleek and hungry bird of prey, it made him beautiful.

Rose's jaded heart shivered, warm. She liked a good fight before sex. And now, with this grotesque mark on her forehead, his flesh didn't burn her. When she did finally get her way with him—he'd bested her this time with his lying heaventricks, but she had more than one weapon in her arsenal, oh yes—it could be more fun than she'd thought . . .

Silently, she sneered, kicking the idea away. She'd never demean herself to be his plaything. This angel would go to hell on her terms. Rose's way, or no way.

Which meant she couldn't stand another second of this pestilent mark. The burn already itched, like a virulent rash that wouldn't heal. Next time, it might not be stupid, fuck-addled fledglings who attacked her.

She jumped, and landed before him in a crouch, knife poised. "Thanks so much, Sir Lancelot," she jeered. "Very noble of you. Now take this thing off me before I skin you and rape your rotting bones."

Challenge glittered in his eyes. "Only if you cooperate."

Her muscles ached, fatigue and hunger. She needed blood. If he didn't release her, she'd have to eat in front of him. The idea sickened her. Satan knew, he'd already humiliated her enough. For him to see *that* . . .

She scowled, catching herself. Why did she care if he saw her feeding? "Fine. I'll play. What is it you want?"

A gilded shrug. "Clean energy. World peace. No more reality TV . . ."

"Don't be a wiseass."

"Then don't be a damn fool. You've only got one thing that's any good to me."

Her heart sank. "You want Fluvium."

"Bingo." Japheth folded bulging arms across blood-streaked silver. "Lead me to Fluvium, and I'll take off the mark. When Fluvium's dead," he added hastily, as if forestalling demon trickery. "Not a moment before."

Rose laughed, sick. What else could she do? There was no way. Even if she'd *wanted* to, there was no way . . .

Japheth's eyes narrowed. "What's so funny?"

"You stupid heaventrash, haven't you figured it out?" Rose jammed hands on hips, frustrated. "I lied, okay? Fluvium always comes to *me*! I have no idea where he's hiding. Not a clue."

Japheth stared, still catching his breath.

The bitch tricked him. Again.

His mark glowed sickly blue on her forehead. Crossed lightning bolts, the sigil of the Tainted Host. It reflected in her eyes, a dark indigo gleam. Awful. Beautiful. Corrupted heavenlight, shimmering its way down to hell . . .

"Don't believe you." He refused to uncross his arms. He'd come this far. She wasn't getting away now.

"Fine. I don't care. Keep looking in the wrong places. Suits me just peachy." She tilted her gaze up through dark lashes, challenging.

His fists clenched. He wanted to squeeze that damned insolence out of her. "How do you know this is the wrong place, if you don't know where he is?"

She laughed. "Listen, moron, he doesn't have an evil supervillain's lair! There's no castle you can storm, or whatever you Dark Age dickheads like to do. I just met him in some nightclub. And then some room on Fifth Avenue by the park. He doesn't live there. He doesn't live anywhere!"

Images assaulted him. The filthy demon on top of her, his burning flesh inside her. Her long legs wrapped around him, the air sultry with sweat and sighs . . . Japheth clenched his jaw tight. "So you *are* his whore."

She scowled. "Don't sneer at me, choirboy. Twelve of your prissy brothers came before you and every single one of them was up for a good screw."

"Yeah, well. I'm not them."

"Right. Like you've never dragged some blushing girlie back to your place to slip her a hot one."

"Matter of fact," he said stonily, "I haven't."

"What, not at your place? Or never?"

He glared, frigid. Fourteen hundred years—give or take a few lurid mistakes—might as well be never. "None of your cursed business, whore."

She laughed. "Jesus. I'm talking to the Virgin frickin' Mary . . . hey, hey, don't be hasty, gunslinger." She raised her hands, warding off his glower. "I've never been to his place, okay? If he's even got a place. Believe me, I've looked for the sly son of Satan."

"Then you're no use to me." He conjured his sword, an impatient blue flash.

Her face paled. "Wait—"

"Go quietly and it'll be better for you." He flitted closer, keeping his gaze steady on hers. But his feathers itched, disappointed. Was that fear, glimmering deep like underwater flame? Killing just another cowering devilslave wouldn't be nearly as sweet . . .

Another trick. Don't look at her. Don't listen to another word from her pretty poison lips. Just stab her through the heart, and walk away . . .

She jumped back. "I said hold on, asshole. Maybe I can still help you."

"How? There's only one way you're any use—"

"I told you, I don't know where he keeps himself!" For the first time, stress cracked her voice. "We're just minions to him, even the Chosen. We're not his buddies. He doesn't hang with us. He just appears out of nowhere and frightens the crap out of me."

"Sorry. Do better." His sword tip kissed a crimson line under her chin. "Unless you like this, hellspawn. Had enough, is that it? Want me to put you out of your misery?"

She winced, feminine. "Ouch. That hurts, you know—"

"Five seconds."

"I can give you the coven master!" The words rushed out of her. "Caliban. He's strongest of all the Chosen. He'll know how to summon Fluvium."

"Are you sure?" He jabbed the point harder.

"Of course I'm sure!" To her credit, she didn't back off. But her face shone pale, her dark eyes wide. "I'm just small fry. Caliban is something else. He's the guy you want. I'll show you. Just promise you'll take your stinking mark off."

Swiftly, Japheth considered. The West Village was a big place, infested with muties and Manhattan virus leftovers and all manner of hellspawn. He'd need Rose's help to find this coven master in time for Michael's deadline.

And if she was tricking him? He'd have her blood. Pin her down, impale her on his steely shaft, watch her writhe . . .

He didn't budge. "I'll take it off when we find Fluvium. Not a moment before."

"Promise you won't kill me afterwards, and you've got yourself a deal."

His guts heated. Of course he'd have to kill her afterwards. The beautiful bitch was demonspawn. Chosen. Not just a helpless infected bloodsucker, but Fluvium's willing disciple.

But . . . he needed her help. His soul was within reach. Without her, he'd never earn his way back to heaven.

His fingers clenched, painful. Lie to her. Smear his honor in the dirt. Stain his heart with sin.

Or lose this chance forever.

CHAPTER 9

"You have my word."

The lie burned like demon's blood in his mouth. His stomach went watery. Holy mercy, he'd never felt this naked. Surely she'd see the untruth, shining from his face like a torch . . .

But a satisfied smile curled her lips. "Deal. Now put that sword away before you hurt yourself."

Heaven's precious light. She'd believed him.

Trusted him. Kept faith in the word of an angel.

His cheeks lit warm. This was surreal. He should be triumphant. But he just wanted to shake her. Slam some sense into her, scream at her to run from him, that he was a monster, to open her goddamned eyes before it was too late . . .

He stepped aside, and flashed his sword away. "Afraid, vampire?"

Sullenly she rubbed her bleeding throat. His mark glowed sickly on her forehead like a disease. "Just biding my time, heavenscum. I never promised I'd *like* helping you."

"Consider the feeling mutual." His feathers curled, uncomfortable. Mocking her didn't make him feel better. Already he'd compromised his honor. His skin slicked filthy with his lies. God, he wanted to flash away from here. Dive under the shower, scrub that horrid untruth from his skin until he bled raw.

She shrugged. "Whatever, hero. First time we met, you kissed me senseless. Go ahead, pretend you don't want to get naked with me."

"Careful what you conjure, bloodsucker. I could rip you apart." But his gaze strayed to her hair, the way her braid swung in warm midnight air. Her smooth, feminine throat. Her t-shirt, riding up over her hip, that lickable flash of bare skin. Her magnificent breasts, so firm and full. Hell, yeah. They were amazing, the nipples poking at her thin t-shirt. Still hard, from the fight or fear or . . .

"Hello? My face is up here?" She pointed, giving him a triumphant grin.

He gritted cold teeth, willing the hungry itch in his balls to fade. Hell, he wanted everything to fade. The guilt, the vile longing, the way his skin sparkled under her sultry dark gaze. "Mock me and it'll be worse for you."

"C'mon, it'll be fun. I like shy boys. We can go slow, if you don't know what to do . . ."

He grabbed a fistful of her hair, and crushed her against the wall.

She gasped, her full lips parting. He wanted to lick them. Her breasts swelled against his chest plate. Her rich curves taunted him, pressing into his secret places, springing skin and blood and feathers alive . . .

He knew what to do, all right. And it tormented him to the bloody edge of his reason.

A hint of breathless smile. "Get off on hitting women, do you?"

"Don't give me that." He yanked her braid tighter. "You wear a weapon. You're in this war. You fight me, you give up the right to cry innocent."

"Ooh, I bet you say that to all the girls."

Left-handed, he sprang his dagger from the ether, a wicked rippled blade made for double-handed combat. Its edge glittered red like fresh blood. "I said, don't mock me, hellwitch. My glory might not burn you. Doesn't mean I can't make this excruciating."

Her dark stare taunted him. Thick lashes, black like a starless midnight. "It's Rose. Rose Harley. Not 'hellwitch' or 'whore' or 'vampire.' Do me the courtesy."

His blade pricked her throat, one single ruby droplet on the steel.

His mouth watered. He'd tortured hellspawn in heaven's name before. He did whatever was necessary in battle's glory-rich delight, and if sometimes he enjoyed it, well, that was the penance he paid. Hurting hellspawn was his job. Heaven let him keep his gifts for a reason. No one up there cared about his conscience when there was work to be done.

Some angels worked it off after battle, like Dash with his endless parade of tiny women. Japheth never did. Never forgave himself the rush. A cold shower, bruises and aches, never the undeserved pardon of release.

But that single crimson drop of blood staining this woman's throat led him places he'd never dared go. Hot, sultry, breathless places, spicy with sighs and forbidden delights . . .

He swallowed, sweating. To taste her, that salty female flavor, danger and sin and sex melted into one. Liquid moonlight in his mouth, her hot juices running down his throat . . .

His fingers bruised her neck. "Let this be clear between us, Rose Harley," he said roughly. "While my mark lasts, you'll do as I say."

She rolled dark eyes, mocking. "Here we go with the schoolgirl fantasies. How dirty do you like it?"

"Don't be juvenile. You'll lead me to this coven master . . . ?"

"Caliban, moron. Were you listening at all, or just staring at my boobs?"

"Caliban," he affirmed, nudging her chin higher. "Aside from that? I don't want to know you. You don't ask questions. You don't speak to me unless you must. And you sure as hell don't touch me outside of battle. Understood?"

"Perfectly." A twist of sardonic smile. "So . . . will you let go first, or should I?"

"Ooh, very clever." He caressed his blade point across her ripe bottom lip. So taut, such delicate skin. If he pressed a little harder, would it pop, like a cherry? "You think you're tempting me? Think you can make me forget myself?"

"Just helping things along." She leaned closer, and her warm breath ghosted over his cheek. Seductive, scented with coppery suggestion. "Be reasonable, angel. We've both got needs. You're a good-looking guy. Even a frigid imbecile like you must know that. No rule says we can't use each other while we've got the opportunity."

His body ached hard. Suck her warm cursed flesh into his mouth, feel his teeth crunch on her disgusting vampire skin as she moaned his name . . .

His mind reeled, dry and fevered. Heaven, what was wrong with him? This earth rained pretty women. Clever ones, too. Willing ones, even, skin on show, candid glances, whispered invitations on painted lips. But he'd never desired one like this. Never wanted to take a woman and lose himself in her pleasure, her flavor, the salt-sweet softness of her sex . . .

Keep it frosty. She was Chosen. Her hellspells were powerful, that was all. And he'd resist her, like he resisted all the others.

Because the alternative was monstrous. Unthinkable. He'd spent the last fourteen hundred years not thinking it.

Just a demon's spell. That's all. Don't let her win.

He inhaled her hell-spiked flavor, daring himself closer to the edge. "Japheth," he growled, and it rumbled deep and primitive in his chest. "Not 'angel' or 'heaventrash' or 'asshole.' You want me to say your name, Angel Slayer? You can damn well say mine."

She grinned, sharp. "Japheth, then. Don't think it'll stop me cutting out your heart."

A wolfish smile spread before he could quench it. Sweet savior, in another life he could learn to like this warrior woman. It only made her a more formidable enemy.

And never say that Japheth of the Tainted turned his back on an enemy.

"I'd be disappointed if it did. Do you want the truth, Rose Harley?"

"That'd make a sweet change." She ran light fingers over his hips, tempting him closer, harder, hotter.

Her thumb slipped down into the crease of his thigh. He jerked, explosive, and heat crunched his flesh tight. Heaven's blood, he was so hard his head swam. The tough leather between them infuriated him. He wanted to rip it away, feel her clever fingertips working his cock, her fists yanking his feathers, her sweet silken hair spilling over his thighs . . .

Just a helltrick. Didn't make it any less real.

"I want to get you naked." The rough fire of truth erupted on his tongue. Rich like release, compelling, unstoppable. "I want to bite your nipples while you moan my name. I want to wrap your legs around my neck and lick your sweet flesh until you scream."

"Now you've got my attention." Her eyes glittered, greedy. She reached between them, running her palm over him, seeking a way in . . .

"I'm not finished." He banged her head into the bricks, crushing her hand to a halt with his hip. "I want to own you. I want to hold you down and have you, deep and hard and breathless while the world ends and heaven and hell melt into oblivion."

Delicately, he tilted his blade, slicing a shimmering red line under her chin. "But—just so we're clear?—I would rather die a dozen screaming deaths on your hell-fouled blade than touch you again."

He shoved her away, and vanished his dagger on a flashing-blue threat. "So don't test me, Rose Harley. Skinning you alive would be a lot less effort."

CHAPTER 10

And Japheth—gentle name, for an ice-hearted killer—spat at her feet, and walked away.

A scream soured Rose's throat, and she choked it down. Her bruised neck ached like poison, the cut he'd made burning like fire, even without his acid glory. But inside, her female flesh melted for him. And that hurt worse than anything.

She'd wanted him. Not just the faked lust of a vampire hunting prey, or Fluvium's compulsion chewing in her veins. Honest desire, woman for man. And he'd *walked away*.

That didn't happen to her.

Her fists curled tight. She wanted to rake her hair over her face, bury herself in the dirt so this Japheth couldn't see the humiliation burning in her cheeks. He'd felt so sickeningly good against her. Metal and unyielding muscle, so brutally strong she'd shivered in anticipation. And the hard thrust of his cock at the juncture of her thighs had her breathless. She'd wanted to strip naked, surrender, let him do whatever he wanted to her . . .

He'd made her feel like a woman. Not a vampire. Not a monster. Just a woman.

The one thing she'd never be again. Damn him for reminding her.

Her nails scraped her palms, raking them raw. Her skin squelched, vampire healing already kicking in, but she dug deeper, gritting her sharp teeth against the sting.

She'd been alone all her life, no one to help her succeed except a drug-addled big sister and a mother who'd died too young. That made a girl self-reliant. She wanted something, she took it. And she was strong, tall, trained to physical peak from years of rehearsal. Not many men made her feel . . . girly. Feminine. Vulnerable.

But one frigid, commanding glare from *him* and she'd bared her belly in submission. And when he'd said those things . . . damn, she'd felt every word. His teeth tugging on her nipples. His mouth at her sex, licking her, sucking, his strong warrior's fingers invading her . . .

She squirmed. Part of her wanted to weep for the human life she'd lost. Sex used to be fun. She'd liked the flirting, the laughter, the breathless excitement. It wasn't fun anymore. More like a necessary chore. Her desperate liaisons with other vampires were frantic, finished too soon to be satisfying. Even the orgasms were forgettable, just empty release without pleasure, and her own fingers were no substitute, even coupled with . . .

The bloodthirst twisted like an evil fanged serpent in her belly, and she shivered. Every time she fed, she promised herself she wouldn't like it. Wouldn't feel the rush. Wouldn't groan with dark-sweet delight as liquid fire poured down her throat, starbursting in her belly and igniting every nerve ending with evil ecstasy . . .

And every time, her will failed her.

The curse's propagation drive was simple. Vampires fed for the same reason humans fucked: it felt too damn good to stop. But Rose couldn't bring herself to fully quench her thirst. Feeding was too disgusting, soaked in evil memories. She drank only enough to survive, and the human stumbled away, infected, leaving her dizzy and sweaty and so horny she sought out other vampires for release.

Hence the quick, blind screw in some dirty doorway, the hurried reciprocal hand jobs, and failing that, her own empty caress in the dark. A few times, she'd made the mistake of feeding on other vampires for nourishment. It tasted vile. Meaty, lumpy with corruption like the hellcurse itself.

And it didn't sate the thirst.

Oh, no. Fluvium wouldn't make it that easy. Drinking vampire blood only made you thirstier.

She hadn't yet sunk low enough to do what most did, which was drink a human to death while you were fucking them. Caliban said the flavor, and the rush, were second to none, especially if you intensified the thirst with a vampire-blood orgy beforehand. They orgasmed when they died, one last frantic cry for immortality, and the pleasure, he said, was explosive.

Just the kind of sick shit that Caliban—he of the razor-carved scars and wire-barbed flesh—would think was cool.

The idea made Rose want to vomit. But one awful day soon, when Fluvium taunted her beyond endurance and the surging famine swelled up to drown her . . .

"Rose? You with me?" Japheth's cold voice sliced her foul memories apart. He'd wiped the bloodstains from his hands, scraped them from his golden hair. His luminous skin gleamed under the blood-lit moon. In her vampire sight, his green eyes burned like ice. Blue glitter danced in his feathers, hostile. All that explosive passion, channeled into frosty rage.

His composure didn't make her feel better. She flushed, sick, her burned forehead stinging. Unlike her, this Tainted angel had a will of steel. It didn't take a genius to see how he wanted her. He'd shuddered in her embrace, gasped when she caressed him. That hot hunk of male flesh, so hard and ready. Any other man would've taken what she offered. Fucked her. Gotten off in her hand. Pushed her to her knees and used her mouth.

But Japheth had just walked away.

Warm admiration bubbled in her heart, and she popped it with a forced sneer. Typical angel superiority, that's all it was. Easy to keep his dick in his pants when he rated her lower than pond scum. Well, he'd need a will of steel—and balls of steel, too—to resist her.

Her muscles warmed, energized by the moonlight, and she stroked her knife as it lay sheathed against her thigh. All she needed was a little exchange of blood. Willpower or not, he was aching for her. Just one mistake—one tiny lapse in the heat of battle, when his blood sang aflame with glory, when primal instincts took over and his brain wasn't running the show—and she'd have him.

Fluvium would be satisfied. He'd grant her one more month out of hell. And she'd flit off into the night, and do what needed to be done.

Drink. Fuck. Rise again tomorrow, and do it all over, more and again and forever, amen . . .

"Rose? You with me?"

Rose's lips curled, and Japheth wanted to rake that sardonic smile from her face. "Sure," she drawled. "Whatever. Let's get on with it."

Demon magic curled like black smoke around her limbs, wreathing her in misty shadow. She tossed back her braid, and led on.

Japheth followed, nerves still twitching. The crumbling red-brick tenements slicked evil shadows over his skin. His armor felt too tight, a sweltering metal cage. Sweat ran down inside it, and his shirt was saturated. He ruffled his feathers, hunting for a cooling breeze, but found none. Somewhere, a pack of cats yowled like banshees, echoing police sirens, and in the distance, a helicopter's blades thudded, its searchlights scything.

Trusting hellspawn. Christ almighty. It didn't feel right.

But what choice? Tomorrow night, the moon would wax full, and Fluvium's plan—whatever it was—would bear its evil fruit. He'd no time to waste on personal scruples. He was heaven's warrior, alive with holy purpose. His conscience meant nothing.

He meant nothing.

That was how it worked. Michael loathed inefficiency, and never wasted soldiers. But in the end, his angels—especially Tainted angels—were expendable. A renewable resource. Stopping these demons was all that mattered.

Apart from killing this Angel Slayer.

Japheth flexed tense fingers. He'd make this one hurt. She

deserved nothing less. If she'd truly killed twelve angels—and he didn't doubt her—it was his duty to put her down like a rabid dog.

Especially if she really had *touched* them. Made them want her, led them into willing sin.

Ahead, she stalked the rubbish-strewn sidewalk, athletic, lethal in her grace. His gaze glued to her denim-clad thighs. His body heated in memory. Her soft feminine scent dizzying him like opium, hypnotic dark eyes, cherry-ripe lips . . .

He bit his tongue, a stinging penance. Temptation was a two-way street. Yeah, she was beautiful. Desirable. Sexy as all hell. But his own weakness, not her wiles, had endangered him. Some ugly creature deep inside him yearned to be corrupted.

Like any good soldier, she'd merely discovered his vulnerability, and aimed for it.

And that was after fourteen hundred years of self-denial.

Heaven's angels—those others she'd seduced—were sheltered creatures. Unworldly. Against this she-devil? No chance.

Faint contempt soured his mouth. Heaven's children looked down with disdain on the Tainted. What price their superiority now? Still, he flicked his gaze skywards, a swift prayer for mercy on their souls. He knew how swift—how terrible—heaven's vengeance could be.

He fluttered to catch up, lighting beside Rose. "Where are we going?"

"Caliban's den. In the Village. Not far."

"And when we get there?"

She ducked an overhanging branch. "Hell if I know. You're the soldier, not me. Storming the castle is your job."

"Tell me about this Caliban." He flashed his dagger, checking the rippled edge for damage or dirt. It stung his finger, blood oozing. Guess it was sharp . . .

Rose averted her eyes, but not before he saw the flashburn glint of hunger.

Japheth smiled grimly as the cut healed. "See something you like?"

"Don't make me puke." But pink stained her cheeks. In the moonlight, feverish sweat gleamed sickly on her throat.

Great. More trouble. Angels could go days without nourishment. It made them more effective soldiers. But vampires, like humans, needed sustenance. The thought of watching her feed, listening to her sigh as she sated her thirst . . .

"Don't hold out on me, vampire," he said roughly. "Is your hunger going to be a problem?"

She lengthened her stride. "My problem, not yours."

He grabbed her elbow, and it burned his fingers. Not angel on devil. Body heat. She was too warm.

Her pulse pounded against his palm, dizzying. He had a knife in his hand. He could end this right now. Kiss her soft skin with razor steel, thrust it deep and hard into her flesh, feel her groan and shudder . . .

He forced her to face him. "It will be my problem, if you faint on me in the middle of a fight. Don't be shy on my account. A soldier does what's necessary. Don't they teach you that in hellspawn school?"

"I'm fine." She yanked free, kept walking. "Don't waste your fake concern on me. You'll be rid of me soon enough."

"Too soon, if you don't take care of yourself. This isn't the time for a low-protein diet." He shrugged. "Unless you really do have that death wish."

"Ha ha. So funny."

He ducked around another burning car, crisp metallic smoke billowing. "I'm a funny guy. Must be all the starving vampires I've killed so easily."

Rose laughed, and her bitterness stung his tongue. "You're a real comedian. Vampires were people once. They had lives and kids and people who loved them. Ever think of that? Or do you just get off on death?"

Above, shutters banged, a light hurriedly extinguished. Did humans still live there? Probably not for long. On the corner, under a pink neon sign that read FLOSSIES, a pair of muties huddled, slapping each other listlessly with misshapen arms. One had tentacles instead of hands, boneless flesh that flapped limply. Not vampires, or zombie virus victims. Just inbred muties, their genes poisoned by poverty and neglect.

"See those guys?" Japheth pointed with his blade. "Them, I feel sorry for. That's a crappy deal they never asked for. Your lot? They made a choice."

"Is that a fact?"

He flashed his knife away, shrugging his armor loose. "Good versus evil isn't rocket science. You were weak. You don't get a second chance."

"Right." Rose shoved hands in pockets, defiant. "And what choice did you make, Japheth of the Tainted? Why'd they kick you out? Did you covet your neighbor's ass, or something?"

" 'Ass' means 'donkey,' " he said stonily. "Do I look like I . . . Oh, forget it," he muttered. He'd walked right into that one. "You're worse than Dashiel."

She snickered, triumphant. "Who's Dashiel? Your holy-shit boyfriend?"

The guy who'll kick my feathered butt to hell's edge when he finds out I let you live. "Someone you'd better hope you never meet. Now tell me about this Caliban."

She shrugged. "If you insist. He's one of the first ones Fluvium made. Some people even say he's from before."

"Before what?"

"You know, the Apocalypse? Like, maybe he's been around a while. Fluvium's old best buddy."

"Just as charming a taste in boyfriends as you, then."

A scowl. "What's that supposed to mean?"

"I mean, I've met your *master*—" He whetted the word with scorn, and watched her flush. "And he's a gutless, whining rat with no honor. Well done on that. He's a real catch."

"Uh-huh," she replied coolly. "And what does that make you, angel? Clinging to your precious heaven's skirts? Promising forgiveness when there's no such thing? I'd call that some pretty shitty honor."

Japheth eyed her coldly. "I'd never promise you forgiveness, *vampire*. You already threw it away."

Her gaze stormed. "You weren't there. You don't know anything about me."

"Why are we even having this conversation? I needn't justify myself to you. You're cursed. That's all I need to know."

"Yeah. Because judging people is what you do, isn't it? You and your heavenly pals. Who cares if you've got all the facts? You're always right." Rose folded her arms, her eyes crackling with eerie black light. "Well, screw you. Bring on the End, asshole. I'm gonna laugh my hell-cursed butt off while Satan devours you all."

Japheth's muscles clenched hard, all over. He should shove her blasphemy down her throat. But his chest stung inside, tiny razors slicing his heart.

He knew what judgment felt like. He'd taken it full force, the day Michael smashed his face into the dirt. He'd spent the centuries since trying to earn forgiveness.

But Rose had surrendered to a demon. Let him creep into her heart, to satisfy her lust for flesh or power, and she didn't show one scrap of remorse. It wasn't the same.

Was it?

He brushed past, avoiding her gaze. "I'm over the insults. Can we take them as read?"

"Oh, there's a lot more where those came from."

He shot her a cold glare. "Don't forget you're wearing my mark. Without my protection, you're mincemeat."

"And without my help, you're one demon prince short. I can say what I want." She stepped closer, taunting him with a toe-curling smile. "Coward. Loser. Heaven's frigid little butt-boy. Is that big fat sword compensating for something? No wonder you can't ever get laid . . . ooh, that hit home, didn't it?" She laughed. "Celibacy was the worst idea your lot ever came up with. You're a big quivering pile of sin waiting to happen. Why don't you just jump me and get it over with?"

Up for a fight, was she? He'd give her one. A long, hard, breathless fight, flesh on naked flesh, blood and salt and sweet sighs . . .

"If I ever 'jump' you, Rose Harley, it won't be with sin in mind," he snarled, and spun away.

But perfidious heat tortured him. He surely had sin in mind right now. Pin her down. Strip her weapons away, one by one, until she lay naked beneath him in surrender . . .

Rose laughed. "You keep telling yourself that, angel. I'm gonna have you. I'll catch you off guard, mark my words. Before this is finished, you'll be screaming in hell with the rest of us, and your precious heaven won't give a damn."

Michael's words repeated in him like bile, ever more acidic for the truth: *I could kick your rebellious ass to hell right now and no one in heaven would blink . . .*

Japheth clenched his jaw so hard it popped, and he threw a silent prayer skywards. *I'll kill her when I'm done, I swear. Just give me the will to resist her.*

But only chilly silence greeted him.

He was on his own.

Damnation was a two-way street. No one could save him. Only his own icy will.

Fine. He'd resist her if it killed him. Oblivion was better than hell. Better to die Tainted than damned.

He strode up to her, sweeping his wings back. Her height was considerable, for a once-human woman, but he still had to look down to capture her gaze, and his muscles swelled warm with power. He was bigger than her. Stronger.

But any advantage was a dangerous illusion.

"Warning noted," he said coldly. "Now here's one for you. I'm kind of task-focused right now. My forbearance has limits. So don't test me. Don't look at me in some way I don't like. And don't even think about hell-spelling me, or I swear to God, I'll stab you through your devil-rotted heart and chance the consequences."

"Save it. You don't scare me." She laughed, mocking, but her eyes clouded, and a tiny quiver softened her arrogant smile.

Well, hello. That crack in her armor intrigued him, like a drug delicious and forbidden. It made her . . . vulnerable. Feminine.

Breakable.

And the primitive, brutal male creature that fired his instincts burned to protect this woman. To cherish her, hold her close, claim her as his own . . .

"See?" Her lips shone in crimson moonlight, her eyes shimmering. "You don't need to threaten me. Let's be friends. I can't harm you. I'm just a girl."

Loose hair drifted against her bruised cheek. He wanted to brush it away. His fingers jerked upwards an inch . . .

Icy glitter showered from his wings, a cold crackle of reality. That wasn't a hellspell. That was his own goddamn weakness.

"You're not a girl, Rose Harley." Cruelty stung cold poison into his mouth, and like all the best poisons, it tasted good. "You're a monster. You always were. The hellcurse just makes it more obvious."

Pain lit scarlet in her eyes.

Gotcha. At last, he'd found a weak spot . . . but his heart contracted, stinging.

He should press his advantage, rub it in like salt on bloody flesh. But for a bright, shocking instant, he wanted to take it back.

Comfort her, stroke her hair, whisper warm secrets. Make all that guilty fury go away.

He spun away, sweating. Compassion be damned. She wasn't a woman. She was hellspawn. And if he forgot it, she'd be worse than the death of him.

CHAPTER 11

You son of a bitch.

Rose's stomach knotted tight. *Screw him. He knows nothing about me.*

But that didn't make it hurt any less.

Memories assaulted her, the clotted crimson stains on Bridie's bedsheets, the screaming horror when she discovered what she'd done. Fluvium's dark laughter, burning her lips in smoky candlelight.

She could've walked away, that night. Gone home, tucked Bridie into bed, forgotten the whole thing.

But she hadn't. Japheth was right. She'd let the demon take her. Let him seduce her away from her life, just when things had been looking up. Her first on-Broadway show, part of the dance company, even a principal role in one number. Her career was taking off, money was coming in, Bridie was finally sleeping through the night without crying for her mommy.

But it hadn't been enough. Rose had craved excitement, peril, the exotic caress of a stranger.

She'd thrown it all away on a whim. Killed Bridie for want of cheap thrills. What kind of monster did that make her?

Stupid tears stung her eyes. Japheth didn't look at her. Just settled his gilded feathers, muscles clenched tight. Frosty anger, controlled, his glacial eyes glittering. *Asshole*.

Rose swiped away her tears, and cracked off the guilt like tarnish.

Fine. Let him despise her, let him make her feel as worthless as he liked. She had a job to do. Lure him to the darkness. Feed Fluvium his soul, and watch him scream. What she'd done was done. Being sorry for it didn't make one spit of difference.

God had taught her that.

She dragged her hair back, and walked up behind him. Even from this distance, his powerful heat tingled her skin, musky male fury overpowering the cloying incense of angel.

It was alluring, she'd give him that. A make-you-look, take-me-home-baby perfume. Arrogant bastard. Why couldn't he stink, like the rest? Too easy to forget he was a lying son of heaven.

Well, she wouldn't forget again. No matter how sexy he smelled.

She pointed over his shoulder, between overhanging trees to where a streetlight spilled eerie yellow shadows. "See that building? Red brick, with the black window bars? That's Caliban's lair."

Japheth cracked his knuckles, shedding blue sparks. "Fine. Let's go get."

"Wait," she said hastily. His filthy mark still burned her forehead. The idea of a hundred hostile vamps chilled her bones. If she died before Fluvium granted her that reprieve from hell . . .

Japheth sighed, impatient. "What?"

"He's a powerful Chosen. He's got an army of minions waiting to slaughter us. How are you planning to get in there?"

He flicked sardonic feather tips at her. "Through the window, of course. I can fly, remember?"

Rose laughed, shaky. "Not to Caliban's. He's a vampire, not an idiot. How d'you think he's evaded your surveillance all this time?"

A frown. "Explain."

She should have been triumphant. But his naivete just scared her. "His lair's in the basement, dumbass! Out of the sun, away from you lot. Oh, and locked beneath five floors of hungry vampires who want us dead. How's your plan looking now?"

Japheth shrugged. "Like a bit more fun. That's all."

But his blood shifted, uneasy. Clever hellspawn, hiding underground. Japheth was a creature of air, wind, stars. He didn't like dank places beneath the earth. Hot thick darkness, clogging his throat, all that weight crushing in to smother him . . .

Determined, he shook it off. No matter. He still had a few tricks to play.

Assuming Rose wasn't lying. Undermining his confidence, leading him into a trap. But he'd seen her eyes, when she spoke of this Caliban. Sensed her quickening breath, her fragile heartbeat, the subtle darkening of her scent. Caliban aroused something in her, and it wasn't desire or hunger.

More like . . . desperation.

But was she desperate to return to him? Or desperate to stay away?

"Fun?" Rose's eyes narrowed. "Are you insane? We'll be pinned down, top and bottom. Who's got the death wish now?"

"I guarded the church walls while Alaric burned Rome. Think I've never stormed a fortress before? You ready, or shall I leave you behind?"

She folded her arms, defiant. "Ready? For a suicide mission? No, I'm not bloody well ready—"

"Just shut up and follow orders." He dragged her along to the street corner, across from Caliban's building. Overhanging branches hid them from view. Through the leaves, his quick gaze dissected the problem. Five floors, tall iron-barred windows, fire escapes zigzagging down crumbling red walls. Front door, hardened glass and bars, shrouded in darkness. Whatever. Locks were no barrier. The stink, on the other hand . . . blood and shit, ripe vampire stench. A few isolated human screams. Probably, the monsters were eating.

He whispered a holy charm, and his spine tingled, apprehensive. His gifts were fragile, dependent on heaven's grace, and he'd wallowed in enough filth tonight to earn a kick in the ass. Would this be the night they deserted him?

But gentle warmth flowed, enhancing his magical angel-sight. The building sprang alive with faint scarlet glimmers in three dimensions. Demon sigils, glowing like ethereal neon serpents.

Japheth allowed a tiny smile. Low-level protective wards, designed to erupt on contact with his kind. Melting skin, liquefying organs, a little blood-rich agony. Nothing immediately lethal. They writhed in the sultry night like trapped salamanders, slavering for prey.

He realized he still held Rose's arm. Her lithe body, inches away. Her scent licked over him, caressing his most sensitive places . . .

He let go, flushing. Damn her. Give him some nice excruciating demonspells, ones that hurt like they should. More tolerable than *her*. "Ground floor, ten o'clock." He pointed over her shoulder, careful not to touch. "See those demon wards?"

"Of course I see them. I'm a vampire, remember?" Her voice husked, breathless.

Fear? Or something else? Japheth risked a glance. Her dark eyes shone. Her thigh muscles quivered, ready for action. Her fingers hovered over her knife, ready to spring it and attack, and she whetted glinting fangs with the tip of her tongue.

A magnificent warrior. Did she feel it, like he did? Battle's rich rush, senses screaming, fight's golden ecstasy in her veins, only not glory but something else, something evil, the relentless hot poison of hell's power?

What would that feel like?

Sweating, he dragged his gaze away. "The wards are our protection," he said tightly. "We block the exits, go in underneath and trap this Caliban in his own dungeon. Simple enough?"

She looked at him like he'd grown an extra nose. "Sorry to burst your bubble, moron, but demon wards won't protect us from vampires."

"They will if they're on fire."

She stared. "You crazy angel. I don't know whether to be impressed or terrified. You want to immolate the wards?"

"Sure. Why not?"

"Under the noses of five floors full of starving vampires with supernatural hearing? Who'll swoop down and slaughter you before you get ten yards?"

"Something like that." He grinned, satisfied. "Unlike yours, sweet Rose, my faith didn't fall out when I hit the dirt. I still have a few of heaven's tricks stuffed up my armor."

She rolled her eyes. "Jesus, I've signed up with Captain frickin' America."

"Thought I was the Virgin frickin' Mary."

"My mistake." She wiped damp hands on her jeans. "Okay. At least let me explain the layout, so we don't get lost. If I remember right, there's no lobby. You walk in, there's a corridor, and then it branches out left and right into the ground floor apartments. No lights, either. Caliban had them all put out. And the elevator's broken, so we'll have to use the back stairs—"

"Whatever," Japheth interrupted coldly. He knew just how to breach this hell-cursed den. "Just stick close to me, and try not to scream, okay?" And he grabbed her around her slim waist—so deliciously warm, this cursed female—and flashed.

Rose screamed, but the sound tore from her lungs. The ground lurched away. No gravity. No support. Only Japheth, strong and warm at her back, stopping her from falling. Darkness swallowed her. She strained her vampire sight. Nothing.

Tiles slapped her boot heels. She stumbled in hot blackness. The stench of rotting meat assaulted her. Screeches, flesh ripping, blood squelching . . . Demon wards sprang alight, glowing scarlet serpents that struck at her flesh. Their poisoned bites stung like acid. The angelic mark on her forehead hissed indignantly, and caught alight.

She yelled, flailing, but found only emptiness. Japheth was gone. He'd left her. Sent her to some black empty hell to fester alone, forever in torment . . .

Blue light erupted.

Heavenlight, searing bright like the sun. She yelped, shielding her vampire eyes. A dirty corridor leapt into view, broken walls, cracked tile floor . . . and Japheth, golden wings aflare, bathed in furious blue fire.

The demon wards screamed and recoiled, snapping their fiery jaws. Japheth ripped his flaming sword from the ether, and slammed it two-handed into the writhing red demon sigil at his feet.

Unholy screams split the night, and the world burst into flame.

Heavenspells seared, ozone and acid. Flames leapt from ward to ward, exploding them in turn and setting the walls alight. Rose yelled, and dove for the floor, cradling her head, waiting for the agony.

Strong wings enfolded her. Feathers, cool and soothing, the rich scent of male skin. She struggled, raking her hair in panic. Surely, the flames swallowed her. Her flesh was burning. She was just in shock, the trauma too great to feel it. Any moment, agony would erupt, abject and dreadful but just a shadow of the torment awaiting her in hell . . .

But Japheth trapped her against his chest, silver armor warm and steadfast. His crisp golden hair caressed her cheek. His touch calmed her, eased her back into reason and reality. "Peace, Rose Harley," he murmured. "You're okay."

Shh, Bridie. Auntie Rosie's here. Go back to sleep . . . She coughed, her lungs stinging from the smoke. But not scorching. The cruel angelic flames didn't touch her. Those screams didn't belong to her. She wasn't burning.

Relief washed her dizzy. She sucked in great gulps of air, heart thumping hard. She wasn't burning. Not dying. Not headed for hell . . .

But in the gibbering darkness, vampires wailed and died. She could smell them, roasting flesh, singed hair, the sour stink of terror. Paint peeled and crackled, nails popping from the warped boards. Screams pierced the firelit dark. Already, the flames roared higher, to the upper floors. The people up there could still use the fire escape, make it to the street before the building went up. But those down here were trapped. He'd burned them all.

Except her.

And damn it if she didn't feel safe in his embrace. Safe, while he mercilessly slaughtered her kind. What kind of monster did that make her?

A pathetic girly one, that's what. *Jesus. What am I, a damsel in distress?*

She punched his metal-clad chest. Her knuckles split. She didn't care. "Get off me, you freak!"

He released her. Blue flame licked his hair, shedding brutal shadows on his face. His sword glittered eagerly, his eyes neon-green. "You're welcome," he called over roaring flames. "I said I'd protect you. Think I'd let you burn?"

She raked sweaty hair back. "Is this your idea of sneaking in here?"

A cold stare. "I don't sneak."

"You know what? There's totally something wrong with you—"

A vampire shot shrieking from a burning doorway. His long hair was alight, his skin seared to raw flesh by holy fire.

Japheth grabbed him and crushed his throat. He tossed the limp body aside, impatient. "I said, I fight my enemies face-to-face. You wanna stab them in the back like a coward? Go right ahead."

Rose stared, aghast. Such a callous, efficient killer. She jabbed her finger at the dead vampire. "Is *that* your idea of honor, angel?"

"It's my idea of doing my job," he retorted. "Don't see you rushing to save them. You can moralize with me, Rose Harley, or you can stay alive." He pushed past her, heading for the stairs.

The air thinned as he moved away, taking his protective spell with him. Rose sweated. The holy heat already singed her hair. Japheth's wards extended only so far. It was follow him, or be immolated.

She whipped out her knife, and dashed after him.

The stairs creaked, down into dusty darkness. Around a corner, away from flickering flamelight. Already, the burning crackle receded.

Bloodscent reeked upwards, a sticky cloud, and Rose's

stomach growled with fresh hunger. Faintness dizzied her, and
she grabbed the banister to stay upright. *Please, not now* . . .
But Fluvium's evil laugh echoed like a nightmare in the dark
crevices of her mind, and with it chimed famine. So long since
she'd eaten. So many hours since she'd fed this demon
thirst . . .

Ahead, Japheth lighted onto the basement floor. A corridor
stretched ahead, lit eerily by his shimmering blue aura. Bloodstained plaster walls, dust, broken glass. No one else in sight.

Rose licked dry lips, and followed. In her vampire sight,
the basement glowed in scarlet outlines. A maze of corridors
and doorways, licked bright with fear. Moans echoed from
hidden rooms. Demon wards spat angry red sparks. Her
insides shuddered, sick. It was like an alien world, uncanny
and bizarre.

She blinked, confused. She should feel at home here. But
now, under Japheth's spell, she saw through different eyes.
The mark on her forehead stung, traumatized, shivering like a
fevered child with *wrongness*.

Was this how Japheth felt, in the face of demon magic?
Stinging, hot, outraged? Violated? No wonder he wanted to
burn it all.

Her wits muddled, hunger and bewilderment a hot mess in
her head. Where was she going, again? She'd been here before,
right? Caliban's place. Easy peasy. Caliban was a sick mo-fo,
but he liked her. All she had to do was . . .

A deep, black chuckle savaged the night.

Rose gasped, reeling, her mind flooded with images of
blood. Japheth flung up a protective ward, electric sparks
flashing from his fingers. "Stay close."

Rose shuddered. "What the hell is—ugh!"

Air rushed, a ghostly intake of breath that flung her hair in
her face, and all the demon wards snuffed out.

CHAPTER 12

Darkness smothered him, hot and excruciating like hell.

For a moment, Japheth couldn't breathe. His sword slipped from his grasp and vanished. He couldn't see. Couldn't raise a shimmer. His glorylight had died. Surely, heaven had deserted him.

His heart convulsed. Drowning. Dark places. Crushing black air, walls shuddering and closing in . . .

Somewhere, Rose cursed, and sharp metal hissed. She was slashing at the darkness. Fighting. Not afraid of this black and bloodstained place. He forced a prayer to cold lips. *Heaven, give me light. Please. Just let me see while I die . . .*

A tiny breeze of solace fluttered his hair. His feathers sprung taut, showering faint blue glitter.

Thank you. He gasped a grateful breath, his pulse calming. Narrow corridor, uneven tiled floor, walls broken and peeling. Somewhere, a human screamed. Metallic bloodstink clogged his nose. And Rose, knife in hand, balanced on tiptoes.

Her gaze darted, hunting. "Shit," she whispered. "Next time, bring a flashlight."

"Noted." Japheth exhaled, gritty, his nerves on edge. His pretty bloodsucker was brave. Determined. A fighter.

But he had a job to do. Heaven's favor to repay. Best he get on with it. Or next time, there might only be silence.

Rose narrowed her eyes at him. "What's wrong with you? You're sweating rivers."

"I don't like small, dark places," he said shortly.

"Great. Is your claustrophobia going to be a problem?" She mocked him with his own words.

"I manage." He flashed his sword, radiant blue. The light pierced the corridor cleanly. No scarlet demonspells fought back, and he resisted a curse. No more wards to burn. They'd just have to fight their way through.

The wall exploded, and vampires fell on him.

Limbs thrashing, tangled hair, evil glinting fangs. Their eyes shone, luminous with night vision. They clawed ragged nails at his face. Growls, snarls, burning vampire spit flecking his cheek.

Rose yelped, fighting, her blade flashing silver. No time to grab her, get her behind him. He tumbled, kicking, slashing one wing viciously. Breaking bones, splashing blood, the slice of steel. Bodies thumped. Heads rolled. Death's dark caress, swift and inevitable.

Japheth's consciousness receded, a distant shadow. He exulted, nerves sparkling, muscles alive with holy energy. His mind became a computer, his body a machine, fueled on sweat and bloodlust and sweet glittering glory.

Rose backed against the wall, breathing hard. Jesus Christ. They'd burst from the wall in a hail of bloody splinters—*through* the damn wall, seriously?—and now she was pinned down.

The first one came at her, bitten fingers clawing for her eyes. His face gleamed, a sick yellow sheen of hunger. Not Chosen. Just infected human prey.

She blocked his nails with her forearm. "Hey! I'm one of you! Can't you see?"

The vampire just drooled and snapped at her, slashing her arm in twin stinging crimson lines. He didn't recognize her as Chosen. All he knew was the angel's mark—and the rich pounding scent of her blood.

Despair soured her breath. It wasn't his fault. He didn't deserve this wretched life, or the death that was coming.

But it's them or me. She rammed her knee into his guts, and when he retched and doubled, she jabbed her knife deep into his throat, and ripped.

Warmth splashed her jeans, and the twitching body fell.

Another one jumped her, a girl with ratty green hair and a nose ring. Rose slashed backhanded to keep her at bay. It was a zoo in here. The corridor was teeming with them, and the poor bastards just kept coming.

And already, the tiled floor was calf-deep in bodies. Severed limbs. Heads. Blood painted the walls. The stink sickened her. And in the midst of it all, Japheth. Killing things, his golden wings alight with blinding glory. His muscles pumped powerfully, his hair dripped crimson. Silent, swift, diving and whirling and landing bone-crunching blows. A perfect death machine.

Rose swallowed, bitter. He sure didn't have any qualms about sending them all to hell. Did they all deserve it? She couldn't tell.

That was the thing, see. You couldn't tell just by looking. Not that Japheth cared.

The vampire girl snarled, and slashed at Rose with a broken bottle. Glass sliced Rose's knuckles. She kicked, and her boot crunched into the girl's fishnet-clad kneecap. The girl howled and collapsed. Rose crushed the bottle to shards under her boot—no point leaving the others a weapon—and stabbed her foe through the heart. The girl screamed, her spine arching. Terror burned bright in her eyes, and she gurgled and died.

Rose quailed, shivering. She didn't mind the blood. No, her heart was racing, desire and hunger only aching harder. Her fangs hurt, so tight and eager. It wasn't the blood that sickened her.

It was the blanching dread on that girl's face. She'd known where she was going.

A scream skewered Rose back to reality. She jumped, tense, knife ready.

Japheth slammed the last vampire against a wall, his green eyes aflame with battle rage.

The kid's feet kicked six inches off the ground. Skinny limbs, young face. Maybe fifteen or sixteen. He thrashed, but the angel held him effortlessly by the throat.

"Caliban," Japheth demanded.

The vampire spluttered, dark hair wet on his face. "Don't kill me. Please. I don't want to die. I'm just so fucking hungry . . ."

"It isn't you I want. Just tell me where Caliban is, and I'll let you live."

His soothing tone stabbed ice along Rose's nerves. Oldest trick in the book. Japheth would slit the kid's scrawny throat as soon as he'd finished his sentence. Never trust an angel.

The kid's expression melted like marshmallow, and tears flowed. "He's in the sub-basement, okay?"

"How is it defended? Don't cry. Just tell me."

"There's a vault. Like a big steel door with locks and shit. I didn't mean it! I didn't mean to kill them. I was just so hungry . . ."

"Shut up," said Japheth coldly, and dropped him to his feet. "Now run."

Wide-eyed, the kid scuttled away, on all fours like a crab into the dark.

Rose stared, and rounded, fighting not to shout and be overheard. "Are you crazy?"

Japheth raised golden eyebrows.

She wanted to shake some goddamn sense into him. "You let him go! He's gone straight to Caliban. Just how dumb *are* you?"

He glared for silence, and dragged her into a corner. He dimmed his wing light to a faint glimmer, but his eyes still flashed frosty green fire. "Said I'd let him live, didn't I?" he whispered.

Rose pulled her protective shadows in close. Her vampire magic swirled and muttered, unsettled by Japheth's proximity and the mark on her forehead, but the shadows held, shrouding them both in black don't-see-me mist. Not even sound would escape, so long as they were careful. She could hear him breathing, light and even. The tiny crisp rustle of his feathers, the sound as he licked his lips.

"You do know that's supposed to be a *lie,* right?" she whispered fiercely. "You know, like 'I promise I'll call' or 'of course I still respect you'?"

"Lying's a sin, Rose Harley. You might want to keep that in mind."

She yanked damp hair from her eyes, furious. Screw him and his stupid morals. But her ears burned, and she squirmed. All the lies she'd told, the prey she'd seduced with trickery. Once, she'd had a conscience. Now, all she had was hunger and fury.

This angel had been cast down, too. He knew how it felt to scream alone at the darkness. Yet the crazy bastard still acted as if the rules meant something to him.

Fresh guilt soured her mouth, maddening. He had the courage of his convictions, she'd give him that. But the rules were unfair. God didn't care. Heaven didn't deserve her obedience. To meekly accept your fate . . . to say *okay, my bad* and move on, without a shred of resentment . . . it was so messed up, her head spun.

"Unbelievable," she snapped. "Your stupid-ass honor's gonna get us both killed. Will that make you feel good about yourself?"

Japheth just shrugged. "Better dead than damned . . . oh, I'm sorry, you already missed that boat, didn't you?"

"Screw you." She shook her head, disgusted. Every time she decided he was maybe only 99 percent asshole, he grabbed that one percent right back again. With interest.

Unwillingly, she recalled how she'd deceived him the night they met. Pretended to be a defenseless human. Lured him close, seduced him with her scent. Opened her mouth under his wild kiss, tasted his tongue, the hot dark slide of his fingers over her skin . . .

A dirty trick, sure. No doubt he despised her for it. But it wasn't as if he hadn't enjoyed it. She shivered, remembering the brutal force of his desire jutting into her, his tight muscles, the heat of his breath . . . "Huh? What?"

"I said, it's not like Caliban doesn't already know we're coming." Japheth wiped bloody hair from his cheek with one forearm. "And now we've got more info. Seems a fair trade to me."

"I already knew what his defenses were, you moron! I've been here, remember?" She blinked, her vision doubling for a moment. Her stomach ached, and her pulse flitted, light and rapid. The hunger was getting worse. Not good.

"I remembered." He grinned, beastly. "Just thought I'd check. You know, in case you forgot a few details and I accidentally got my head sliced off?"

"Ye of little faith," she mocked. But her guts twisted. Of course she'd planned to lie.

"Yeah, well. Just because I choose to be truthful doesn't mean I don't know the rest of you are full of shit most of the time. I'm an angel, not an idiot."

She steadied herself, light-headed. "Spare me the moralizing. What's the plan now? We gonna just teleport right in there and start slashing again?"

Japheth grimaced. "Not without knowing exactly where I'm going, or how to get out. Like I said: angel, not idiot."

"Can't do your fancy tricks into a locked room?" she scoffed. "What use are they?"

A green stare, warm with amusement. "I can flash into a locked room, if you must know. But not when it's sealed with high-level demon blood wards. And it will be, if this Caliban is as thick with Fluvium as you say."

"How can you be so sure?"

"I could flash in there and explode. That'd prove it. Not my preferred option."

"Wouldn't want you to break a nail."

"Wow. I'm touched. Remember you'll be exploding right along with me."

Her head ached, dizzy. "So why not just immolate these wards, like before?"

"I have to see the wards to burn them." He gestured in the direction of the sub-basement. "Do you see the wards, Rose Harley?"

She strained her vampire eyes until her vision swam. Nothing. "Shit."

"More or less what I was thinking. They'll be ready for us. We'll have to fight our way in." He stepped away from the wall, flicking blood from his blade, and flexed his body, one muscle group at a time, readying himself for another round.

She coughed, self-conscious. Bastard recovered quickly. Probably the same in bed. Come early, come often . . .

Japheth stretched his wings. Muscles tightened and released, his bare skin glistening with bloody sweat . . .

Rose's throat hurt, crusty. He looked good to her. Sickening, how her gaze glued itself to his body for all the wrong reasons. *Teach me to get so hungry* . . . "Or we could get him to come out."

"Say again?"

Faintness rinsed her wits thin. Her gaze zoomed in on the pulse in his throat, the brutal veins swelling in his arms. His hot male scent watered her mouth. Her vampire ears drank in his heartbeat, hungering for more, deeper, harder . . .

Giddy, Rose fought for control. She couldn't drink angel blood. Disgusting, corrosive, poisonous. But she wanted to leap on him, yank that rough golden hair back, sink her teeth deep . . .

Fuck! She wanted to scream, claw the air apart. If only that vampire kid hadn't gotten away. She could have fed from him, just a little. Even desperately horny would be better than this.

Her gaze slicked over her angel's sculpted lips, the bunched curve of his biceps, those strong forearms . . . Her nipples ached hard. Damn, she loved a man's wrists, and this angel— curse him to hell's vilest hole—this Japheth had the sexiest wrists she'd ever seen. Powerful, dangerous, built raw and thick from swordplay, muscle and sinew standing out . . .

He flexed his fingers on his sword grip, and she nearly fainted with need. Who was she kidding? She was *already* desperately horny, and all she had to play with was this maddening angel.

And *she* was meant to be seducing *him*.

"I might be able to get Caliban to come out," she repeated thickly. "He's interested in the Chosen. Wants us to join his little fuck-and-die club. If I tell him I'm in trouble, he might believe me."

"I'm sorry, perhaps we should've discussed this *before* we were hiding in a dark basement full of vampires?"

"They can't hear us, wiseass. Look." She prodded at her wall of shadow. "Cone of silence?"

"Whatever. We don't have all night to argue. The answer's no. It's too risky."

"Risky, my butt. You fell for it, didn't you?" She tossed it out recklessly, expecting him to flip her off.

But Japheth's eyes stormed over like midnight rain. "You want to seduce him, is that it?"

His disdain itched like a rash. "Who died and made you my . . ." *Mother*, she almost said, and sick images of Bridie slicked her stomach. "My big brother? Whatever works, I say. If he's horny, he's hungry. If he's hungry, he's vulnerable. I distract him, you grab him, job done. You've got no qualms about torture. How else are we supposed to make him talk?"

His arms clenched, swelling, like he was about to burst. "I won't let you . . ." He swallowed, calm, but his eyes flamed dark. "It's not honorable," he said finally.

As if that made any goddamn sense at all.

Her head ached. Her palms itched. Fight or feed, she didn't know which she wanted more. "It's a better plan than you've come up with."

"I won't order you to defile yourself." He stared ahead, steadfast, but color blossomed in his cheeks. He looked shy. Uncomfortable.

She wanted to punch that bashful blush from his face. "*Order* me? Jesus Christ in a fricassee. If you even *think* about giving me orders I'll—"

"You are not my slave to do with as I please," he snapped. "Want to wallow in corruption? Do it on your own time. It's not honorable. You're not doing it. End of story."

"And what do you care about my honor?" She kicked angrily at the floor, and pain speared up her toe. It only fired her frustration. "I'm hell-cursed, aren't I? What's one more sin?"

"Not. On. My. Watch." He jammed his teeth together so hard, his jaw popped.

"But we need Caliban! How d'you think we're gonna get

him? Stroll up and knock on the door?" She yanked her braid over her shoulder. "Damn you, Japheth, you're worse than a jealous boyfriend."

Murder ignited in that fierce green glare.

Rose laughed, incredulous. "Ha! You are so busted. Say it's not true. I dare you."

He jerked a step towards her. Her pulse quickened. His hot musky rage flowed over her, dizzying. His fists clenched, cording those sexy wrists even tighter. Suddenly, provoking him didn't seem such a smart idea . . . but her insides melted with unwanted longing.

No one had ever cared what she did before.

But the demon in her heart licked hungry lips. This was her chance. He'd kissed her once. She'd not let him escape unscathed again. Her fingers tightened on her knife hilt. She wanted to stab him so bad. Thrust her blade in, twist it, dip her lips into his blood . . .

"Go on, say it," she taunted. "You don't want Caliban touching me. You're jealous. Say it's not true, if you can."

He swallowed, hard.

Triumphant, Rose edged closer. He didn't move, and her body thrilled with anticipation. He was hers. She'd won. She parted her lips, leaned in . . .

CHAPTER 13

Lord, he couldn't stop staring at her mouth.

He wanted to taste it. Force those cherry lips apart, take her tongue with his, kiss her until she couldn't breathe, until her mind scorched to mush with desire and she knew only him. Until every last thought of touching that foul monster in the vault was burned from her brain.

Jealous? He was *insane*.

He cupped her chin, stopping her from coming any closer. "If I were," he said roughly, "it'd be unwise to provoke me, Rose Harley."

Her dark eyes danced, victorious. She was practically purring. "That's not a no."

Japheth whirled away, quivering. He hadn't said *no*. Hadn't coldly brushed her off. What was one more lie? He'd already dragged his honor through the shitpile. *You have my word,* he'd said, and she'd believed him. What difference was one more untruth?

But little by little was how damnation happened. A slippery slide to hell. And the idea of some scum-shit bloodsucker touching her . . .

He closed his eyes, willing his throbbing blood to subside.

When he'd wrapped her in his wings upstairs, shielding her from the flames, he'd done so with a wince of distaste. He couldn't help the way his body reacted to her. Touching her was wrong. So he'd steeled himself against attraction, intoxication, drunken lust.

But he hadn't been prepared for what happened.

Her breath against his feathers *soothed* him. Her warm flesh both threat and solace. He was turned on, sure. Just being near her made him hard, but . . . it was more shameful than that.

Holding her had felt . . . right. Good. The way things should be. Protecting her lit sweet flames in his heart, and they burned still, mingling with his heaven-sent glory until he didn't know one from the other.

Glory and earthly obsession. They felt like the same thing. How was he meant to tell the difference?

This Rose Harley would be his undoing. He'd never felt anything like this. If this was a hellspell—and what else could it be?—he was in serious trouble.

Because he had no damn clue how to fight it.

What if it isn't a hellspell? A wicked murmur, mingled with dark laughter. *What if it's just . . . you?*

Japheth shuddered. No way. Not true. He wasn't like that. He'd only ever wanted glory for heaven. Only ever that . . .

You think feathers and a flaming sword make you special? Always so reasonable, sin's insidious whisper. *You're a man. You're supposed to want to protect her. Jesus, you're supposed to want to fuck her. It's natural. There's nothing wrong with you.*

The world's ending, Jae. Lighten up.

But his muscles burned, his wing bones cramped and ached, bumps broke on his skin. Slicing up those vampires had only ratcheted his nerves tighter.

He flexed shaking fingers. No, he didn't deserve to relax. Not the way he'd handled this. He'd broken the rules, and if this pain—this *jealousy*, for heaven's sake—was his penance, he'd accept it.

Yes. Let Rose seduce Caliban, if that's what she wanted. Japheth would watch while she touched this other man. Look on mute while she bared her sweet body for this vampire's vile hunger. He'd even watch while she lay with him, if that's what it took. Listen to her moans as they sated each other. Smell their mingled fluids, the sweat, the iron-rich blood.

And when they'd gotten the information they needed? He'd tear the hell-cursed bastard's limbs off, and watch him die.

Rose grinned at him, still waiting. "C'mon, angel. Would it hurt so much to admit you like me?"

"Whatever," he said coldly. "Do what you like. Make a whore of yourself, I don't care. But all you dirty hellspawn look the same to me. Don't get too tangled up, or I might accidentally slice off the wrong head."

Asshole!

Rose's fingers itched to claw his eyes out. But she wanted to claw her own face, too. Frustration bubbled in her throat. She didn't care what he thought of her. So why did it hurt when he called her a whore?

She tossed her braid back coolly. "Fine. Should be fun. Just pay attention, flyboy, and don't interrupt me when I'm about to get off." She flexed aching shoulders. "Now hit me."

"What?"

"I'm about to stumble in there and tell Caliban you took me by force. It'll be more convincing if I'm a bit dented. Now hit me."

Japheth snorted. "Not a chance."

"No time to mess around, angel. Lay one on me, and don't you dare pull your punch because I'm a girl."

"No." But his knuckles flexed white.

She laughed. "You know you want to. It'll feel good. Work the edge off that permanent hard-on of yours."

"Rose, I won't—"

Rose punched him. Hard, sweet, on the side of his perfect jaw. *Crunch!* Her finger bones rattled. But a grin plastered her face. Damn, that felt good.

Japheth stumbled, and recovered with a swift wing flare. He licked his bloody lip, and his eyes flashed hell-green. "Careful what you conjure."

Rose hit him again. Cheekbone this time, her nails splitting his skin. She lined up for another one.

Crack! The hard floor smacked into her back.

Her ears rang. She choked, dizzy. Her left cheek felt twice its normal size. She scrambled up, clumsy.

Gently, Japheth steadied her. "Feel good, vampire?"

"Screw you. You enjoyed it." Rose shook her head to clear it. "Again."

He tilted her chin up, examining her bruise. His fingers were light, soothing. She winced, and he jerked his hand away. "Looks authentic enough."

"Think I can't take more?"

"I'm sure you can take whatever I give you." His murmur slid shivers under her skin, and in an instant, she was deeply aware of his fragrant male heat, the nerve-twisting double entendre in his words. "But I'm not sure I can."

Warmth pooled inside her, unwilled but sweet. Her fangs ached. Curse him. Who was seducing whom here? She wanted to press close, find his desire and stroke it, let him kiss the stinging pain away . . . "Look," she said thickly, "I didn't mean to—"

"You think you can make me hurt you?" Acid dripped from his voice. "Think you can seduce me into sin? I may want to kill you, Rose Harley—believe me, nothing would please me more—but you won't tempt me into torturing you for fun. Should I slice off a leg, rip off an arm or two? Perhaps I should force you. Would that be *convincing* enough?"

She jerked away, hot. "Yeah, you'd enjoy that, wouldn't you? Taking a defenseless woman by force? That'd really take the edge off that hard-on."

"I'm not even going to dignify that."

"Whatever. Don't see you wringing your hands over all those other vampires you tortured to death."

"That serves a purpose," he retorted, but his wings showered fierce golden rain. "I don't do it for kicks."

She laughed harshly. "Right. Who do you actually think you're fooling, Japheth? Because it sure as shit ain't me. I've seen your eyes when you wield that sword. You *enjoy* hurting them. You *like* that they're going to hell and you're not."

"You know *nothing* about what I like." His feathers frosted, his glacial tone chipped sharp. Hell, ice was practically dripping from the walls.

She laughed again . . . but sultry memories melted, warm sweet syrup in her belly. She knew what he liked, all right. The taste of her tongue, her fingers stroking his cock through his jeans . . .

Her mouth soured at his doublethink. He wanted her. Wanted everything she offered. Hell, he was halfway to the dark side already.

He just didn't have the balls to admit it.

Dark knots tightened in her belly. Just one more straw. That'd be all it took to break him. He'd fall into her deadly trap and drown, and enjoy every moment of it.

So why was she disappointed?

Whatever. She speared him on a mocking grin. "Hey, don't be bashful. You're a sick son of a bitch. That's okay with me. Hell, I'd even like you, if you weren't such a self-satisfied asshat. You want to glory in suffering? Fine. Just don't *lie* about it. It's so pathetic."

And she stalked into the dark, shaking.

CHAPTER 14

Down the sub-basement stairs, darkness swamped her utterly.

Rose shivered in the heat, straining her vampire sight. She could see, of course, the shadows filtering into smoky shapes, the glinting red edges of corridor and doorway. But this darkness in Caliban's lair was more than lack of light. It was alive, crawling over her like a hungry creature, creeping stealthy fingers under her clothes, between her legs, down her throat to strangle her.

She clamped her mouth shut, and tried not to breathe, and kept descending.

She couldn't hear Japheth behind her. Was he coming? Bastard moved silently when he wanted to. Hunger made her faint, her head swimming. Her anger still flared at his insults.

But who cared? Caliban could feed her. Maybe even help her get rid of this horrid angel's mark. She had only Japheth's word that until he released her, the mark was permanent. For all his lofty words about lying being sinful, he could still be winding her up.

But Caliban might kill her on sight. Best to stick with the plan until she got inside, and could explain to Caliban about the mark. Then, and only then, she'd see the color of Japheth's truth.

And if he'd lied?

Her teeth clenched tighter. If he'd lied, she'd do more than feed him her blood. She'd rip the dirtbag apart and laugh while he fell screaming to hell.

At last, her feet touched smooth floor. The stink thickened, blood and sour human fear. Wails and sobs lit the air like fireworks. Her vampire night sight outlined a wide space, the entire basement's breadth. At the end, Caliban's iron door lay barred, floor to ceiling, like a huge old-fashioned bank vault with a big levered handle. Prison bars lined the walls left and right, and behind them, humans squirmed and groaned and beat their fists against the steel.

Caliban's party snacks. *Cattle*, he called them. Men, women, children, too. Most were naked. Some writhed on the floor, gripped by unholy nightmares. Others flailed and screamed, fighting each other. Still others slumped against walls or bars, close to death, their will sucked away.

Rose swallowed hungry spit. The scent of food made her head whirl. Weeping wounds marred the humans' skin, knives or spikes or vampire teeth. She could see the blood. Their heartbeats pounded in her ears, hammering a sick chorus, driving her on like insane jungle drums . . .

No. Her nails sliced into her palms, the sting ripping her trance apart. She gulped air, seeking fresh strength. *I won't give in. If that angel can resist me? I can resist this.*

Woodenly, she dragged her singed hair loose from the braid. Her swollen eye ached. Blood stained her clothes, her face was bruised, her forehead scorched and weeping with Japheth's Tainted sigil. Convincing enough.

She sprinted down the room towards the vault door, stumbling and catching herself. "Caliban! It's Rose. Rose Harley. Open the door." She banged on the iron, below the tiny inspection slot. The door boomed like a massive bell, echoing into silence.

"Caliban. It's me. I'm in trouble. Some dirty angel, he grabbed me. I've got this stupid thing on my skin, it's . . ."

The inspection slot snapped open. Smoke drifted out, harsh with drugged smoke. Gleaming yellow eyes inspected her. A low female voice lisped. "Rose Harley. You're not welcome here."

Not Caliban. Just another Chosen, a minion like her.

Rose lifted her chin, showing her bruises, the mark, her sallow starved skin. "The building's on fire, okay? Open the door, Lily. If that angel finds me, I'm a dead woman. Let me in!" She hammered harder, hoping Lily would think her demented, driven insane by the angel's mark.

Lily's gaze darted left and right. Japheth's glowing ass better be well hidden. "No one comes in. Least of all you."

"Then send Caliban out. Jesus, Lily, I'm starving here. I'll do whatever he wants this time. He can have me. I promise . . ."

Black smoke crawled from the slot. It surrounded her, coalescing. She choked, but couldn't help inhaling, the sour taste of charcoal and meat. Her thoughts spaced out, bright and distinct, like she'd sucked on a crack pipe. An effortless rush soaked into her muscles, so good she gasped and melted to her knees, dizzy . . . and hard arms lifted her, laying her on her back on the sticky floor.

"Rose . . ." Caliban's deep whisper echoed, stretching to eternity. Dreamy, she blinked.

A dark face, riddled with pin piercings, spikes and sharpened wire. Long dreadlocks, knotted with tiny bones. Black eyes, whirling with starlit crazy. He wore tight jeans and no shirt, his wiry muscles gleaming damp with fever. A steel razor wire collar circled his sinewy throat, the wicked barbs slicing through his fast-healing flesh. It was adorned with a gleaming black gemstone, wreathed in smoke and glowing like moonlit midnight.

Rose shuddered. People said Caliban was once a voodoo priest, raising dull-eyed zombies from the grave to do his bidding. Others said he was a fucked-up crack dealer from Queens. Either way, the dude was a total whackjob.

"My beauty." His deep Haitian lilt stroked her lazy nerves. She struggled to stay alert. He was dangerous. He could turn to *smoke*. Only demons could do that, right? How had he learned that trick?

"Caliban," she said, with what she hoped was a disarming sigh. She eyed the smoking black gemstone, and covered a shudder. It stank of Fluvium, rank and raw. "Some dirty heavenshit is coming for me. You have to help me . . ."

"What's this?" Caliban touched one fingertip to her mark. His barbed-wire bracelet grazed her cheek. "Our lord won't like this."

She struggled not to recoil. Caliban's sick rituals were legendary. The evil vampire thirst was a religion to him. He thought Fluvium was God, and drinking was worship. And he taught his eager disciples to be just like him.

"I told you. The asshole marked me. I ran away. Now everyone tries to kill me." She fell fainter into his arms. Her breasts pressed against his naked chest, and unwanted memories of Japheth made her squirm. Her angel was so strong, smelled so good. Her nipples had hardened at his barest touch. But Caliban's flesh raised no reaction, beyond disgust. His scent—blood and burned resin—made her retch.

She covered it with a splutter. "I'm so hungry. I'm sorry. I know I was . . . disobedient. But I can't . . ."

"Hush, baby girl." Caliban stood, and looked down at her, long locks falling on his razor-pierced nipples. Every time his muscles moved, that sharp wire cut him again . . . but as she watched, his uncanny flesh healed, fast even for a vampire. Fluvium's charmed gemstone was increasing Caliban's powers. "You have no right to come here. You refused me. You grieve our blood lord's spirit, Rose. I should rape your girly ass and leave you in pieces for the crows."

Rose shuddered. She'd seen Caliban naked. Knew those barbed-wire ornaments on his chest weren't the only ones . . .

"I know I deserve that," she lied thickly. God, she wanted to throw up. "But please, I've changed my mind. I need you."

His eyes gleamed. "You know my price."

"Whatever you want—"

"Say it." Caliban's hollow, inhuman tone scraped her spine. "Convince me you believe, my beauty. I'll have no blasphemers here."

She knew what she had to do . . . but humiliation flamed deep in her belly. Japheth was hearing this. He'd think she meant it. That she actually wanted these horrid things.

But no time for stupid pride. She had to make Caliban believe it. Say it, and make it good, and hope her angel came for her before that barbed wire went somewhere she wouldn't like . . .

Boldly, she focused on Caliban's dark eyes, and imagined.

Crisp golden feathers, teasing my bare nipples. That soft gilded hair on my face, rich hard angelflesh under my lips. He tastes of coffee, musk, glorious skin. He's kissing me, sliding his strong hands on my ribs, my ass. I wrap my legs around him, he's kissing my breasts, sucking them, oh God it feels so . . . and the hot iron blade thrust as he takes me, fucks me, rips me apart and exposes my raw insides . . .

"I want the blood." Her voice husked with hunger. Angelflesh stinging her fangs, the sweet saltiness on her lips . . .

"Worship with me, Caliban. Please. Let me drink you until I can't bear it, and then you can torture me. I'll come when you say. I'll take it wherever you want. I'll fuck the cattle and drink them to death with you."

She forced down sour bile, struggling to focus. Japheth's tongue between her legs, licking, sucking her into his mouth, while she wrapped her arms around his rock-hard thighs and licked the blood from his skin . . . "I'll even . . . do that thing you like, with the dead ones. Just let me taste you. Please. For our lord."

"Very good, Rose. Most convincing." Caliban loomed over her, a monstrous shadow. His knotted hair scratched her face. He smelled of iron and empty hatred. His spiked lips cut her cheek, and she flinched, but he grabbed her hair, holding her still. "But I don't believe you."

Rose's heart hammered. Surely, he could smell her fear. Her mind gibbered. *He can taste it. He knows I'm a traitor.* She wanted to scream, yell at her angel to get out of here before it was too late . . .

But it was already too late.

Caliban jumped astride her. She tried to break free, but he pinned her down, wrists and thighs. Jesus, he was strong. "You stupid whore." His fangs clicked out, wickedly barbed. "Tricked by an angel. What did you think, that I'd take that stinking burn off if you spun a few lies?"

Her mind lit sharp, desperate. Maybe he hadn't guessed about Japheth. Maybe he just thought she was jonesing for blood. "It's not a lie," she stammered, playing for time. "I . . . I can't live alone anymore. I tried, but I can't. It's too lonely. I want to be part of the coven. With you."

"Let's see." He dragged one big hand across his abdomen. The razor bracelet sliced his flesh. Blood trickled. "Ahh." His eyes gleamed yellow, and he wrenched her mouth open with one thumb. "Worship, bitch. And you'd better enjoy it."

Blood gushed over her lips. So hot. So evilly delicious . . . She gagged, spitting, but the hunger howled like a beast in her guts and she couldn't help but swallow.

Oh, fuck. Sick hunger gripped her. She swallowed harder, thirstier. It didn't sate her. She just wanted more. Liquid fire, filling her mouth, obliterating reason and dignity, leaving only thirst, and her drumming pulse, and the dark-fire delight of demon-spelled blood.

Her nerves raked raw. The thirst wouldn't ease. If Caliban gave her a human, she'd tear the thing's flesh apart, wouldn't stop until she'd wrung the body dry.

Caliban laughed, monstrous. The charmed gemstone at his throat flickered with unholy flame. "That's it. Our thirst is pure, Rose. It's beautiful. This is what we are. Learn to love it."

Oh, God, help me. The prayer choked her, and the black silence only sharpened her horror. It was like Fluvium all over again. Her body screamed with thirst. Her flesh ached to be satisfied. Her nerves cried out for punishment, agony, torture, any sensation at all to feed this insatiable yearning . . .

Satan's sweet blood, she'd been such a screaming idiot.

To think that an angel—any angel, but especially Japheth, with his fuck-you-hellspawn morals and iron-cast will—would help her now.

He already despised her. He'd think even less of her now. Probably, he'd already gone.

Despair swamped her, a cold black tide. Caliban had claimed her. He'd use her, drink from her, throw her in with his human cattle and make her eat them. Kill them and make her do horrible things with their bodies. And then, he'd kill her, and eat her flesh raw, and she'd fall screaming into hell.

Well, screw that. Defiance lit a baleful bonfire in her heart. Japheth had abandoned her. But she wasn't ready for hell. Not yet.

Grimly, she punched her nausea down, and arched up to sink aching fangs into Caliban's chest.

He grunted, throwing his bestial head back. She sucked, blood trickling over her chin. More warm wetness spread in her lap, staining her jeans where he rubbed against her. She could feel the ugly spikes where the wire he wore there had pierced him, made him bleed. The thought of taking *that* inside her made her shudder . . .

But the demon inside her exulted, and her body burned like hellfire for release. This demonic lust was insane. She didn't want to fight it.

But she had to.

She grabbed his hair, dragging herself upwards. "Yes. I understand now. This is what we are."

Caliban sighed, guttural, and pulled her onto his lap, wrapping her in his arms. "You can't fight it, my beauty. We are thirst. Our lord demands it."

She folded one leg around him, and bared her throat like prey. "Then drink me."

His eyes flashed yellow, and he reared his head back to strike.

CHAPTER 15

Rose ripped the fiery black gemstone from Caliban's flesh.

Skin and sinew tore, a flash of scarlet flame. Her fingers burned. Caliban screamed, smoke erupting from his eyes.

The air writhed with fiery worms, bewildered demonspells unexpectedly released from their enchanted prison. They darted blindly, screeching, snapping at anything that moved, and their rage sizzled the air to acrid steam.

The explosion blew Rose backwards onto her ass. The gemstone in her hand smoked, and she hurled it away with all her strength. It hit the wall and exploded, raining flames.

Caliban flailed, his hair afire. He raked at his eyeballs, but they melted down his pin-pierced cheeks like custard. He howled, and the darkness answered, an evil echo that stripped her blood raw.

Rose scrambled up, heart pumping. Demonspells nipped at her, gnashing their spectral teeth, enraged by her Tainted mark. She swatted them away, and whirled to run.

Frosty blue light erupted in a fireball.

She screamed, her marked forehead burning afresh, and a fiery blue-gold whirlwind grabbed Caliban and flung him twenty feet across the room.

Caliban slammed against the prison bars. Bones cracked. And Japheth unfurled his wings and landed in a blinding blue halo. The floor quaked and splintered beneath him. Lightning forked along the bars, and ozone stung, laced sharp with the angel's rage.

"Talk to me, worm." Thunder cracked in his voice. He slammed Caliban's head into the bars, and his left fist clenched around a spike of blue flame, his Tainted sigil burning uncontrolled. "Or your eyeballs won't be all that melts."

Rose's heart swelled, fierce. Her body still bled and burned. Thirst still tore her throat. The horror of what she'd become still stained her soul, and she wanted to dig deep underground, find a cold dark cavern where sunlight never shone.

But her angel hadn't deserted her. He'd come for her, in all his brutal, quivering, magnificent fury.

And she didn't know whether to be ecstatic or terrified.

Japheth's palm sizzled on Caliban's unholy flesh, and he screamed silent exultation to the sky.

Heaven forgive him, he wanted to scrape this twisted thing's skin off. Rip those evil piercings from his body one by one and watch him burn. If only the hell-sick gutterworm wouldn't enjoy the pain.

To see Rose at Caliban's mercy like that . . . Japheth's muscles jerked so tight, his fingers cramped. It was all he could do not to dive in and chew the bastard's rotted brains out.

Maybe half a minute, it had taken his clever vampire lady to trick Caliban. The longest thirty seconds of Japheth's life. Watching her slide her lithe body on him, part her sweet lips for that monster's blood . . . Jesus, he'd almost bitten his tongue in half. Her husky groan of longing was excruciating, maddening, both the worst and the sexiest fucking thing he'd ever heard. Holy mercy, he'd nearly spilled himself in his leathers without a single touch.

But now, glory soaked his blood, ecstasy and agony and delirium in one. Rose was safe. And this sadistic vampire scum squirmed at his mercy.

Japheth grinned, rabid. Penance later. Time for holy work.

And damn him to hell's deepest dungeon if he wasn't going to enjoy every second of it.

Caliban howled, his eyes weeping red. Fresh crimson flowered from his wounds. God, he stank, crap and corruption and his demon master's foul malice. "I can't see! Show yourself, heavenscuuummmm . . ."

"Right here." Japheth jammed a thumb into Caliban's burned eye socket. "Where's your master, asshole?"

"Sataaan!!" Caliban squealed. Sinews popped tight in his neck, and he gurgled. *"Masterrrrr!!"* His ruined vampire flesh crawled, trying to repair itself. But the damage was too great. Without his gemstone, his magic failed him.

"Satan's still in the pit, dimwit. And Fluvium's not listening. Your lord doesn't care about you. Where is he?"

An evil chuckle. "Ha ha. Go fuck yourself. You and your cringing *sheee*-bitch!" But Caliban's dark skin shone, clammy. His forehead twitched, and his sweat smelled goaty, rank with terror.

Like most sadists, in his heart this Caliban was a coward. Reveling in power over others to hide his fear.

Not like Rose Harley, who'd jumped into the fire with open eyes. She must have known what it'd cost her. Just remembering her anguish broke fresh sweat on Japheth's palms.

Now, Rose's cheeks glistened with fever, her eyes unnaturally bright. She attacked Caliban, fingers like claws. "Don't even speak to me, you evil motherf—"

"Peace, Rose Harley. Back off. I'll deal." Japheth shrugged her aside, but gently. Hell-bound she might be. Didn't mean she wasn't the bravest woman he knew.

He slammed Caliban's skull into the bars once more. "Go on, vampire. Insult her again. See what happens."

"She-bitch," repeated Caliban, and giggled, unhinged.

Japheth hissed a guttural charm.

Eager heavenlight rained, and tiny smoke tendrils curled from Caliban's skin. Angry hellspells boiled in response. He scrabbled at them blindly. "The darkness, it eeeeats meee! Can't seeeee . . . !"

Grimly, Japheth forced Caliban's chin upwards, and spat into his face. Heavenlight bubbled, spreading over the vampire's body in an angry blue cloud. And the hungry hellspells howled, and speared for Caliban's living flesh.

Some sank stinging teeth into Japheth's fingers by mistake. They exploded, blood splashing. The others snarled in frustration, and dove back to Caliban. Easier prey. And without Fluvium's gemstone to wash off the heavenfire? Caliban was fair game.

"You want your sight back, monster?" Japheth demanded.

Caliban flopped uselessly. The fiery snakes were eating his skin. "Can't see them. Let me seeeeee them!"

"Tell me where Fluvium's lair is, and I'll give you back your sight." Japheth slapped his face. "Are you listening? I have that power. You know I do. Where's Fluvium?"

"The park!" Caliban gibbered, drooling. They'd eaten through his cheek and were starting in on his tongue. "Central Park, near Bethesda. A coven gathering there. Just give me my eyeeees!"

"On your knees, hellshit." Japheth kicked his kneecap. Caliban screamed and fell, and Japheth yanked his head back with a fistful of bloody hair. He'd promised. And he always kept his word.

Holy rage lit his feathers sky-blue. *For laying your hate-grimed fingers on her. For the look on her face when you touched her. For breathing the same air as her, you black-hearted freak.*

"I didn't say 'eyes,' moron," he growled. "I said 'sight.' You want to see? Take a look at hell." And he slammed his palm into the vampire's forehead, and screamed his rage to heaven.

Blue light thundered, an ear-splitting echo of centuries-lost wrath. The walls shook and crumbled. The hellserpents shrieked bloody slaughter, and exploded in a hail of red.

Caliban shrieked, a blood-frothing nightmare erupting before his sightless eyes. And he kept on shrieking, while the heavenlight ate the flesh from his bones.

CHAPTER 16

Rose reeled, dizzy. *He's killed the son of a swine. He's really killed him.*

Flames crawled higher, over the ceiling, the floor, along the opposite walls. Trapped humans yelled and hammered on the bars. Their bloodstink blinded her, and she struggled to resist. To focus on the unbelievable truth. *I'm not dead. Not torn apart. Not howling like a beast in a rain of blood.*

I'm safe. Because of an angel.

And I'm really, desperately, fucking hungry. Oh, Jesus.

Drool slithered down her chin. Her body ached. She'd swallowed Caliban's blood. Chosen blood, cursed by Fluvium himself. Vampire blood only made the longing worse. And nothing now would quench her thirst, except . . .

Her legs must have grown a life of their own, because she was sprinting towards the iron cages. Blind, tripping over her own ankles, skinning her knees on the concrete floor, but sprinting, drawn to her prey by hunger that tore her guts, by the ripe, rich, redolent scent of human blood.

The people were screaming. The sound wrapped around the pulse in her ears, caressed it, whipped it ever faster, into a frenzy of thirst. Pupils dilated with fear, mouths hanging open, ragged hair and splitting lips and skin ripped with cruel hooks that stretched and tore . . .

A beastly howl erupted from her throat, and she hurled herself at the glowing hot iron bars. She scrabbled wildly for the locks, a gap, a way in. Heavenlight blinded her. Flames raked her face. She didn't care. She didn't feel the pain. Only the blood, forever and always . . .

Cool golden feathers swept her up, effortless, holding her tightly against a hard silver-metal chest plate. "Be still. I've got you."

Deep within the bloodthirsty monster that had claimed her, Rose's bruised human heart screamed for Japheth's touch. The soothing brush of his wings, his comforting warmth. But the monster sneered, vengeful. Her angel wouldn't save her from this. He had what he needed from her. Surely now, he'd send her crashing to hell.

"Get off me!" A shriek, some uncanny voice not her own. She fought him, thirst and fear clawing evilly in her belly. "I'm not your slave, angel," she snarled. "Just go back to heaven and let me be."

But Japheth's big arms trapped her, unyielding like a hot-muscled cage. His heartbeat echoed in her chest, and her own pulse sprinted harder, but she couldn't escape. "Peace, Rose Harley," he murmured, and whispered a prayer, and his icy light crashed in to engulf them both.

Japheth flashed into his darkened apartment, Rose in his arms.

Shit. He hadn't thought, hadn't considered where to go. Just knew he had to get her out of there, away from those living bodies she craved. He could have chosen a thousand places in Babylon alone, yet . . .

His mirror-lined walls leered, hurling his reflection back at him like an accusation. Blood was clotting in his hair, trickling through his wings, the weeping burns of demonspawn knitting on his skin. Situation normal. But this bleeding, sweating, shivering *thing* he cradled in his arms . . .

That wasn't normal.

He strode inside, keeping his gaze down. He didn't care much for mirrors. His reflection wasn't something he liked to look at. But he made a point of it, every day. Just to be sure he could look himself in the eye.

Right now? Not a good time.

But averting his eyes from wall-to-wall mirrors just meant he was looking down at *her.* She shuddered against his chest, her wet hair plastered to his silver armor, lashes curling on her bloody cheekbones . . .

He swallowed, dry. Everywhere he looked, his mistakes glared back at him.

"Lights," he ordered, and down lights bloomed, gleaming on the marble kitchenette, gloating over his black-lacquered piano. The floor-to-ceiling windows glinted, neon and car headlights from Madison Avenue twenty floors below. "Air-con, sixty-five degrees. And turn the humidity down."

Rose muttered in his arms, delirious. Sweat ran on her face, soaked her hair. Her clothes were a clotted mess. She breathed shallowly, her breasts crushing against his chest. Her skin glowed with fever. She was burning, consumed by starvation and demonic need she couldn't control.

Japheth shuddered, alive in all the wrong places. Sweet mercy, he could smell her, skin and sweat and salty female arousal. Her soft feminine moans as Caliban fed her still crawled in his memory, slithered into his blood and wouldn't let go. That vampire's foul hands roaming her body, tugging her t-shirt up, a glimpse of smooth ribs, her swelling breasts. Her fangs, so beautiful, curved and glittering sharp, slicing into Caliban's flesh, her deep groan of relief as she sucked . . .

Christ almighty. How had he ever thought he could take it? To watch her suffer and writhe? He needed his bloody head examined. Watching this proud woman humiliate herself wasn't penance. It was torture.

Well, now it was over, and here she lay, muttering in his embrace. And brutal indecision tore him in two.

What are you doing, Jae? This time, the whisper in his head sounded suspiciously like Dashiel. *Why bring her to your place? You've got what you need from her. Kill her, and get on with the job.*

He closed his eyes, blocking out those reproachful reflections. He knew where to hunt Fluvium now. Rose's usefulness was ended. He should slit her pretty throat, leave her to burn . . .

But instinctively, his arms tightened around her, and guilt and sorrow mixed bitter absinthe in his heart.

He'd given her his word.

His stomach wrung cold. What a weak, pathetic thing a promise was. Just a blade's bright flick, and it'd be done. He could get on with the business of demon slaying, and forget her. Scour these thrilling, delicious, disgusting hours from his mind. Frost his nerves cold, the way they should be, and never think of her again.

Never imagine her fingers crushing his feathers. Never dream of her tongue in his mouth, her breasts against his chest, her hair a rough silken temptation in his fist . . .

She shivered violently in his arms—so light, this female thing, despite her fighting strength—and he bit down savagely on his lip to focus his wits.

Kill her, hunt Fluvium down, win his redemption. Simple.

But his heart swelled, choking him with dumb, stubborn honor that cold common sense couldn't rinse away.

He'd given her his word. He'd *promised* her.

And never say that Japheth of the Tainted won his way back to heaven with a trick.

But you already promised you'd lie to Gabriel, his mental Dashiel argued. *Can't have it both ways.*

"That's different." He spoke aloud, and it echoed, stupid, mocking him. But it *was* different. He'd promised Michael ignorance, an honest shrug when pressed for information. Not a barefaced untruth . . .

So don't kill her, if it makes you feel better. Dash's imagined scorn stung. *You're an idiot, for what it's worth, but it's not too late. Dump her in an alleyway and forget her, before you do something even more monumentally stupid.*

"Too bloody late for that," Japheth muttered. Heaven, his head ached. And now he was talking to himself. When had this gotten so damned complicated?

A good plan, right? Return her to the Village where he'd found her, scorch away his Tainted mark. Wash his hands of her, like Pilate on that windswept stone balcony in Jerusalem.

But her fever-soaked body trembled in his arms. Her scent enveloped him, her pulse fluttering like a wounded bird's against his chest, and that primitive male creature inside him growled like a stubborn guard dog and wouldn't let him pass.

He groaned, frustrated, but it was no use. He couldn't do it. Couldn't leave her to die. Left alone, delirious, unable to find food or shelter? Die, she surely would.

His mind spun drugged circles. This was all his fault. He could've found another way to trick Caliban, but he'd let Rose drink the foul creature's blood. She starved because of him.

Not because she was hell's creature, doomed to die. Because he'd *used* her. Screwed if he'd go to his fate with that on his conscience.

Yeah, the voice in his head muttered, and this time it wasn't Dash, but his own cynical self-loathing. *Call it honor if you want, hero. It's not like you want your cock in her, or anything.*

"Fuck you," he muttered, and the nasty word felt good. Yes, saving her was a sin, and deep in his heart, the part of him that was terrified of oblivion shrank cold.

But no worse than the sins he'd already committed. Sins like lying. Lust. Neglecting his duty.

His determination firmed. Yeah, Rose Harley would die. But he'd give her an honest death. She deserved that much, for what she'd suffered. An honorable death, so far as cunning hellspawn had honor. He'd look her in the eye on the battlefield and drive his flaming sword through her heart.

Not let her flicker out from starvation in some grime-splashed alleyway.

Blood dripped from his feathers, spotting the floorboards. His pale sofa cushions glared at him, pristine, daring him to dirty them by laying her down. Normally, his apartment's familiar smells—glass, leather, wood polish—comforted him. Safe smells. Incorruptible. Tonight, they accused. *What's she doing here? Stinking hellspawn. Get her out . . .*

He laid her gently on the cushions—not the first time he'd made a bloody mess in here—and hit his knees beside her. She whimpered, pawing at her blood-soaked clothes. Her eyeballs rolled back, white like a corpse's. Japheth's warrior's instinct kicked in, trained by centuries of demon-poisoned battle. She was ill. He should strip her, check for injuries, wash her in case of infection . . .

He cleared his throat, gritty. Woman. On his sofa. Naked. Naked *vampire* woman, on his sofa. Not happening.

He unclipped her knife holster from her thigh and dropped it. Sweaty hair plastered to her cheeks, and he wiped it away, trying to hold her rolling head still. She arched her back, running palms over her breasts, down her flanks. Spreading her thighs so she could touch herself through her jeans. *Oh, hell.*

She sighed, pressing harder, the other hand raking her knotted hair. "Mmm. I need it. I need it so bad."

"Rose," he whispered, hoarse. *Week-old corpses. Clubbing baby seals. That slimy stuff that grows on the sewer walls . . .* Holy shit, was she unzipping her jeans?

Sweating, he grabbed her hand and forced it away. Forced away the rich scent of her flesh. God, he could practically taste her, that musky female flavor . . . "Rose, wake up. You're safe."

She grabbed his hair, both hands. He jerked back, cold and alight at the same time, but she held on. "Come to me," she breathed, struggling to drag him down. "I'm so fucking hungry. Let me taste you."

CHAPTER 17

Oh, Lord.

Japheth tried to pry her fingers free, but she nuzzled her face under his chin, hunting for his pulse. Her tongue teased his skin, dizzying. Suddenly all he could think about was her cherry-sweet mouth, her lips gliding over him, kissing, sucking . . .

His veins throbbed, a dark sparkle of hunger. *Glory, or hellspell? Can't tell. Don't care.* God, he wanted her to taste him. Wanted to feel the sting as she bit into him, the dizzy rush of blood when she drank . . .

Roughly, he jerked away, trapping her hands in his fists. "Rose, snap out of it. I'm poison to you. You'll die." But his thoughts shattered, shards spinning to dark and dangerous places that smelled of blood.

She wasn't snapping out of it. She was licking his throat. Sniffing at him. Trying to suck his pulsing vein into her mouth. And he couldn't take much more.

If he didn't feed her, she'd die. Or drink his blessed angel blood, and die. Or strip him naked and screw his brains out and *then* drink his blood and die. Either way, they'd both finish up in hell.

Unacceptable.

But his nerves shivered at the thought of her fangs ripping living flesh. Disgusting. Deliciously compelling. Grotesque, in fact. Could he really let her kill another human so she could survive?

He gnashed cold teeth. Screw his conscience, for once. He'd made this bed, and he'd damn well lie in it. Pun most definitely not intended.

He forced her hands still. "Rose, listen. I'll bring you food. Just hold on a little longer. Can you do that for me?"

She just muttered, eyes rolling, and with a thudding heart, he flashed out.

Tumbling in mid-air, five hundred feet above dawnlit Babylon. Japheth pumped his wings hard to gain altitude. Fresh breeze invigorated him, dragging his dirty hair back, fingering over his sweaty skin, making him feel clean for the first time since he'd laid eyes on her.

But his skin tingled. His muscles ached for her loss, and urgency tugged his feathers tight. Must get back to her. He didn't have much time.

The Park spiraled below, shadows pooling under the trees. He turned north and headed for the burning wreck of Harlem, where fires still glowed like hungry eyes in ruined apartments and offices. The Manhattan virus had hit hard there. In their newly declared *state of extreme emergency*, city hall and the state governor (advised by a crisis committee of heavenly host, picked by Michael himself) had petitioned the White House to call in the USAF to firebomb the infected areas with incendiaries.

Ash and the stench of burned flesh had hung over Babylon for days. They'd also collapsed the northbound subway tunnel and burned three of the bridges to the Bronx. So much for a precision strike.

Japheth surveyed the scorched earth dispassionately. Craters, charred shells of buildings, twisted steel. He'd done worse in heaven's service. At least they hadn't turned the entire city to salt. That devastated a place for centuries. Nothing ever grew again.

Of course, no one—especially not Michael's angels—had

bothered to evacuate the healthy before calling in the Harlem air strike. You couldn't pick and choose with a demon's curse. It was all or nothing. Innocent monkeys had to be sacrificed.

But discomfort prickled his stomach as he inhaled sickly sweet smoke. Collateral damage, hell. It was just expedient. Convenient. The easiest way out.

In Caliban's stifling black vault, Japheth had let those trapped people burn. All infected with the vampire curse, already marked for hell. He could've set them free. He'd chosen to put them out of their misery. Same as every other vampire he'd slaughtered.

But some hadn't looked miserable. They'd looked angry. Determined. Fighting to escape.

Fighting to live. Even though they must have known their hours would be short, blood-soaked, a tortured nightmare. They had still wanted to live.

Like his deadly Rose Harley, the Angel Slayer, who right now was melting to a fevered puddle on his sofa. Hellspawn or no, she raged against her fate. And here *he* was, aloft on a crazy-ass mission to save her . . .

One objective at a time, soldier. Japheth crackled his wings with static, snapping off his compassion like a brittle shell. He'd fight to live, too, if howling forever in hell was the alternative. Didn't make her noble.

He dipped his left shoulder and wheeled, over the tall apartments of Central Park West. Barricades crisscrossed the streets, lined with National Guard and NYPD in riot gear. Rifles bristled. Searchlights dazzled, and he ascended on a powerful sweep to avoid whipping helicopter blades. Damn things were a flight hazard. Compared to an angel, even modern fly-by-wire machines flew blind, their trim sluggish. They had no thrum of air over sinew and skin to guide them, no scents or warm updrafts, no flicker of each individual feather to warn them of danger. Just electrical threat systems, to which any feathered flying thing looked pretty much like empty air.

The helicopter thundered beneath him, oblivious. He spiraled upwards, and when the machine had moved on, he drifted down towards Seventy-second and Broadway, scenting the air for the thing he sought.

And soon enough, in a darkened maze of buildings and alleyways, where the street lay littered with broken glass and bricks from some forgotten riot, he smelled it. The peculiar metallic tang of human fear.

He swooped lower. No lights shone. Darkness choked the streets, the grid failed or sabotaged by anarchists. Lonely flames flickered in a single upstairs window. A pack of starving dogs attacked a Dumpster, and scattered as he landed, not quite hungry enough to brave his strange glittery aura.

Japheth edged past the Dumpster, zoning in on the scent. Shadows crept. A cat scooted from his path. Heartbeats echoed from all directions, a rainbow of human auras flashing in his magical angelsight. Swiftly, he blocked them out, focusing on the ones he wanted. Two of them. One weak and fluttery, the salt-oxide stink of fear, like someone had pissed on a pile of rusty razors. The other heartbeat was exhilarated, rich with adrenaline, emanating a strange furry smell like a goat . . .

He swooped through a window beneath a rusted fire escape, and grabbed the man by the hair.

Not vampire, or mutie, or zombie virus victim. Just a skinny lunatic, waving a switchblade and giggling as he did things to the terrified girl chained to his kitchen table.

The asshole's skull made a satisfying *squelch!* against the wall. His switchblade clattered to the dirty linoleum. He howled, and Japheth punched him. "Shut up, dogshit."

The guy drooled, semi-conscious, and bled onto his APOC-ALYPSE NOW t-shirt. He stank of sweat and wet fur, that peculiar scent of *crazy* that never changed. Japheth had smelled it many times, over the centuries. A little French girl called Jeanne, who wore plate armor and a sword she could barely carry and hadn't believed him when he explained she wasn't the chosen one. A fat little cross-eyed fellow in Whitechapel who liked to slice up prostitutes, a mad monk in St. Petersburg who hypnotized rich men's wives into screwing him and enabled a revolution.

This guy here? Just a crazy man. Insignificant. Dime-a-dozen thrill killer, by all the signs. A predator, about to become prey.

Japheth's mouth watered. This was . . . a good thing.

Sparks shot from his fingertips, and the handcuffs on the girl's wrists and ankles snapped open. She sat up, wooden. She was half-naked, filth smeared on her skin and in her blond hair. Her mouth was stuffed with her own panties, and she fumbled the tape off with trembling fingers.

Japheth eyed her curiously, still gripping the guy by the hair. She was pretty, he noted. Brave. Vulnerable. It didn't affect him. Not like *she* did. What was he supposed to do now, hug her? She didn't look like she wanted that. Hell, in her position, he wouldn't want to be touched either. "You got friends, lady? Somewhere to go?"

She nodded, tugging her torn dress, and her eyes kindled wild. "You fuck him up, hear me? You *fuck* that son of a bitch *up good!*"

The guy sniggered and drooled.

"Oh, I intend to." Japheth slapped a blistering palm onto the asshole's forehead, laced with enough screaming madness that the guy frothed at the mouth and fainted.

Japheth studied him, disgusted. The idea of Rose having to touch this shitbag—*feed* from him, bite his goat-stinking skin, suck his diseased blood into her mouth and *swallow*—the thought churned his stomach cold.

But Rose was hellspawn. She'd made her choices. And the prey deserved to die. That was what mattered.

A black metal pistol lay on the gore-streaked table. The square barrel shone slick and wet. He could imagine what the guy had been doing with it. He plucked it up and held it out to the girl, frosty. "Don't leave home without it."

She kept her distance, eyes shadowed.

"Take it, lady. He can't hurt you now."

She snatched the pistol, and held it awkwardly, like she'd never shot before.

Who the hell lives in Babylon and doesn't own a gun? Japheth showed her, impatient, coaxing her hands into a secure two-handed grip. "Safety. Sight here. Squeeze, don't yank. Next time some animal tries that? Put a bullet in his head." And he hefted the guy's limp body over his shoulder, and flashed out before she could try out any of her newfound skills on his prey.

CHAPTER 18

Rose tumbled in an endless, burning pit of thirst.

Darkness ravaged her. Need tore her open inside, exposing her raw flesh and torturing it. She wailed, and raked ripped nails over her skin, but it didn't stop the yearning. Every nerve ending hung ragged, teased to horrible agony by the emptiness inside. So empty, she'd never be filled, no matter how she howled and bit and hurt herself . . .

"Rose."

She moaned, helpless. A trick. No one was there. No one to save her, touch her, give her what she needed so very badly . . .

"Rose." Insistent this time. Fingers brushed her hair. She grabbed for them, desperate, until they folded over hers, soothing, stroking her face . . . She caught the crisp spice-latte scent of feathers, and choked on a scream. Japheth. She snapped ravenous fangs, but caught on nothing, and she ground her jaw in frustration . . .

"Rose, wake up. Time to eat." Something nudged her lips. Delicious salty scent wafted. Skin. Human skin, a delicious arterial pulse, thundering beneath the thinnest of layers.

Disgusting. Delectable. She loathed it. She needed it. The

thirst groaned inside her, rich with desire. She was wet, aching, her breasts heavy, longing for release . . .

But the human lay limp. Unresisting. Unconscious.

She reeled, confusion salting her desire. *Jesus Christ. He's feeding me. He's brought a human, and he's feeding me* . . .

Shame wrenched her heart. *I can't do this. Not in front of him* . . .

But the redolent skin brushed her lips again, offering like a lover, and her control shattered. Sobbing, she arched her neck. Her fangs strained, juddering in anticipation. She cracked her aching jaws wide, and struck.

The skin broke, and blood erupted into her mouth.

Oh my god. Delight exploded inside her. Her thighs quivered, like that lover was licking her clit and wouldn't stop. It *spurted*, that liquid sunshine, squirting in time with her heartbeat, and with every swallow, the knot in her belly twisted tighter, deeper, hotter . . .

"Peace, Rose. It's okay." A distant voice cut through her trance. God, she was moaning, she'd buried her hands in this limp human's ragged hair, his blood ran down her chin and her chest . . . The human wriggled feebly, and his heartbeat galloped in panic.

But it only made the blood taste better.

"Drink it up. Go on, now."

She drank harder, sucking as deeply as she knew how. Pleasure thrummed like harp strings. Her stomach swelled, tight, but she didn't care. Her nipples sprang hard, every movement a torture. Her sex ached, and with every suck, she flexed her body and her sensitive flesh rubbed against her jeans and nothing ever felt so good . . .

She gasped, hungry for more. The prey's heartbeat skipped, now, weak, fighting to stay alive, and she knew she didn't have long. But her pleasure teetered on a precipice, ready to fall into screaming completion . . .

Cold-wire dread pierced her. She should stop. He was dying. It wasn't right . . . but she was nearly finished, she was going to come, God, she was going to *explode*, and all because Japheth had . . .

Like an ice bath, the thought shocked her heart still.

Japheth had fetched her this prey. And now he watched, while she killed a man and had an *orgasm* over it . . .

She ripped her teeth free, and shoved the dying man away. Her shuddering flesh wailed in protest, the tension crippling her, but she bore it. God, it was awful, his limp limbs, his rolling eyes, his sweat . . . "No more," she gasped, eyes watering. "Please, no more."

Japheth held the gasping woman in his arms. He'd never seen hunger like it. Never seen a creature overcome by thirst, her eyes inflamed, fever raging like a bonfire to consume all sense. She'd moaned, wallowed, gorged herself on that despicable killer's blood.

And then she'd stopped.

He couldn't fathom it. She'd given in. Surrendered to the darkness, yearning for the shattering release that only feeding to the death could bring . . . and she'd *stopped*.

Japheth fought ugly confusion. He'd felt the strength in her muscles, sharpened to inhuman power by demonspells and thirst. Easily, she could've sucked out the last drop of life.

Only one explanation fitted.

She didn't *want* to kill.

Was she trying to impress him? Doubtful. He'd seen the disgust in her gaze. Female curiosity, sure, but mostly hellspawn's hatred for everything holy. Besides, that thirst of hers was . . . passionate. Urgent. All-consuming. No space left for reason or calculation.

A vampire who refused to kill her victims. Astonishing.

Warmth breathed unbidden on Japheth's icy heart. Brave, this Rose Harley. Strong. In the face of overwhelming temptation, she'd resisted. And she'd won.

He closed his eyes, blocking out the glaring light.

He knew what that felt like. Longing for things you shouldn't take. Denying your secret desires. Letting what you craved slip away.

Control. Self-denial. *Not* how evil was supposed to behave.

In his lap, Rose writhed and fought, tears slipping on her cheeks. "Help me." Her broken plea made his bones ache. "Please, just get him away!"

Her anguish stung him into movement. Swiftly he scooped up the bleeding body—still breathing, he noticed dimly—and flung it away. It skidded across the floorboards on a patina of red fluid. He didn't care. Always, a mess to clean up in this job.

But nothing compared to the mess she lay in. Blood, tears, his melted wits. It wasn't right. She didn't deserve to wallow in gore.

He swept her up, and swooped to his bathroom.

White lights sprang on as he entered. Too strong, glaring on the mirrored walls. No dimmer switch. He'd never wanted to turn them down before. Soft lighting was an indulgence. Either you needed to see, or you didn't.

But Rose was shivering, weak with fever. Limp and vulnerable in his arms. She stank of blood, sure, but beneath the filth he tasted hot salt. She was ashamed. Humiliated. Mortified.

His pulse quickened, disbelieving. *She can't care what I think. She loathes me, everything I am.*

But that burning brine on his tongue didn't lie.

"Lights off," he ordered, and they obeyed, throwing the room into shadow. Only the light from the living room angled in. He ruffled his feathers, shedding a soft golden glow. Better.

His inner Dashiel snorted. *Take care, kid, your soft side is showing . . .*

He jerked the glass shower door open with a wingtip, and lowered her feet to the white tiles.

Rose stumbled, bleary-eyed. "Wh . . . ?"

"Hey, girl." His voice cracked on the unaccustomed gentleness. This was weird. He'd never put anyone in his shower before, least of all a woman covered in blood. A beautiful, troubled, deeply humiliated woman, who addled his senses and stirred his desire, no matter how he pretended it wasn't happening . . .

"Where are we?" She blinked, confused, like she'd woken from a nightmare. Her fangs had slipped away, sated. She didn't look monstrous. Just a blood-smeared girl, numb with shock. A girl who needed protection, and comfort.

He still had his arm around her. Her warm breasts pressed

against his chest. His body tingled all over. God, she felt
treacherously good. Sweet, not to be at odds with her for once.
To share something more than snarky retorts.

That she trusted him enough to let him bathe her.

Hot glitter stung his feathers, and he fought it, shaking. He
wanted to peel off those blood-soaked clothes and rinse her
clean. Slide his hands through her dripping hair, over her
breasts, her ass, kneel between her tight warrior's thighs and
taste the trembling flesh between . . .

Hell of a way to repay her trust.

Japheth swallowed, struggling to recall her question.
"Uh . . . we're at my place. You're okay. Stand up for me." He
leaned over to ease her boots off, one by one. Her socks were
mismatched, one pink and one gray. Old, torn, like she'd
scrounged them from somewhere. He peeled them off. Her
pale feet looked so tiny and delicate.

She leaned against him, exhausted. The bloodstains didn't
bother him. They only made her more vulnerable. He straight-
ened, awkward. "Um . . . I'm going to put the water on. You,
uh . . . you say if it's too hot, okay?"

Shit, he didn't know how to do this. Didn't know how to be
kind. Sweet mercy. *What happened to you, Jae?*

"Shower," he whispered, "soft, hundred and ten."

Hot water rained on Rose's upturned face. Not the cold
spiky spray he was used to, but a gentle, soothing flood. Blood
washed over the white porcelain, swirling in scarlet rivulets
down the drain.

Clumsily, he stroked her hair, pulling out her ruined braid,
rinsing out the gore. It felt nice, the hot water tingling his
hands . . .

Rose murmured, fumbling at his fingers, and immediately
he let go, mortified. Surely, she'd raise those snapping dark
eyes and cut him down with a sarcastic remark.

But she didn't. She just stared, hair plastered to her cheeks
under the flood, an unnamable dark tide rising in her eyes.
"Why?"

"Huh?" The best he could manage. The sight of her, soaking in bloody rain, stabbed guilty blades deep into his heart.
What he'd done was wrong, on so many levels.

But the poisoned ache felt right.

"You fed me." She coughed, blood staining her lips. "You helped me. You could've just left me to die. Why?"

Replies flitted through his brain, all of them unspeakable. *I felt sorry for you. I lied and I'm trying to make amends. I didn't want to leave you. I remembered what it felt like to kiss you and I didn't want* you *to leave* me . . .

God, this was ridiculous. Hatred, he could cope with. Anger. Desire, even, just an obstacle to be overcome or avoided. Pain, merely penance for his weakness. But this cursed *compassion* . . .

His thoughts clattered like falling rocks, until his head ached trying to comprehend. *It's not possible. We have nothing in common, this demon's child and I* . . .

But even as he hammered the lie into his brain, he knew it for what it was.

They were the same. She fought her ugly hunger, just as he did. In the face of hell-dark impulses, she'd kept her dignity. Tried her best not to give in.

Didn't that mean she deserved a second chance?

His heart cracked, and seething horror poured out.

No. That evil revelation was the devil, whispering foul lies in his empty soul. He wanted to bleed, break, scream his confusion to heaven. Claw his eyeballs out, blind himself so he wouldn't see what glared before him.

But he couldn't unthink that awful thought.

And he knew this brave woman deserved better than empty platitudes he'd learned by heart centuries ago. She deserved the truth. Even if it ripped his absent soul to bleeding.

So he swallowed, and iced his nerves, and gave her the best answer he had.

CHAPTER 19

"Because you don't deserve to die like that."

An angry retort clogged in Rose's throat.

Not *you disgust me, hellspawn* or *go to hell* or *damn you to endless torment for your sins, witch.*

Because you don't deserve to die.

Her eyes dazzled, and she shivered in the warm water. God, he was beautiful, bathed in that soft golden shimmer. Those wild green eyes, his hair tangled, his feathers glimmering with tiny rainbows. Water trickled down his bare arms, over his wrists, glinted on his sharp cheekbones. But shock drew his face white. He looked like the ghost of Jesus Christ himself had just screamed some horrible secret in his ear, and her heart ached for his sorrow. She wanted to hold him, stroke that golden hair, murmur worthless promises that everything would be okay.

But he was a merciless demonslayer who hated everything about her. A trick. It had to be. That candid sympathy in his eyes couldn't be real. If she showed weakness? He'd just snarl, stab her with some sarcastic remark, leave her alone with her guilt.

"Bull*shit*." She slapped her palm on the mixer, and the

water ceased, leaving her cold and wet. "What's the catch? Since when does an angel feed a starving vampire?"

"No catch. Just good sense. After Caliban gave you all that . . . well, you were . . ." He fidgeted. "I had to feed you or you'd die. I didn't do it for fun."

"Yeah, right." She laughed, bitter. "At least Caliban was an honest sadist. You're the worst kind of asshole, you know that? You know I can't be saved and you're just rubbing it in."

But Japheth didn't flare up. "Think what you like."

The dark, unwanted truth in his gaze assaulted her, and she trembled. The night Bridie died, she'd sobbed, screamed, slashed at herself in punishment, but the horrid vampire skin had healed and she'd just screamed harder in terror. And then she'd fallen on her face in a bloody mess, and prayed.

She'd never really believed in God. Sure, maybe something was out there, but the kind of God who intervened in people's daily lives? Not happening. But that night, in Fluvium's evil-soaked bed, she'd had her mind irrevocably changed.

The demon had ripped her soul open, hurled her screaming into the fiery chasm of truth. And she'd believed, with every cursed fiber of her heart. She'd begged, implored, sworn herself to God's eternal service, and she'd meant every bloodstained word . . . if He'd only undo what she'd done.

Faith was enough, the preachers said. She'd seen it on enough billboards and newsfeeds to know that. Religious mutters had crawled out of the woodwork since the Apocalypse hit, if they ever really were in the woodwork, what with the gangs of zealots who roamed the streets and the fundamentalist lunatics in city hall and the White House. *Believe in me, and you'll never die*, they said. *You shall know the truth, and the truth will make you free.*

What a vicious lie.

And now this Tainted angel was joking about it. While she was weak, her head aching to explode, her body still shuddering with the remnants of her vile hunger.

Angrily, she scraped wet hair from her face, but it only stung her with memories of his touch. He'd stroked her gently, cleaning her, easing the clotted tangles free. How long since anyone had touched her like that? For a dream-sweet moment, she'd relaxed into his arms, enjoying his warm silver breast-plate against her cheek, the dark male scent of his wet feathers, still coffee and spice but somehow . . . earthy. Even *human*.

Her bare feet itched, indignant. He'd touched her while she was vulnerable. Ambushed her personal space while she was off-guard, and damn it to the foulest pits of hell if she hadn't *liked* it.

She wrenched water from her hair. "Don't do me any more favors, okay? I didn't ask for your help and I don't need it."

"Yeah, you do."

"Go to hell." But her voice faded, breathless. He was so close. She wanted more of that gentle touch. Her skin still crawled in memory of Caliban's evil caress, and she wanted it gone.

His wings sparked, and static arced on the wet wall. Her skin tingled. What was that, anger? Embarrassment? Regret, even?

She didn't care. She felt all of those things and it didn't help one bit. She just wanted the past twelve hours to dissolve, like the horrid nightmare it was.

Her guts still twisted into painful knots, the tension in her muscles unbearable. Her whole body ached like fire, longing for contact, any contact to banish those evil sensations. Her lips were raw, stinging. God, she wanted him to kiss her. The fresh taste of him, hot and male and spiced with danger, his smooth lips taking hers, the hot demanding sweep of his tongue . . . So clean. So fresh. The heady flavor of absolution . . .

Impulsively, she edged closer, into his eerie wing glow. It sparkled over her, beauty and grace sinking deep. She shivered, goose bumps prickling. Maybe it was a spell. Maybe he was pouring on the holy-crap euphoria to test her. She didn't care. It felt so . . . innocent, passionate. So good, she quivered, melting inside like warm honey.

Unholy hell. If this is what heaven's like? Sign me up, baby.

Japheth's eyes shone brighter. His arms clenched, muscles tight . . . but he didn't back off. "Rose. Listen. I . . ."

"Don't talk." Daring, she stroked one finger along the rough silken edge of his wing. Her fingertip sparkled. So soft, yet steely. Delicate, yet . . . lethal.

His feathers quivered taut at her touch. She slipped her finger further into the layers. The crisp plumes tickled her palm.

He clenched his jaw, so hard it popped. "You don't understand. This isn't what you think. We can't . . . oh, shit."

She sank all four fingers and thumb in deep, and *squeezed*. Yeah, baby. She'd wanted to do that since the moment she'd laid eyes on him, and his reaction made the wait worth it.

He growled—yeah, like an animal, and if that wasn't the sexiest damn thing she'd ever heard—and his aura flashed scarlet like sin. "Careful."

Boldly, she burrowed her fingers deeper. "Stop me if you don't like it—oh!"

The tiled wall thudded against her back. He crushed her with his massive body, and wrapped those gilded feathers over her, both threat and caress. "I didn't say," he murmured, with a dark edge that flushed her faint, "that I didn't *like* it."

He stroked her cheek with his knuckles. His big thigh pressed between hers, coaxing her to open for him. Her breasts ached against his armor. Such a brutal creature, her angel, hard and rigid all over, silver and muscle and bone . . .

Rose's head whirled, drunk, and all thoughts of resisting fled. She'd decided long ago that she'd have him. It was just a matter of when.

And now seemed like a fucking good time.

And what will you do then? Fluvium's slick compulsion wriggled inside her like a worm. *You owe me an angel's soul, Rose. Don't forget that, while you're getting all breathless and moany. Take his blood. Feed him yours. This dirty nectar-licker is mine . . .*

Japheth rubbed his cheekbone on hers, with a slow purr-growl that thrilled her. His hair tickled her face, drowning her with his deadly fragrance, sweetness and steel.

Screw Fluvium. This one's for me.

She stretched up on tiptoes, searching. "Kiss me."

"No." But his body strained, his chest heaving . . .

"Hell, yes." She caught him, just a tiny brush of lips, and he jerked tighter against her, helpless. "You want to. Forget all this for once. We're the same, you and me . . ." She eased against him, tempting him, squeezing his thigh between hers—oh yes, right there, fuck, he felt so good—and leaned up to glide her lips across his.

CHAPTER 20

He recoiled.

Just an inch. But it shattered Rose's dream like glass.

Her head pounded. He didn't want to kiss her. Didn't like touching her. She'd just swallowed a gutful of fresh human blood. She probably tasted like a slaughterhouse. Disgusting. He'd spit at her, be sick, push her away like the soiled demon-trash he thought she was.

Heat rushed from her belly to the top of her head, scorching everything it found on the way. He was just a man like all the rest. He let his dick do his thinking. She was a woman, he was horny, end of story.

To think she'd imagined he wanted *her*.

He'd even tried to trick her with all that bullshit about not deserving to die. Just a *pick-up line*, for fuck's sake. And now his hands were finally on her, he'd gotten squeamish about the blood and freaked out.

She'd actually thought he meant it. And she'd been ready to abandon her mission—or at least postpone it—so she could be with him. She'd risked her life—her chance to escape eternal torment—and it was all a lie.

But Japheth doesn't lie. You know that . . .

Rage lit through her like a flashburn. "You know what? I changed my mind. I'd rather have the corpse, if it's all the same to you."

Japheth staggered backwards, his shredded thoughts obliterated by his thudding heartbeat.

So close.

He had had her in his hands. Feathers on her skin, her scent in his mouth, all thoughts of sin burned to ash. This magnificent woman assaulted his reason, swamping his senses until his world drowned in wanting her.

And then he'd frozen. Not guilt or disgust. Just witless confusion. No idea what to do next.

He'd always just . . . used them. Taken what he wanted, just as they'd used him. Never mind that it had been centuries since he'd even touched a woman. Longer since he'd done it for its own sake, just to make her feel good.

And he deeply, madly, hungrily wanted to pleasure this one.

But all he knew was how to get it done. How to get it over with for both of them. Quick, breathless release, a few minutes' work and everyone's happy. That was what he was good at.

Not long, slow, torturous sighs, the kind of lovemaking that lasted for hours.

Not that it mattered. She'd clearly come to her senses. And now she glared at him like he'd just crawled from a demon's dung heap.

Sweet heaven's mercy. A demon's slave, looking at *him* with disgust. He needed his bloody head examined.

He backed off, slipping on wet tiles. Bloodstained water puddled everywhere. His reflection in the vanity mirror glared at him, edged with bright malice. His feathers still stung, aroused. He tried to slick them back, but they wouldn't subside, any more than his straining erection would subside. Nope, he'd be carrying that one around for a good hour, if he was lucky . . .

Mind on the job, soldier. He sucked in a lungful, fighting to cool his blood. He had a corpse in his living room. A demon prince to hunt, once the sun slipped down. And a vampire in his bathroom, who he was responsible for. Who needed . . . stuff, like girls needed. The kind of stuff he didn't keep on hand.

He'd made this mess. Time to clean it up.

"Stay here," he said coldly. Both gratifying and scary, how easily he could slip his icy cloak over the seething heat inside. "Take a shower. Towels are in the press. I'll get you something fresh to wear."

"The hell you will." Rose folded her arms over her wet t-shirt. Holy Jesus. Like a second skin, licking every gorgeous curve . . .

"Just stay here, okay? I need to clean up your mess. There's a bleeding body out there, in case you've forgotten." Cruelty stung his words. Like she'd forget that, the way she'd growled and moaned and sucked blood from that body like a monster . . .

Hurt flashed in her eyes. It didn't make him feel better. "Fine," she snapped. "Whatever. Just don't expect me to be here when you get back."

"Oh, I think you will be. The locks are formidable. And we're on the twentieth floor. Unless you can fly . . ."

She scowled, but she had to know it was true. "Screw you, angel."

He smiled, sharp. "I state a fact, you tell me to go fuck myself. Looks like we've returned to normality."

"How nice."

"Not a moment too soon."

"Suits me." She narrowed her eyes at him, mocking.

"Fine."

"Whatever."

God, he wanted to smack her smug face off. Or kiss her mouth until it bruised.

He flung up his hands in mock surrender, and stalked to the bed. His body still quivered, feathers and muscle and bone. She'd see it, laugh at him, make some snarky comment and he'd leap over there and strangle the bitch, like he should've done the first moment he saw her . . .

First things first. He needed to change. He shouldn't go out covered in blood . . . but he kept his clothes here, in the bed-room. And the idea of stripping off in front of *her* . . .

His courage quailed, courage that had stood firm on a thousand battlefields. He clenched his fists, rolled his neck, popped a few taut vertebrae. It didn't help. Inwardly, he growled, frustrated. "Do you mind?"

"What?"

He made a turning-about motion with one finger.

She laughed. "What are you, shy? I've seen it all before and better, hero."

"Then it won't matter if you don't look, will it?"

"Jesus, you really are the Virgin frickin' Mary." But she did turn away. Lounging on one foot, like she couldn't care less. Damn her.

He vanished his wings with a red-sparkled snap, and swiftly as he could—his fingers seemed to have thickened and gotten clumsy while he wasn't watching—unbuckled his armor and shucked off his filthy shirt.

She wasn't watching him. He knew that, right? She wouldn't sneak a peek. But he could still feel her gaze on him, sizing him up, drizzling liquid lust over his skin like warm oil . . .

Uh-huh. His pulse raced. He didn't dare glance around. Did she like what she saw? Did he turn her on, the way she did him? It sure seemed like it, the way she'd rubbed herself against him a minute ago. The way her lips eased apart, tilting up breathlessly for his kiss . . .

Or all just a vampire's lie?

He unclipped his boots, kicked them off. As he unbuttoned his trousers, his cock strained towards his fingers, aching for sensation. Sweat popped on his skin. He'd never so badly wanted to touch himself. Thrust himself into his fist and put an end to this hell-cursed need . . . but release was self-indulgent, the easy way out. He would endure. And besides, *she* was watching. Not cool.

Not cool at all.

He found some fresh trousers in the drawer and pulled them on. Shit, he nearly couldn't button them, he was so hard, and the tight leather squashed him uncomfortably. He reclipped his boots, yanked on a black t-shirt and flashed his wings back in.

His feathers ruffled and settled. They still had blood in them. So did his hair. The healing magic burned the cursed mess off, of course, but only to a certain extent. He could really use a shower.

Yeah. With *her* standing there? Not in a thousand years.

Without looking at her—and certain her eyes were fixed on him, laughing—he strode out into the living room. Daylight angled in, slanting shadows over the gore-stained floor, the body, the mess of blood on his sofa. He flung the corpse over his shoulder, and flashed out.

His boots thudded down in a burned-out crater in Harlem. Smoke twisted like black demonwisps, crawling over the charred remains of buildings. The broken shells of apartments hunched like old men over the melted concrete sidewalk. Early-morning shadows crawled long, stretched by the wind that fingered his damp hair.

Eerie silence. Just the crackle of burning rubble.

He slung the corpse to the ground. It twitched, and its chest convulsed, trying to breathe.

Dude wasn't dead. *Great. What am I supposed to do with him now?*

He lifted the guy by the hair, and cold reason jumpstarted his brain. Maybe because he was away from *her*, his mind functioning without any help from his hard-on. His choices glinted, crystalline. *Let him suffer? Or put him down?*

This human had sustained deep vampire bites. He'd soon be insane, dead and in hell, or infected with the curse. Add to that, the evil raping prick was already crazy as a shit-house rat . . . Japheth didn't like what might happen when he woke up and realized what he was. The things his new powers could do.

You fuck him up good, hear me? That abused girl's voice resounded in his head, and he wrapped one hand under the human's chin and *crunch!* snapped its bleeding neck.

Consider yourself fucked up good, asshole. He dropped

the body in a pile of ash and splintered steel. It slumped, already blank-faced in death . . .

Warning spidered over the back of his neck.

He whirled, feathers crackling. Nothing. No movement in the sharp early shadows . . . but his nose twitched. Honey-scent. The cloying sweetness of heaven.

He flashed his sword, ribbons of blue flame. "Show yourself, soldier."

Gravel crunched, and from behind a broken brick wall swooped a shining copper-winged angel.

She landed gracefully, and folded shimmering wings with a haughty snap. Flawless dark skin, smooth cheeks, her cocoa-brown hair clipped neatly back. She wore a spotless gray suit, and she halted three feet away and aimed her delicate curved sword at his throat.

But Japheth barely registered any of it.

He saw only disdainful eyes, the deep brown of a wood-land pool. Beautiful, the way an angel should be. Her coppery feathers pristine, glowing, alight with holy fervor.

The way he'd once been, when they'd lain side-by-side on that starlit beach long ago.

He tried to talk, but his tongue thickened, useless. "Esther. Uh . . . what a surprise."

His thoughts twisted, diving deeper into blackness. He'd once been like her. And now here he was, dumping a corpse. A vampire's half-dead prey. With that vampire's almost-kiss still burning on his lips.

Give yourself a break, his inner demon argued. *She hasn't spent the last fourteen hundred years greasing around in the dirt down here. Easy to be sinless, when you live in heaven.*

But the empty hollow where his soul once lived cried out in forgotten agony. Could he ever go back? Did he even belong there?

His bones shivered. He knew the rules. Knew what was right and what was sinful. But his treacherous heart whispered otherwise, luring him to evil . . . and he'd followed it.

For the first time in centuries, the crippling doubt surged full strength, drowning his faith on an ugly tide. *What the hell were you thinking, Jae? You'll never win redemption. You're*

*evil, pure and poisonous. You lie, you murder, you're a slave
to your lust, and what's worse? You're too damn proud to
admit you're a sinner. Michael cast you down because you
deserved it. Your stink corrupted that hallowed garden. You
don't belong there. You never did.*

You belong in hell.

"Japheth." Esther eyed his pet corpse, her pretty mouth
curling. "What in heaven's name are you doing?"

Anyone could see the corpse was vampire prey. Torn
throat, pale bloodless skin. His guts heated, scolding. Memories of that awful day centuries ago ate at him like hungry
worms. Esther's disdain, the first hot slither of her hatred, the
hollow cracking pain in his chest that could only have been his
heart . . .

"Nothing," he said roughly. "Cleaning up a mess. Did he
send you to check up on me?" That'd be just Michael's style.

Esther crouched to examine the body. Dust kicked up
beneath her wings. She wrinkled her nose. "Vampire bites.
Honestly. Do you have to wallow in the shit you've dropped
yourself in?"

"Wow. Great to see you, too. Michael's manners are rubbing off on you." Probably, the archangel was screwing her.
Michael screwed all his minions at some time or another.
Strangely, the idea didn't hurt. But still his heart stung raw,
like she'd torn the skin off and rubbed it in salt.

Wallowing in it was exactly what he'd done.

He'd lied. Tortured, killed for revenge. Indulged his lust.
Rubbed himself on a hungry vampire, slimed in her victim's
blood . . . and come a devil's sly whisper from *forgiving* her.

"Shall I tell him you've gone completely insane?" Esther
dusted her hands clean, and raised her sword again. "Or are
you going to tell me what you're doing with a vampire's leftovers?"

He vanished his sword with an angry blue crackle. "None
of your damn business. Done sneering at me, or is there a
point?"

Esther didn't disarm. She just studied him coolly, and
flicked the tip of her blade. A lock of his hair sliced free. "My,
my. Is that blood in your hair?"

"There'd be blood in yours, too, if you ever did anything useful." His stomach sickened, cold. He didn't remember her like this. In his dreams, she'd been warm, laughing, starry-eyed. Not this proud statue.

But he hadn't dreamed about Esther for a long time. She'd faded from his memory, like everything else in heaven. Pale, empty, a ghost bereft of substance.

Unbidden, an image of Rose Harley burned into his mind. Rose certainly wasn't pale. No, she bled color, excitement, rage, dark-sweet delight. She wasn't afraid to feel . . .

"Oh, I don't think that's demon blood, Japheth. Any more than I think you're just cleaning up a mess." Esther propped one spotless hand on her hip, and bit her lip, thoughtful.

He remembered that gesture. It used to make him smile. Hell, he used to make *her* smile. Both so bloody innocent, convinced they'd live forever. That heaven would go on, and on, and nothing would ever change.

Well, now he knew better.

The world wasn't perfect. Everything changed eventually. And no one—not him, not Esther, not even Michael—lived forever. Not if this Demon King and his crazy-ass disciples had their way.

Crap, he didn't have time for this. Plans to make, demons to hunt. And Rose still needed him. "Look, this is real nice and all, but . . ."

"Don't play innocent." Esther's laugh clanged like cracked glass bells, off-key. "I saw you."

"Come again?"

"You really should draw the curtains when you have your little demonspawn girlfriends over." Her brown eyes gloated, bitter and bright. "Anyone might see in."

He flushed, mortified. She'd tell Michael the whole sordid story. As if he didn't have enough problems right now.

He strode closer, challenging her. "And what did you see, Esther? Go on, let me have it. Or are you so damned perfect that you don't know the words?"

Her pretty lips tightened. "It was disgusting. How far you've sunk."

His guts bruised inside, like she'd punched him. He

laughed. "Why do you hate me so much? I never hurt you. I never asked you for anything. We used to be friends. What changed?"

"You deceived me!" Flame glittered on her coppery wings, red and green.

"That's ridiculous." His head swam, confused. He didn't remember. What foul sins was he guilty of now?

"I trusted you! You pretended to be good, but you lied, Japheth, Michael cast you down. He's never wrong."

"But I didn't . . ." He bit his tongue, cutting off the denial. Excuses were useless. What was done was done.

Esther's lovely eyes brimmed. "They're not complicated rules. You do as you're told, you don't make mistakes. It's not supposed to be a trick!"

"The rules." Christ, he was shaking again. The orders he'd believed in since he was made. The ones he'd unknowingly broken.

The rules that said Rose Harley was irredeemable.

"Yes!" Esther hissed. "The rules. Made by *God*."

Her blind innocence jabbed spikes under his skin. "I asked Him, you know that? The day I was Tainted. I begged Him to show me how I could atone for my sins. You know what He said?"

Esther twisted her mouth, silent.

"Nothing," Japheth said stonily. "Not a damn thing. It looks pretty simple, doesn't it, from where you stand? Where everything's clean and tidy? Well, I'm alone here, Esther. I'm figuring it out as best I can. Think about that, the next time Michael hands you your morals on a plate." And he turned aside, icing his anger clear.

But Esther tossed her haughty chin. "I don't know, Jae. Not screwing a vampire slut seems pretty simple to me."

He arced back to her, burning. "Don't judge me. You know nothing about what it's like . . ."

His throat corked shut. *You weren't there,* Rose had said. *You don't know anything about me . . .*

A sick ache hammered between his eyes. That was different. Wasn't it?

But he couldn't defeat the truth. Heaven was a blur, a

shadow. A picture he'd kept for so long, all the colors had faded to gray. Earth was the real world now, hot and bloody, sparkling with ecstasy and excruciations and heart-wrenching emotion.

God, it was terrifying. All that *feeling*. He'd run scared from it for as long as he could remember.

But he'd never felt more alive. Never closer to the edge. And he'd sacrifice all that . . . for what?

To be like Esther? Mind shuttered? Eyes blinkered, seeing only what she wanted to see? Or was that just the demon in him, whispering foul lies? Worse still, his own wretched black heart?

Esther was right. He was lost. Corrupted. Evil inside . . .

Sparks showered from his feathers, and with a gut-wrenching screech, his rage exploded.

The ground shuddered. Thunder rolled, black and threatening. Wind whipped his hair back, his muscles swelling so tight it hurt. Corrupted scarlet fire blazed behind his eyelids, and he struggled to hold it in. Oh, Lord. He wanted to howl, pour his living fury into the air, ignite it and destroy everything in his path . . .

Esther backed off, sword ready. "Belay that, soldier," she snapped, but her voice shook.

He closed the distance, trapping her against a charcoaled brick wall. "Yeah, it's an ugly sight, isn't it? A filthy Tainted angel. Feel superior now?"

Her gaze darted, hunting for escape. "Japheth, listen—"

"No, you listen." He flashed out his dagger, and thunder boomed in his ears, deafening. She'd bleed the same as him. Die the same. What the hell made her so much better than he? Shaking, he leveled the tip an inch from her eyes. "Tell Michael whatever the hell you want, Esther, I don't care. But you don't spy on me anymore. This is my life and I'll go to hell my way. Get me?"

Her eyes narrowed, dark. "And if I don't? What will you do, kill me?"

He wanted to. God help him, he burned to carve that smug superiority from her brain.

He shuddered in denial. Just revenge. A petty indulgence.

It'd prove nothing. It wasn't Esther's fault he was Tainted. Her kind would still sneer at him. He'd still be banished from heaven.

And few greater sins could stain his soul than killing one of heaven's angels.

Japheth gritted his teeth, and vanished his dagger. "Just don't ever spy on me again." And before she could taunt him into falling, he flashed out.

CHAPTER 21

Rose slammed her fist into the dribbling tiles.

Crunch! Pain lanced. She didn't care. It felt better than the acid shame scorching holes in her heart. She punched the wall again. Blood oozed, and the shock jolted up her arm. *Damn that angel to the filthiest pit of hell.*

She raked wet tangles from her face, and shivered. She wanted another shower. The soft warm water had soothed her sharp-cut nerves. She wanted to strip off her filthy clothes and rinse clean, for the first time in what seemed like weeks.

But the water just reminded her of *him.* The whole place stank of him. Damn if she'd accept one scrap of comfort he offered.

Urgency gripped her. She had to get out before he returned. She'd break the locks, climb out the damn window if she had to, but she wasn't staying here one moment longer than necessary.

Her clothes dripped watery blood onto the tiles. She yanked a towel from the stack and wrapped herself. The towel was clean but thin, not soft and scrunchy. Heaven forbid he might actually enjoy himself.

Ha ha. That was a good one. Heaven probably *had* forbidden it. More fool him for obeying their stupid rules.

She squeezed her hair, releasing a rush of wet warmth. The mirrors showed her reflection in the dim light. Her eyes were bruised with fatigue, her cheek still reddened where she'd taunted him into hitting her. Her lips were drawn back, sharp fangs edging out. Ugly. Good. She hoped he'd seen it.

She blotted her wet clothes. Pink stains spread on the white towel. That'd have to do. She had to get the hell out of here . . .

With a hissing crack, the lights extinguished.

Evil smoky blackness crawled down her throat. She choked, and struggled, but poisoned shadows trapped her. The darkness was impenetrable. She couldn't see a damn thing. Even her vampire sight was blocked. She was utterly blinded, helpless. No escape.

Invisible hands slammed her head into the glass wall, an unseen voice gloating with triumph. "Hello, Rose. Did you miss me?"

Her skull clanged. She gulped, dizzy, but couldn't suck in any air. Her lungs convulsed, deflated like sealed plastic bags, but somehow that awful scent of storms and ash invaded her throat. Hot wires of panic threaded her veins. Her demon prince had come for her. And he didn't sound happy.

Fluvium smacked her head into the glass again, harder. His hellfire breath stung her cheek like crawling ants. "What, no answer? Tell me you're not two-timing me with an *angel*, Rose. You're breaking my fetid little heart. Perhaps you've changed your mind about that visit to hell, hmm?"

The old terror tore her guts apart. Just his hands on her brought back revolting memories. She wanted to fight him, claw his face, say *get the hell off me, you lunatic*, but images of the torments he'd promised her blazed into her mind like a hell-charged inferno, and her defiance singed to ash. She coughed up black grit, sick. "Please, master, it's not like that . . ."

"It looked like that, Rose. It looked a whole fucking lot *like that*." Fluvium's steely fingers plucked at her fangs from the blackness. The roots crunched painfully in her gums, and blood leaked over her parched tongue. "Perhaps I'll yank these out. I don't think you need them anymore. Seems to me you'd rather suck his cock than his blood."

"I'm trying!" She spluttered, flailing in a fruitless effort to escape. Like a paper cut, the small pain was unbearable. "You have to believe m—"

"But I don't, see?" Invisible fingers forced her jaw wide, and his rough fist shoved down her throat. Tears poured from her eyes. God, it hurt, stretching flesh that was never meant to stretch, knuckles forcing in, down . . . "I think you're a lying whore, Rose. I think I was stupid to want you for my consort. Shall I take back what I gave you, hmm? Would you like that? I can rip your power from you as easily as I put it there, you ungrateful little tart."

She couldn't breathe. Her ribs stretched, agonizing. She dry retched. Nothing. Just Fluvium, raping her, his cruel fingers scraping her insides. The devilcreature lurking in her belly writhed, eager, its fangs snapping for Fluvium's fingertips. It wanted to go home. To leave her helpless, at her angel's mercy . . .

"No!" The scream burst from her lips, shocking. Abruptly, her throat was clear.

The lights flashed on, dazzling. She whirled, scrabbling blindly for her lost weapon. Fluvium was gone.

But his threat lingered, a leering ghost that taunted her to black desperation.

She crumpled, panting. Her belly ached with suppressed sobs. This would never end. She was Fluvium's slave, and his bidding was law. No way out.

And to please him, she'd make Japheth's soul her prey. Doom him to eternal darkness. In a black, dirty world teeming with monsters, he was the only monster who'd shown her a glimmer of compassion. And she'd betray him.

A midnight wave of despair swamped her, dragging her down into darkness. Her heart wailed, drowning, but the weight was too great. No escape. She was an evil, cursed creature, doomed forever to treachery and lies.

So she'd better start acting like it.

She blinked back savage tears. Japheth despised her. Yet for a few moments, he'd tricked her with his talk of redemption.

He'd softened her brittle heart, weaseled into her consciousness as something other than a loathsome enemy. It was time to cut him out.

Time to kill.

And when her icy golden-feathered tormentor returned, she'd show him no mercy.

Japheth flashed into bright Mediterranean sunshine. Heat wicked his feathers dry, pleasant after sultry Babylon. He landed on the blinding white patio. Brilliant blue ocean stretched to a sharp horizon. The swimming pool glittered, dazzling, and below him, the cliff side fell sharply away to a rocky beach.

Uneasy, he hopped up the steps to the white stucco villa, its broad glass doors laid open wide to the sun.

Inside, cool sand-white tiles drifted towards a marble breakfast bar. Beside the wicker sofa lay a daybed, and on the soft ochre cushions sat the woman he'd come to see.

Lovely oval face, keen eyes, the smoothest skin on earth. She wore a single-piece chocolate-brown swimsuit that showed off her curving hips, generous breasts, taut fighting muscles, and her long olive-skinned legs glistened in the heat. Sunlight teased her glossy black hair, flashing it with pink and green like a mermaid's tail. Her sleek black wings shone with the same iridescent fire.

Even Japheth's well-trained pulse jumped a beat. Iria of the Tainted was gorgeous. Like, supermodel status. And she wore it casually, comfortable in her skin. Didn't care that people figured she must be dumb as a dead fish and just used her gob-smacking beauty to get whatever she wanted. No, Iria didn't give a fling of demonshit what people thought. Women all over the world probably loathed her.

Japheth just envied her indifference. "Hey."

She glanced up, and frowned. "What the hell do you want?"

Okay, so they weren't friends, not really. The words *ice-hearted* and *monster* had passed her lips on more than one occasion. But she was cynical, worldly wise, didn't give a rat's ass for authority. The only person he could think of who might get it.

He forced a weak smile. "Okay. Straight to the point. Can I, uh . . . borrow some of your clothes?"

Iria tossed aside the silver breastplate she'd been tinkering with, and stood, stretching. She noted his drying hair, his bloody feathers, and amusement sparkled in her dark green eyes. "Always figured you for a bit strange, dude, but seriously? I don't think you're my size."

Walked right into that one. His skin heated, and he couldn't help averting his face. Blushing like a girl. Classy. Iria ate hard, arrogant men for breakfast. She wouldn't even taste the blood if she swallowed him. "It's for a friend, okay?"

"*You've* got a friend who needs *my* clothes." Iria's eyes crinkled. "As in, a *woman?* Christ on the bleeding cross. Someone page the hellbeast's PA, there's a snowstorm coming his way."

"Tee hee," he remarked acidly. "My sides are splitting. I asked for clothes, not comedy."

She grinned, naughty. "After fourteen hundred years without a shag? You can suck it right up with your soda, my friend."

"I didn't say I was sh—"

"Right. Whatever. Obviously you can't see the look on your face, or you wouldn't even bother to lie." A teasing grin. "Now tell me. This *friend* of yours, she can't buy her own clothes, because . . . ?"

"It's complicated." He could've bought some clothes. He lived on Madison Avenue, boutiques and label stores wherever you tripped. But the choice confused him—he didn't know dick about women's fashion, but Rose didn't seem like a designer-label girl—and thinking about her body made him sweat. Besides, talking to Iria had seemed like a good idea at the time . . .

"I'm sure it is." Iria stretched her wings, and sighed. "Don't say I never do anything for you. Closet's that way, take whatever you want. Time I culled last season anyhow."

"Thanks." He dipped a swift bow, and turned. Bad idea to come here. He'd just grab some clothes and take off . . .

"Not so fast." She laid a cool hand on his arm. "Answer me one question first."

"It's really not im—"

"Do you know what you're doing?"

Her gaze skewered him, unrelenting . . . but the concern filtering deep in her eyes undid his silence.

She knew what he was like. Knew when he acted strangely. She might think his self-denial ridiculous—she'd scoffed at it often enough—but she knew it mattered to him. And the Tainted looked after their own . . .

"No." It was as if a wall of steel melted around him, exposing his raw-burned flesh to the world. "I have no idea, Iria, and it's scaring the shit out of me."

His voice broke on the final syllable, and what spilled through the cracks wasn't embarrassment or self-disgust but hot-sweet relief.

He shuddered, terrified. God, he was falling apart.

"Christ on a cracker," said Iria, breathless. "The end of the world really is nigh. Sit down, Goldilocks—no, don't think you're getting away. Sit the fuck down." She planted her hand on his shoulder and shoved, and his butt thumped into the cushions. She arranged herself opposite, crossing endless brown legs, eyes gleaming in anticipation. A manic beauty-queen therapist. "Now fess up. Is it a human?"

"Worse," he admitted.

"Ooh. An angel from upstairs, then? One of Mike's holy babes, right?"

"Worse."

She blinked. "Holy motherfucker. What is this, demon-freak week?"

He flushed fire warm. "She's not a demon—"

"Look, you can spare me the juicy details of your sex life, okay?" Iria warded him off with upheld palms and a theatrical shudder. "Are you asking for my advice?"

He sighed, defeated. "I guess I am."

"Then I have four words for you." She rested elbows on slim knees, all her amusement fled. Just heartfelt truth. *"Love isn't a sin."*

Bloody horror clotted in his throat.

Yeah, he wanted Rose. Thought about her. Couldn't carve her from his mind. That didn't mean he had *affection* for her. "Don't be ridiculous," he said tightly. "This woman, she's . . . she's just screwing with my mind. That's all it is."

"Then why are we even having this conversation?"

He shrugged, jerky, but he couldn't meet her eyes.

Iria touched his knee, just an affectionate flutter of fingers. "Look, I can't tell you what to do. No one can. But take a long stroll in the hall of mirrors, my friend, because if you ask me, something's rotten in the state of Frosty-ass. Last week, you would've shaken this off without a second thought. What's changed?"

He didn't know what to say. Because nothing had changed.

Nothing. Except redemption was truly within his reach. And he'd throw it away, for . . . What? A kiss that lasted a few seconds? The dark delight of illicit fire in his blood?

Jesus fucking Christ, he *seriously* needed his head examined. "I don't know," he admitted, past teeth clenched cold. "She's different. That's it. I don't get it."

"Then it's time you found out, instead of running in the other direction." Iria's gaze spiked him, deadlier than her crossbow bolts. "I don't pretend to understand what goes on in that messed-up head of yours, but I do know you can't fight your feelings by pretending them away."

Sweat popped hot bubbles on his skin. He'd rather fork his own eyeballs out. At least physical pain was simple.

Then do it. Temptation licked his bones. *Take the easy way. Kill the bloodsucking bitch, and you'll never have to deal with the mess. She'll be gone. Finished. An ugly memory.*

But poisonous roots of doubt wriggled into his heart, and he couldn't yank them free.

Iria sighed. "Listen, I've gotta go. Mike called, apparently there are some asses in Bhutan that need kicking. Are you—?"

"Can I ask you something?" It came out in a rush, before he knew what he wanted.

A shrug. "Fire away."

"Do you believe in redemption?"

She laughed, her beautiful chin lifting. "Do I seem like I want back into Club Holy?"

"No, I mean . . . when you were Tainted, did they . . ." He tried to swallow, but his chest felt stuffed with bricks. "Did you understand?"

Iria tossed shimmering black hair. "I should hope so. It was right after I told Michael to go fuck himself."

"Oh. I, uh . . . guess that'll do it." But his stomach sank. He hadn't said anything, that chilly day. They'd fought a battle, won a victory. He'd done his job. That was all.

I know what you are, Japheth. Think you can hide from me? Think again.

A shadow flitted demon wings across Iria's face. "Yeah. Wasn't funny at the time, let me tell you. I guess you missed the Crusades, huh?"

"Mongolia," he admitted. "Michael still had the shits."

"Know how you feel. Anyway. Holy Land, twelfth century. Real barrel of laughs. We were all set up to rape Jerusalem, on the Pope's side this time—shit, I don't even remember what year this was, we'd climbed that fucking tree so many times— and Michael and his host had it all figured out. I was there in King Richard's tent, Japheth. I heard Michael tell that bunch of prayer-mad knights and lords exactly how they'd take the city. When we got there, the hellshits slaughtered us."

Japheth shrugged tightly. "It happens."

"Not like this." She gave a helpless little laugh. "They knew we were coming. Envywraiths had possessed Saladin's army, you see, and Michael had done a deal with them. The city, in return for ratting out their demon prince. The scaly mothers sliced and diced every one of those God-fearing knights and lords until the sand was drenched in scarlet. Angels, too. His own heavenly host, Jae. All to get a piece of this one demon prince who'd pissed him off."

Iria recrossed her legs. "So when the blood dried? I told him what I thought of him. Next thing, I had dirt smashing into my teeth." She mimicked Michael's cruel diamond-cutting tones. " 'Word of advice, Iria of the Tainted. Know your place. And it's wherever the fuck I say it is.' "

For a moment, Japheth closed stinging eyes, a silent prayer for the lost. But rebellion was a sin, and Michael was the boss. You didn't ask questions. The heavenly host had a simple chain of command, archangel to officer to common soldier. You obeyed, or you were punished. And he'd always obeyed. Right until the end. "I'm sorry."

"Are you? I wasn't. If Michael's shitty honor makes me a sinner? Sign me up, brother." Iria folded dark wings against the ochre cushions. "I did wonder, though, why they put up with him. Gabriel and the rest, I mean."

"That's one of those questions you don't ask. It's just because."

"No," said Iria simply. "It's because they need him, to do the jobs they can't. Jobs like hunting out this Azaroth and his Dark Apocalypse while thousands of humans die horribly. The same reason Michael needs *you*."

Japheth's skull clanged, a newly resonant chord. He knew that, of course. Dirty jobs were what the Tainted Host were for. But . . .

Iria smiled softly. "Their precious rules cripple them, don't you see? Without us, they can't win. Well, I say screw their rules. It doesn't make 'em better than us. Think about that, next time you're flagellating your sorry ass over your girl."

She's not my girl, he almost snapped. But futility glued his tongue still. While Rose Harley languished in his apartment, with his mark burned into her forehead? Most definitely *his girl.*

But he shivered. He'd already debased himself for her. She'd already crawled under his skin. Cutting her out was gonna hurt. Blood would drench the floor before he was through, and it wouldn't all be hers.

Iria was right. Time he stopped pretending he hadn't screwed up. He had to deal with this crazy emotional shit, before he daydreamed his way into a demon ambush and got his sentimental ass killed.

Before his treacherous heart landed him in hell.

But what did that even mean? What he felt was . . . admiration. Protectiveness. Tenderness, even. How could he fight that? Why should he have to? Weren't they good things?

"Ooh, I see cogs turning in there." Iria's eyes twinkled, rain-sparkled forest leaves. "See? Auntie Iria's not such a bitch on wheels after all."

He flushed. "I never said—"

"No, you never said. Full points for keeping your mouth shut all these years, sweetie. But *hiding* your feelings was never your problem, was it? Maybe you should try letting them out for a change."

Inwardly, he shuddered. Last time he'd let his feelings show, a building caught fire. Things were gonna get broken.

But it was better than the alternative. Better than losing himself in the dark sultry splendor that was Rose Harley, and ending up howling in hell.

Iria stood, and retrieved her breastplate, dusting it off with one glossy black wing. "Now I've *really* gotta go. You're not invited to this Bhutan shindig, eh? Mike got you washing his underwear, or something?"

"Or something." He caught her wingtip as she passed. Her dark feathers were smooth and cool in his palm, her perfumed scent a revelation. "Iria?"

"Hmm?"

"Thanks." It burned his throat, unaccustomed softness. But it felt good.

A dark-lashed wink. "You're welcome, you frosty-assed son of a bitch."

CHAPTER 22

Japheth flashed out of Iria's dressing room—he'd taken a small pile of her clothes, jeans and a few shirts or something—and she gazed after him, absorbed.

For a legendary two-thousand-year-old demon slayer? The guy had no fucking clue.

She snorted, and buckled on her breastplate, tugging her undershirt straight. Seriously? He was like a little boy, asking his mom if it was okay to play in the mud. The kind of wild, rage-filled kid who got upset and broke things, because he didn't know how to cry.

A handsome, muscled-up kid, mind you, with crushable golden hair and wild eyes, who smelled like caramel latte and sex. Hoo boy. She didn't envy him, trying to fend off the ladies while he walked around Babylon in that panty-wetting package. But a kid nonetheless.

And it turned out the kid had a heart.

Who knew? She'd always thought Japheth as chilly inside as he pretended on the outside. And now he was dating—ahem—what prim and proper matrons used to call *an unsuitable woman*. Better than a soap opera.

Not a human, or an angel. *Worse*, he'd said. Iria frowned.

Holy crapola, Goldilocks better not be banging a demon. She'd
have to tell Dashiel, and shit would surely fly . . .

Linen rustled, and a man leaned in her bedroom doorway
on one forearm. Her bed sheet was wrapped around his hips.
He messed his strawberry-blond hair, muscles fighting in his
bare chest. "Morning, beautiful."

"Uh-huh." Iria eyed him critically. Long legs, slim waist,
abs of steel. Not bad. Prettier than the usual tourist trash who
frequented this island. She did like that hair. And a sexy Nor-
wegian accent. He'd felt good, trembling between her thighs.
"More like afternoon."

"Yeah. I guess I slept in." A sheepish smile, timid little
brother to last night's cocky grin.

Iria's nose tweaked. They were so cute, when they met
their match. She'd pulled him from the dance floor in some
neon-lit nightclub, the playboy all the girls swooned over and
all the guys secretly wanted to beat the shit out of. So confident, in his black leather coat and perfectly fitting jeans. He'd
thought he could tease her, play her, make her beg for him.

Her smile darkened, sultry. They all thought they could
play her. But who always ended up doing the begging? Not this
little black-winged angel. "Yeah, I guess you did, uh . . . ?"

"Thor."

Like the god of thunder. Right. "Yeah. Of course. Thor.
Look, Thor, I've gotta go. You can show yourself out, right?"
She buttoned her smooth leather pants and bent to pull on her
boots, flashing him a sweet view of her snugly clad rear.

He slipped a warm hand over her ass, easing between her
thighs. "Where you off to so fast? I thought we might stay in.
Play a few more games." He nuzzled warm breath into her
wings. "That thing you do with your feathers on my cock?
When you tie me up? That is *so* hot."

Yeah, right. She wriggled her toes into her boot and
snapped the clips tight. *Hot* was the tone of his voice as he'd
pleaded with her to have mercy on him, fuck him, let him
come. *Been there, done that, this one's broken. Bored now.*
"Gotta work. Not that it's any of your business."

"So be late." He kissed the back of her neck. "You're so
fucking sexy in silver."

She smacked the last clip to tighten it, and shoved him away. "Save it, kid. Momma's busy."

She strode into the sunlit dayroom and plucked her silver crossbow from the kitchenette bench. Already polished, the wicked bolts fresh and sharp. She flexed her muscle groups experimentally. All fluent, nothing twingeing. She was a professional. She took care of her weapons.

Citrus excitement sparkled in her mouth. Michael had mentioned something about fearwraiths in Bhutan. She liked shooting fearwraiths. Their spells shivered every nerve alive, every muscle aquiver with sweet terror. The danger turned her on. Anything she'd done with baby Thor last night was insipid by comparison. Cutting arrogant men down to size was fun, sure. She liked dominating them. But the fight . . .

Iria slung her crossbow over her shoulder and tied back her hair. Just her and the boys, on the hunt. Trillium, by choice. The others were more conventional, if no less deadly. But Trill was all cunning and craft, a dirty fighter, fiercely competitive, matching her kill for kill. It was a heady rush, better than drugs or booze or lazy power games with strangers.

So much better than anything she could get around here.

She sighed as she strapped her forearms with leather bracers, ready for battle. Jesus. She really needed to find a decent man. A real man, who could give her as good as she gave.

Not that she was Bridget fucking Jones, or anything. She had a life. But hell, she was sick of bedding children. That's what Thor and his like were. Babies. Mastering them was too easy. Give her a decent fight any day. So long as she won in the end.

Know your place, Iria of the Tainted. Michael's ugly words echoed back to her, and the old anger flared, whetted bright by a centuries-old grudge. She knew her goddamned place, thank you very much. And it was on top.

Thor, lately the god of *fuck-me-Iria* if not of thunder, leaned his elbows on the marble bar. Sleek, half-naked, beautiful. Boring. "When do you get back? I thought we could catch some dinner. I know this awesome seafood place . . . ?"

"Not likely, kid. Don't forget your clothes, they're . . ." She glanced around, perplexed. "Somewhere." She wiggled her fingers in a wave, and flashed out to Bhutan.

Emptiness, no sound, no temperature. Subconsciously, she homed in on Michael's diamond-sparkled aura. The archangel burned bright in the ethereal darkness, the space between *here* and *there*, leading her to him.

Wind swirled, and her boots crunched in wet pebbles.

Blinding white snow dazzled. She blinked away tears. A broad snowy plateau stretched for miles. In the distance, a towering escarpment of white-capped rock clawed for the sapphire sky. Atop it, cut into the mountain, a turreted monastery keep reflected the sun, stones glittering like coppery mosaic. To her right, a precipice dropped a thousand feet, and snowflakes danced upwards on freezing wind.

Iria sniffed the thin air, invigorated despite the altitude. Fresh, sparkling, but soured with a faint ashen stink. Demons lurked here. Today was their day to die.

Michael stood on a rocky spur, a flash of icy brilliance, brighter than the snow. He swept the looming horizon with piercing eyes. He wore battle armor, blinding silver, cuirass and twin vambraces, and the sun shone behind him, shedding a glittering winged silhouette edged with ice-blue flame. "Glad you could join us."

Iria shrugged. "You know me. Wouldn't miss a fearwraith swarm." But she eyed the empty plateau, and chill tinkled like glass along her spine. This was a big operation, vital to the cause. Yet she saw no heavenly host.

Not one.

Plausible deniability? Shit. That never boded well.

"So glad you're entertained." Michael floated down and landed, feathers snapping. His unsettling sweet scent pierced the breeze. Her mouth watered. It made her crave hot chocolate syrup, and churned her stomach with brine at the same time. But that was Michael for you.

The archangel glared at the slipping afternoon sun, as if he could halt its slide. Maybe he could. "Where the hell is Trillium?"

Getting drunk and laid? Keeping the hell away from you? "I'm not his keeper. He'll be here—"

"Someone speak the magic word?" Trillium flashed in, an explosion of red-green feathers and wry panache. Intriguing tattoos spiraled on his muscled arms—how he kept them there with his fast-healing angel flesh, no one knew. Sunlight gloated on the golden ring piercing his eyebrow. Blood still crusted his armor from his last battle, like he'd not bothered to clean up, and his rough leather trousers were ripped, just under his left butt cheek. He stank of cigarette smoke and sweat and impish mischief.

Iria shoved him, amused. "Dude, you *reek*. Don't you ever shower?"

Trill dipped her a green-eyed wink. Brutal muscles bulged in his arm as he ruffled his sweaty orange hair. "And wash off all this manly dirt? You know you like me this way."

She snorted. "Not in this lifetime, buddy." But it was a good smell, she had to admit. A trustworthy smell, no perfume or scrubbing to disguise what really lay underneath. Over the years, men had perfumed themselves with varying levels of sexiness—patchouli was a long-standing favorite of hers—but through centuries of rapidly changing fashion, Trill had smelled like Trill, uncouth habits and attitude intact . . .

Her nose wrinkled, a whiff of lavender. Yeah. He also smelled of some girl, the latest teen pop star's brand of sickly perfume. Classy. Not exactly Chanel or Dior. "What is that, candy? Jesus, Trill, this isn't Regency England. It's illegal if they're still in school, okay?"

"I'm sorry, did someone say *cougar*?" Trill flashed his swords and spun them in twin flaming violet arcs, dancing a few lethal warm-up steps. "No doubt yours was barely out of diapers this time."

"Younger men are sexy these days," she lied loftily. "They've got class, and stamina. Unlike some crusty old fuckers I could mention."

Purple light played over Trill's limbs as he flexed, stretched, flipped a sleek somersault. "I am not *crusty*," he retorted. "I look hot for my age. Guys like me are in jeans ads."

"Hair replacement ads, more like. Dude, you've been on Viagra since before the fall of Rome. A wonder you can still get it up at all."

He turned a one-handed cartwheel and landed on both feet, wings aflare. Getting it up notwithstanding, he had a great ass. The hard muscular curve peeked through the hole in his pants. More than scrumptious enough for a jeans ad. He grinned, and vanished his blades with a showy purple crackle. "Let's see who's got the bigger hard-on, then, soldier. First to a hundred wraiths buys the whiskey?"

She couldn't resist an answering grin as she unslung her crossbow to check it one more time. "Two hundred, or you don't taste a drop."

"My lovely, you are *on*."

Another burst of light, and Jadzia appeared, dusting stray feathers from her armor. Her creamy-white wings fluffed, untidy, and her pale hair was braided askew, like she'd done it in a hurry. "Shit," she muttered, yanking it straight.

Trill grinned. "Now the party's started. Hey, Lady J."

Jadzia strode over, wiping slim hands on her trousers. "Sorry I'm late."

"So am I." Michael fired her a freezing blue glare. "Finished putting on your face? Shall we get on?"

"Sure." A cool Jadzia smile. "No problem."

But Iria frowned. Jaz's clear voice lacked its usual confidence. Her classically pretty face flushed warm in the frigid sunlight. Not that Michael would notice . . . but Iria recalled Japheth, sitting on her sofa wearing that *what-the-fuck-just-hit-me?* expression, and her feathers crawled.

Jaz was seeing a demon. Iria had caught her at it, or as good as, a few weeks ago in a burned-out Babylon office block. She'd assumed it was over now, just a brief dalliance, a hot forbidden fuck to spice up life in the shadow of eternal oblivion.

But Jaz didn't look like a girl with no man problems on her mind.

Iria's nerves coiled tight. She glanced at Trill and Michael, but neither had noticed a thing. Shit. Sometimes female intuition sucked.

She sidled closer, and nudged Jadzia with a wingtip. Jaz stared pointedly at the snow. *Damn it.* Iria's palms itched. She wanted to whisper comfort, ask if everything was okay. But Michael was talking, something about fearwraith tactics and the best killing technique. You didn't interrupt Michael. Not if you wanted your skin intact.

Iria nudged harder, insistent, and at last Jadzia's cool blue eyes met hers.

Shadows swirled there, dark with desperation.

Iria's heart sank. Jesus. Not only hadn't she ended it, she was up to her bloody neck in it.

Fuck. She dragged her attention to Michael, but her mind sprinted laps. Jadzia was a good, faithful girl. But demons were wily. They milked information you didn't even realize you were leaking. If Jadzia had let slip about this mission . . . if she'd murmured even a single word, while her hell-cursed lover teased her breathless . . .

"Iria? Am I boring you?" Michael's gaze snapped, an ice-blue whip. Her nose popped, and she tasted blood.

"Sorry. I'm with it. Carry on." But her bones chilled. What if Jaz had compromised them? Knowingly or not, the result was the same. The demon prince forewarned. Their surprise advantage lost. And the snow would melt crimson with Tainted blood before the day died.

But if Michael learned Jaz was sleeping with the enemy . . . well, there'd be Tainted blood in the slush, all right. Dripping from Michael's blazing sword.

Double damn it.

"Two hours of sunlight left," Michael said, and Iria forced her attention sharp. "That's our advantage. The wraiths won't mass until twilight, as usual, so don't be waiting for shadows to cover you. Just get in there and secure your positions. And remember, you can't flash. The place is wrapped in hell-fucked spellwork, Azaroth's doing. Otherwise the damn Guardian could come to us, and we wouldn't be freezing our balls off in this forsaken snowy shitheap. It also means you keep your feathers stowed, unless you want a hundred screaming imps diving down your throat. With me?"

They all nodded.

"After that, you know the drill. Each swarm has a queen wraith. Put some holy fuck-you into that bitch, and the rest will burn. Questions?"

Trillium linked his fingers, cracking tattooed knuckles. "What about this demon prince? Lucy-Loo, or whatever he's called?"

Michael allowed an ice-cracked laugh. "Luuceat. Prince of Fire."

"Whichever. Who gets to rip his skinny ass to demon jerky?"

"I'm getting to that. Trill, you and Iria take the wraiths. Jadzia and I will lure the prince inside, where he's most vulnerable."

Jadzia cocked an eyebrow. "And how will we do that, exactly?"

"We let our defenses slide, of course. Luuceat will overwhelm the Guardian easily enough. He wants the vial, we're going to give it to him. Up to a point, that is." Michael gave a chilling smile, devoid of feeling. "The point where I tear his greasy arms off and stuff them up his ass."

Trill scowled, good-natured. "Typical. You get all the fun."

"What about the Guardian?" Iria asked, doubts still howling like unquiet ghosts in her mind. "How does she feel about this plan?"

Michael shrugged, and diamonds tinkled into the snow, winking in the sun. "More authentic if she doesn't know."

"You mean she's bait."

A glacial stare. "She's part of the ruse. Sweet Salome. The perfect distraction."

"But—"

"The Guardian is expendable," Michael snapped. A snow cloud gusted, stinging Iria's face. "I don't care if Luuceat makes a strawberry fucking milkshake out of her. Nothing matters but the vial. If that wrath gets spilled—even by us—the whole damned mission is pointless."

"But—"

"Stow your attitude, Iria. What part of *hell on earth* are you still not comprehending?"

Iria's fists clenched. Michael had betrayed the Tainted Host in the past. Shit, he'd betrayed everyone, at some time or another. But fuck if he didn't sound sincere this time. The archangel's eyes burned clear with icy-blue rage. If there was one guy you could count on to win a fight, it was a pissed-off Michael. But if Jaz's demon stud had betrayed their plans to Luuceat . . .

Shit. They were all going to die.

She cleared her throat on sour guilt. *Jadzia's screwing a demon. She's told him everything. And now she'll never trust me again* . . . But the words clogged her tongue, and try as she might, they wouldn't come loose.

Jadzia's blue gaze homed in on Iria's, pleading. Her pretty lip trembled . . . and then her mouth firmed, and she flashed her sword, planting its point in the snow between her feet. "I'm ready," Jaz announced, looking Michael directly in the eyes.

Cool. Composed. Not a quiver of fear.

Not the stance of a traitor.

Iria's resolve wilted. If Jaz was going in unafraid? She'd take her chances. And if demons jumped out and fried her gullible ass . . . well, at least she wouldn't go to oblivion having betrayed a friend.

Iria slung her crossbow over her shoulder. "Me, too."

"You got it." Fire gleamed in Trill's eyes.

Michael vanished his wings, a plume of dazzling white, and swept all three of them with a razor-blue glare. "How gratifying you're all in agreement. Now lock and load, people, and let's unfuck this sorry situation."

CHAPTER 23

Rose awoke to the sound of a rippling waterfall.

She groaned, shifting. Something banged into her skull, and her eyelids cracked apart.

Glossy white tiles, hard and cool through her damp jeans. Jeweled raindrops glittered on a tall pane of glass.

She'd hit her head on the shower screen. Japheth's bathroom. She'd passed out in the shower? Damn, she must have been exhausted.

She rubbed her bruised temple, and memory glared, indignant. She'd tried to kiss him, and he'd rejected her. And then Fluvium . . .

Her blood thumped sickly. How did Fluvium get in here? Surely Japheth had put up wards. Explosive angelic traps to keep demons out. So what was it, a dream? It sure as hell felt real . . .

She shivered, and clambered up, bare feet sticking to the tiles. Her clothes were still plastered to her chilled skin. Where was Japheth? Why had the bastard left her here? She palmed her eyes, fighting a raging headache. It didn't matter. He'd be sorry soon enough that he hadn't killed her when he'd had the chance.

The waterfall sound swelled louder. She leaned on the tiled wall for a moment, dizzy. What the hell was that . . . ?

Her vampire ears pricked. Not water. Music. Clear, crystalline notes, rippling up and down, uncanny sound quality . . .

Goose bumps licked her forearms, and she rubbed them. But curiosity itched, too. He'd left her fresh clothes, she saw. Folded neatly on his bed, jeans and a t-shirt, similar to what she already wore. Two sets, in fact, like he couldn't decide between blue and black. He'd even brought socks.

Like she wanted anything he'd brought her . . . but despite the shower, her body crawled with filth, real or imagined. Her skin tingled with longing. Clean clothes would sure be nice.

Swiftly, she peeled off her damp jeans and shirt. Her bra and panties were damp, too, but she left them on. They'd dry soon enough. The new t-shirt said VERSACE in golden letters, and smelled of Chanel No. 5. It fit okay, a bit big around the boobs, but it'd do. The fabric stretched smooth and clean over her skin, and she sighed in sweet relief.

The blue jeans were tight and too long—whose were they, anyway, a supermodel's?—but she stuffed the bottoms into her boots. Her knife lay on the bed. She buckled the sheath around her thigh. It felt good to be armed again.

She smoothed the jeans over her butt, enjoying the crisp clean feeling. But that eerie music still ebbed and flowed. Tugging her hair back as neatly as she could, she tiptoed from the bathroom.

In the living room, late afternoon light scarred the floor with stark orange shadows. The cityscape glared, blinding sunset reflecting in the west-facing glass across the street. Great. She'd slept all day. Who knew what he'd gotten up to without her?

The music grew louder, climbing the octaves. Sunlight licked the dark granite breakfast bar, two shiny metal stools, spotless sink and tapware. Bloodstains still crusted the pale sofa, but guess-who had meticulously polished the floor. His silver breastplate lay sparkling on the boards. And the human she'd fed from . . .

She shuddered in memory. He'd been alive when she stopped. She was sure. But the body was gone.

And Japheth sat at his piano, playing. Meticulous rhythm, not a note out of place, a rapid melody in baroque counterpoint, twinkling and tumbling like a rocky river. Golden hair fell across his forehead. He stared at his fingers with deadly focus, as if he forced the notes from the instrument with sheer will alone. His precision razored the air, lovely but lethal. A lot like Japheth himself . . . but in those achingly beautiful notes, everything he locked away so tightly in his heart poured out.

He played rage, loneliness, weariness, sorrow, long dark centuries of denial. The perfect chords swelled, vibrated, imbued with pain and emotion they were never meant to carry . . .

Tears sprang in Rose's eyes. She hugged herself, and cleared her throat. "That's beautiful."

Abruptly, the sound clanged silent.

He looked up, blank. Lost. Confused. Like he'd forgotten where he was.

Then his eyes cleared, and shadows crept in. "J. S. Bach," he said grudgingly, like it was a shameful admission. "It's . . . been a long time, I guess. I'm rusty. Sorry." And he slid from the stool, tucking his wings in stiffly. Scraping his hair back. Slowing his breathing. She could practically feel those icy barriers, crunching down around him.

"Don't stop." The words ambushed her, pinned her down before she could defend herself. "I mean, don't mind me, if you're practicing . . ."

Her old life flashed before her, endless hours of painful repetition, aches and muscle strains, blisters, the same moves over and again until she'd rather claw her face off than do that damn step one more time . . .

But she always did it one more time. And then again, and again. You didn't get better, unless you did it one more time.

Sure, he'd had centuries to learn. But you didn't get to play like that without putting in a lot of work.

She shivered, rubbing her bare arms. It was a side to him she'd never imagined. She'd thought all he cared about was killing. But no, he had to be a fucking artist as well. Unwilled, her interest tweaked sharp. A bundle of surprises, this Tainted angel . . .

Her heart stung, a stab of panic. She didn't want him to be a real person. Not when she had no choice but to steal his soul. But she couldn't rip that image of him at the piano from her mind. Couldn't unhear that heartbreaking sound, so mathematical and precise, yet swelling with suppressed emotion. Screaming like a caged animal with everything he didn't dare let himself feel.

Block it out, Rose. He loathes you. And he's losing it. Look at him. This is your chance. Just get him naked, take what you need, and get the hell out of here . . .

Compelled, she shuffled closer. "Play me something else."

Japheth's fingers lingered on the piano's gleaming black lid. "That's not a good idea."

"Your favorite. Please." She dared him with her steady gaze. "Come on, angel. Let it out. I won't tell."

A dark glance, unfathomable. And slowly, he sat, tidied his feathers, and began.

Rose caught her breath. She knew this one, even after just a few bars. Beethoven, the "Moonlight Sonata." The part everyone recognized, with stirring arpeggios and a plaintive, desolate melody that pierced her jaded soul. So beautiful. So . . . lost. And the way he played it . . . like he tore his heart open and bled into every phrase. Unspeakable, bewildered feeling, molded into music. He stared at the keys, emerald eyes shimmering, and his handsome mouth quivered, as if he knew he was draining himself to death but couldn't stop.

Oh, hell. Heat swelled her eyelids. She tried to blink the tears back, but they wouldn't obey. Damn it. She didn't want to feel for him. Didn't want to see him like this, lost and alone and so heartbreakingly real.

But too late. She'd dared him, and he'd called her on it. Fuck, had he ever. He played exhaustion, famine, desperate sadness, the heartbreaking agony of loss. Her knees buckled. She clutched the breakfast bar, drained. She wanted to crumple to the floor and weep.

The final minor chord chimed, and faded into screaming silence.

It wasn't fair. This angel's heart overflowed. He felt so much, it flayed him raw and bleeding, and he fought so hard to keep it in that it was destroying him, shard by icy shard.

For so long, Rose had felt nothing. Nothing, except thirst, and rage, and black delight in other people's pain. She'd imagined she cared about her victims, suffered for them. What a hateful lie.

All she cared about was misery.

Acid threatened to dissolve her eyes. Her skin caught fire. She couldn't face Japheth's gaze. She wanted to crawl into a hole, disappear, hide her ugly face from the light.

But the sun poured in, hateful, and she couldn't escape the blinding truth.

She was ugly, and he was beautiful. And she'd throw him to the howling wolves of hell, just so she could delay her own torment for a few sad little weeks.

She was a monster. And for the first time since the curse took her, her steely heart scorched with shame.

Japheth stared at the piano keys, but didn't see them.

The music still tore through his blood, thundered in his pulse. He sweated. His feathers stung hard. His skin was surely melting from his bones. And still he wanted to dive into the empty sky and scream until his heart exploded.

He couldn't deny this anymore. For fourteen hundred years, he'd cried, hungered, hoped, laughed, wanted. All without uttering a sound. His icy barriers in place, a glacier safe and solid around his heart, with only glory-rich slaughter to prove his pulse still beat at all.

But now the ice was cracking. He could feel it, just as he had on the day Michael cast him out. That swift, sharp agony deep inside his chest.

His calm was crumbling. And Rose knew. He could *feel* it. He could feel *her*.

A hot fist mashed his guts, and he trembled, like he never had in battle. God help him, he wanted to flee. To run and hide like a coward.

With a supreme effort, he dragged his leaden gaze upwards.

Tears smudged her dark eyes red. She wiped her nose, rough. And then she laughed. "I suppose you think that makes you special."

That cruel twist of her mouth stung him like envy. "What? No, I—"

"Well, it doesn't." She shoved her hands in her jeans pockets. "Don't fool yourself, angel. Heaven doesn't care about your god-damned bleeding heart. It won't save you. You make one mistake, and suddenly nothing else you've ever done matters a damn."

His lungs burned. He couldn't breathe. Didn't want to face her. Didn't want to listen.

He jerked aloft, landing by the window. He glared down at the city, the failing sun glinting on glass and metal, and his fists crunched so tight they shook. He wanted to punch the damn window to splinters. "What would you know about mistakes? You made your choice. Live with it."

She strode up to him, eyes storming dark. "You'd like to think that, wouldn't you? That I made a *choice*? So you can pretend you're the only one who got fucked over by heaven?"

"Actions trump words, Rose Harley," he said roughly. "Saying you're sorry isn't enough. You make your choice every time you flash those fangs of yours."

She planted herself in front of him, trapping him by the window. His feathers tingled with her body heat, but he refused to back off. He'd face his enemy head-on.

"Yeah," she said scornfully. "And you know all about that, don't you? You fed me that blood. Did you enjoy that? Did you get off on watching me gorge myself?"

His guts roiled. She'd refused to kill, pushed that dying man away from her.

A soldier does what's necessary. Those words chimed ugly dissonance now. She'd taken only what she needed to survive . . . "Don't give me your innocent act. You've played the whore with me since the moment we met, and you don't show one scrap of remorse. Not one bloody bit."

She snorted. "Yeah, right. About as much as you show when you're slicing a vampire's head off."

"That's different. At least I haven't given up on myself."

Her face drained pale. "Excuse me?"

"You want absolution? You can start by acting like you give a shit. I believe in redemption. I *work* for it. What do you believe in?"

She laughed, and it grated his skin. "Believe? That's a joke. I believed in your God, and look what it got me."

His wings fired blue, the burning rage of injustice. He wanted to squeeze sense into her, make her understand. Silence her with bruising kisses until she surrendered. "You drank that demon's blood, vampire," he growled. "You chose this life. So guess what? You don't get to complain. You don't get to blame God for your weakness. You want forgiveness? Earn it."

"Forgiveness?" She shoved his chest, knocking him back. "Forgiveness is a dirty lie. I begged on my fucking *knees* for one tiny glimmer of mercy. All it got me was damned."

His heart sliced raw. He'd screamed to the sky, that ugly day when he fell. Raked his skin with filthy nails, the pain ugly and incomprehensible. Dirt in his feathers, on his face, everywhere, itching like poison but scrape as he might, he couldn't get it off. *Help me,* he'd prayed. *Tell me what to do. Give one more chance . . .*

But only black silence had echoed.

Blood thundered in his head, splitting agony. He wanted to crack his skull open, let this insanity explode. "Go on, then," he spat. "Blame God, if it makes you feel better. Doesn't change the truth."

"Right. And the truth will make me free. Isn't that what your asshole Book says?" Sunlight flashed on her hair, imbuing it with ethereal fire.

But her beauty just spiked his bones with rage. She was healthy. Strong. Intelligent. She had everything, and she'd thrown it away. He turned aside, insolent. "What if it does? What do you care?"

She grabbed a handful of his feathers—*sweet heaven, woman, stop doing that*—and pulled him around to face her. "Try me," she snapped. "Go on. If you know so much about me? Show me your stupid truth. I'm ready—ugh!"

He slammed her back against the window with one forearm. The glass shuddered. He didn't care. Let it break. Let them both fall forever.

"You want the truth?" He was shaking, his voice, too. Her body trembled sweetly against his, and he burned. Have her, kill her. He didn't know the difference. "Being a demon's whore is what got you damned, Rose Harley. And until you take some goddamn responsibility? No one will *ever* forgive you. Especially not me."

CHAPTER 24

He let her go. His lungs burned like poison. Christ redeemer, he was still too fragile. He couldn't control his rage, and his heart swelled with the dumb urge to apologize.

But she just stood there, trembling. "So that's still what you think of me, is it? A demon's whore?"

"You're Chosen, aren't you?" He ruffled sweaty feathers, overheating. "Infected directly from the source? You expect me to believe you drank his blood from a glass?"

"Don't you want to know what happened to me? Do you even care?"

His throat tightened. Damn her for asking a direct question. "Make your lame excuses to someone else," he said tightly. "It doesn't matter—"

"I killed my sister's little girl."

He gulped, and his rage withered cold.

He'd never had children, of course. Never someone who relied on him for everything. But he'd known the sorrow of fallen comrades, soldiers who fought at his side. He'd lost friends when he fell. That was bad enough. But to lose a child . . .

Rose's mouth crumpled. "Bridie. She's six. She lives . . .

she lived with me, while her mom . . ." She swallowed, and swiped her eyes roughly. "Well, my sister's in prison, it's a long story, and you don't actually give a shit, so . . ."

Japheth touched her shoulder, stopping her from turning away. "I'm listening." Soft. Gentle. The best he could make it.

Rose gazed up at him, sorrow brimming black. And she sighed, weary, and leaned back against the glass. "One night, I . . . I was celebrating." Her voice was small, lost. "I'd started a new job, see. I'm a dancer, and this show, it was . . . well, it was everything I'd ever wanted." Distant light brightened her face, long-forgotten joy. "So me and my friends, we went out, and I left Bridie with my neighbor like usual. I didn't normally stay out so late, I'd come right home, but that night was special, so . . . They put her to bed, and . . . that was the night *he* took me."

Shadows haunted her eyes. Her chin trembled. Jesus, she was trying not to cry. "The next morning, I woke up in my apartment, and . . . Bridie was dead. Gone. There was blood all over the place . . . and I . . ."

He tried to speak, but his throat squeezed shut. What the hell was there to say? *I'm sorry* was stupid, futile.

Rose banged her fists against the glass at her sides. "You think I wanted that, angel? *It was an accident!* I made a mistake! I screamed for forgiveness until my heart bled out, and you know what I got? Nothing. So don't give me crap about responsibility. If your God wanted me, I was there for the taking. He abandoned me."

I didn't mean it. It was a mistake . . . How he'd screamed it to himself, so many times, like bloody ruts worn into his brain.

But raging at fate was useless. He'd learned that the hard way. "Hell of a mistake," he said harshly. "*Don't screw a demon*. It's not rocket science."

"I got drunk and went home with some guy," she retorted. "Maybe that doesn't happen on your perfect little island? But it's not a capital offense. Next thing I know, I'm waking up in a pool of blood."

"So you did screw him, then." Japheth gritted his teeth on incoherent fury. The insane desire to lick her clean, kiss the

demon's foul breath from her body. Thrust himself deep inside
her and make her scream his name to the sky, show the world
to whom she belonged . . .

Right. He struggled to ice his shattered dignity. This stone-
age jealousy thing was getting old real fast. Next he'd be dragging her off to his cave by the hair.

"He tricked me!" Her voice rose, grating. "I was an idiot,
okay? I was celebrating. I was lonely, if you must know. I was
flattered that a guy like that would want me. *Mea* fucking
culpa. You think I wanted what he did to me?" Her eyes
flamed dark with rage. "You think I asked to be *violated*?
Fuck you, angel, you have no goddamn *idea* what I went
through."

Her scent dizzied him, a dark and dangerous drug. He
wanted to swallow more. Madness wrapped itself around his
mind, wispy and glowing like a wraith. *This is crazy. I don't
believe her. Can't believe her . . .*

He growled, and in hot frustration he grabbed her by the
arm and slammed his left palm into her forehead.

No. Don't want to. Can't invade her like this . . . But he had
to know.

The angel's mark on her skin flashed, azure bright,
responding to the touch of his sigil. She gasped, reeling, but
he held her upright and flung a desperate prayer skywards.
Heaven, help me see. Show me the truth.

Visions swamped him, so clear they dazzled. Fluvium, his
crazy eyes shadowed behind a crafty spell, just a soft-spoken
guy, deadly handsome but human. Rose's womanly perfume,
flowers and spice, mixing with the dark musk of the demon's
skin. Their limbs entwining, mouths molding wet, his fingers
pinching her nipples, her long flexible legs wrapped around
the demon's hips as he eased within her, her low female moans
of delight, rising, peaking, breathless . . .

Japheth gasped, choking on pure sensation. His feathers
stung, too sensitive. His skin burned. His pulse tortured him,
banging in his ears, making him hard and aching. It was too
much.

He tried to pull back, but his senses dragged him down,
deeper and darker until he *felt* her inside him, a wailing, tor-

tured ghost that possessed him and wouldn't let go. He *was* her, lying on those rough cushions. The stale flavor of vodka and cigarettes, flickering candlelight, drunk and swimming out of his mind with delight . . .

The pleasure won't stop. It's too much. He's got his fingers playing on my clit—sweet Jesus—and his cock is so deep inside me, fuck, I can feel it, he's splitting me open, emptying me, letting me wash out over him . . . It hits me again, a shockwave of raw sensation that cripples me. I cry out. I've never come this hard in my life. It's astonishing. I'm so exposed, so vulnerable. And the sound he's making, guttural, hungry, deep inside his chest like . . .

Oh, Jesus. I moan, helpless. I'm coming again. Again, and again, more and forever and it hurts, God, it rips me apart . . . I can't endure it. "No," I gasp. "Don't. Stop." But he won't stop. My legs are thrashing, I'm twitching like electric shock. I'm out of control. I gasp for some air, and he presses my face into his shoulder, my teeth gnash down and . . . oh, fuck. That's blood. That's skin, crunching in my teeth. I'm BITING him, he's bleeding, it's running over my face and into my mouth and I want to be sick. I choke. It splashes, hot and thick, painting my face, my breasts.

And he . . . he just laughs.

Holy crap, I've BITTEN him and he's laughing.

And I realize I'm afraid.

I'm panicking. This isn't fun anymore. Blood spills down his chest from my bite marks. And he's dragging my mouth back onto the gash. He's very strong. I struggle and spit it out, dizzy. "No," I splutter, "don't, what the hell are you . . ." But the blood spurts into my mouth, hot and coppery, disgusting. He forces it in, stops me from breathing. Stars dance in my eyes. I have to swallow or I'll suffocate. My throat convulses, and the stuff hits my stomach, crawling, writhing in my guts like a burning snake . . .

"Ahh." His fingers dig cruelly into my skull. He's crushing me. He won't let me move. "Drink me, Rose. Take me in. You'll live forever."

He's still inside me, still caressing my flesh, but now I'm crawling inside like worms, it's so disgusting . . . I'm helpless.

I have to swallow more and more. And this psychopath is enjoying it. I can feel how hard he is inside me, how his breath catches every time I swallow and I'm sick and I'm fucking terrified and oh, God, I want to die. I want him to strangle me and get it over with. I just want this to stop.

I'm crying now. Begging, every time he lets me choke in a breath. "Please . . . Let me go . . . I won't tell anyone . . . We can fuck some more, you can do whatever you want . . . You can . . . you can hurt me. Just not this. Not this . . ."

But he won't stop. And finally his back arches, impossibly flexible, and with a beastly roar he comes, spilling acid deep inside me. It hurts, like some vicious animal is chewing me out inside. I scream. Blood froths, and something black and disgusting like a slug squirms its way down my throat. Horror drowns me. He's killing me. My heart's going to explode. I'm going to die. I struggle and choke until my eyes water, but there's nothing I can do . . .

Dizzy, Japheth staggered backwards. His palm ripped from Rose's forehead, leaving a second burn. And ugly truth sizzled into his brain.

Fluvium had tricked her. Forced her to drink from him, while she suffered unutterable torment.

He stumbled to his knees, and his rage exploded.

Blue lightning flashed, a smoking crack of thunder that split the window in two. Acid ate his bones, his muscles so tight they screamed. Hunt Fluvium across this black hell of a city and peel the dirty motherfucker's skin off. Wrap Rose in his arms, comfort her, stroke her hair and whisper that she was safe now, that he'd never let anyone hurt her again.

As if another man could erase what the evil bastard had done to her.

Anguish stabbed his heart, a rough demon-steel blade. Her wounds would never heal. The horror would always be there, lurking inside, waiting to consume her.

But terrifying icy logic slashed through his sympathy. Fluvium had tricked her. Taken her against her will. The curse wasn't her fault.

And if it wasn't her fault . . .

He reeled. The floor shuddered. The cracked window lit

with forked blue static, and he struggled to deny it, hold it in like he had for centuries.

You will know the truth, and the truth shall make you free.

He couldn't unsee what he'd seen. Couldn't unknow what he knew.

With every fiber of his stolen soul, he believed in redemption. Because his heart was pure. He could still make up for whatever he'd done. So if he could still earn a second chance . . .

The bottom crashed out of his world, and he fell.

If I can earn redemption . . .

. . . then so can she.

CHAPTER 25

Rose staggered, her forehead smoking, and drowned in a burning ocean of horror.

Her brain twisted in knots. *No. Not that. Don't let him see . . .*

But too late. Fluvium's dreadful assault had replayed in her mind like a disgusting horror film, and Japheth had seen it all.

He knows.

Toxic shame mushroomed in her guts. She squeezed her eyelids on stupid tears. She shouldn't be ashamed. It wasn't her fault . . .

She covered her mouth, sick bile boiling in her throat. Japheth was a guy, for fuck's sake. They didn't get what it was like to be a woman. He probably thought she'd brought it on herself. What did she expect, when she flirted, wore a short skirt, showed her tits? When she came onto a guy like that? She'd gone to his bed willingly enough to start with. Japheth would think she'd asked for it . . .

The floor shook, and her sharp vampire nose smelled a storm.

Wind swirled her hair back. Tiny blue lightning forked on the window, crackling in Japheth's golden feathers. The floor shook. He quivered, every muscle wrenched hard, and the air shimmered black with power about to explode.

Rose stumbled forwards, wild. "Japheth, hold it together. You'll kill us both!"

He screamed between gritted teeth, and wrenched his wings around him. Clenched them tight, shivering, static arcing bright. And with a snap, the light died. The air cleared, cooling. The wind subsided, leaving only a broken window and the smell of rain.

He relaxed, shuddering, and his eyes flashed open.

Rose shivered. Wetness glistened on his icy cheekbones. He was weeping, shaking, on his knees at her feet, and yet, she'd never felt so . . . threatened. Raw. Exposed . . .

She swallowed, hot. She wanted to go to him. Run her hands through those golden feathers, let him stroke her hair, take comfort in his embrace . . .

She crossed her arms, defiant. "I suppose you think I asked for it, huh?"

He didn't speak. Just stared.

Humiliation swelled her belly warm. *Damn him.* She wiped her eyes roughly with the back of her hand. "Right. Thanks for that vote of confidence—!"

Twin blue flashes, *boom-boom* like deafening drums, and he stood upright, buckling on his silver armor. His expression was stony. "Stay here," he said coldly, yanking the buckles tight. "I'll come back for you when I'm done."

"What do you mean, 'done'? Where are you going?" Frustration nipped like rats. He never talked. Never explained himself. Inscrutable as a fucking iceberg.

But her stomach twisted. She didn't want to be alone. Not now. Not with that horrid memory torn afresh in her mind . . .

At last, he faced her, and his chilly gaze froze her spine. "Central Park. Bethesda, to be exact. I'm going to do what I came here for. And you're not coming." He strode to his fridge and yanked the door open. Light spilled. He grabbed a bottle—iced water—and drank it dry. Crushed it, tossed it in the garbage. "When I'm done, I'll take the mark off, and you can go."

"No!" She blocked his path. Useless, she knew. He could

flash out anytime, leave her here alone. "You can't leave me behind. You need me!"

He took her by the shoulders. Yanked her close, pinned her with his cold stare until she shivered, and tensed, ready to fight . . .

"Do you really think I'd take you down there?" He cupped his warm hand on her cheek, and his unexpected gentleness undid her. "After what he did to you?"

Her throat stoppered. Disgust, she understood. But this . . . "I—"

"Not a chance." He stroked her unruly hair back. Just one fingertip, the lightest of touches. His gaze flicked over her mouth. Back up to her eyes. Her pulse skipped warm.

And then he effortlessly picked her up, gently by the shoulders like a child. Turned. Set her down, out of his way.

His eyes hardened, green ice, his frosty barriers crashing down. "I work better alone," he said, chilly as ever. "Stay here, and don't do anything stupid. I'll be back for you." He flexed his wings, a rain of gold, and vanished.

Japeth flashed into the Park, dark and silent. Stones crunched under his boots. The long paved Mall stretched before him, a dark tunnel through threatening elm trees. Smoke coated his tongue. Here and there, flames cackled like witches, and shadows crawled, closing in. Twilight had swamped the city quickly, thickened by gathering storm clouds, and the hungry darkness muttered and shifted.

Leaves whispered on a hot, malicious breeze. Rows of stately statues loomed. Some artistic crazies had taken their liberties, and the bronzes were splashed with paint and blood, their faces twisted. Someone had drawn fangs and a horrible green leer on Christopher Columbus's upturned face.

Stinking heat stifled him, his shirt and feathers already soaked with sweat. A solitary moan creaked from the trees. He didn't chase it. Ever since the first sign, the Park was a refuge for muties, virus-mad zombies, people driven crazy by the portents and the heat. Whoever lurked here was already prey . . . or predator.

He'd been right not to bring Rose.

His heart still hurt for her, alone with her terrors. But this place dripped with hunger and fear. An ugly battle zone, temptation versus will. She'd faced enough torments for one night.

And soon, he'd be rid of her. The thought laced his blood with a sharp honey-sweet ache.

He hopped the metal fence and crouched beside a tree trunk, dimming his wing glow to a pale shimmer. In the distance, a fire roared. He could hear the threatening crackle, the hissing smoke. At the top of the Mall, through shadows that writhed and fought like living creatures, orange flames flickered. Not just a smoldering trash can. A bonfire. A monstrous inferno, sucking in air low and fast, and when he listened hard, he caught shrieks of laughter.

Sickening images of blood and flesh raided his mind. Rose, sobbing, the horrible metal taste of gore . . . He flared his feathers, impatient. Dive in at full speed, tear the asshole's face off . . .

But Fluvium was insane, not stupid. Not like he wasn't expecting an attack. No need to take chances.

Luckily, Japheth knew someone who never said no to a fight. But his phone slipped in his sweaty palm as he fumbled it out. Dash saw through him like glass. If he asked about Rose . . .

"Japheth, my good son. What's the rumpus?"

"Some killing for you," Japheth whispered. "You up?"

"Actually, I'm . . . kinda busy. Can it wait?"

"Say again? Who are you, and what've you done with the real Dashiel?"

A sigh. "I hate to brush you off, kid, but I'm in sort of a one-off situation here. Try the others?"

"Sure. No problem. I'll, uh, call you later." Japheth ended, perplexed. *One-off situation, my ass.* Probably making out with some little baby doll . . .

But his damp feathers prickled, uneasy. Dash's voice had sounded forced. Like he was covering something . . .

No time to figure it out now. He tried Ariel's number. Voice mail. Likewise Trillium. Maybe they were all in Bhutan, with no cell service.

He sighed, frustrated, and texted all five of them, just in case. Trill, Jaz, Iria, Ariel, Lune. *If you're bored, come down to Bethesda and slice up some vampire butt. xx JJ*

He switched the phone off, and peeled his nerves to chilly awareness. Slicked his feathers sharp. Filled his lungs, stretched his limbs for fighting flexibility. His body sprang alive, every muscle poised for motion, every instinct yearning for prey, and ice-cruel delight shimmered in his veins.

Here, now, in the velvety blackness before battle, the truth about Rose Harley's making didn't matter. His bleeding obsession with her didn't matter. He was made for killing hellspawn, and he'd wouldn't stop until every last one was slaughtered.

And when I'm done? Will I kill her, too?

He sniffed the wet black shadows for scent—so piquant, this black and bloody air—and drifted on ghostly golden wings towards the fountain.

Bugger it.

Dashiel sweated in the over-stuffed leather armchair, his jeans sticking to his ass. His bones itched for the fight, the glory hit, sensation's sweet rush to fill the emptiness . . .

But he flicked his phone to silent and stuffed it away. "Sorry," he muttered. "Kids are acting up. What can you do?"

Gabriel just stared, hard and gray like rain.

Dash shivered, and tried to hide it. He hadn't seen Gabriel for what, two hundred years? Still looked like a fucking Ivy League gangster. Immaculate dark suit, silver tie, storm-gray feathers spread behind him in his massive office chair. His face was remote, commanding, and his crisp steely hair rumbled with threatening shadows. The brothers archangel, all freakishly identical. But if Michael was ice, Gabriel was thunder.

Twitchy son of a bitch, too. Michael was an asshole, sure, but he was an angry, bloodthirsty asshole with a sword. Dash got that. Gabriel, *au contraire,* was the Plan in a sharp Italian suit, making him an offer he couldn't refuse. Even this office was right out of *The Godfather,* with its antique sofas and dim green lamps bent low over the leather-bound desk.

Late California sun poured through the open French windows, shedding golden shadows on the heavy-pile carpet. Warm frangipani perfume drifted in from the garden, and distant Los Angeles traffic hummed and wailed. Gabriel didn't like Babylon. He liked to stay spotless, and L.A. was a bit less edgy, despite the dengue quarantine, the armored barricades, the trigger-happy PD.

If Gabriel even visited earth at all. Half the goddamned problem, if anyone ever asked Dash, which they didn't. The hierarchy had their heads in the sand up to their feathered asses. Gabriel had only agreed to see him because Dash exchanged a few sly words with one of his minions. Nice girl, legs up to here, flirty blond wings. The words had included *fuck me* and *harder* and *oh, God, more.*

Probably he'd go to hell for that, eventually. But hey, you played the cards they dealt you, and in their wisdom, apart from demon slaying, they'd made Dash good at only one thing.

"You were saying?" Gabriel glanced at his silver wristwatch, impatient.

Like an archangel didn't always know innately what fucking time it was. Dash folded his arms, bracing for a face full of thunder. "It's about Michael."

Gabriel's mouth twitched. "What about him?"

"When's the last time you spoke to him about this vials business?"

"Recently."

"Recently enough to know he's not taking any heavenly host to Bhutan?"

A steely glare. "Michael's war games are his own concern. I don't presume to tell him how to run them—"

"Well, maybe you should." Dash pretended not to see Gabriel's left wing flaring in irritation at the interruption. "He did the same thing in Babylon last month when Vorvian was spreading the zombie virus. And when we caught Quuzaat at the blood sabbat? Michael's demon thrall was right there in the middle of it." He paused. "You do know he's got a demon thrall, right?"

"I expect he has several," Gabriel said coldly. "I'm not my brother's keeper."

"Including a skanky little redheaded painmuncher who lives in a cage under his bed?"

"Michael has hot blood." Impatient storm clouds darkened around Gabriel's wings. "We all have our flaws. God forgives us."

Emphasis on the *us*. Asshole. "Really? Did I miss the mercy bus? Shit."

"Don't be flippant."

"Then don't be so damn stubborn, Gabriel. Fact is, Mike's not taking this Apocalypse seriously, and neither are you. With all due respect, Seraph," Dash added silkily.

Code for *you're a fucking idiot, Gabriel.*

Due respect, my ass. What's he gonna do, Taint me again?

Gabriel swooped to the gilded mirror behind the desk, and glared a hair-crackling rebuke at Dash's reflection. "And with all due respect to you, *angel*—" He salted the word with sarcasm. "Don't question my brother's authority. Especially since it was he who saved you. If it were up to me, you'd be screeching skinless in hell right now."

"Like Lucifer, you mean? That one was up to you. Michael wanted to fry his sniveling innards on egg bread and eat them for lunch. How disappointed do you think he'll be if the prick gets sprung from the pit for a second go?"

Gabriel's eyes blackened, and icy breeze flung Dash's hair wild. " 'Thou shalt not bear false witness,' Dashiel. I trust you're not dragging your charming Tainted friends into your seditious delusions."

"My Tainted have the goddamn sense to figure it out for themselves," Dash growled. "Tell me, why did you hide the vials away with Guardians, instead of just keeping them yourself? Could it be because you wanted to keep them away from Michael?"

"Watch your pride, minion. It betrays you."

Dash clenched his fists to still them. God, he wanted to punch some bloody sense into him. "You're not *listening* to me. I was there, on the ground in Babylon. We watched these demon princes in action. This threat is real—"

"Are you sure?" Storm clouds roiled in Gabriel's feathers, swelling him to half again his size. Dash's hair prickled in static-charged breeze. For a guy who supposedly didn't fight worth a damn? Gabe was fucking scary. "We've lived through 'signs' before. They were never real. You think a bunch of upstart demons can pervert the Plan? Polish up your faith, soldier. I believe it's tarnished."

Dash lit up, landing with a thump. "Have you met Azaroth, Seraph?" he demanded. "I stood on the burning walls of Gomorrah and watched him drink twenty thousand souls in a single night. His thirst can't be quenched. And he doesn't get off on it. He doesn't have a weakness like the others. He just *consumes*. The fucker keeps right on drinking, and with every soul, his strength grows. If he gets his hands on the rest of those vials? The suffering will be beyond even your nightmares, Gabriel, and don't tell me you don't dream some shockers when the witching hour comes."

Gabriel's thundery gaze stabbed deep. Agony jolted Dash's bones. A massive weight crushed down on him. His muscles strained, tendons popping, but like an invisible, mighty hammer, the archangel forced Dashiel to his knees with nothing but will.

Blinding voltage crackled around Gabriel's fingers. Outside, lightning split the summer sky, and his voice resounded in thunder. "Michael has my full confidence. Don't mention it again."

And darkness swept Dash away.

Burning desert sand crunched under his knees. Sunlight scorched. He blinked, watery. A sandy plain, the desert horizon shimmering with haze. Rocks scattered, soot-scarred remnants of some ancient brick ruin. Gulls crowed. Down the slope, in the distance, a mirage flashed . . . or a lake.

An inland sea, its shores marked white with rocky cliffs. Salt crusted the surface, a sparkling crescent. He could smell the toxic tang of sea water.

The Dead Sea. Gomorrah. No one could say Gabriel didn't appreciate irony.

Standing on the endless sand, Dash shielded his eyes from the blasting sun. He tried to flash out. Nothing. Just blank darkness. A sharp archangelic slap on the wrist for his attitude. And it was already morning. He'd lost hours.

He laughed, parched. It wasn't the first time. The glory would come back. Always did. But for now . . .

Already, sweat soaked him. Heat haze shimmered like ghostly laughter, mocking him with the empty echoes of twenty thousand lost souls and grim memories of death.

The Demon King had devoured the souls. But Dash had done the killing. And the time for reckoning was way overdue.

Azaroth, you ugly son of hell. I'm coming for you.

Wearily, Dash cracked his aching neck, and walked.

CHAPTER 26

Rose watched Japheth disappear in a stormy blue flash of light, and banged her fists against the cracked window.

He'd left her here. He'd actually gone to hunt Fluvium without her. *How the hell am I supposed to trap him now?*

But chill spiked her blood like wire. Fluvium was strong. Crafty. Ruthless, armed with lies and clever tricks. And Japheth was . . .

She swallowed. Japheth was too damned honorable for his own good. His compassion was frighteningly real. What if . . . ?

What if Fluvium kills him?

The skin on her arms crawled cold, like corpse-munching worms wriggled under there. No. She couldn't let that happen. For a terrifying moment, the promise of redemption had flashed in his eyes. And it wasn't just angel's lies.

For one shocking, magical instant, Japheth had *believed* in her.

Empty, Rose stared out over the neon-lit city. Her vampire vision glittered bright, a loving caress in the darkness. Yells and screeching traffic echoed. Muzzle flash scintillated, a burst of automatic gunfire. Searchlights razored the sky, and whipping helicopter blades kept pace with her frightened heart . . . and cold common sense slashed her warm dreams to bleeding ribbons.

If Fluvium killed him, she'd have failed. And Fluvium never rewarded failure. When the demon moon waxed, he'd shove her screaming into hell.

She couldn't let that happen.

Never mind that she couldn't stop thinking about that lost expression in Japheth's eyes. That she wanted him naked, hot and breathless beneath her, those lush feathers wrapping her thighs, his mouth tugging on her breasts. That she wanted to kiss him, swallow him, drag him into her. Make his quest for redemption her own . . .

"Fuck." Rose yanked her hair, itching. Damn his false compassion. If she wanted to live, she needed to kill this magnificent liar herself. Tempt his soul to the dark side, push his trembling body down beneath her and take everything he had.

And she couldn't do it standing about in his apartment, feeling sorry for herself.

Determined, she strode to the door. The locks—three of them, stainless steel deadlocks polished bright—glared menacingly at her. She shook the door. Solid as granite. She fashioned shadows and let them crawl, fingering the locks, slipping inside . . . and stinging angelfire zapped, a vicious electric shock.

"Ow! Shit!" Her muscles spasmed, an agonizing fit. Smoke hissed, and all the hair on her body stood on end. She recoiled, reeling her shadows back in. Cramp still clawed her arm. She flexed it, working the shock out. Damn, that hurt.

She strode to the kitchen, and rifled through the drawers. No keys. Maybe the bedroom.

Only the bathroom lights on in there, the way she'd left them, and the bedroom was dim. His latte scent still sweetened the air. "Lights up," she ordered. The bedroom lights didn't obey. Probably only responded to his voice.

Damn, this angel was paranoid. Hardly likely to lock her in and leave the keys behind. If there even were any keys. The locks were probably magical . . .

Still, she hunted through his spotless wooden bureau, pushing aside his clothes. Neatly folded to the point of obsession, of course. Practical, good quality but not too nice. Like he didn't want to indulge himself.

Her fingertips lingered over a soft dark shirt. The kind he wore under his armor, sleeveless, the smooth fabric absorbent to soak up sweat and blood. The midnight color would look good against his clear skin, his rich golden hair. He chose dark jeans, too, neat, not torn or worn thin as per the fashion these days. And as for his other fighting gear . . . She brushed the back of her hand over a pair of leather trousers. The roughness tingled her skin. That sweet coffee scent, but this time darker, hair and male skin, the musk of secret sweat . . .

She pulled away, uncomfortably warm. For a guy who didn't care what he looked like, he looked damn fine.

Either that, or he was just as vain as the rest of them, and lied about it.

Whatever. She slammed the drawer shut, and walked away. No keys. She couldn't break the locks. And this was Babylon. No one took chances on security, especially not Captain Paranoia here. The door and frame were steel cored. Even with her nimble limbs and enhanced vampire strength, she couldn't kick it down.

Only one other way out.

She strode into the living room. Mirrors whispered shadows at her, rustling. The windows were locked, of course, the edges of the folding glass doors sparkling with the same angelspells that nearly blew her goddamn arm off . . .

By the piano's hulking silhouette, broken glass flashed.

She bent, her heart thumping. A few shards sparkled gem-like on the floorboards, next to a long crack that split the window from floor to ceiling. She fingered it cautiously. No spells. Nothing to burn her. And the two thick glass slabs weren't flush. A quarter-inch sharp edge glittered like a blade in the down lights.

Her pulse quickened. Japheth had broken the window. Just a few minutes ago, when he did that scary lightning thing. He'd broken it with anger, disgust, explosive emotion that clanged in her ears like bells. And he'd left her a way out.

She peeked over the edge, dizzy. God, she'd always loathed heights. He had a narrow balcony, just enough to stand or sit.

Beyond, twenty floors of nothing plummeted to the street. She peered sideways, cheek pressing the glass. His was the corner apartment. To one side, a sharp edge and howling nothing. To the other . . . well, the next balcony was a long way away. But maybe—just maybe—not too far to climb.

She swallowed, sick. He'd left her a way out, all right. If she dared. But risking certain death was better than doing nothing. At least her fate would rest in her own hands. And if she fell . . .

Rose tightened her trembling mouth. Her palms were clammy, and she wiped them on her jeans. If she fell, she'd just go to hell a few hours sooner.

She grabbed a stainless steel barstool, and hurled it with all her vampire strength at the cracked window.

Wreathed in as much shadow as he could muster— which was to say, he'd vanished his wings lest their fire betray him, and damn it if Rose's can't-see-me spell wouldn't come in handy right now—Japheth crouched in an elm tree, perched on his toes, and gazed down on the blood-soaked horror of Bethesda Terrace.

A huge bonfire roared on the terrace's roof. Black smoke billowed, a fetid cloud that stung and poisoned. Corpses littered the tiles. They clogged the steps, piled two and three deep, slumping across the cloistered railing. Throats torn out, crimson flesh open and bleeding. A few had broken ribs, their chests torn asunder, hearts missing.

Some weren't dead, and tried to crawl away. But they didn't have the strength. Their naked bodies shone sickly blue, drained beyond survival, and their weakened limbs just slipped in the rivers of blood.

It clotted the ground, inches deep, soaking off the terrace's edge into the grass. The meaty stench made him retch. But worse, the reek of hellcurse. Vampires leapt and capered. Dozens of them, charging about like mad insects, red eyes gleaming. Most of them were naked. All were covered in gore.

Some clambered over the corpses on all fours, licking and sniffing for live ones. Others danced, and howled, or rolled and gurgled in the sea of blood, or balanced on the railing, tilting their outflung arms like trapeze artists and shrieking in delight. A few groped each other among the corpses, fucked, savaged each other's bodies with hungry teeth. One ripped strips of flesh from a corpse and ate them, feeding the strands into his mouth like crimson-dripping spaghetti.

Japheth fought crawling nausea. How had they lured these humans here? Did they have a stash of them, like Caliban, locked in cages awaiting their screwed-up pleasure? Or was some viler magic at work? He sniffed, sorting through the scents, rolling back the thickening bloodstink in search of demon magic . . .

There. His senses yanked taut, like hooks ripping through his skin.

A summoning spell. The demon prince was luring his prey. Wafting his foul allure on the smoke, tempting humans to horrible death and even more horrid damnation.

Clever. Japheth sniffed the evil scent again, memorizing it. Random infections were unreliable. Luring humans en masse was a quicker, surer way to make vampires. The demons were ramping up their plague-spreading mojo.

His feathers sprang, sharp hackles of threat, and he jumped, wafting to the ground. He ghosted towards the forest's edge. Shadows muttered and nipped at his ankles. He kicked them away, his warrior's instincts automatically calculating his chances, the best approach, the enemy's likely strengths and weaknesses.

They were eating, glutting themselves. Likely they'd be in a stupor, their reaction time dulled. And threatening storm clouds obscured the moon. This was good. Moonlight increased the demons' power, and the shadows would hide him a few moments longer.

Sure, hiding was dishonorable. It lent his craven enemies dignity they didn't deserve. But if he happened to move quietly, and Fluvium's horde were too wrapped up in their ghastly slaughter games to smell him coming?

Japheth allowed a hungry grin. That was their problem.

And Fluvium was here, all right. The toxic strength of those hellspells promised that. By dawn, his evil gibbous moon would be full.

Dark desire flashed in Japheth's veins, indistinguishable from glory. These ravenous hellshits were evil. Weak. Slaves to their selfish desires. You didn't see them fighting the curse, trying to hold themselves back. They deserved nothing less than swift damnation.

But Rose Harley was strong. She'd rejected Fluvium's sick murder games. Defied Caliban. Refused to kill even one man to sate her hunger . . .

He bit back a caustic curse. Wasn't it enough that his mind was awash with her, his blood still burning for her kiss? Did he have to *like* her as well?

And why not? She's strong. Resourceful. Determined, makes the most of her strengths. The way a fighter should be. She's a top chick. If she was an angel, you'd admire her, like you admire Jadzia and Iria and the others. What's wrong with that?

Yet Rose was still—wasn't she?—irrevocably bound for hell.

It doesn't seem fair.

The word clanged in his skull like demonbells. *Unfair* was dangerous ground, especially when you were Tainted. Rules were rules. Fairness didn't come into it. Raging at the injustice didn't change the truth.

And the truth was that sins—whatever their genesis—had to be paid for.

Like he was paying for his.

Michael made the rules. Kill Fluvium—just one more dead demon, after so many dark centuries filled with dead demons—and Japheth's payment would be done.

He hopped a few feet into the air, and drifted from the shadowy forest onto the terrace.

The bonfire leapt higher, roaring in indignation at his intrusion. The heat scorched his face, seeped under his skin, and like an angry hawk, the hellish light struck for his glory-drenched feathers.

Instinctively, they flashed blue.

And a dozen pairs of insane vampire eyes swiveled like searchlights, and fixed on him.

CHAPTER 27

Japheth flashed out his sword, a blinding blue blaze, and prayed holy fire.

Wind sucked along the ground towards him, and around him, a six-foot sphere erupted into flame.

A shimmering blue shockwave of wrath boomed outwards. The hell-spelled air boiled in fury. And twelve vampires screamed, flesh melting from bones.

He exploded into action.

Nine seconds to slash off their heads. Swift, precise, calculated to the last slice.

He landed in a mess of blood. His fireball dissipated, eaten by furious hellspells. He whirled, the breeze snapping his bloodstained hair back, and dived down the terrace steps into blackness.

Hell.

Sightless, oppressive heat. Only the stink and the screams of damned creatures to guide his way. He lit his angelsight, a rich cordite flare, but the smoking hellspells blinded him.

Shit. His wing glow smothered under wailing black shadows. Vampires screeched and chewed at his legs, gripping with unearthly strength. He stabbed, slashed off limbs, broke bones and necks.

One jumped on his back, hacking at the roots of his feathers with something sharp and jagged. His blood splurted. Crap, that hurt. Disoriented, he crashed into a pile of corpses. They flopped, stinking, and he tumbled face-first into a heap of rotting flesh.

Ew. He spat, acidic. The vampire on his back fell with him, and he flipped to his feet in the dark, jammed one boot on the thing's scrawny throat by pure instinct, and stabbed his blade through its heart.

It screamed, and gnashed its fangs, and died.

Fresh glory flamed in his blood, and he fought on.

Was it a minute, an hour before he cleared the terrace? He didn't know. He knew only muscles flexing, heart pumping, feathers sweeping and slicing. His sword sang sweet death, a malicious melody that crooned in his veins like a lover's sigh.

Bodies fell. Bones crunched. Screams shimmered, and he sliced them off, delicate and precise. Blood splashed in his eyes, and he sizzled it away. His fingers ached on the sword's sticky grip. But finally, light spilled into his world.

He blinked, adjusting swiftly. The bonfire glared balefully from above the terrace's seven archways. *One for each perverted sign. Poetic.*

Catching his breath, he stepped out onto slippery tiles. The thickening stink watered his eyes. What was that bubbling sound? Thick, claggy like the *pop!* of boiling mud in a geyser . . .

The flames roared higher in sick triumph, illuminating Bethesda Fountain.

The wide round pool overflowed with blood. It slopped over the edge onto the tiles. Around the marble rim, lotus flowers rotted black.

He edged closer. Vampires splashed and glutted themselves in the pool. One girl squatted in her torn dress, dipping her face in the blood, gulping it in. She spewed up a clot of black strings, torn flesh. It splashed into the pool and sank, and she kept right on drinking.

Japheth swallowed, sour. Yeah, that was about the grossest

thing he'd ever seen. But something was strange. These creatures hadn't filled the pool with their dying victims' blood. It
was pouring from the central bronze basin, where the statue
of the angel stood.

Pumping up from the fountain's pipes.

He stared. *Angel of the Waters*, she was called, long robes
flapping in imaginary breeze, wings flared back. Named for
the holy healing waters of Bethesda. It was in the Book. *An
angel went down and troubled the water*, it said, *and whoso-
ever stepped in was healed . . .*

Now, the bronze angel was stained with gore, a cruel
thorny crown jammed around her forehead, and . . .

Atop her head sat the demon. Perched on his pointy butt,
swinging his legs. He wore a tailcoat and a dented top hat, and
he sang at the top of his voice, some vile hell-twisted language
that spidered Japheth's skin cold.

*And the third angel poured out his vial upon the rivers and
the fountains of waters, and they became blood . . .*

Fluvium had cursed the water supply. Tipped in his vial of
perverted wrath and poisoned the mains with the vampire
curse. And the stench of hellmagic was overpowering. It
scratched with acid-drenched claws, a living thing trying to
peel layers from his skin and devour them.

This curse was one kick-ass son of a bitch.

Japheth shuddered, sick. Any human who drank this
water—who tasted even a single drop by mistake—would
become vampire.

Rose crouched in the bushes, wreathed in sultry
vampire shadows. It had taken her nearly half an hour to climb
from Japheth's window, break out of the adjacent apartment,
and run down here. She hoped she wasn't too late.

Screams tore the air, the ragged sounds of death and splitting flesh. Beneath the terrace, the darkness lit with electric
blue flashes. Japheth was killing vampires.

The slaughter raked her nerves, iron claws on glass. So
much killing. So many human lives, wasted.

I'm so sick of all this death.

Surprise glimmered warm at the thought. She enjoyed her powers. Relished her unholy vengeance. She'd thought she'd never get enough, never kill or maim or destroy enough to make up for what had happened to her. But now . . .

Cautiously, she peered out. A huge bonfire roared on the terrace, leaping dozens of feet skywards in a monstrous plume of smoke. Even from thirty yards away, black grit crunched her throat sour.

But the stink of blood was worse. It splurted from the fountain, down the angel statue, into the pool and over the sides. The vampires slopped in it up to their ankles. Some of them rolled in it, licking the tiles . . . and atop the bronze angel, the demon swung his legs, and sang his hell-weird song, and laughed.

I'm one of these monsters. Rose's guts wrenched, and she vomited into the dirt. Her eyes poured, burning. She wiped her mouth. A reddish stain soaked the earth, her most recent meal, and it made her retch again. *I belong with them . . .*

But all that blood in the fountain didn't make her hungry.

What they were doing wasn't hunger, it was madness. Sick satisfaction in others' suffering. And she wanted no part of it. Not now. Not ever.

But she watched Japheth explode from beneath the terrace, a ball of spitting blue flame, and her guts twisted. If Fluvium killed Japheth, she'd have failed. She'd be in hell the instant that demon moon swelled full. And if Japheth killed Fluvium—it seemed frighteningly possible—then . . . what?

She'd still be cursed, her sins unforgiven.

Japheth had promised not to kill her. And so far, he'd kept his word to the letter. But what did she have to look forward to? Hell? Oblivion? Endless nights of this bloody torment, again and forever until the End?

Either way, she was screwed.

But the prospect of hell still fired cold bullets of terror into her heart. Pain unending, skin peeling back, acid teeth gnawing eternally at her joints. And Bridie, screaming at her, hacking at her heart with tiny claws, *You killed me, Auntie Rosie, I'm in hell and it's all your fault . . .*

She steeled herself, polishing her hatred afresh. Forgiveness was a sick joke. Her sins were irredeemable. Japheth had to die. She'd force her cursed blood down his throat if she had to. At least then, she'd know what was in store for her. One more month away from Bridie's accusing eyes. For that, she'd . . .

Rose swallowed. For that, she'd do anything.

Even send this beautiful angel to hell?

She crept from the bushes. Her thighs creaked, tense. Sweat dripped between her breasts, soaking her new t-shirt. Where was all his so-called compassion when God cursed her? *Too little, too late, angel. You lost this game. I'm damned, and it's forever.*

She padded down the grassy slope towards the fountain. On her left, the firelit terrace loomed. Vampires pranced and giggled among piles of corpses. They groped each other, kissing, biting, coupling frantically. They seemed madly delighted to have a vengeful angel in their midst, and they pointed and screeched with unholy laughter. One guy was jerking off, concentrating furiously, scraping up handfuls of clotting blood to lubricate himself.

Rose swallowed bile. She'd seen worse, in Caliban's filthy coven. At least the guy wasn't doing a dead body . . . *oh, Jesus.* She retched again, guts aching. *Ew. Don't look, Rose. Just keep your eyes on the demon.*

She crept closer, beside the sloping wall. Onto the gore-stained paving. The fire's roaring heat roasted the tiny hairs from her cheeks.

"Maah!"

A little vampire boy pointed at her, banging a chewed human bone on the ground. His belly was swollen, and tiny fangs sliced his lips. "Maah!" he yelled into the din, and smacked at her legs with his bone. "Wa-maa-*maaah!*"

Fuck. He'd give her away. She'd have to . . .

Her heart hollowed cold. He was just a baby. Too young to understand what she was, to know what the angel's mark meant. He only knew she was strange, upsetting, not like the others.

God have mercy, he was only two or three. Was he really bound for hell?

Bridie's in hell. The demon's voice crept stealthily into her heart. *Oh, yes, Rose, she surely is. Screaming and bleeding and suffering in hell, forever and always. You sent her there. Why not this one? Kill him, and get on with it.*

Trembling, Rose lifted a finger to her lips, and widened her eyes at the boy, like it was a game. "Shh . . ."

The cursed boy grinned back. "Shh," he agreed happily, and stuffed the bone's end back into his mouth.

Her pulse racing, she crept silently on.

A few feet away, Japheth shook blood from his hair, breathing hard. She crouched by the cloistered arches, wreathed in shadow. He'd taken some hits. His smooth skin was clawed and bitten. Blue glitter rained, and his wounds healed, his magical angelflesh doing its blessed work.

He flared his blue sword brighter. "Get your ugly butt down here, Fluvium, and let's get this over with. Don't make me come up there."

Rose's throat clenched hard. He was brave. Determined. Uncompromising. All the things she admired in a warrior. But it didn't matter. Not when hell awaited her.

She had to be there when he fell. Overpower him herself. Then, maybe, Fluvium would let her have him, and she'd win her respite.

The betrayal stung bitter in her mouth. But she had no choice. Jump out, flatten him, pin those handsome golden wings to the ground . . . She crouched, heart thumping, poised to attack.

The moon lurched through a break in the clouds, huge and bloated like a bloody midnight sun.

The vampires howled as one, an insane wolf pack keening for prey. The sound tore strips from Rose's soul. Not quite full, that gore-soaked moon. Just a sliver away from brimming with demonic power.

But Japheth staggered, thrown off balance. He shielded his eyes, flashing his blade up to defend against the piercing hell-cursed glare.

The demon just cackled, and jumped. He landed like a cat, on all fours on the slick tiles. Beneath his tailcoat, he wore demon armor, a suit of studded black leather. A spiked leather collar was tucked around his throat, and his long hair stuck to his cheeks in bloody crimson ringlets.

The blood sloughed aside as he wiped the knots back . . . but the hair underneath was crimson, too.

Not midnight purple. Red.

Rose stared, chilled. Red hair. Pointy face, sharp little chin, eyes black as hellshadow.

"Oh, this is fucking priceless." Zuul giggled, black eyes alight with glee. He doffed his top hat, ironic, and frisbeed it away. "Are you looking for the Prince of Thirst? Too late, Blondie. Job's all done."

Jesus Christ in a pumpkin pie. We're screwed.

CHAPTER 28

Bloody dominoes crashed to their deaths in Japheth's mind.

Caliban lied. Fluvium's not here.

So where the hell is he?

"Wh . . . ?" Japheth's tongue withered. He tried again. "Then where?"

"Doing the next bit, of course." Zuul skipped closer, shrugging off his bloody coat and throwing it into the fountain. "The Apocalypse isn't all fun and games, you know. We've gotta work for it."

"The next bit? What next bit?" Japheth fought to drag his wits from the sludge, regain his icy composure. This was bad. This was very bad. Michael had given him only until tomorrow's waxing moon to kill Fluvium. If he had to start searching all over again . . .

He backed off a step, scenting for threats. The vampires still cackled and danced and ate. Enjoying a good joke, no doubt. They didn't attack. More interested in the blood. This hellcurse was potent.

"What next bit?" Zuul mimicked his question. "What do I look like, a fucking search engine? Do your research. If you wanted to pour holy wrath into Babylon's water, where would you go?"

His mind sprinted through barely remembered trivia. Babylon had three water supply tunnels, six hundred feet beneath the earth, below the subway and the sewers. One via Brooklyn under the East Side. Another through Midtown to Staten Island. And one under Central Park . . .

Poison them, and all the fresh water in Babylon would be contaminated. Taps, fire hydrants, everything. Bottled water would never be enough. Everyone would die of thirst . . . or become vampire.

"Bravo!" Zuul gave him a sarcastic round of applause. "Give the dumbass Tainted angel some cotton candy. Better still—" He snapped his fingers, a puff of charcoal smoke, and pointed over Japheth's shoulder. "Skip the fucking candy and let's have some fun. Grab her."

Too late, Japheth smelled that warm female perfume. His heart somersaulted, sick.

Rose Harley.

He whirled, vengeful sword at the ready. *Kill her. Save her.* He didn't know.

But already, a pair of Zuul's minions had grabbed Rose's arms, dragged her from her hiding place. Not vampires, to be easily sliced. Hatesuckers, seven feet tall, their ragged hair knotted around monstrous bare shoulders. In the moonlight, their hulking troll-like forms shone pale, like reanimated corpses and as strong. Their magically enhanced muscles bulged, brutal and top-heavy.

Jesus in a jam jar, they stank. How had he not noticed them?

But Rose's proximity blinded his judgment, a stinging black sandstorm that ate away at his reason. He couldn't think. Couldn't move.

Could only meet her gaze, her eyes wide and black with terror.

Rose struggled in their grip, futile. She scrabbled for her

knife, but they tore it away. The bigger one's skin was lumpy, peeling with hateful warts. He gripped a spiked club in one huge fist, and bashed Rose in the face with it. She cried out, spluttering blood.

Japheth yelled, fireballs erupting from his wings. *Screw it all to oblivion.* If he attacked, they'd just use her as a shield . . .

Zuul sauntered up to Rose. "That's an ugly scar you've got there." He poked at the angel's mark, and winced, shaking his smoking finger. "Ooh! Nasty. Let's cover it up." And he exhaled, a black ashcloud that swarmed like angry gnats over the mark, obscuring it from view.

Rose screamed.

Japheth's limbs quivered tight. The hatesuckers' spells leached poisoned loathing into his veins. His body burned. God, he wanted to chew the ugly bastard's skin off and kick his bleeding corpse.

But the sight of Rose's beautiful face, now a mass of bruises and burns, eclipsed the magical hatred like a rock blotting out the sun.

Her lovely dark hair fell in her face. Her vampire flesh stretched and writhed, fighting to heal, but already, the hate-sucker's poison crawled under her skin, a spreading black web of corruption.

Don't. The calculating part of Japheth's mind whispered cold reason. *They're provoking you. Let it be . . .*

The warty hatesucker grinned, and poked her with cruel fingers. "Tasty," he gurgled, and slurped his rotting tongue over her cheek.

To hell with it. Japheth screamed a filthy heavencurse, and leapt.

But hissing demonspawn hands locked into his feathers. His body jerked backwards. Something hard smashed into the back of his skull. Pain sliced, cold and calming, but too late. More hands grabbed him, impossibly strong, dragging him to the ground.

His knees hit the tiles, slipping in clotted blood. Someone wrenched his sword hand, hard.

Crunch! His fingers broke, and the sword cartwheeled from his grip.

He cursed, and grabbed for it. His bones reforming, a stinging flash. But the ether just howled, empty, curetted like a charred husk by the demonspells.

And *slam!* His cheek smacked into the tiles.

Shit.

Countless heavy hands pinned him down. They gripped his wrists, his ankles, his aching wing bones. Too strong for vampires. Their rank white bodies reeked, bitter. More hatesuckers. Great.

He kicked. Bone splintered. A creature howled, and someone kneed him in the kidneys. The pain blinded him, and he coughed up bloody bile.

Zuul crouched before him, filling his vision with that crazy-ass grin. "Distract you, did I? With the pretty vampire? Thought as much. Ha ha! When Michael finds out you're screwing her, he's gonna kick your feathered ass straight to hell."

Japheth managed an ugly smile, but his mind calculated, sensed, analyzed. *Where's Rose? Can't see. They're too heavy to shift. Can't flash a blade. Maybe beg another heavenspell . . . could be pushing my luck . . .* "Didn't I crush your skull last time we met?"

Zuul faked a delighted shiver. "Fuck, yeah, I remember that. Honestly? I felt violated. But I didn't quite get off. Can you crush it harder next time?"

"With pleasure." Grimly, he flexed his arms, testing, but the hatesuckers just squeezed him tighter, cutting off the blood flow. Screw them. They'd give an opportunity. And he'd be ready . . .

"All mine, I assure you." Zuul stood, and dragged Rose forwards into Japheth's limited field of view.

His heart leaked sorrow. She looked so . . . damaged. She'd already endured so much, and now she had to take more. He'd not let their mistreatment of his lady go unpunished. Oh, no, he most certainly would not . . .

Zuul tweaked her bleeding nose. "I say, pretty girl, you're a mess. What a shame. Never mind, it'll heal. Eventually. In the meantime, what shall we do with this sorry feathered freak show, eh comrade?"

Rose spat at him. "Fuck you."

"Well, yeah, I was kind of planning that. You, me, my whip collection. But that won't get the job done, will it?" Zuul frowned. "I'm sure Fluvium said something about damnation, eternal torture, the usual blah-blah."

"Since when do you follow Fluvium's orders?" Rose glared at him, that lovely defiance blazing like starshine despite the bruises. "I've always liked you, Zuul. You're just as powerful as Fluvium. Let me go, and I'll help you skin him alive."

A brave effort. Did she mean it? Hell, he didn't know.

But Zuul just frowned more, feigning confusion. "Satan's hairy hard-on, I've got Alzheimer's. Someone walk me back to the hospice. Was it curse the angel? Or the vampire?" He scratched his blood-crusted head. "Hmm . . . Oh, I remember now!" Malice lit his hell-black eyes. "It's both!"

Rose kicked, but the hatesuckers held on. She snarled, fangs glistening. "Don't you lay a hand on him, you skanky cocksucker. He's worth a thousand of you."

Japheth's nerves peeled raw. She was tough as nails. So damn beautiful, it broke his heart.

"Is that what he told you?" Zuul snorted. "Bloody angels, always dick measuring. At least mine still works, honey. Blondie's has likely rotted off from neglect." He danced a giggling quickstep. "Ha ha! Come on, admit it, that was funny."

"Hilarious," Rose growled.

"I know! I'm here all week! But—" Zuul held up a finger, admonishing himself. "All this joviality still isn't finishing the job. Text in now, viewers! Who gets voted off the island tonight? The feathered freak? Or the lovesick vampire bitch?"

Japheth's throat squeezed shut. He couldn't breathe. Couldn't speak.

Couldn't say *take me and let her go*.

Rose's instincts wrenched in two. She'd longed for this. Worked for it, for the last few excruciating days. Finally, this lying angel would get what he deserved.

But now that the moment had come . . . her heart ached. Not like this. Not him.

He was the only one who believed she could be saved.

If even Japheth is damned, what hope is there for you, Rose? Let him get the curse. God doesn't care. At least Fluvium might take pity on you . . .

But his haunted green gaze wouldn't let her be. Wouldn't let her forget his brutally gentle caress, the rage that bled from his heart when he had seen her shame . . .

He hadn't hated her. Hadn't pushed her away, cursed her for hellspawn, insisted it was all her fault. He'd flashed straight down here to kill the monster who'd done it to her. Like he cared that she'd suffered.

Guilt crashed over her, a bitter wave. It filled her lungs, forcing away the air, but she couldn't claw to the surface. Couldn't stop drowning.

And this time, she had no one to blame but herself.

You don't get to blame God for your weakness, Rose Harley. That demon whisper twisted Japheth's words with jagged delight. *God didn't do this. You did.*

Zuul laughed, manic. "Oh, gosh, I think I just came in my pants. You should see the look on your face, vampire. You were about to attack him, weren't you? Ready to cook him up in a hot temptation pie? Hand him over to the prince, to save your own sorry skin?"

Her throat clogged. She couldn't deny it. Couldn't find one fucking word.

Don't look at him, Rose. Don't see him hate you.

"And now you feel *bad* because you've gotta look him in the *eye* while you screw him over? Bleeding Christ, don't they teach new minions anything these days?" Zuul shook his head sadly. "Lesson one in demon-baiting, honey: be careful what you wish for."

Dimly, she felt the hatesucker's warty hands crushing her shoulders. It hurt, those bones scraping together. His fat fingers poked at her belly, her breasts. Her half-healed face still ached. She didn't care. She deserved to suffer . . .

But defiance still blazed, a cold hard kernel in her heart. She wasn't ready to give up yet.

Zuul was treacherous, mercurial, did anything for kicks. Maybe she could bribe him to help her. "It isn't like that." It hurt her bruised lips to talk. "Fluvium gave me special orders for this heavenscum, that's all. I get that you want your share. I'm sure we can come to some arrangement . . ."

"You and me?" A scornful laugh. "Don't think so, honey. I don't do Fluvium's sloppy seconds . . . well, I guess that's a lie, isn't it? But a Tainted angel's whore?" He mimed sticking a finger down his throat. "Gross. I can smell the self-righteous stench from here. Who knew? I've got standards after all! Ha ha!"

Her hatesucker pal giggled, fresh spit splashing her hair. *Yuk*. She recoiled, but he pinned her tightly, and his magical disgust radiated over her like black sunshine.

Her blood boiled, the spell irresistible. Fuck, she hated them all. Zuul for trapping her. The hatesuckers for hurting her. And Japheth for screwing with her mind.

For confusing her about a simple mission, with his maddening logic and magnificent, godforsaken honor. For being so damn beautiful, for making her want him when he was the last thing on earth she could have.

For making her want to *be* him, when she never could. Not after the things she'd done.

She struggled, hurling vile, wordless curses that blistered Zuul's face.

"Ouch." He grinned at her knowingly. "This is too funny. Lesson two, darling: it's always too late to back out."

He whirled, spreading his skinny arms wide. "Let's go to the phones! Who's your choice tonight, viewers? It's . . . Japheth! Yes!" He kicked the angel's shoulder, igniting a black crackle of fire. "Guess what, heavenshit? You're voted off!" He pointed dramatically. "You're fired! Please leave the house! You are the weakest link! Good-bye!"

On the ground, Japheth just grinned, beastly.

"No." Rose's voice strangled. "No, wait, we can figure something out—"

"*Bzzt!* Too late! Voting's closed." Zuul grinned, rubbing long hands with glee. "Pick him up, lads. Let's see how much he can drink before he drowns."

CHAPTER 29

The hatesuckers grabbed him in their warty fists, and plunged him face-first into the blood.

Hot, thick, disgusting. His head slammed into the pond's marble bottom. He couldn't break free. His skin was on fire, the evil blood hissing like a hungry devil. He scrabbled for a heavenspell, an immolation, anything to get these vile hate-suckers off him for just a moment . . .

But his talent scuttled away into the dark, smothered in blood and doubt, and fear scrambled in to fill the emptiness. He'd screwed up. Heaven couldn't help him. He couldn't even flash out, not with Rose still at Zuul's mercy. And the burning blood licked over him, crawling through his hair, into his ears, under his eyelids, up his nose . . .

Japheth's stomach convulsed. *Christ. Don't vomit. Don't . . .*

Acid bile exploded into his throat. He couldn't spit it out. Couldn't open his mouth. If even a drop of this horrible stuff went down his throat . . .

What if it did? Would it be so bad? The whisper coiled around his heart, a serpent with cool, calming scales. *An end*

*to all this fighting. Aren't you tired of fighting, Jae? Aren't you
sick to your heart of denying what you want?*

His cheek scraped the marble. He fought not to gulp for air
that wasn't there. After fourteen hundred years, he was weary
to the bone. Of not understanding, of fumbling in the dark. Of
following rules that didn't make sense, the blind keeper of an
empty ritual.

*Then suck it in. Drink it up. Join them, and you could have
her, Jae. You could have everything you ever wanted.*

But I want heaven! Stars spun before his eyes. *I want to go
home . . .*

Do you really? So reasonable, this devil voice. *Or do you
just want to stop hurting?*

A scream bubbled in his chest. He didn't need oxygen. He
knew that. Didn't need to breathe but every minute or two to
stay alive . . . But hot panic chemicals flooded his body, wild
and demanding, licked with golden temptation. He wanted
it. Wanted that dark coppery flavor, the heat, the sweet delight,
to *consume . . .*

His lungs stung and spasmed. His diaphragm contracted,
desperate to drag in air . . .

*Drink, Jae. Swallow. Drown in it, and you'll never have to
deny yourself again.*

No. Horror clawed him ragged. *I don't want to want like
this! I loathe it. It's foul. Make it stop. Cut my heart out, I
don't care. Just say I'm not past saving. Don't let me be
evil . . .*

Dark laughter slicked his throat. Already, his jaw weakened, his lips easing apart . . . *Too late, Jae,* that demonic
voice whispered, sparkling with bright diamonds like an archangel's curse. *You* are *evil. You always have been.*

Black hatemagic swarmed over Rose like angry
piranhas. Zuul's minions pinned Japheth down, face-first in
the bloody fountain. Up to his chest in it, his wings thrashing
in a hail of blood. The hatesuckers were laughing, crimson to
the elbows, their massive chests soaked. One had a long lank

braid of hair, and it hung over his shoulder, licking into the gore.

Zuul just stood there, arms folded, and smiled his slick demon's smile. "Wow," he shouted, "that's nearly a minute. Amazing, viewers! Can he last another? Text 'die, heavenshit!' if you think so!"

Japheth's massive muscles strained, but the hatesuckers ground his guts into the marble, squeezing away his strength. If he sucked in even one mouthful . . .

No. Clarity flashed in Rose's heart like ice, burning away the fog. *I can't let them do it. Not like this . . .*

She cared what happened to him, for fuck's sake. Where was her fire? Her hatred, the only thing that kept her safe? He was an angel, a deceitful messenger of her despised heaven. Everything he stood for was a dreadful lie. All he desired was her suffering. He *deserved* this . . .

The two hatesuckers who held her giggled, watching the fun. One of them had a hard-on, and he rubbed it against her ass, enjoying himself. Rose barely noticed. She gritted her teeth, trying to grind away this horrible sympathy that wrenched tight like hot wire around her heart . . .

But it wouldn't break. *We're ugly. Japheth's beautiful. I can't let them destroy him.*

She coiled her thigh muscles like whips, and kicked the hatesuckers in the face.

Both of them. She swung her legs up like clubs, folding her body at the waist and using their grip on her shoulders for leverage. Her tendons shrieked with the effort. She was supple, ultra-flexible, agile, able to take a beating and carry on. To dance eight shows a week, she needed to be tough. Skip even one show for a bruise or a strain, and there was always some other ambitious, talented girl chomping at the bit to take her place.

Christ, how long ago that seems.

Her boots connected. *Crack!* Bones broke. The hatesuckers howled, confused, spitting blood and teeth . . . and their grip on her shoulders slipped.

She whiplashed to her feet, and sprinted for the fountain's marble edge . . . and Japheth's fallen sword.

She dived for it. Tumbled, the bloody tiles scraping her knuckles. The blade was dark, bereft of flame or life. But it was still sharp. And she was one pissed-off vampire.

Her fist closed around the warm hilt. She rolled to her feet, and launched herself at Zuul and his two sniggering buddies.

Her other two warty pals were already howling, waving their bulging arms, their waxy white faces a mess of blood and bone splinters. She grinned, fierce. *Howl away, assholes. This little girl got the drop on you. How's that feel?*

She swung the blade two-handed as she ran, and *schllp!* The long-haired hatesucker's pale head sliced off and splatted into the red pond. His braid cartwheeled and followed, sliced neatly in half.

Zuul whirled, rage burning around him in a cloud of black ash. The other hatesucker froze, shock dulling his eyes, and in a blur of bloody gold, Japheth exploded to his feet and tore the thing's head off with his bare hands. He hurled the head into the grass on a rich angelic curse, and it burst into flame.

Rose's heart thumped. He was filthy with blood. It clotted in his hair, soaked his wings, ran in a crimson wash down his face. It sizzled to smoke, his burned skin healing. If he'd swallowed some . . .

She screamed in wordless disgust and swung her sword at Zuul.

Japheth sprang forwards. "Jesus, Rose, don't drop your guard—"

Too late, she saw the wicked green fire blazing in the demon's eyes. But she couldn't stop her stroke. Couldn't halt her forwards motion.

And quick as a striking viper, Zuul hurled a fistful of ash into her face.

She choked, blinded. Bitter grit coated her tongue. Her sword whistled wild, flinging her off balance. And white-hot agony bladed deep into her belly.

She staggered, and screamed. Her vision shorted out. Ice and fire, excruciating. The stinking ash dissolved, and with an evil grin that froze her blood, Zuul twisted his poisoned dagger deeper into her guts, and ripped it out.

Time slowed, a stop-motion horror film. Her fingers flashed

numb. The sword clattered to the gory tiles. And she stared down in dizzy shock at the blood flowering on her t-shirt.

"Ooh, I bet that feels good," Zuul hissed, and in a puff of hell-spelled glitter, he vanished.

CHAPTER 30

Rose choked, and dropped to her knees. Blood bloomed on her belly, her thighs, her clutching hands.

Japheth's heart stopped.

Just for a moment. But long enough for the silence to cut through his throbbing pulse.

Gut stabbed. With a demon blade. Poison already chewed through her body.

Zuul was gone. The hatesuckers howled, beating their chests with bloody fists, and advanced on her. And the vampires—until now busy screwing and moaning and sloshing about in the blood—screamed as one, and sprinted for the fountain.

The hell-bright moon glared, scorching Japheth's skin afresh. His heart jerked, and started again. And his warrior instincts screamed alive.

No time for doubt or self-loathing. Rose was dying. These foul creatures would feast on her corpse. And she'd fall struggling into hell.

Not on my watch.

He scooped her up, and flashed out.

Blackness swamped them, sweet relief. He almost hadn't

dared try it. For all he knew, his magic had withered, along with his righteous intentions. But still, heaven chose to help him.

He laughed, sick. Good intentions. The road to hell. He'd heard that one before.

Rose shivered in his arms. So warm against his chest. So human.

Disoriented, he jumped from the ether, not caring where he landed. Grass crunched beneath his feet. Scorching red moonlight, the dappled shade of elms. Beyond, in the distance, the tall apartments of Fifth Avenue. Cabs whizzed by under neon-bright virtual billboards. A guy sold hot dogs next to the police barricade. A skinhead in jeans and no shirt brandished a machete, yelling nonsense, out of his brain on hellcry. A Kevlar-armored riot cop shot him, and he collapsed. She took his machete. No one paid attention.

Still in the park. Whatever. He didn't smell vampires. Safe, for now.

He laid Rose on the soft grass. She muttered, sweating, her breath shallow. Her lashes fluttered. A sick greenish hue glowed from her skin. Blood oozed from her belly. Lots and lots of blood.

He scraped away the dirty ash that clotted the mark on her forehead. His hands were bloody. Shit, he was still drenched in it, despite his angelic healing. He wiped his face with his forearm. Rose's t-shirt—the one he'd borrowed from Iria, how long ago that seemed—was soaked. He ripped it apart, exposing her skin from waist to breasts.

Holy Jesus. He stared, sick. Surely, even her cursed vampire resilience couldn't heal *that.*

The wound was ragged, deep. He could see muscle, dark and inflamed, and beyond it the soft shapes of organs. Mottled black corruption sank cruel roots into her flesh. The torn edges were already rotting. He'd seen enough demon-poisoned wounds to know what happened next.

She was going to die.

God, he wanted to flash out, run away, hide from this awful sight. *What the hell do I do now?*

But he already knew.

Defiance blazed in his heart, bright like unseasonal sunshine, inescapable like fate. He didn't bother to pray. He knew healing humans was forbidden. He had the power, more or less. Just not allowed to use it. Another of heaven's senseless rules. Suffering was all they wanted.

Well, screw them. Heaven was obsessed with death. He wanted to live. And Rose deserved to live, too. Not flicker out in a blood-stinking park with a demon's poisoned blade in her guts.

Does that make me evil? This time, he did pray, searching his heart for the truth. *Does feeling something other than hatred when I look at her make me a monster?*

Then send me to hell. I'm ready.

He conjured his dagger. It slapped into his hand, a strange, dark flash of violet. The heat seared his eyes, a heavenly warning.

But it was too late for warnings.

He slashed the blade across his palm, letting the blood sacrifice flow free. His Tainted sigil burned bright, that same weird purple glow.

More blood. More death. That should make them happy.

He clenched his bloody fist, and raised his gaze to heaven. *I don't know what I did to make you shun me. I don't know why you're helping me now. But my will is my own, Lord. I'll accept the consequences. Don't take this choice from me.*

If I ever pleased you at all? Grant me this before I go.

And he pressed his bleeding hand to his vampire lady's flesh, and gave her back her nightmare.

God, it hurts.

Rose groaned. Ugly fingers of pain grasped inside her, clawing ever deeper. Piercing flesh and sinew and organs, jamming into crevices, forcing up inside her bones, and no matter how she pleaded, they wouldn't stop.

Fever stifled her breath. *Don't want to die. Don't want to go to hell. Please. Just let me breathe . . .*

Her guts convulsed in a fit. Her body quaked. She gasped, warm and blessedly fresh air, and her eyes snapped open.

Darkness, still and quiet, the sultry heat of Babylon.

She blinked, her head aching. Dappled foliage loomed, rustling in hot breeze. Warm arms cradled her, protective. And the pain . . . the pain was fading. Those horrid fingers receding, crawling away at last.

Japheth's eyes glowed dark, strange, almost purple. "How do you feel?"

He was still smeared in blood. Some had burned away, but it still stained his hair, clotted in his feathers. Her face felt sticky against his breastplate.

But he was so warm. Not the ugly heat of heaven's wrath. A clean, good warmth that sank deep into her body to soothe her. To *pleasure* her.

God, she wanted to sleep forever in his embrace. Squirm closer, nestle her head under his chin, inhale his precious scent . . .

But memory faded in, clearing like a fogged mirror. Zuul had knifed her. Demon poison. Which meant . . .

Frantic, she rubbed her belly. It barely ached. The wound was tender, soft, bruised. But it no longer gaped open. And her breath no longer stung her sinuses. Her broken face was healed, too.

Her heart crushed tight. *No. No, no, no . . .*

"What did you do?" she whispered.

"Doesn't matter. You're safe." His murmur vibrated through her body, warm and wonderful. Something gentle brushed her hair, spreading shivers all over her body. *A kiss. He just kissed me . . .*

She squirmed from his arms, and scrabbled up. "A moment ago I was dying. What did you do, Japheth? Tell me!"

"It's nothing." His hot ultraviolet gaze pierced straight to her heart. Her heart pounded. God, he was beautiful. Like a wild animal, hard-packed muscle and glossy skin. The mess crusted in his hair only made him more desirable. And then he had to go and . . . and . . .

"It damn well isn't nothing!" She was shaking. He'd lied for her. Killed for her. Poured out his secret heart, let her see inside. And now he'd committed a heinous sin, just to save her pitiful life.

She was ugly. He was beautiful. And he'd broken every rule in his stupid book for her.

"You're alive," he said harshly. "I couldn't let you die. There, I've said it. What else do you want from me?"

Her chest swelled tight. Fuck, she wanted to cry, scream, yell her rage to heaven or hell or anyone who'd listen. But no one would. God didn't care. Unless . . .

Unless he's right, and redemption is real. It's real, and I've already blown my chance . . .

She clenched her fists, furious. "How dare you make that choice for me? I don't want this. Take it back."

"Say again?" He glided to his feet. So effortlessly graceful, her angel. So maddeningly perfect.

"Take it back." She was trembling inside. She needed to pee. "You healed me. So unheal me. Undo what you've done!" Her voice cracked, and she squeezed her eyes shut for a moment. She couldn't cry. This wasn't about her tears . . .

But he already stroked her hair, tilted her chin up. "Don't. Please. What's done is done. And you're here. With me."

Oh, Jesus. She blinked, fierce, but she couldn't stop the burning liquid flowing. Shame pierced her, keener than Zuul's demonsteel. "It's not done! You can go back. You believe in forgiveness. You have to!" *You're the only one who believes there's any hope for me . . .*

He laughed. Bitter, delighted, utterly confused. "I don't know what I believe anymore. I only know what I feel."

Rose's spine tingled, warm and frightening. "Don't even go there—"

"I feel for you, Rose Harley." He didn't look away. Didn't let her escape. "I'm angry for you. I'm afraid for you. I'm . . . hell, I don't even know what this is, okay? If that makes me evil, then . . ." He shook his head, wordless. Like he didn't know how to go on.

"Angel, you don't know what evil is. You're not even close! It's what we do that counts. Actions trump words, isn't that what you said?" The injustice of it all melted her will. She'd raged against her own damnation, cursed God for a liar. But this angel . . .

He hadn't seduced a demon or killed a child or drunk the

blood of innocents to stay alive. He'd only wanted to help her. And now . . .

"I was wrong!" His eyes flared darker, a strange passionate fire that shivered deep inside her. "Don't you see? For fourteen hundred years, I've tried to stop feeling. I can't do it. They were right to cast me out."

"Don't be ridiculous." Rose dragged him back when he tried to turn away. "Look at me!" she demanded. "You're smart. You're kind. You're braver than anyone I know. You care, angel! That's more than anyone can say for me. And now you've broken all your stupid, fucked-up rules, because of me!"

"I did it *for* you, Rose. That's not the same. You're not to blame."

"Is that a fact?" The stubborn set of his jaw maddened her. "Take responsibility, you said. Well, watch me, because here I go. Yes, I hell-spelled you. Yes, I tempted you. You're a man, it's not difficult. And you fell for it. It wasn't your fault!"

"Yes, it is." Flat. Harsh. No denial. "It was a test, and I failed it. Life is temptation, Rose Harley. Not everyone falls."

God, she wanted to shake some sense into him. Punch him in the face. Kiss him until he melted in her arms, until he forgot about temptation and heaven and hell, and just . . . "Bullshit," she said desperately. "You can't absolve me just because you feel like beating yourself up. God, you really hate yourself, don't you?"

He lifted his arms, mocking himself. "What's there to like? I'm here, aren't I? On earth? They cast me down, Rose. I'm not worthy of heaven. And now I've proved it."

She closed the gap between them. He wasn't getting away, not this time. "And why did they cast you down, Japheth? You never told me. What did you do that was so terrible?"

"It doesn't matter." Harsh, unforgiving. But his gaze slipped. He wouldn't look at her.

"Oh, no you don't." Furious, she grabbed his chin, forced him to look. His eyes were shadowed, bleeding with emotion he had no way to control, and it broke her heart. "You've seen my shame, angel," she said steadily. "You didn't run from me. Let me do the same for you."

His face paled like moonshadow. His eyes glittered wet. He swallowed, and tried to speak. But nothing came out.

Rose's wits shorted out, burned like electric shock. And everything she thought she knew about him disintegrated into mocking hellsmoke.

"Oh my god," she whispered, the shadows of the Park closing in. "You sorry son of a bitch. You don't have the first clue."

Japheth wanted to scream, but his throat swelled shut. He wanted to flash out, but his wits dissolved in a confused mess, and he couldn't move. He just stood, petrified to the spot. Unable to escape her piercing dark gaze.

The taste of his own blood filled his mouth, bitter and disgusting, like the evil elixir it was. Somehow, he must have sucked in air, though his teeth clenched so hard he felt one crack. "I did everything they asked of me. I was a soldier. I followed my orders. That's all I did! And one day it just wasn't enough."

Rose stared, her dark eyes bottomless. Her face trembled, white. And then she lifted a shaking hand, and scraped a crusted lock of hair from his cheek with one fingertip. "You are more than enough, believe me."

He jerked away, sweating. He didn't deserve her touch. Didn't deserve the way it felt. "It wasn't enough to make up for what's in here." He slammed a fist over his heart. The silver crunched. It didn't hurt enough. *Never, ever enough . . .*

Rose's face shone in the half light. Her dark eyes, her luxuriant hair, the tempting curve of her lips. His heartbeat quickened. Lord, she was infernally beautiful. The longing she aroused in him was excruciating. Just looking at her blackened his wicked heart. But he couldn't tear his gaze away.

Slowly, she let her forearm rest on his shoulder. Tangled her fingers into his hair. He stiffened. He shouldn't let her touch him. Shouldn't *long* for her to touch him . . .

But she was so close. He wanted her closer. Wanted to drag her against him, feel her body tremble under his hands. Inhale her wine-dark scent, taste her rich soft skin, forget sin and hell and heaven and lay her down beneath him, succumb to this sweet velvet darkness . . .

Her gaze smoldered, knowing.

He flushed. She knew how he craved her, the dark and evil things he wanted to do. Surely, she'd run from him . . .

But she didn't move. "I see into your heart, angel," she said steadily. "Let me tell you what's in there. Compassion. Courage. Honesty. Dedication to duty. That's not evil." A sweet chuckle. "Trust me, you are way out of evil's league."

He choked on sick laughter. "How about jealousy? Lust? Selfishness? I seem to remember those on a list somewhere—"

"Screw your lists, okay?" Rose clenched both fists in his hair, and shook him, frustrated. "Are you blind, or stupid, or just one stubborn fucking angel?"

"I don't—"

"You want me to spell this out for you?" She dragged herself closer, so her body collided with his, her face just a breath away. "Shut up and kiss me, Japheth, before I strangle you," she whispered, and pressed her lips on his.

Sweet poisoned flame consumed him.

Oh, hell. He crushed her in his arms, like he'd wanted to from the moment he laid eyes on her. She yielded to him, eager, and when her lips opened under his he couldn't help but kiss her deeper. She tasted of salt and tears, bitter yet sweet and alive. He folded his wings around her, showering them both in hot dark glitter that kindled flames deep inside him.

Forbidden fire.

He didn't care.

He groaned, helpless, drowning in her sultry female flavor, the delicious sting as she yanked his hair tighter. His feathers bristled, a hot frisson that speared desire straight to his balls. His vision blurred. Already he was hard, hot, ready. Shit, that happened fast. She was so small in his hands, strong yet delicate, her muscles playing sweetly against his palms. Her slim body trembled under his touch. She felt so fine against him. So good. So . . . right.

Dimly, far distant, some frigid, forgotten part of his heart protested. *Heaven's grace, am I so lost?*

But he already knew the answer.

* * *

Rose gasped, and gave herself up to his fire.

His heartbeat thudded against her chest, a sweet caress. He tasted so good, of flame and blood and dark passion. Everything she felt. Everything she was. His feathers sparkled, and the static crackled over her skin, heightening her senses. He kissed her boldly, asking no permission, just taking her as she loved to be taken, deep and demanding and so hot she melted inside, hurting for him. God, he was so raw. So fierce. All his unshackled emotion pouring out into this one kiss.

It frightened her.

It made her greedy for more.

His wings enfolded her, a hot velvety embrace. She wrapped one thigh around him, and when he pulled her in tighter she hopped, folding her legs around his hips. Damn, he felt good there. So hard and ready. He cupped her ass in one hand, supporting her with strong wings, and kissed a trail of hot tingles down to her collarbone. *Oh, God.* She'd forgotten what it was like, this honest, innocent need . . .

"Rose. You're so beautiful." His whisper sparkled warmth into her blood. Not very original. She didn't care. He meant it. That was all that counted.

His thumb brushed her bare ribs, under her ripped t-shirt. She arched, inviting, and he didn't need to be asked twice. He kissed her belly, up to the hollow between her breasts, and when he pushed the stained fabric aside . . . *oh, fuck.* Her nipple swelled hard in his mouth. So hot. So good and strong. He suckled her, deep pulls that coiled exquisite tension deep in her belly. Her fingertips tingled. His body between her legs, his mouth on her breasts, his hands gripping her ass . . . Jesus, she was going to . . .

Urgent, she thrust her hands between them, searching for him, trying to get him inside her before she . . .

He laughed, almost a growl, and lifted her away. "Nuh-uh. I know my limits, my lady. You won't get out of this that easy." And he swept her off her feet, wrapped in fragrant golden feathers.

In a hot violet flash, she lay beneath him, hot starlight dazzling her eyes. Crisp grass tickled her back. In the half light, his strange eyes glowed, violet tinged with green. Her body thrummed, breeze playing delicious games over her skin. He was so light, for such a big guy. His weight barely pressed down on her, his delicate angelic bones built for flight. Yet all that hard muscle, his brutal strength, the burning pressure of his pulse . . .

Exquisite fear sharpened her desire. Boldly, she arched against him. She loved his hard male shapes, his rough-silk texture. "Won't I, just?"

"You want to fight me?" He inhaled her scent, lips brushing her throat, and swear to God, he *purred*. "Try it."

She shoved his silver-clad chest. He caught her wrists, pinned them down, one each side of her head, and arched his golden eyebrows, a hot challenge.

Just what she liked. She kicked, lashing, her excitement building. Easily, he pinned her thighs with his, absorbing her struggles with powerful muscles that flexed to take the impact but never gave. He forced her legs apart, eased his body between them, promise and threat. She could feel how hard he was for her, and her flesh ached. *Sweet Jesus. Take me now.*

He grinned, fiery. "Surrender? Or must I torment myself all night?"

God, she wanted him so hard, her eyeballs hurt. But her heart hammered, shaky. He'd trapped her easily. His strength far outstripped hers. She'd been fooling herself that she could overpower him.

He could have killed her anytime. Fucked her. Hurt her however he liked.

But the old fear didn't paralyze her. His victory only fanned her desire. He wasn't Fluvium. He'd never do anything she didn't want.

She trusted him. And that was a victory for *her*.

She licked dry lips, her pulse aflame. "Torment *me*."

His eyes blazed dark. He flared his wings, a fragrant golden cocoon that shut out the world. And then he bent to kiss her.

Mouth first, deep and slow, drawing out her desire until she moaned, drunk on his heady flavor. She could feel his body trembling, alive with urgent need . . . yet he took his time with her, sought her pleasure, tested it. His kissed his way down her throat, sucking her throbbing pulse, nipping playfully at her collarbone. By the time he reached her breasts, she was wild, writhing with need. She laughed, breathless. "You bastard. Sure you don't do this often?"

His only response was to kiss her more. Her nipples ached in the midnight heat of his mouth. Pleasure dizzied her. Delicious summer breeze played over her skin, tuning her to an ever higher pitch. She barely noticed that he'd let her go, that he had slipped one hand down to play over her belly . . . but then magically her jeans were undone, her flesh bare to the sultry darkness and his fingers slipped warm into her secret places and he was *touching* her . . .

"Oh, fuck." She arched, delirious. He stroked her with such exquisite care, searching, finding what she liked. It was too much. It wasn't enough. As if she'd never been touched before, and had only just now learned what sweet pleasure touching could be.

She thrust her hips forwards, desperate for more, and dragged him back up for a kiss. "More. I want to feel you."

Mmm. Deep inside her, the demon curse groaned, waking from slumber. *More, Rose. You've got a job to do. Take him now, and his soul will be ours . . .*

Cold shock almost spoiled her high. *No, I don't want to. Leave us be!* She fought the demon, wild, even as her mouth molded to Japheth's, her breasts aching against his silver-clad chest. He dipped one finger deeper into her folds, playing the tip over her entrance, and the exquisite sensation nearly toppled her over the edge.

But the pleasure was sharp, cruel. Polluted with hunger for blood. *No!* she screamed silently. *Get away. This is mine. He's mine!*

The creature just laughed. *I want his blood, Rose. You want his blood . . . and his SOUL . . .*

She tilted her hips, desperate to take him inside her, banish this evil creature that tempted her to darkness. "Yes. Touch me."

"Look at me." Japheth pulled back, and their gazes locked. She shuddered, pleasured by the passion that burned there.

Slowly, he eased his finger in. Deeper. More. Until he could go no further, and then he started to move, caress her, draw her on.

Oh, God. She was so tight, so wound up with frustrated desire, it felt like he was fucking her with his cock, every sweet thrust parting her with delicious precision. She wanted to explode, blast away this horrid hungry creature inside her . . . Her flesh throbbed, tension coiling so rapidly, it must surely break . . .

Desperate, she focused on the sensation, the cruel-sweet delight of her angel inside her, stroking her most secret places, that little spot in her flesh hardening, resonating, ready to shatter . . .

Evil laughter shook her. *You can't be rid of me. I'm part of you. The thirst is what you are. Feed, Rose. It'll feel so good . . .*

Her fangs sprang out, greedy. The demon's spell chewed up what remained of her reason and spat it out in bleeding chunks . . . and suddenly, all she could smell was blood.

God, she was so hungry.

His pulse vibrated through her, quickening in harmony with her own. She could feel it in his fingers, where he touched her inside. Against her thigh, where his male hardness strained. In his trembling lips, as they brushed her cheek, the blood throbbing in the sweet words he whispered to her. "Let go for me, Rose Harley. I've never wanted anything more."

She fought it, frantic, but her eyes dragged themselves to the broad muscled curve leading to his shoulder. Such fragile, delicate skin. The vein pulsed beneath it, hot and delicious . . .

Her vision misted scarlet. Wildly, she arched her neck, baring her face to the greedy moon. Her fangs strained, aching, triumphant as the first shockwave of orgasm sparkled from her belly towards her toes. "Oh. Yes. Yes!" She was coming, his fingers leading her, his scent drowning her, and she wanted his blood in her mouth so very badly . . .

She stretched hungry jaws, and deep in her heart, the wicked demon smiled. *He'll taste soooo good . . .*

CHAPTER 31

"Sweet Lord in heaven, what are you *doing*?"

Japheth sprang to his feet, and instinctively swept Rose up behind him.

She cried out, stumbling against the protective shield he'd made with his wings. Dizzy, he fought for breath. Sweet heaven, he'd smelled that. Felt her tighten and pulse around his fingers. She'd come for him, her beautiful body shuddering exquisitely . . .

Sword on the grass, too far away. In a blur, he scooped up his darkened dagger. "I warned you, Esther. Back off."

Esther landed lightly, fluttering her coppery wings. Her immaculate gray suit settled around her. "I knew it," she announced with a sneer. "You're having *sex* with her. That's disgusting, Japheth. Is there anything you won't stoop to?"

"I told you not to spy on me." But his pulse raced, out of control. He was drunk on Rose's scent, her spicy female skin, her hot slick wetness . . . Lord, he'd been so close to wrapping her sweet thighs around him and slamming into her. To feel that delicious flesh on his cock, feel her surrounding him, so close, dissolving together, becoming one . . .

Shit. Blind lust just wasn't enough for him, was it? He had

to go and *feel* something. And that made it so much worse . . .
or better . . . ?

Esther's mouth curled. "Yeah. Because me spying on you
totally makes sticking your dick in some foul hellspawn bitch
okay."

God, he wanted to claw that supercilious expression from
Esther's lips. Slam her face into the dirt and scream *yes, it is
okay, hear me? It's okay because I care for her. I* feel *something. Is that so awful?*

Is it?

Behind him, Rose fought to escape the trap of his wings.
"Who are you calling 'bitch,' you uppity feathered tart?" she
yelled. "How about you get the fuck out of my face?"

"You heard the lady," Japheth growled, satisfied. Damn, he
loved Rose's attitude. Especially when, for once, he wasn't on
the receiving end . . . and at his satisfaction, a tiny blue glimmer licked his knife's edge.

His heart skipped, baffled. Heavenfire. They hadn't
shunned him. Not completely. Did that mean . . . ?

"Is that how you teach your little playthings to talk?
Michael was right. You can't be trusted." Esther flashed her
sword, lighting the park with a blinding white crackle.

His warrior's nerves sprang tight. He backed off a step,
cradling Rose behind him. "What are you doing?"

"Finishing what you should have started." Esther advanced.

Instinctively, Japheth raised his guard. His rippled blade
dripped moonlight, a bloody curse. He sucked in chilly
calm, ready for the fight. "Back off, Esther," he warned frost-
ily. "You won't get a second warning."

Esther twirled her fiery blade, spite glittering in her eyes.
"She's hellspawn, Japheth. She dies. Get out of my way."

Rose struggled, and tore from his grip. "Let me at her," she
snarled, and dived forwards.

Esther grinned, smug, and struck.

White fire flashed. Rose cried out, blinded. Esther danced
in on coppery wings for the kill. And Japheth's heart screamed.

He didn't think. He didn't breathe. He just dived, his
angelic senses sparkling with rage, and his centuries-trained
blade hit home.

Rose tumbled to the grass. The flaming white sword cartwheeled, an inch from Japheth's cheek. And Esther's pretty mouth gaped in shock.

Dumbly, he looked down. Blood drenched his arm to the elbow.

Angel's blood.

The blade was sharp. He'd made sure of that. And he'd buried it to the hilt in Esther's heart.

Esther gurgled. Blood bloomed on her gray suit. She gasped, mouthing silent words, and then her lips twisted, a last, satisfied smile.

Japheth's throat squeezed cold. The knife squelched from his grip. Her glittering body thudded into the grass. Twitched. Lay still.

But her final words slashed deep into Japheth's benighted heart.

Go to hell, sinner.

Cold reality smothered him, in a deep icy place without air or light.

He'd killed Esther. Murdered a lieutenant in Michael's heavenly host. That, Michael would never forgive.

He fought for air, but darkness crawled in to choke him. All the stupid things he'd said and done over the past two days cackled like sadistic witches from the shadows.

God's blood, he'd been so blind. So *stupid,* he didn't deserve to live.

So he'd kissed a girl. Touched her. Wanted to have her. Other angels did that all the time. Look at Dash, and Trill, and Lune, for heaven's sake. Lune had practically married his.

Surely, Michael would've forgiven him, so long as the archangel got the dead demon prince he'd asked for. Heaven knew, Michael harbored enough lust of his own.

But killing a precious angel warrior, to save a vampire's life? When more than ever, heaven needed all the warriors they could get?

That was unforgivable.

Surely, now, his dagger's flame would die.

Acid guilt stripped him bleeding. Lust for a woman was one thing. But he'd let his hunger for Rose lead him into a grievous mistake. *Fight with your brain, not your hard-on,* Dashiel liked to say. But sweet hellfire, he'd drowned in her. Lost his wits in her sultry body. A vampire's body.

After centuries of self-denial, he'd finally indulged his lust—touched her, tasted her musky nipples, pushed his fingers inside her and caressed her and made her come and, fuck it all, if he didn't stop thinking about that, he'd make a mess in his trousers—and it had brought both of them only tragedy.

Esther was dead. Rose was still damned. And he . . .

Well, he'd only proved what a selfish, black-crusted thing his heart was. And screw him with a pitchfork if he'd let the filthy thing rule him for a moment longer. Heaven had offered him a chance. This time, he wouldn't waste it.

Beside him, Rose struggled to her feet. Esther's wrath had blinded her only temporarily, and she blinked, rubbing her eyes. "What happened—oh, shit." She stared at the corpse, dumb.

Her t-shirt was torn, and her breasts were half-bared where he'd tugged her bra aside. Her nipples still shone pink and hard from his kisses. Her jeans lay undone, her smooth belly naked, and the neat hair between her legs glistened with her female wetness . . .

Japheth tore his gaze away. Calmed the swift thumping of his heart. Poured liquid frost into his blood, until his aching heart froze over.

"She's dead," he said icily. "Isn't that obvious?"

"Did she get you? Are you hit?" Rose hurried up to him, reaching to touch his cheek.

He averted his face, just an inch.

Her mouth tightened, and slowly, she let her hand fall. "So it's like that, is it?"

God, he wanted to reach for her. Embrace her, fold her in his feathers and take her away from all of this . . .

Keep it frosty, angel.

"Dress yourself," he ordered coldly. "We've a demon prince to catch. And this time, I'm not leaving you behind to screw it up."

Angrily she tugged her t-shirt to cover her bared skin. "Listen, I'm sorry your friend's dead. It was an accident. That doesn't mean you have to be such a prick, right after we—"

"She wasn't my friend. And *we* didn't anything."

"Right. Typical fucking guy. Let's not talk about us having sex. Suits me."

"Fine."

"Whatever." She snapped her jeans closed, wriggling her beautiful hips. "So who was she, then, this Esther? Your angel girlfriend? Why was she watching us?"

"Just someone I used to know. It doesn't matter." Rose was lisping, he noted distantly. Fangs glittered in her mouth, playing over her lush bottom lip . . .

He'd been too absorbed in the desperate delight of touching her at last to take much notice . . . had she snapped them out while he kissed her? Ready to bite him? To take his blood?

His bones rattled cold. *To take my soul?*

He wanted to be sick. Christ, he was so dumb it was a minor miracle that his sorry flesh still soiled this world. He'd actually thought she'd *liked* it.

Of course she enjoyed it. That cynical voice taunted him. *She hungers for you. Not as a woman. As a demon's thrall. She wants your blood. Your soul . . .*

No. Ridiculous. He'd felt her, tasted her, seen the fire in her eyes. What they had was real. It had to be . . .

He yanked his blade from Esther's fallen body. Her blood gushed only weakly, her life force spent. He wiped the blade clean on the grass, and a faint blue flash twinkled along the edge. It meant nothing, right? Just an echo of what he'd lost.

Esther's lush dark hair was already fading. Her wings dimmed, their coppery richness draining to lifeless pewter. *Her soul's in paradise.* The thought clanged dully. *But her body's just . . . dirt. Ashes. A bloody smear on the grass.*

He'd been fond of her, once. Long ago, when they were both so innocent. That was ashes, too. He plucked a feather from Esther's flaccid wing. It sparkled faintly in his fingers, a bitter reminder of home.

"What are you doing?" Rose watched him, fidgeting. She didn't know what to say, how to act.

Good. See how you like it.

"None of your business." He tucked the feather inside his armor, and retrieved his sword. It lay cold in his hand, dark, threatening. He slung it over one metal-clad shoulder, and held out his arm. "Come here."

She edged closer, her gaze guarded but warm.

"Not for that." He pulled her roughly against him, wrapping his arm around her waist, and his body reacted, a flush of heat that nearly staggered him. She still felt amazing. He wanted to groan, inhale her, tilt her mouth up to his. He wanted to hold her. Cherish her, keep her for his own.

Call it penance. He looked down at her coldly, while his heart wailed bloody anguish. He was good at hiding his feelings. He'd had centuries of practice. "Hold on. We're going back to my place. I need to do some research."

"Like what?" Rose's voice sounded small. Lost.

His bones ached with sorrow. "Water tunnels. They're deep underground, but they have access valves. That's where we'll find your master."

"Japheth—"

"Just don't talk, okay?" Like it wasn't hard enough to clear his confusion, crystallize what was important.

His fingers tightened on his sword grip. He was happy to try to flash himself. Worst thing that could happen was he'd have to walk. But the thought of flashing his weapons away chilled him to the marrow.

They won't come back. Heaven's already decided you're unworthy . . .

He chased the treacherous voice away. Better safe than screwed. At least this way, he could be certain he'd have cold steel. He'd need it, to kill Fluvium. And if he wanted Michael to keep his promise, Fluvium had to die. Tonight.

Anticipation tingled his blood like snowflakes. Yes. Battle, he was good at. Not this exquisite torture. So screw it. Battle it was.

Kill the demon prince . . . but how? His angelsteel was failing. His faith was . . . well, it was what it was. But he'd fought worse odds. Somehow, he'd find another way.

And when the demon's dead, what then? Will you kill Rose, too? Like you know you should?

He squeezed his eyes shut on unexpected tears. *I can't. She's too precious. I gave her my word . . .*

But his jaw clenched, painful. This was the Apocalypse. The world didn't care about his honor. His conscience didn't matter a damn. All that mattered was Fluvium, and the vial, and his fragile angelic soul.

And the ugly, bittersweet ache in his heart only reminded him how perilously close he'd come to losing them all.

God, he was so cold.

His stained-glass gaze sliced chilly blades under Rose's skin. His arm around her felt hard, unyielding, not giving an inch. All those frigid barriers had slammed back into place. She could practically feel the frost crackling the air. Nothing remained of that passionate creature who'd touched her, whispered her name, drowned himself in her kiss.

He'd taught her so much. Proved to her that honor was worth something, that her actions still mattered, that the decisions she made could save her soul . . . and now he'd turned on her.

The man was gone. The frosty warrior angel was back. And he loathed her more than ever.

"Don't forget your promise." Her words rang hollow. "We kill Fluvium, you take this mark off, I walk away. Agreed?"

Agreed, whispered the demon inside her. *And then we chew his lying throat out, and feast on his flesh . . .*

She shivered, desperate. God, she'd so nearly fallen. To drink, to ease him into darkness, slide him inside her and drink up his soul . . .

She forced her aching fangs to retract. Japheth had earned better, even if killing that uppity angel bitch had frightened him away from making love to her. Damn it. Her body still ached for him, empty. In those few precious moments she'd felt . . . real. Alive.

Human.

Japheth flicked his distant gaze over her face. A frigid green blast of *keep away*. Even that dangerous ultraviolet glimmer had faded, leaving icy emerald that brooked no doubt. He wouldn't be touching her like that again anytime soon. Anytime ever.

Useless frustration clenched Rose's fists. The disdain in that Esther woman's eyes frothed old hatred back into her blood. *What was she to him, anyway?*

His heart was so fragile, under all that ice. Had Esther hurt him, once? Bound him to her by some frightful oath? Fucked him, even? They had rules about that in heaven, most likely. They probably had to get married, or something. Fuck. Was he cheating on his angel wife with her?

Whatever. She was glad the bitch was dead. Glad. If it left him free to find someone else.

Someone else. But not a vampire. Not Rose Harley, the demon's slave.

Her guts sickened, like they were stuffed with rotten worms. If only she could rip the curse from her body. Ram her hand down her throat, tear the demon creature out, prove she wasn't the monster Japheth despised.

A lump swelled hot in her throat. God, she wanted to fall on her knees, scream her guilt to heaven. Beg for just a scrap of forgiveness, if only it'd give her one more moment of his regard.

But she clenched sharp teeth, and the prayer crunched to dust.

She'd never be human again. She was cursed. What was done, was done.

You want absolution? Japheth's words ricocheted in her skull. *You can start by acting like you give a shit.*

Fine. Screw Fluvium and his deal. Japheth had earned his life. They'd kill the demon prince, and she'd walk away. Just like that.

The hot curse-thing inside her chuckled. *How virtuous of you. If Fluvium's dead, Japheth's soul will earn you nothing. It's easy to pass on lunch when you're not hungry . . .*

"Agreed?" she repeated, impatient.

Japheth gave her an arctic smile, colder than midnight. "Agreed."

CHAPTER 32

Twenty minutes later, Japheth leaned over his kitchen bench and spread out the fuzzy chart of Babylon he'd printed from his computer. "Pay attention," he snapped over his shoulder.

"Uh. Sorry." Rose edged to his side, flushing. His arm brushed against hers, and it tingled. Her resolve to be Rose the Ice Queen with him wasn't going well.

Her gaze kept drawing to his strong forearms, his muscles flexing as he moved the paper so she could see. His luminous angelic skin, eerily perfect, no scars, yet . . . experienced. Her sex throbbed, hot. God, his wrists were . . . his strong, tapered fingers . . .

The irony blistered her throat. She'd spent the last two days seducing *him*, and now . . . maybe it was just because they hadn't finished what they'd started, but she'd never in all her days been so aware of a man.

His tiniest movement mesmerized her. Her skin prickled as he moved his shoulders, silver armor sliding against skin, the soft silken rustle of his feathers. He shifted one crisp wing, and his clean and angry scent washed over her, dizzying. How was it fair that he smelled so damn fantastic?

She exhaled, hard. She didn't want to smell him. Didn't want to be reminded of what she'd lost . . .

Her attitude withered. What was this, a crush? She'd always been a one-night girl. Kick 'em out before the bed gets too warm. It wasn't even as if they'd had mind-blowing sex . . .

Warmth rippled up her body, a sweet echo of his touch. Okay, so she'd had an orgasm. She usually needed a tongue between her legs for that. But Jesus, this guy had barely kissed her and she was already thinking second date . . .

Inwardly, she snorted at her stupid daydreams. Clearly, a second date was not happening. No-way-never with a cherry on top. *Mind on the job, girlfriend. J-Rose is going nowhere and you know it.*

But the awareness that crept under her skin at the fragrant flush of his body heat insisted otherwise. Loudly.

Japheth favored her with a chilly glance. Hot night breeze swirled into his apartment through a jagged hole in the glass, and stifling Babylon summer poured in like treacle, overwhelming the air-conditioning. His damp golden hair shone in the heat, slicking on those ridiculous cheekbones. "Nice mess you made of my window," he remarked acidly.

"Shouldn't have locked me in, then."

"You were supposed to stay put."

The way he looked at her—distant, utterly restrained—chewed her nerves ragged. Fire lurked under that icy shell. She knew it. God, he was so close. His lips glistened, tempting. If she leaned just a little, she could . . . Mmm. Yes. Flash a few helltricks, get him under her spell. Shove him to the floor, strip him off, ease that long thick cock inside her, ride him . . .

Her mouth watered. Before, she'd used her magic to try stealing his soul. Now . . . well, it wasn't his soul she was fantasizing about. God, yeah. His frosty ass would warm up soon enough . . .

"Rose?" The cold word shocked her from her daze.

She shrugged, sweating. *You can't have him, Rose. Let it go.* "Movie mistake. No one ever stays put. You were saying?"

A few shards of a smile skipped across his face. "Water tunnels," he said, and returned to his map. "Three of 'em, reinforced concrete, six hundred feet below the surface. They feed into a network of pipes that supply fresh water to the whole of Babylon." He pointed. "Bethesda Fountain is here. That's connected to tunnel number one, under the West Side. And . . ." He leaned over to flip on the kitchen faucet.

No water flowed.

The faucet choked, and shuddered . . . and blood exploded from its mouth. It splashed the sink, clogging the drain. A fetid stink drifted.

Japheth grimaced, and shut it off. The pipes groaned in protest. "I'd call that already contaminated, wouldn't you?"

Rose peered into the sink, disgusted. The gore reeked of curse, a mix of spoiled flesh and shit. "Gross. Is that happening all over the city?"

"I hope not. Zuul said 'the next bit,' right? Fluvium's not finished. There are still two more tunnels. One there—" He indicated a line crossing the East River to Roosevelt Island. "And one there." A circular shape encompassing downtown. Japheth frowned. "If you were a demon prince with a vial of wrath, how would you poison this system?"

"You're asking me?"

A cruel smile. "You know him better than I do, vampire."

Rose bristled. "You know what? I totally understand why you never get laid."

"Do you? I doubt that. Didn't seem like it in the park when you—"

"Don't even go there." She leaned over the map, trying not to think about smashing his face in. Or kissing him. Or kissing him, and then smashing his face in . . . She cleared her throat. "So . . . where does all this water come from?"

"Upstate. Bunch of reservoirs and aqueducts."

"So if I'm him—" She painted the words with sarcasm. "Why wouldn't I just poison those? Why mess about with finding a way into the tunnels, when I can corrupt the source?"

"Because he's only got eight hours until the full moon, that's why. The system is gravity-fed. That means no pumps. It takes at least a day for the water from the reservoirs to reach Babylon." He tapped the paper, impatient. "No, he's in the tunnels. They're underground. The skanky little sucker likes that. But which one first? And where?"

Rose peered closer at the chart. The tunnels looked like subterranean snakes, writhing beneath the surface. "Okay, wiseass. Imagine I'm the demon. How do I get into these tunnels?"

"There are vertical shafts that bring the water up to the distribution network."

"So why can't I just tip my crap into one of those? Wouldn't that poison the whole thing?"

Japheth considered, surveying the chart with hard eyes. "They're two hundred feet underground," he said at last. "He'd have to get down there first. And the water's flowing upwards under pressure at that point. The poison would be washed back up into the system and dissipate after a few hours. No, he'll do this the most efficient way."

Rose laughed, shaky. "Don't wanna burst your bubble, angel, but reason doesn't fly high on this guy's radar."

"And that's why he'll do this properly." Japheth shrugged, feathers sparking. "I've met your master, Rose Harley. He likes to make people suffer, and the more people, the better. He won't waste his precious wrath on some fleeting disaster." A grim smile. "Oh, no. He'll want the entire catastrophe. Everyone in Babylon either cursed or dead. And that means all three of these tunnels."

Rose dragged her hair back, and her fingers caught and pulled. Her braid had dissolved, somehow, into a nest of knots she'd probably have to cut off . . . Hmm. She yanked tighter. "What if we cut off the water?"

"Say again?"

"They must be able to shut these tunnels down, right? For maintenance or cleaning or whatever?" Her heart quickened. "He's only got a few hours to get this done. So who cares where he's going to be? Why don't we just stop the water flowing? No water's better than cursed water, right?"

Japheth shot her a fierce smile, echoes of his lost passion. "Clever as well as pretty. How nice for you."

Stupidly, she flushed. "Save it, dickhead. How do we do that?"

"I have no idea."

"Well, that's a big help."

"Have a little faith, vampire." Japheth pulled a phone from his pocket and thumbed through the contacts. "We don't have a cabal of angels running city hall for nothing. And there were terrorist threats in Babylon long before Azaroth got wrath-happy. We have guys who know about this stuff. Let me make a few calls, get the lowdown."

"O-kaay." Rose eyed him quizzically. Still weird, the idea of angels with cell phones and computers, hanging about in city hall and the PD, telling everyone how to run things. Fore-stalling hell on earth.

She shivered. Easier just to pretend the End wasn't coming. That was how everyone got through the day. Sort of like Japheth and his emotions. Just pretend the whole fucking lot of them away. *See ya. Thanks. Bye.*

Everyone except those End of Days freaks, partying in the streets like there was no tomorrow. If she and Japheth failed, here, now, to stop Fluvium spreading this curse? There really would be no tomorrow.

The thought sobered her. But it fired sweet seduction in her blood, too. The world was ending. Who cared about heaven or hell or sins? No point wasting the days the world had left with pointless moralizing.

"Hey." Japheth stalked over to the window, talking into his phone. "It's Japheth. Yeah, that one . . . Listen, can we trade insults later? I'm doing a job for Michael and I need . . . No, it can't wait. Will you just put Simeon on . . . ? Simeon, yeah. Because I need an engineer, that's why, and you're obviously a moron, so . . . Well, go get him, then, genius. I'll hold. Thanks ever so."

He leaned one strong forearm on the glass, gazing out over the street. His feathers glistened, luminous, streaked with moonlit red. Beautiful. She wanted to touch them again. Revel in his body heat. Make him gasp, groan, feel his pleasure. Prove they were both real, alive, here and now while the world ended.

Spend their last few hours making love, instead of fighting battles that couldn't be won. There were worse ways to go.

Suddenly, she wanted that more than anything.

She hugged herself, steamy. "Umm . . . Excuse me? I'm kinda useless here. What can I do to help?"

Japheth glanced over his shoulder. "Come again?"

Did he just say that on purpose? She cleared her throat, husky. "I said, is there anything I can do?"

He flashed a cold grin. "Stand there and look sexy and think up excuses to get me into bed?" Not an invitation. A rebuke, sarcastic and cruel. "You can do that, can't you?"

"Valve chamber," announced Simeon, ten minutes later. "Up here, near the city line. That's where I'd go."

He peered shortsightedly at the chart, and Rose sighed. This white-haired angel was no warrior, evidently. More like an office worker. Tie loosened, shirt sleeves rolled up, and his skinny forearms hadn't seen the sun any time recently. He smelled of dust and old paper, like a crusty librarian who spent too much time reading in the dark.

"Van Cortlandt Park," Japheth read, frowning. "In the Bronx. Great. Nothing like a den of muties and virus zombies to make it easy for us. Why so far up the line?"

"There's a reservoir up there that feeds all three tunnels." Simeon shrugged, ruffling dusty white feathers. "In a round-about way. I could get technical, but that's the gist of it. And the valve chamber controls the flow. It's quite near the surface. The best place to introduce a contaminant, if you're into that sort of thing. And the only place you can shut off the water."

"But one's tunnel's already contaminated," said Rose. "We saw the fountain at Bethesda. And look." She pointed at the bloodstained sink. "Doesn't that mean Fluvium's already been there?"

Simeon squinted at her, like she was a spider on his shower screen. "Must we have *her* in here?"

Rose bristled. "Hey, I'm doing my part. Must *you* be such a self-righteous son of a—"

"Just answer the lady's question," snapped Japheth.

Rose snorted inwardly. *Lady. There's a turnabout.* But it felt all warm and squishy inside that he'd defended her. Damn his frosty ass to hell.

Simeon sniffed, haughty. "The answer is no, in case you weren't paying attention. The water down at city hall is still clear. So if both Madison Avenue and the park are poisoned? That's not the tunnels. That's the aqueduct."

"The what?" Rose and Japheth said simultaneously. He glared at her. She glared back, sardonic. Jesus, at this rate they'd tear each other's throats out before they got anywhere near Fluvium.

"The old aqueduct. It's a different system altogether, using water from a different reservoir. Probably your demon's using it as a test. You see, when they upgraded at the turn of the century—"

"Okay, Simeon." Japheth cut him off. "We get it. Valve chamber. How do we get in there?"

"An elevator. I can get you the key—"

"I don't do tiny metal boxes," Japheth said stonily.

Rose snorted. "My hero."

"Screw you," offered Japheth coldly. "What else is there?"

"Well . . ." Simeon's feathers curled. "There's the emergency stairs. It's two hundred fifty feet down . . ."

"Perfect." Japheth stuffed the chart into his pocket. "Now get your dusty butt back to city hall. All those contingency plans for poison, biological agents, whatever other threats you disaster guys dream up? I want it all happening in the next three hours. Evacuations, bottled water, fire hydrants feeding from the Hudson, whatever. Drag the fricking mayor down to Bethesda and rub her face in it, if you have to."

Simeon's pasty face paled more. "I'm just a consultant. I don't have the authority—"

"Then get the authority," snapped Japheth. "All you heavenly asshats have Michael's number, don't you?"

The other angel smirked, superior. "Matter of fact, we don't need it."

"Hooray for you. Just do whatever you have to." Japheth buckled a silver vambrace around his right forearm, and slid his rippled dagger into it. He slung his sword over his shoulder with a metallic scrape, and hooked Rose on a cold glance. "You," he announced. "You're coming with me."

Oh, yes I am. The thought of meeting Fluvium again—this time with an angel on her side—speared dark vengeance into her blood. But her skin crawled at the thought of Fluvium leer-

ing at her. Sliding that rapacious gaze over her body. Feeding
her curse with his silken words. Touching her . . .

She smoothed her hands over her ripped t-shirt, shivering.
It didn't cover much of her anymore. "Can't I change first?"

"What you gonna do, take a shower?"

"Oh. Yeah." She'd forgotten about the contaminated water.
Cold fear knifed into her bones, and her teeth rattled. She
couldn't be exposed in front of that psychopath. Not again . . .

Japheth's glacial gaze cracked. "You don't need armor,
Rose Harley," he said stiffly. "He can't hurt you where it
matters."

She licked her lips, speechless. He saw through her. Felt for
her. She knew it. But . . .

His mouth hardened, and the moment fled.

She coughed, and tied the torn ends of her t-shirt into a
knot over her sternum. At least she wouldn't be flashing her
boobs everywhere. "Guess that'll have to do."

"Stop fluffing and get over here, woman," growled Japheth,
extending his arm to her. "As if you don't know you look
perfect."

She sidled up to him, flushing. *Damn. Asshole or not, he
still smells fantastic.* "Got kind of a hard-on for this, don't
you?" she grumbled as he folded her into his metal-clad
embrace. "Shouldn't we take some time first? Come up with
an ambush plan?"

"Ambush?" Japheth laughed, a dreadful eagerness that
tingled her skin warm. "I think you're missing the big picture.
All that messing about at Bethesda? That was a *diversion*,
Rose Harley. You don't actually believe we'll get to the chamber before him, do you?"

CHAPTER 33

Iria coughed blood into the glittering snow.

Bleeding Christ on a cross. These fearwraiths were all over the goddamn place.

On her knees, she leaned two-handed on her crossbow, catching her breath. The last glare of sunset had blown out like a candle flame an hour ago, and the darkness swarmed, biting and scratching and exploding at whim into flame and terror. She'd killed hundreds. They all had. But the ethereal little squeezers kept coming.

She climbed wearily to her feet, sheltered from sight by wind-whipped snow. They'd crept in under cover of daylight, taken key positions, just as Michael had planned . . . but the wraiths were just so many. She hadn't seen Jadzia, or the Guardian. She only hoped their plan was working.

She tightened the spring on her crossbow, wiping away gore and demonslime. Her bolts were magical, a gift from distant heaven that hadn't deserted her when she was Tainted. Her supply never ran out. Damn good thing, too. Swords were difficult against fearwraiths, who clawed inside you with their nasty little spellfingers, chewed at your confidence until it wilted. The crossbow let her keep her distance, thrive on the thrill of fear . . .

Above her, atop the ancient stone monastery wall, Trillium yelled, his voice shredded by the gale. A curse, most likely, wraiths exploding left and right. Iria readied her bow, and sprang up onto the wall.

Her boots crunched onto the parapet. Snow swirled, blinding, but she detected that bitter fearstink, so strong she gagged. The queen wraith. At last. *Come out, you bitch. Let me see you . . .*

Stairs, leading upwards onto a wide stone rampart. She took them two at a time, stealthy. A baby fearwraith dived for her, and sank gritty teeth into her wrist. She smashed it against the stone. It fell limp, and she hurled it away.

She reached the rampart. The snow was clearing, and overhead, starry sky peeked through gaps in the clouds. The monastery tower loomed, a forbidding black silhouette against the mountain.

In her ear, her phone buzzed, incongruous. Cell reception at twelve thousand feet. Who knew?

She tapped her tiny earpiece. "I'm kinda busy," she snapped, darting her gaze left and right. Where was Trillium?

"Iria . . . damn time. . . . you for an hour." Dashiel's voice crackled, dropping in and out.

Twin wraiths knotted themselves around her throat. She hurled them away and fired a shining silver bolt. They exploded in mid-air, splashing fearful muck. Ha. Like target shooting, only better. "Could use your help, Dash. Where are you?"

"Jerusalem," yelled Dash.

"What the hell are you doing in Jerusalem?"

"Don't ask. I'm . . . Michael isn't . . . you have to . . ?"

She wiped fresh demonslime from her face, the burns healing. Her eyes darted sharply to a red-green flash at the tower's wall. Trillium, laying into a pack of wraiths with twin swords blazing. His laughter swirled on the wind, and she grinned. He'd always loved a fight.

She sprinted, wings stretched back. "Say again? I'm losing you, Dash."

"I said, you've gotta . . . the vial. Gabriel said . . . Don't let him . . ." The line popped, and dropped out.

Shit. Iria leapt, sweeping her wings around and kicking another wraith to swirling smoke. Dash was talking to Gabriel? About the vial? Sounded important. But no time to bother about it now.

Beneath her, Trillium whirled, his dappled wings afire. Wraiths squealed and exploded. The smoke stung her eyes. She landed on slushy stones beside him, and he grinned at her, orange hair poking up like a porcupine's spines. He clashed his crossed swords, and sparks flew. "Just in time, my lovely. I saved the queen for you."

She grinned back, excitement twingeing sharp. Her crossbow sprang alight with emerald fire. "Don't do me any favors, hero. First to two hundred, you said."

He crunched a screaming wraith under his boot. Slime splurted, eating into the bricks. "Ew, gross. Two hundred? I lost count."

"I didn't. Whiskey's on you."

"Needed an excuse to buy you a drink anyway. I'm intimidated by your gorgeousness." His smile twinkled. "Y'know. Shy little boy like me."

"The hell you are." His inked muscles swelled brutally, pumped up from the fight, and his manic eyes blazed. *Shy* and *boy* weren't words that sprang to mind.

"Okay, maybe not. But you are, warrior queen. Gorgeous, that is. Did I ever tell you that?"

"Screw you." But secret pleasure tingled inside her, and she glanced away, mortified. He'd never said anything like that before. Fuck, her cheeks were warm. She was *blushing.* Iria didn't blush. Ever. *I'm gonna kick his crusty jeans-ad ass . . .*

A blood-rotting screech tore the air. She cursed, dragging herself back to the real world. Smoke billowed. Her skin crawled with magical fear. And the queen wraith slithered from a ragged hole in the ether, with a sharp *snap!* as the rift sealed shut.

Long, lizardlike, shimmering like a ghost, leathery fins trailing and a long spiked tail crusted with sharp scales. The queen snarled, her long crocodile jaws slavering, three rows of needle teeth dripping with acid malice.

Ash rained, laced with bone-chilling terror. Trillium

yelled, and leapt, shielding Iria from the caustic shower with a purple-flamed wing. But too late. She gasped, and the choking spell hit her full in the face.

Shit. Iria staggered, sick and cold. She trembled. Her pulse stumbled to escape. Her breath strangled. She needed to pee. Every sense screeched at her to run, hide, dig a hole and disappear . . .

Trillium dragged her up, his fist in her feathers. His voice thundered in her ear. "Stay with me, Iria. Fight that bitch!"

She growled, and cracked the fearspells off with a sparkling green heavencurse. Black charcoal shards rained, aflame. Thwarted, the queen wraith screamed, and struck.

Whippy like a serpent, and as fast. Fangs sliced Iria's cheek. She jerked away, blood drops flying, and clawed for the queen's eyes. Trillium stabbed, twin blades like forked lightning . . . but the queen whiplashed, screaming, and his flaming swords slashed empty air. Triumphant, the queen gaped foul jaws around Trillium's feathers and bit down.

Blood spurted. His wing bone broke, a horrible sound like crackling sticks. Trillium grunted, his face draining white. The queen crunched harder, shaking her head like a rabid dog. The sword clanged from his numbed right hand, and he fell.

"Get off him, you bitch!" Iria screamed. But the queen just grinned, her mouth full. Her spiked tail swept a wide arc, trailing black hellflame. Iria dived, vanishing her crossbow, and grabbed that thrashing tail.

Razor scales sliced her hands bloody. Iria yelled, and pulled harder. Christ, the bitch was strong. The queen thrashed, trying to fling Iria skywards, but she held on, driving downwards with her wings, and ground the tail into the stone with a crunching thud.

And Trillium roared his ancient battle cry, swung his left-hand blade, and sliced the queen in two.

The monster screamed. Trillium tore his dripping wing from her mouth. The severed tail fell, twitching, smoke wisping from the hacked-off end. And Iria scooped up Trill's fallen sword, and drove it two-handed into the queen's rolling eye.

The steel pierced the head like a needle, effortless. The

point slammed into the stone beneath. The queen wraith howled and thrashed and exploded into smoke.

And all around, tiny wraiths caught alight, shimmering for a few seconds before they fell like ashen stars, and winked out.

Kill the queen and you kill her children. Good bloody riddance.

Iria panted, searching for her burning breath. Blood coated her armor, her hands, her hair. The fear-rich smoke nipped at her skin, but she crackled it off. With a hiss of indignant heaven-spell, her torn hands healed.

At her feet, Trillium bled on his belly in the snow. His left hand still clutched one fiery sword. He shifted his broken wing and blood trickled down his dirty breastplate into the slush. Torn feather ends puffed, drifting in the breeze.

He groaned, still on his face, and kicked up his feet. "Can I get a hand here?"

Iria slipped her hands under his arms, and heaved him up. He was warm, almost fevered. He stumbled, and she steadied him, holding his bulky shoulders. He smelled of Trill, musky hair and fresh male sweat. A good smell.

His broken wing drooped limply, uneven. He flexed it, and more sweat beaded on his pale face. "Ouch. Fucking glory. Taking its goddamn time." He still managed a lopsided grin, green eyes sparkling bright. "You did good, lady."

"In better shape than you." Unwilled, Iria's fingers lingered. His wounds would heal. She knew that. But still, she wanted to wipe the blood away, soothe his bruised flesh. His injury was her fault. If she hadn't fallen apart in the middle of the fight . . .

Her guts twisted. She forced her hands still at her sides. "Listen, uh . . . Thanks. For . . ."

"No problem." Trillium fidgeted. "Forget it."

She'd like nothing better. But he'd saved her life when her courage failed. It needed to be said. "No, look, I . . ."

"It happens." He rubbed a filthy hand in his hair, making it stick up. "We got through it. No one's perfect."

The old anger rippled in her veins, flashing her back to cold reality. *I am.*

I was, until you ruined it. If you hadn't distracted me with your goddamned crazy flirting, I would have seen that fucking queen coming and none of this would have happened . . .

He'd caught her vulnerable. And Iria of the Tainted didn't do vulnerable. Not now. Not ever.

"I guess not," she said coldly. "One more thing, Trill. I'm not some little girl you need to protect. If you ever push me behind you in a fight again? I'll shoot you in the back and clamber over your corpse." And she shouldered her shimmering crossbow, and strode away.

CHAPTER 34

Two hundred and fifty feet below the earth, the heat was stifling.

At the bottom of the metal stairs, a single electric light gleamed on the wall. Some kind of maintenance tunnel, concrete walls closing in. At Rose's feet, train tracks gleamed along the wet floor, stretching off left and right, vanishing into hollow darkness. Water dripped and trickled. Somewhere in the distance, water rushed and thundered in massive pipes, vibrating the floor.

She wiped back damp hair, squinting into the dark. Her vampire sight showed . . . nothing. No one.

And that was creepier than the piled-up corpses at Bethesda.

It had taken an eternity to descend, her footfalls clanging impossibly loud. Or at least, so it had seemed. Japheth had drifted ahead of her, spiraling down on a warm updraft, sword in hand. The steel gleamed, a cold angry blue. Was it her imagination, or did the flames waver?

She shivered, despite the sweat. No time to worry about Japheth's crisis of faith. Fluvium and his hateful plan were all that mattered. Bloody water, dripping with the vampire curse. All those unwitting victims, damned. Howling with bloodthirst, fighting like animals for survival. They'd eat each other, and when it only made them hungrier, they'd do it again, and again, until . . .

Rose's guts watered. She hadn't thought she cared. *Let 'em die,* she'd have snarled. *Heaven doesn't care. Why the hell should I?*

But now, her benighted soul screamed at the injustice. People didn't deserve to die like that. And she wasn't ready for the world to end. For the first time since she'd been cursed, she saw a future. And damn it if she'd let that slip away now.

Ahead, Japheth beckoned. He pointed at the darkened ceiling, where a wheeled hatch was barely visible. "The valve chamber's directly above us. I can hear movement. There's at least one person in there."

"Don't tell me. Your plan is to burst in there in full sight of everyone?"

That familiar grin, wild with fight and glory. "Now you're getting the hang of it."

Her palms itched in frustration. God, she wanted to punch some sense into him. "Sure can't fault your balls, angel," she admitted grudgingly.

"Uh. Thanks. I think." His gaze darkened. "Listen, if we don't get out of this alive—"

"Oh, no, you don't." She warded him off with one hand. "Don't be giving me your preachy bullshit now—"

"*If* we don't get out alive," he insisted, "I just . . ." His cheeks colored faintly. "You don't make this easy, do you? Half the time I want to throttle you."

"You're a real romantic, you know that?"

"Let me finish." His gaze locked on hers, so candid it hurt. "The rest of the time . . . well, I guess I like you, Rose Harley. Angel, vampire, whatever. You're . . . refreshing."

She tried to laugh, but a stupid lump cramped her throat. "Yeah? And how's that?"

"You laugh at me." He shrugged, awkward. "I don't have a lot of friends. Mostly they've given up on testing me. It's been . . . nice." And he leaned over, halting, as if on some unwanted impulse, and kissed her.

Warm, chaste. Just a gentle kiss on the cheek. But it stabbed cruel blades of longing into her heart. And then he pulled away, and the blades ripped out, bleeding.

Nice? Rose choked on dumb wetness that trickled down the back of her nose. As in, *It was nice, but it's over. I'm just not that into you. Call me if you ever need anything.*

Fuck.

Her throat ached. She wanted to scream, tear the walls down, rage at this stupid injustice and the blind rules that crippled his heart. *He's just a man. Can't they let him be, for an hour? For a moment?*

"Friends?" she scoffed, trying to keep it light. "Jesus bawled like a baby. With friends like you . . ."

"Yeah. Who needs 'em, right?" His haunted smile undid her . . . but her blood chilled, too. Was that a glint of guilt? What secrets did he keep now?

But before she could react, he'd turned away.

Japheth cranked the wheel one more time, and yanked the ceiling hatch open. The hinges creaked, and fiery light knifed in.

He could already smell the curse. Fluvium was here. Doing this alone was a bad idea. But he'd called Dash. No service. And the others were all still in Bhutan.

Still, part of him *wanted* to do it alone. Fluvium was his, and only his. And this time, Japheth knew exactly where Rose was. He wouldn't let her distract him.

Not until you have to kill her, Jae. How's that working out for you?

He gritted his teeth. He could just . . . let her go. Pretend she'd escaped. Look the other way for a second while she disappeared. Who'd ever know?

You'd know, whispered that voice, and try as he might, Japheth could find no answer.

He'd know, all right. And heaven saw straight into the tarnished depths of his heart. There'd be no hiding. No pretending his dishonor away. After fourteen hundred years of truth? He was the world's worst damn liar.

So why the hell had Rose believed him?

Because she wants to, that's why. She wants to believe you'll save her. She's screaming out for help, and you'll use her up and toss her bleeding into hell. Nice work, angel. Very noble . . .

He gripped the hatch's edge and vaulted through into the light.

He landed on a metal catwalk, barely wide enough to flare his wings. A long narrow chamber, metal walls glistening in reddish light, bunches of three-foot-thick steel pipes snaking into the distance. The pipes were pierced at intervals with bolts and wheeled valves, flanges and welded ladders, gauges and safety warnings.

Damn, it stank. Dirty charcoal gritted his mouth, crawled over his damp skin. Hellsmoke blanketed the ceiling, only four or five feet clear of the floor, and the walls shuddered, threatening, closing in . . .

Breathe. Don't freak out. Cold. Quiet. Nothing to fear . . .

Rose grabbed his hand, and he heaved her up beside him. She clambered over the edge, and wiped the ash-slick mess from her hands. "Demonslime. Yuk. Why do we have to be so gross?"

"Could be worse. At least he's not poisoning the sewers."

Her nose wrinkled. "Thanks for that."

"Just stay behind me until we see what's going on, okay? And peel your eyes for the vial. If that stuff gets spilled, it won't be pretty." He crept beside the big bunch of pipes. Sweat slicked his warm sword grip. He should wipe it off . . . but too soon, he reached the end of the huge pipe, where it curved at a ninety-degree angle and plunged through a hole in the floor deep into the earth.

Ahead, an evil bonfire roared, spreading a pall of black smoke. The fire stank like pork crackling. Those were bodies burning. Human bodies, charred and broken, flesh melting from the bones.

His sword flared brighter, angry. Not an illusion. A hungry, righteous blue gleam, howling for demon blood.

His muscles ached for action. Hot glitter tingled into his skin, obliterating everything but his pulse, his senses, the ruthless undercurrent of rage. *For me. For Rose. For all the lives you've ruined.*

He gasped as it took him, that black urge for slaughter. Horror, passion, dreadful heat in his blood. His muscles swelled. He was hard, quivering, on the wickedest of edges. In that moment, he knew how Dashiel felt. Glory, a beautiful drug, liquid ecstasy in his veins. Fight, fuck, bleed, die. All the same.

Japheth drifted around the corner, sword in hand, more hungry beast than angel.

Rose peered around the corner, and her throat parched.

Blood everywhere. Pooling on the floor, splashed over the curling pipes, dripping from the ceiling like an evil cartoon house of horrors. Her vampire senses growled. Torn human flesh, heartbeats like panicked drums, half a dozen or more in close proximity . . .

But where were the vampires? Who was doing all the killing?

Ahead of her, Japheth crept, wrapped in sparkling blue death. She strained, hunting that evil rhythm, the sweet harmony of vampire heartbeats . . .

Her ears prickled. A single pulse, swift and light. Just one vampire? For all that blood . . . ?

The smoke pall rolled, and parted, and velvety black compulsion crawled up Rose's throat to throttle her. She stumbled back, sweating, but too late.

Atop the mass of welded pipes sat Fluvium.

Leaning on one elbow, legs outstretched. Firelight caressed his night-purple hair. This time, he'd dressed like a dude from a Sergio Leone Western, complete with moleskin shirt and tall spurred boots, a red bandanna knotted around his neck.

He grinned at her—such ugly, gloating eyes—and tipped his dusty cowboy hat. A pair of antique six-guns hung from crossed belts over his hips. "Well howdy, partner. Just in time! And you've brought me a gift!"

Japheth spat, and it burned a smoking hole in the steel. "Happy birthday, hellshit. Come get it."

Excruciating movie reels of hell seared into Rose's brain.

Fluvium's evil smile, the exquisite pleasure of his touch, the steaming horror of blood . . .

She wanted him. She loathed him. Salty sickness watered her guts. She tried to speak, say anything to forestall her master's wrath . . .

But Fluvium glared at Japheth, and the stinking air shimmered black. "But it's not wrapped properly, Rose. He's not cursed! I give you one simple task, and you screw it up. Honestly. What did I ever see in you?"

And swift as a striking hawk, he hurled a glittering hellspell.

"Heads up!" Japheth's aura flashed bright in warning.

But too late. Gritty fire exploded over Rose's face. The hellspell cackled, crawling up her nose like tear gas. Her eyes poured. She choked, waving frantic hands, but she couldn't help it. Her legs buckled. Her knees hit the floor, a sick jolt that pierced her bones like a hot blade, and she screamed.

I'm not cursed.

Japheth shuddered, his sanity cracking.

Fluvium's hellspell crawled over him, into his ears, up his nose, into his mouth. Pain, witless confusion, blindness. Demons' tools. He fought it, a flash of blue fire that seared the grit from his skin. But his thoughts scrambled, a lunatic's crayon scribbles.

Rose meant to trick me all along. He sent her to tempt me. She's still his creature.

But I'm not cursed . . . ?

He didn't get it. All that mattered was the vial. And he couldn't see it. Not in Fluvium's hand. Not on the floor. Not by the jumbled pipes.

Okay, then. He dropped his sword, swept his wings back and leapt.

Slam! He collided with Fluvium, knocking him flat atop the pipes.

The demon's body was hard, whippy with muscle. But Japheth was stronger. He grabbed a flailing wrist, and slammed it down on the pipe. *Crack!* Fluvium's forearm snapped. Bare skin sizzled. Japheth whipped his dagger from his vambrace, and jammed the point under the demon's chin.

Hatred boiled in his veins, and sweat poured from his face. God, he wanted to slit the prick's throat and bathe in his boiling blood. *That's for making her scream, hellshit. For making her a monster . . .* "Where is it?"

Fluvium struggled to breathe, but his eyes glinted with rainbow glee. His hat had fallen off, and his purple hair glared wild. "Where's what?"

Japheth banged the demon's head into the steel. His knife sliced deeper, and poisoned blood steamed. "Where's the vial, asshole? Before I gut you like a fish—"

Fluvium winked, and vanished to ash.

Japheth thudded into the pipes where the demon had lain, and his blade screeched on empty steel. He whipped into a backwards somersault, landing with a twist on the steel floor . . .

Crap.

Fluvium leered at him from the catwalk. His broken arm had mended, and Rose knelt at his feet, shivering in a puddle of blood. She stared, blinded by wicked demonspells, seeing only the nightmares the bastard was feeding her . . .

Fluvium bent over to lick her ear, and traced one long gun barrel against her cheek. "Mmm. She tastes good, don't you think? Perhaps I'll eat her, if you don't behave."

Japheth's fist clenched, so hard his dagger's hilt warped. So easy, to sacrifice others for the mission. To let this woman suffer so the world could be saved.

It wasn't fair. But it had never bothered him before. He'd never wanted to forget the mission, save the girl, scream a final fuck-you prayer to heaven.

"Get off me!" Rose struggled, fighting to stay lucid. But Fluvium planted a hand on her shoulder, effortlessly forced her down, ground his foot on her calf until something crunched.

Rose's face drained white. But she wouldn't scream. She gritted her teeth, shaking with the effort. "Son of a *bitch*!"

Fluvium nipped the side of her neck. Blood oozed. He

licked it, lingering. "Play nice, minion, or I'll flay the skin from your face until you beg me for death! Sound fair?"

Japheth crouched, tense. *Sword at the catwalk's edge. Try a flash? Jump him? Throw, and hope I hit something that's not her? All shitty options. Where the hell is that vial?*

"You afraid of me, demon?" he threw back, stalling. "Why don't you let her go and fight me face-to-face?"

"Because you'd win?" Fluvium's laughter clanged. "How dumb do you think I am? No, we'll do this my way. And I've got such a surprise for you both!"

He spun his six-gun into its holster—did he practice that?—and whistled, a ripping shriek that curdled Japheth's breath. "Come out, sweetling," Fluvium called. "Come meet the family. And mind your manners, like Daddy showed you."

Japheth primed his senses, ready for whatever foul hell-beast the demon had summoned.

A dark shape crawled on all fours from the shadows. Its small, naked body dripped crimson. Wet ringlets dangled over its forehead. Slitted eyes glinted wickedly in the firelight. Its tongue lolled, drooling, and it licked its sloppy fangs and grinned.

A girl.

A little vampire girl. And in one hand, it—she—clutched a bloodstained golden bottle.

Japheth stared, his pulse thudding. He'd seen a holy vial before, at Quuzaat's dirty sabbat. Ten inches high, round like a globe at the bottom and narrowing to a long spout at the top . . . and it *burned*, angry white-hot flames that licked up the little vampire's arm.

But the girl-creature didn't flinch. She just crouched in loving firelight, and gazed up at Fluvium with wide wet eyes. "Daddy," she lisped, fangs too big for her mouth. "I'm hungry."

"I know, darling," Fluvium soothed. "We'll feed you in just a second. First, come say hello to Rose." His grin sharpened, cruel. "You remember Auntie Rosie, don't you, Bridie?"

CHAPTER 35

Razors sliced living flesh from Rose's brain.

A howl split her ears, some horrid cacophony straight from the stinking bowels of hell, and her mouth gaped wide.

But she was already screaming. And Bridie—this *thing* the curse had made of her precious child—just grinned at her, and giggled. "Auntie Rosie," it gurgled, blood drooling on its dimpled chin. "Let's play hide-and-seek! When's Mommy coming home?"

"Aww, that is *so* cute!" Fluvium grinned. "Seriously, I'm dying from the fucking cuteness over here. Isn't she adorable?"

Dimly, Rose heard Japheth curse, sibilant words in some ancient language that seared her skin with unholy fire.

"You sick bastard. You did this to her!" Her voice ripped ragged, and she leapt up to tear Fluvium's face off with her bare hands . . . but her sprained calf shrieked, and folded. She collapsed, dizzy with agony.

Fluvium laughed, his hair smoldering. He got off on her pain. "Oh, no, Rose. It's much worse than that." He yanked her hair, dragging her ear to his lips. "*You* did this," he hissed. "Don't you remember?"

"No." She formed the word, but no sound came out.

"You ate her. You were so *hungry*, isn't that right?" Fluvium whined, mocking. "Poor *you*. You couldn't *help* it. You stumbled home in a sweating fever of thirst and there she was, so sweet and tasty and innocent. She smelled so good, didn't she?"

Rose struggled, drowning in bloody memories. She'd thought Bridie was dead. Already in hell. But this . . .

She'd made her sister's child a vampire. Infected her with this horrible thirst, and turned her into a monster.

Her tortured soul wailed, writhing, crucified on ugly spikes of truth. Japheth had given her hope. She'd almost believed redemption was within her reach.

But her hope was an evil lie.

They'd never forgive this. Not heaven. Not her sweet Tainted angel. Not anyone.

"Her little heartbeat pounded in your ears." Fluvium was on his knees beside her, rubbing against her, reveling in her pain. His breath came hard and fast. "She ran, didn't she, Rose, she tried to get away but you were too big, too strong. She had no chance. You tore her little throat out and then you fainted, didn't you? You passed out, and I took her. And now she's mine . . ."

She yelled, hoarse, anything to block out his horrible, hypnotic voice. Someone was screaming her name. Over and over, shouting for her. Was it Japheth? It was so distant, just a ghostly echo, lost in creeping horror.

She was damned. Lost. She'd go to hell forever.

Nothing could change that.

Then save her instead! She howled a silent prayer, pleading with anyone who'd listen. *Save Bridie! She's only six. She doesn't know any better . . .*

Bridie crawled forwards on all fours. Her little hands slicked in the blood. The golden vial in her fist—yeah, that, Rose had almost forgotten it—banged on the rippled floor. "I'm hungry," she announced again, gazing at Fluvium expectantly.

Rose shuddered, broken. She'd heard a single vampire heartbeat. Just one, among all those victims. Bridie had killed them all. And she was still hungry.

"Of course you are," Fluvium said fondly. "Have you finished all those ones already?"

Bridie nodded proudly. Like she'd completed her homework, or braided her hair.

"All by yourself? Such a big girl! We'll get you some more, I promise. But first—" His gaze gleamed with sudden purpose. "Let's play a game! Give me that vial, sweetie."

Bridie giggled, and held it out to him.

And golden heavenlight tore the skin from Rose's eyes.

Driving angel wings blasted her face with hot breeze. She screamed. Bridie screamed, too. Japheth hit the floor in a flurry of gilded feathers, flinging Bridie onto her face in the blood.

Lightning flashed, a deafening howl of thunder. And Japheth rolled, and lighted to his feet, the vial clutched in his hand.

Holy flame ripped up Japheth's arm, bathing him in bloodthirsty glory.

Hot, glittering, everything he'd ever thought he'd lost. The vial pulsed in his hand, feeding his life force, stroking his senses to sweet pleasure . . .

He shuddered, on a perilous edge. His flesh tingled, energized like magical quicksilver. Current arced along the catwalk, and the cursed air boiled in fury.

Inside the burning golden vial, liquid sloshed. Wrath in earthly form. The most powerful heavenspell in creation. The vial wasn't empty. Which meant Fluvium wasn't done. He could still be stopped.

Just sacrifice Rose and the child, and it'd be done. Fluvium dead. The vial safe. Mission accomplished.

He flashed his sword, a blinding strike of sky blue. With this vial in his hand, the power was his again, like he hadn't felt it in fourteen hundred filthy, Tainted years.

He crouched, ready to dive at Fluvium and chew the sick monster's skin off.

But Rose's heartbreak shredded his nerves, an overvoltage

of rage that sizzled his righteous fervor to ash. None of this was her fault. She'd suffered enough.

His fingers clenched on the burning vial, and it lit him up like fireworks. But his heart still stung, defiant. She didn't deserve hell.

Hot blue warning whispered in his veins. But he ignored it. There had to be a way to save her.

His voice reverberated, echoed in myriad harmony. "Rose, come on. Nothing you can do here."

And he reached out a flaming blue hand for Bridie.

❦

Rose stared, openmouthed, as her angel exploded in heavenly blue fire.

He'd help her. Try to save Bridie. He still believed there was hope for her . . .

Current crackled from the vial, up Japheth's arm, arcing along his golden wings. The air stung with ozone. His eyes blazed with purpose, and he reached for Bridie.

But the little girl spat bloody flames, and scuttled away under the pipes.

"Bridie!" Rose stumbled to her knees. Her sprained leg squealed. She crawled, slipping in the gore, and stretched her arm out, desperate, grasping for Bridie's outflung hand . . .

A flash of stinking ash, and Fluvium swept the child into his arms and darted away. "Get off her, bitch. She's mine now."

"No!" Rose screamed, mindless, and dived for Bridie. Her little girl, in that foul beast's embrace. The horror was too much to bear.

But Fluvium just grabbed Rose's hair, lightning quick, and slammed her into the floor.

Her breath squeezed out. She gasped, but her lungs wouldn't fill. Her eyes bulged, and she lay there, helpless, gulping like a grounded fish.

And Fluvium faced Japheth, a knowing grin on his handsome face. "Ooh, didn't count on that, did you? Now give me that stinking golden piss pot, or they both die screaming."

* * *

Shit. Time for Plan B.

"Go ahead," Japheth growled. "The vial's mine. You lose."

Fluvium propped Bridie on his hip. "Nice try, angel, but I don't think you can watch them die. I've seen how you look at my little wife. You can save her, Japheth. She can be yours. All you have to do is give me the vial."

His vision misted red. Temptation mesmerized him, a crawling velvet hellspell. He could keep her. Hold her, love her, make her his very own . . .

But the vial's strength powered through him, and he shook the spell off, a crackle of lightning. "Your filthy magic won't work on me. Now choose, demon. A clean death on my sword? Or shall I shove this glory down your throat and strangle you with it?"

Fluvium nipped at Bridie's little wrist, and she giggled as he licked the blood. "I choose door number three, angel. Give me the fucking vial, or I drink this little bitch's blood dry."

Rose yelled, a heart-ripping cry of misery.

The water's already contaminated, Jae. That serpent voice, sweet poisoned reason in his head. *Remember Bethesda Fountain? The Sign is done. You can't stop that now. What's a little more blood, compared to her pain? Give Fluvium the vial and let her live.*

He gnashed his teeth, trying to sever that ugly temptation. If Fluvium poisoned the rest of the pipes, two million people in Babylon would succumb to the curse.

Why should you care about them? They sure don't give a shit for you. But Rose does, dumbass. Can't you see that? How can you let her die? What kind of monster are you?

The selfish screaming in his heart shocked him cold. That was the demon in him talking. The evil inside . . .

I'm not a demon, Jae. Sorrow, bleak and cold like storm water. *I never was.*

I'm you. I'm fourteen hundred years of pain and emptiness and stupid suffering you didn't deserve. I'm the part of you that hates them to their fucking marrow for what they did. And you can't ever cut me out . . .

He shuddered. Two million deaths. Heaven's children, burning in torment. Hell on earth.

Sweet revenge.

And for a bloody, shocking moment, he relished it.

Mercy, it was unthinkable. Impossible. He couldn't surrender God's holy wrath just to soothe his selfish rage.

But Rose trusted you. How can you let her die? And this little girl, poisoned by a demon. Don't they deserve to live a little longer?

The vial glowed white-hot in his hand. His fingers quivered, aching to the bone. The hollow where his soul once lived boiled over, sorrow and confusion and bitter loss, and he screamed his anguish to the unseen sky. *I can't do this! I can't make this decision. I'm not strong enough.*

His knees buckled, and he fought to stay upright. *You win, okay? You've beaten me. Just tell me what to do . . .*

But silence resounded. Deep. Cold. Never ending . . .

Crunch! Something hard crashed into his wrist. Pain arrowed up his arm.

And the sword dropped from his broken fingers.

Stunned, he stared into Rose's face. Pale, tear streaked, her eyes shadowed black. She'd kicked him. Right on the point of his wrist. Such a delicate dancer, his warrior beauty.

Blindly, he scrabbled for his knife, but it was gone. He'd dropped it when he'd tackled Bridie. And now Rose gripped it, jabbing the point into the vein in his throat.

CHAPTER 36

Rose quivered, but she held the knife steady. *I have to believe I'll be forgiven. I have to believe.*

I have to.

Her foot still hurt where she'd kicked Japheth's wrist. Her angel was strong. But heaven's steel could kill an angel, just a surely as a demon's blade. And Japheth's rippled knife didn't burn her. He'd made sure of that, when he gave her his mark.

Her treachery sickened her. But it had to be done.

"Let her go!" Her whisper boiled into a scream. "You can have him. I've done everything you asked! Just let my little girl go."

Fluvium laughed, gloating. "Good work, Rose. I knew you'd come through for me. Do you like that, angel? She's been working for me all along. And now I've got you right where I want you."

Don't look, Rose. Not his eyes . . .

But her gaze sucked upwards, ineluctable.

Beautiful, this angel's eyes. Brimming bright with passion and sorrow and unspeakable emotion. It pierced her, stabbing through the fuck-you armor of hatred and violence she'd so painstakingly built up.

He didn't see a hellslave, or a monster. He saw *her*.

Her heart twanged, like hot wires broke inside.

But only Bridie mattered. She'd failed her de facto daughter once. Never again.

She jabbed the knife point deeper. Blood oozed. It must have hurt—God, she felt it herself, as if the blade lodged in her own flesh—but Japheth didn't flinch. Didn't shift that ultra-green gaze from hers.

He just flexed his shattered wrist, and it healed, wreathed in blue flame. "Ouch," he said softly.

He didn't mean the broken bones.

I'm sorry! she wanted to scream. *I had to. It's not you . . .*

But there was no time. No space. No reason. He'd never forgive her. Never understand that saving Bridie was more important than her life, or her soul.

The end of the world didn't matter. If she could just save Bridie . . . *then hell won't have won.*

She flung a frantic glance at Fluvium. The demon still supped at her little girl's wrist, slurping in contentment. "Mmm. I've gotta say"—he licked gory chops, and Bridie laughed—"she tastes damn fine. A bit like you, Rose. I can see the resemblance. I wonder if she feels like you, too? Y'know, inside, where it's soft and warm . . ."

"Shut up!" Rose yelled. "You win, okay? Just let her go."

Fluvium kissed the child's nose tenderly. "Of course I win. What did you expect? Now bring me the vial."

Japheth spat at him. "Coward. Come get it yourself, and see what happens."

"Give her the vial, angel," Fluvium snapped, "or I eat this child and your bitch of a girlfriend stabs you in the throat. I believe that's what you call a lose-lose situation."

Trembling, Rose reached out, and wrapped her fingers around the vial.

Japheth's hand twitched. Such a strong forearm, roped with muscle. She'd always liked his wrists. His aura glowered in the firelight. But he didn't fight her. Didn't flash his sword.

He just let her take it.

It didn't make her feel better about fucking him over.

A soldier does what's necessary. His words from hours ago

echoed, hollow. *A life for a life? I have to give up one to have the other? Where's the justice in that?*

The golden vial spat angry fire in her hand, a vow of awful retribution that shivered her soul. Without Japheth's mark, she'd surely have fried on the spot.

She held it out to Fluvium, sick.

Triumphant, he took it, eyes gleaming. It howled, crackling with furious voltage. But Fluvium was a demon prince, one of hell's chosen few. His magic crawled over him, an ethereal black shell, deflecting the wrath with a smug hiss of smoke.

"Lovely," he remarked. "Here you go, Bridie. Run along and play in the pond I made you."

"You're sick," Japheth growled. "At least have the balls to do it yours—"

"Shut up." Fluvium's tone was mild, but white-hot sparks spat from his fingers as he lifted the girl gently to the floor. "Off you go, sweetie."

"Where's my pond?" Bridie said eagerly, waving the vial in her little fist. Fluvium's spells shielded her, too. A few golden drops splashed, and sizzled holes in the floor.

"Oh, did I forget? My mistake." Fluvium strode over to the array of pipes, and slammed his fist into the steel.

Demonspells crackled. The metal buckled, and shattered. Water burst out, drenching Fluvium in a powerful spray that hit the ceiling and showered left and right.

Somewhere, an alarm screeched. Fluvium ducked beneath the fountain, jammed his hand into the hole and tore the cracked steel apart.

The pressure eased. Water flowed fast, bubbling onto the bloody floor. "There you go, darling." He lifted Bridie onto the pipe, her little legs swinging. "And remember what I said. A little at a time. Don't waste it. Otherwise the pretty magic won't work." He kissed her cheek. "You want the pretty magic to work, don't you?"

Rose's bones crunched cold. "No. Don't make her . . ."

Bridie grinned, toothy, and tipped up the vial.

Wind shrieked in righteous protest, blowing Rose off balance. But it just whipped the evil bonfire higher. Japheth whispered something. *God help us,* or *the Lord is my shepherd.* Or maybe *fuck you, Rose Harley.* She couldn't hear.

Thick black liquid globbed from the vial's neck, and dribbled into the pipe.

And the spilling water turned to blood.

Fresh, thick, crimson. The magic bubbled and spat, licking the blood with gleeful black flames. And like a writhing, living thing, the liquid sucked itself back into the pipe and rushed downstream, towards the thirsty city.

The bonfire screeched in triumph. Flames billowed, pouring black smoke, and the air lit bright with hungry hellfire that snapped and writhed.

Rose coughed on acid grit. Japheth hissed in pain as the snaky hellthings chewed his skin. He lashed out with heavenspells, but the creatures swarmed over him, flinging him backwards, pinning his limbs to the wall like living shackles of fire.

Fluvium laughed. Fresh power glowed from his body, surrounding him in a howling aura of devilmagic. "Hah-*oooh!*" His exultant yell clanged louder with each echo, an eldritch curse. "Just like turning water into wine, except better. That Jesus dude always did lack imagination. Whaddaya think, Rose? A good joke?"

Bridie splashed her hands into the gushing blood. "I'm hungry," she repeated. "When can we eat?"

You unleashed this, Rose. What price getting this genie back into its bottle? She gripped Japheth's knife tighter. "You've got your angel, Fluvium. Now give me Bridie."

Fiery hellcreatures squirmed over Japheth's body. It had to hurt like a motherfucker, but he just shook his head, and gave her a weary *told-you-so* smile.

Fluvium grinned.

Rose tensed, her heart pumping . . . and Fluvium struck, serpentine.

Not for Japheth. For her.

His iron grip chomped around her wrist. She struggled, but her heart sank into chilly depths of despair. Ever since that first night, he'd been too strong for her.

"Sit the fuck down," he ordered, and threw her onto the floor.

Her injured leg thumped sickly. She tried to scramble up, but her limbs were pinned to the floor, sticky black hellspells like an evil spider's web.

And Fluvium strode up to Japheth, and smiled. "Enough screwing around, heavenshit. Let's get it on."

Crazily, Japheth laughed.

He couldn't remember ever screwing up quite this badly. Getting Tainted? That was nothing. *Michael's gonna tear my skin off, layer by layer. I'll bleed slowly to death, and miss the end of the world. Bummer.*

"Bring it on." He growled, and spat a heavencurse, the foulest he could muster.

A flameball exploded in Fluvium's face. His skin dripped, flesh melting over bone . . . but he just snarled, and shook himself, and his skin repaired with a black-smoked hiss.

"Don't do that," he snapped. "It's not nice."

Japheth strained his burning muscles, trying to rip his living shackles free. No use. Ragespells, they were, and they fed on his own deep-seated anger. Heaven knew, he had enough to feed an army.

He tried to flash weapons, sword, dagger, another ball of heavenspell. But the fiery demon serpents just chewed up his magic and spat it out in bleeding shards.

Pain sheeted, blinding him. *Holy Jesus. Let it flow, keep it in.* He couldn't give them the advantage of his weakness.

But Rose lay bruised and broken, stuck to the floor with black webs. It took all he had not to swallow that stinking ragefire, succumb to temptation and rip Fluvium's head off with his teeth.

The roaring flames and fighting hellspells deafened him. Blood gurgled in the pipes, drawn deep underground, the pressure forcing the cursed liquid faster and faster.

And little Bridie just smiled.

"Pay attention!" Fluvium backhanded him across the jaw. "I'm disappointed in you, Tainted. All you had to do was fuck her, and she would've taken care of the rest! A bite here, a suck there and you're done. Hell of a way to go out, let me tell you.

Did you know she can do the splits? And those titties . . ." He fanned himself. "Hoo boy. Four words, my friend: *fuck of the century.*"

Japheth snapped at his face, missing by inches. "Don't talk about her like that, scumlicker. Don't even dirty her name with your hell-rotted tongue."

"Oh, I've dirtied more than that." Fluvium twirled a lock of flaming purple hair. "You could have been there. But no, you had to do it the hard way. Fucking angels. Always a pain in my ass." He yanked Japheth's chin up. "Put him on his knees," he ordered.

Burning spells dug molten spikes into his limbs, tearing at his joints until he relented and sank to his knees. Dizzy black stars flashed in his eyes. Sweet Jesus, he was going to pass out. The pain was like nothing he'd known . . .

"Leave him be!" Rose struggled against her ethereal bonds. "You got what you wanted. Just kill us and get it over w—ukh!"

An ashcloud hit her in the face, choking her silent.

Fluvium licked Japheth's cheekbone, gloating. "I think I like you like this. Do you beg, angel? Do you plead for your miserable life?"

"Not bloody likely."

"They all say that. They're all wrong. Tell me, when Michael cast you down, did you scream for mercy?"

A bitter spark of amusement pierced the pain. Oh, he'd screamed, all right. But not for mercy.

Across the room, Bridie clapped her bloody hands. "Can we, Daddy? Can we make him?"

"Soon, darling," Fluvium murmured. "Be patient. Because I can be, angel. I can be very patient indeed."

Japheth gritted bleeding teeth. Too much to hope that Fluvium would simply kill him. And it already hurt so much he could barely breathe.

But torture was good. Pain, he could handle. Easier than the bewildered agony in his heart.

The world was ending. The vampire curse would consume the city. And all he could think about was the bleeding woman on the floor.

Clarity dazzled him like sunshine. Would he truly let them all die to save her?

In a heartbeat.

Everything he'd feared about himself was true. And he didn't give a damn.

"Try me," he spat. "I'll die before I ask you for anything."

"They all say that, too!" Fluvium hopped on one foot, delighted, but then he frowned. "Actually, no. Most of them say *oh, God, yes!* or *harder!* or *don't stop, please, don't stop!* But that's before we get to the good part. You remember, don't you, Rose?"

"Screw you," Rose spluttered. "Hope your dick rots off."

Evil images shimmered of Rose, pinned to the bed, choking on Fluvium's blood . . . "Try that with me and you'll die in pieces," Japheth hissed.

Fluvium laughed, his teeth smoking. "Never mind, angel. You're not my type. All those feathers make me sneeze. And besides"—he planted a stinging kiss on Japheth's lips—"I've already figured out your weakness, lover boy. Want to test it?"

And he bared cruel barbed teeth, and slashed them into his own wrist.

Black blood dribbled over his hand, thick with corruption, and with a gloating grin, he held the wound over Japheth's face.

Blood dripped, and soaked his cheek, and burned.

God, it was disgusting. The stink sickened him. His skin melted, bubbled, desperately healing itself and burning again. He fought to escape, to avert his face. But the demon's spells twined smoky fingers of malice in his hair, rooting him to the spot.

Fluvium smeared his bloody wrist against Japheth's lips. He cocked his silver six-gun with his other thumb, and jammed the barrel up under the angel's chin. "Drink it, angel. You know you want to."

Rose yelled again, struggling furiously. "Japheth, for God's sake. Spit it out!"

Dizzy, Japheth clamped his lips tight. They blistered, crackling. Christ, this was worse than the fountain. Worse than any other torture Fluvium's sick imagination could invent.

Because he knew what was coming.

And Fluvium knew it, too. He could see the triumphant fire in the demon's eyes, the sexual pleasure flexing his muscles tight. The Prince of Thirst delighted in pain.

But he delighted in damnation more.

"Say it, angel," Fluvium's smile glittered, exultant. His pulse beat an evil rhythm against Japheth's lips. "Beg for my blood. Implore me to own your miserable soul. Or I swear on Satan's sweet vengeance, I'll eat both of your little bitch-whores right before your eyes, and drag them with me to hell."

The blood ate into Japheth's face. His lungs howled for air. The pain minced his reason . . .

But shining truth blazed in his heart. *It's over. The Sign is done. You lose. Simple choice, Jae. Let Rose die.*

Or let her live.

Baleful heavenflame howled through his veins. Everything he'd been created for screamed at him to stop. *You're ours. You can't. You won't . . .*

Icy determination set like diamonds, unbreakable. *You cast me out, remember? You made me what I am. I can. And I will.*

Wrath shredded his veins, a swift and terrible threat. *Do this, and you'll never come back.*

The awful truth stabbed his heart like a demon's sword, and fourteen hundred years of poisoned self-hatred gushed out to drown him.

I don't care.

I don't belong there. I don't want to go back. Not now. Not ever.

Dreamy, he let his jaw relax. Softened his aching mouth. Licked his blood-soaked lips.

The acid stung his tongue, liquid fire. Coppery air rushed into his lungs, caustic with hellflame. It tasted good.

It tasted like freedom.

And he shut away the distant screaming in his heart—easy,

after so many years of frosty denial—and speared Fluvium on a ghastly grin.

"Please," he gasped. "I beg you. I want your blood. Give it to me."

And Fluvium laughed, an awful black chuckle straight from the pit, and let the blood spill.

Hellflame filled his mouth, dark and sweet, hunger and desire and passion and everything he'd spent his life pretending he didn't feel. Violet flame licked his wings, and his feathers sparkled electric. His muscles burned with unholy power. Already, the glory in his blood faded, screaming, eaten alive by some blacker, more beautiful magic.

Japheth shuddered, exultant. Light erupted, a shimmering ultraviolet shockwave, echoing in the iron room like a hell-forged bell. It felt right. It felt . . . good.

He gulped, meaty blood spilling down his chin, and drank.

And drank.

And drank some more.

CHAPTER 37

Jadzia shuddered, sweating cold, and gazed down upon hell.

Dead monks littered the prayer room floor. Limbs spread-eagled, splintered bones thrusting through flesh. Guts torn open, ribs split apart to expose torn hearts. Weapons scattered, here a crossbow, there the melted remains of a sword.

They'd fought. It hadn't mattered.

And now hundreds of hungry fearwraiths shrieked and feasted on the corpses, their ghostly bodies swelling fat like leeches.

Jadzia clutched the stone balustrade, sick. In the centre, a space had been cleared, the bodies piled carelessly aside. A makeshift altar, painted on the floor in blood. A fire roaring at one end, belching black smoke, the foul stench of burning flesh. Four devil-sharp iron spikes, driven deep into the stone floor. Wicked hellflame licked the metal white-hot. And crucified, on her back with limbs stretched in an evil four-pointed cross, lay Salome, the Guardian.

Still alive.

Naked, the spikes piercing wrist and ankle. Stretched beyond endurance. Her silver-white hair was filthy. Blood oozed from her wounds, burning, and her angelic flesh tried to heal, but the hell-spelled spikes tore it afresh, over and over. Her silver wings had been ripped off, and poisoned so they wouldn't grow back. Her body sweated green with infected agony.

Salome was beyond screaming. She just whimpered, and the sound scraped Jaz's heart raw.

Beside her, on the stone, sat the holy vial. Still full, glowing bright with glorious wrath.

And dancing around her, a giggling dervish, the demon, Luuceat.

A fat little wart of a man, maybe three feet high. His greasy bald head shone in the firelight. He wore no clothes. He'd rolled in Salome's blood at some point, and it dripped from his plump body in clots. He held one severed wing, admiring its dying glimmer, and plucked the feathers off one by one with fat fingers. They burst into flame, and he tossed them aloft, watching them fall like shooting stars and go out.

"So pretty," he hummed. His sing-song voice grated in Jaz's ears. "Just a little longer, pretty angel. The time will soon be right. You'll soon burn. Save up a nice big scream, won't you? Luuceat likes it when angels scream."

Jadzia shuddered, chilled to the core. Were demons all like this? Did Shax do stuff like this for fun, when he wasn't bringing her flowers and kissing her hair? Was her sweet, shy demon a vile torturer?

Beside her, Michael crouched in midnight-blue shadow, and grinned. "Plan worked out well, don't you think?"

Jadzia nodded faintly. Sweat itched inside her armor. The vial was full. The Guardian still alive. She supposed that was a success. But . . .

Michael's ice-blue hair glittered in the dark like broken diamonds. "Don't fret. It'll soon be over."

"I hope so."

A flicker of disapproval that stung her breath. "Trust me," he said smoothly. "I didn't bring you here by accident, girl. I like you. You've done good work. Perhaps you've made up for your sins, hmm? Just stay with me on this one, and we can talk about it. Do you trust me, Jadzia?"

"Yes." She hoped it didn't sound too breathless. *Did he just promise . . . ?* No. Too much to hope for. She'd only been Tainted a hundred and fifty years. The others had served much longer. Much harder . . .

And the others aren't dating a demon. If he finds out about that . . .

Her chin firmed. Michael wouldn't find out. She was careful. And she feared more that Dash and Lune and the others would find out. Especially Dashiel. He'd picked her up when she was broken, eased her pain, taught her to survive in a world where glory was a whim and the sky just blackish silence. She wanted Dash's good opinion more than anything.

Anyway, she and Shax weren't *dating*. Right? They were just . . . talking. Meeting in secret. Stealing forbidden kisses on moonlit beaches.

They didn't count, those dark and breathless things they did in her dreams.

She forced a smile, but her skin burned, like she was naked, exposed before her archangel with everything on show. She'd kissed Shax, just a few short hours ago. Let him stroke her to breathless desire. Surely, Michael could smell it on her. See the guilt in her eyes, taste the sweet demon kisses on her breath. Hear her wild pounding heart . . .

But Michael just smiled, raw. "Good." And he clenched one massive fist, and whispered to heaven.

Holy fire erupted, blinding, and poured down into the chamber like silver-blue lava. The air sang with holy vengeance. The feasting wraiths screamed and exploded. The fire consumed them, roaring, raging over the dead monks until nothing remained but stink and smoke and black-scorched stone.

And then, in a breath, the fire snuffed out. Silent. Leaving the demon and his crucified angel, and the vial.

Jadzia gasped. She'd seen Michael's tricks before. Of course she had. Didn't make them any less cool.

Michael jumped, a swirl of glacial wings. Wind buffeted. The demon prince cursed, and shielded his beady eyes. The archangel landed, and the stone floor quaked and shattered beneath him. "Luuceat, I presume. I don't think I need an introduction."

Jadzia swooped down, dizzy, landing a few feet behind her archangel. Blue fire glimmered in his broad feathers. He towered over Luuceat, more than twice the demon prince's height. Probably twice the fat little bastard's weight, too.

She wasn't needed here. Michael was going to wipe the floor with this sniveling slimehead. And the fourth vial would be theirs.

Does that seem too easy?

Luuceat smiled, lickerish. His beady black eyes gleamed, and he made a fulsome bow. "Ah. At last. Luuceat's been waiting for you. Azaroth told him you'd come."

Jadzia shivered. Great. Another megalomaniac moron who talked about himself in the third person. *Just die, scumbag, and we can all go home.*

Before you lay eyes on me and tell everyone I'm a traitor.

She shuddered. Luuceat was a demon, with a demon's snide intuition. Surely, he could see . . .

Michael flashed his sword, a blinding blue crackle of thunder. "Nice crucifixion," he remarked. "Stylish. Only that's my angel you're plucking, shitface, and I don't recall you asking my permission."

Sparks flickered between Luuceat's sweat-shiny palms. An ugly grin split his fat face. "Come get her, then." He giggled, and exploded into towering scarlet flame.

It roared, the column of fire the demon prince had made. Black smoke billowed, and the red inferno shaped itself into a human figure, tall and long limbed, flames peeling in ribbons as it moved. Its fiery feet hissed on the blackened stones, leaving long glowing footprints the size of platters.

And where the fire walked, it *spread.*

Two, four, seven, twelve Luuceats sprang alive, ringing poor crucified Salome and her vial in a fiery guard. Jadzia stared, her wits dazzled blind. Which was the original? Which was real?

The tall, lanky fire demons roared as one, an ugly harmony. Gouts of flame poured from their mouths.

The heat seared Jadzia's cheeks, blew her braided hair back. She flashed her sword, grim. Didn't know which one was real? She'd just have to kill them all.

Michael laughed, and ice crystals hit the shimmering hot air and melted. His muscles swelled, his blade sprang bright with sky-blue wrath. "Sweet trick, demon," he snarled, and crouched, his diamond wings flashing. "Now I get to kill you over and over again."

And Jadzia leapt into the fight.

CHAPTER 38

Pinned to the metal floor, Rose screamed. Wordless, insensible, horror, crackling like ice crystals in her heart.

Her precious angel was drinking Fluvium's blood. And already the curse was eating him.

His aura glared, not honest angelic blue but a poisoned purple glow that scorched her eyes. His wings rippled with violet fire. Black lightning crackled from his feathers, forking from floor to ceiling. The shock clanged through her bones, a powerful clap of thunder.

And still, he drank more. Clawed at the demon's arm. Sucked the blood deep.

Fluvium staggered back, ripping his bleeding wrist from Japheth's grip. "Holy motherfucker," he gasped, "you meant it!"

Rose's thoughts whirled. He'd expected Japheth to let her die. To save his angelic soul at all costs . . .

"Take it back," she yelled, desperate. "I won't let him. Take it back!"

But Fluvium just laughed, shrill, mad.

And Bridie laughed, too. "Look, Auntie Rosie. Pretty magic!"

The angel—or whatever he now was—crouched on all fours, growling. He clawed at the floor, powerful muscles shaking. Strings of blood drooled from beneath the tangled hair hiding his face. His wings juddered, and as she watched, that gorgeous glimmering gold bled out, replaced with luminescent purple that shimmered in dark rainbows.

The angel's mark on Rose's forehead sizzled, and smoked, and healed over.

Japheth raised his head. His eyes burned, unholy, no longer emerald green but wild with ultraviolet rage. Hideously, he laughed, and wickedly curved teeth erupted from his gums. "Surprise," he growled. "I win."

The writhing hellspells around him blazed in scarlet delight, and with a satisfied snarl, he broke free. He was one of their own. They'd let him go.

And he dived for her, and swept her into a fiery feathered embrace.

She struggled, blind. The hellspells that trapped her on the floor cringed, and dissolved under his touch. He wrapped her in his powerful arms. His skin smelled of fire. She swooned against his metal-clad chest. His feathers caressed her like perfumed velvet. And the wonderful, terrible heat of his curse called to her, seductive, irresistible. His pulse thundered deep in her ears, vibrating through her, awakening dark desire.

"Peace, Rose Harley," he whispered. "I've got you."

Her heart bled, aching. So much like himself, yet . . .

He thrust his hand out, hissing a few sibilant syllables. Violet fire crackled from his palm, and from the bloodstained floor, his weapons vanished in a sting of scarlet sparks.

Fluvium shot at him, a gun in each hand. Bullets whistled, clanging harmlessly on the walls. He cursed, flung his empty guns away, and sprang with a poisoned scream, conjuring his serrated demonblade.

Rose screamed. Japheth hugged her tighter, whispering dark words, and the world vanished in sparkling purple ash.

* * *

Dazzling red moonlight swirled. Wind screamed, scratching at Rose's skin, plastering her hair back. Burning claws pierced her guts. Surely, she was falling into hell . . .

Glass exploded, stinging her face, and a wooden floor thumped under her boots.

She staggered in Japheth's embrace. His apartment, moonlight glaring through the shattered window. Angelic charms crackled white lightning over the glass. Japheth hissed at them, fangs gleaming, and they dissolved to white smoke, and vanished.

She shoved him away, catching her breath. "What the fuck did you do?"

"Isn't it obvious?" He spread shimmering violet wings. Moonlight danced over him, lovingly, painting him in crimson shadows. So beautiful . . .

"You stupid bastard." She kicked the wooden sofa table, furious. It skittered across the floor, and she picked it up and hurled it at him, not caring what she hit.

He swept it away with one wing. It hit the wall and clattered to the floorboards. "We're alive, aren't we?"

She yanked viciously at her knotted hair. God, she wanted to tear it all out and strangle him with it. "You're cursed, angel! Don't you get that? What happened to your precious forgiveness?"

"There is no forgiveness!" He grabbed her arm to make her stop.

She shook him off.

He grabbed her again, both wrists this time. "You were right." A dizzy, defeated smile. "Heaven doesn't care. No one cares, Rose Harley. The world's ending. We're alone. There's only us."

"No!" She twisted free, and hit him, right across his beautiful face.

He didn't flinch. Just shoved her backwards. "You and me, Rose. What should we do about that?"

She hit him again. He pushed her backwards again. She stumbled, and righted herself, and then her back thudded into the wall and he grabbed her chin and assaulted her mouth with his.

His teeth collided with hers. Hot, hard, insistent, like he didn't give a damn. She tasted blood, the delicious dark fruity flavor of the curse . . . Desire flashed over her like sunburn. She wanted to drink him, swallow him, sink her teeth into his sweet flesh and suck him into her at last . . . and now, there was nothing to keep them apart.

Enraged, she swung at him again, and landed a fistful of feathers. So silky and crisp and hot. She yanked them, hard.

He growled, muscles swelling all over. He was so big, his body tense and burning against hers. His strange dark-light aura licked over her, a hot velvet tongue. *I did this!* The last scrap of her reason howled, broken. *He's cursed because of me. It's all my fault . . .*

"You can't," she whispered.

"I can." He trapped her against the wall, one hand either side of her head. His metal-clad chest crushed her, a dangerous thrill that fired her blood wild. "I made my choice. I'll live with it. And for once in my life . . ." He brushed a hot kiss over the corner of her mouth, and warm tingles spread down her neck, into her breasts, all the way to her fingertips.

God, he was so hard all over, muscles and metal. So brutally male. Her breasts ached for his mouth, and she couldn't help but arch her throat, offering. "Mmm?"

He teased his lips over her throbbing vein, just a tiny sting of teeth, and heat spiraled inside her, exquisite hunger for more. "For once in my life, Rose Harley," he whispered, "I'm going to take what I want."

CHAPTER 39

Her insides melted, aching with cruel desire. It was mad. It was stupid. The world was ending, Bridie was a prisoner, Fluvium would curse everyone in Babylon before the night was through . . . but rage and desperate guilt ravaged her blood like fiery liquid vengeance and all she could think about was sensation, ecstasy, sweet oblivion . . .

She grabbed two fistfuls of feathers, and yanked him closer. "Me first," she snapped, and ambushed his mouth with hers.

Her lips bruised. She didn't care. She kissed him harder, hungrier. He tasted of fire and blood. His scent drugged her, hot male skin and the rich flesh-fire of the demon's curse. Ash stung her nose. She buried her fingers deep in his feathers, so crisp and warm. She wanted them all over her, stroking her naked skin, teasing her nipples, brushing between her legs . . .

She groaned as he responded, tongues mingling, fighting, the sharp sting of his teeth drawing blood. He sucked on her tongue, hard. Sweet Jesus, that felt good. Faintness washed her thin. Already, he attacked her bare midriff with hungry hands. His thumbs stroked her ribs, slipping under her knotted t-shirt to search for her breast.

She arched, wrapping one thigh around his hip, and he growled and tore her t-shirt in two.

The warm air kissed her bared skin, a fevered dream. God, she wanted him to touch her. His mouth scorched her throat. He tortured her straining nipples with his thumbs. Pinched them, cruel and sweet. She groaned at the sting, that delicious pleasure-pain, just what she needed.

Just what she craved. And when he ripped her thin lace bra aside and suckled her nipple deep into his mouth, she gasped and writhed and delirium swallowed her whole. *There's no heaven. No forgiveness. There's only us . . .*

Crimson flame flashed, engulfing her in bitter ash . . . and her back thumped into something soft and firm. A quilt. His bed, the soft down lights shimmering blue.

He crouched over her, wings flared, aglow with strange dark fire. She grabbed his fiery hair and pulled him down to her breasts. His kisses tortured her, his tongue drawing her hard into his mouth. God, she wanted him inside her. He was already undoing her jeans. She raked hungry nails over his hips, drawing blood. The smell of it only fired her desire hotter. She fumbled in haste for his buttons. His cock sprang into her hands. She gasped at the feel of him, so smooth and iron hard . . .

She stroked him, squeezing, and he growled and nipped at her. Blood trickled between her breasts, hot and stinging. He licked it up, a swathe of shuddering delight. "There's only us, Rose. I want to swallow you. Be with me."

"Yes." Her sex ached hard, tight, wet. She wanted to swallow *him*, take him inside her any way she could before this fragile magic broke . . .

He yanked her jeans down her thighs. The fabric caught on her boots, and with a grunt of frustration he tore those off, too. He'd probably broken her laces. She didn't care. Urgently, she wrapped him in one naked leg, flexing her hips to feel him. He thrust a hand between them, caressing her swollen wet flesh. God, she couldn't breathe. She still had her panties on. Damn, clothes were such a nuisance. She struggled with them, fingers knotting. The fabric tore. Whatever. She dragged the ruined satin away, and at last, her slick heat connected with his hot hard flesh.

Oh, fuck. He was only rubbing against her, and it felt . . . She squirmed, desperate. Tension already throbbed deep within her, a taut wire ready to snap. It'd be a miracle if she lasted more than a few seconds . . . Bracing himself on flaming violet wings—fuck, he could do this with no hands—he pulled her legs around him and filled her with a single hard thrust.

Oh, my God. So deep. So hot. She arched into him, straining for him, locking her legs around his smooth hips. He eased back, and drove deeper, and gave a half groan, half wicked laugh. "Rose Harley. So perfect." And he flexed powerful thighs, and rocked back onto his knees, taking her with him.

She landed astride him, and he plunged deeper, hotter, right to her very core . . . Hell, yeah. Hot dizziness washed over her. His cock was fucking perfect. Her female muscles rippled around him in delight, already tightening . . . His wings wrapped her in eerie dark flame, and it sank into her skin, glorious warmth tingling deep.

She gripped his shoulders, lifting herself, sliding back down. He slid his big hands on her hips, helping her ride him, and she closed her eyes, breathing in the scent of his crisp hair, drugging herself senseless on his glorious hot flavor . . .

"Look at me." Breathless, shaking. Like he didn't have much time.

"No." She buried her face in his shoulder. She didn't want to look. Didn't want to remember what she'd done to him . . .

"Rose . . ."

"Don't talk." Her nipples brushed his metal-clad chest as she worked him inside her. She shuddered, tension building swiftly. He felt so raw. So wild, guiltless, free . . . and on the third thrust, her pleasure exploded.

She cried out, dizziness and exultation. Her flesh pulsed around him, an explosion of tension and rage and sweet desire. He kissed her, tasting her tongue, crushing her against him. . . and then he groaned, deep and primal, and sank his cursed teeth into her shoulder.

Blood spilled warm, and he licked at it. *Oh, yeah.* She moaned, helpless, insane with dark delight. And then he *sucked.* Her blood boiled, hot and cold at the same time, flow-

ing, pulsing, loving. Her pulse sang, delirious rhythm. That
glorious pressure, pulling like a burning tide, surrendering . . .
He swallowed, and shuddered, and with one more, impossibly
deep thrust, he growled and spilled himself into her. She felt
it, heat pulsing, his cock pumping inside her, and it felt so
good . . .

It ambushed her, hot on the tail of her first orgasm, so
intense her vision shorted out. It soaked her, twisted her,
wrung her out in throbbing shockwaves. She rode it, gasping,
pain and pleasure mingling in sweet delirium.

Holy fuck-a-duckling. She fought faintness, trying to catch
her breath. He eased his sharp teeth from her flesh, licking her
softly. His tongue felt so good on that bite. She wanted him to
delve it deeper, ease himself inside her torn flesh, swallow
her . . .

He crushed her close, folding her in his strong arms. His
lips brushed bleeding and raw on hers. Sweet kisses, breathless, hearts pounding in unison. "More," he whispered.

And she wanted more. His flesh still pulsed inside her, the
sweet rhythm of shared blood still pumping pleasure through
her body. She didn't want to move. Not now. Not ever.

Stupid tears burned behind her eyelids, and she cursed and
fought them back. *Jesus, don't cry* . . .

But he just kissed her tears away, impossibly gentle, and
her heart overflowed. His feathers caressed her spine, slid
along her naked flank, and he eased his hand between her legs
to find her wet. She flinched in anticipation. Surely, she
couldn't take more. But when he found her clit, and slowly
stroked it, gentle pleasure bloomed inside her all over again.

"Oh . . ." She arched into his hand, dizzy. His cock was still
inside her, and her flesh rippled softly around him, squeezing,
clenching . . . God, she couldn't come again . . .

Violet strangeness gleamed in his eyes. He smiled, secret,
so beautiful it hurt. "More."

She shuddered, close to that delicious edge. Oh, yes, she
wanted more. Wanted to taste him all over, bury her face in his
feathers, get drunk on the wine-dark fragrance of his hair.
Slide his cock between her lips, make him moan, lick the vein
in his thigh until it pulsed hard against her lips, and then bite

down and let the blood spill, into her mouth, over her face, her breasts. Spread her legs and let him taste her there, lick her, suck her clit until she broke apart and then lie down beneath him and have him fuck her to oblivion.

But discomfort wormed under her skin. She'd done this to him. Her precious angel had lost his faith. They were together only because she'd let him fall . . .

What the hell did it matter? After what she'd endured, she deserved some indulgence. *There's no heaven. There's only us* . . .

Fierce anger fired her blood hotter. She eased herself against his fingers, rubbing, drawing ever closer. He was still half-hard, and the feel of him inside her stroked her to selfish pleasure. God, he felt so good . . .

But her ears clanged, the evil discord of *wrongness*. He'd unlocked her shackled conscience, and try as she might, she couldn't lock it up again. *I can't. I shouldn't. It's not right* . . .

Rose shuddered in his arms, and pushed his hand away. "No. Stop it."

"Uh." Japheth barely had sense to understand her. He still couldn't breathe. His pulse still jerked wild, his skin still burning, his flesh still exulting with the insane delight of loving her.

Sweet heaven's grace, he didn't remember it being like this.

Her magnificent scent licking him all over, jasmine and flame and gorgeous woman. Her honey-smooth skin under his palms, the curl of her lashes on her cheek, her breath warm on his lips as she sighed in pleasure, the delicious throb of her hot slick flesh on his. She'd been so tight as he entered her, such delicious resistance, enfolding him, clamping down on him . . . the taste of her blood, slicking over his tongue, that was . . . and just the feel of her strong, lithe body as she moved, taking her pleasure . . .

His cock stirred within her. Already, fresh blood pumped there. He wanted to take her again, push her onto her back and pin her down and take his sweet time in making her scream . . .

But he gulped in a cold breath, and let her push his hand away. "What? What did I do?"

"Nothing." She scrambled back, off him, dark eyes sparkling wild. "Everything. We can't do this. It's not right."

His heart skipped. Hell, she was beautiful, those long naked legs, taut stomach, smooth breasts, the nipples still hard and pink from his mouth. Her tangled hair shone. She had a tiny brown freckle on her belly, just below her navel. He wanted to kiss it. Blood trickled down her shoulder, over one breast. His teeth marks glistened crimson where he'd bitten her, and the thought of *that* was so fucking sexy he wanted to dive on top of her and take her all over again . . .

"It feels right, Rose Harley. That's all I care about."

"Don't say that." She was crying now, tears shimmering on her lashes. She climbed off the bed, searching for her clothes. She wouldn't look at him. Like she was pretending he wasn't there.

His heart tore raw. "But—"

"It's all right, don't you see?" Her panties were ripped—had he done that?—and she tossed them aside and fumbled her naked legs into her jeans. "It's not too late for you. It was my fault, what we just did. I seduced you. You're not to blame . . ."

"Blame?" He laughed, breathless. "Rose—"

"Don't you see?" She tugged on a fresh t-shirt. Now, she did look up, and her eyes blazed, desperate with denial. "It wasn't your fault. They'll forgive you. Everything will be like it was. You'll see."

He knew that look. He'd worn it himself enough times. "Rose, look at me."

She turned away, fumbling with her hair.

He flitted up, and swiftly made himself decent. His skin still smelled of her, rich and feminine. A trickle of her blood still painted his breastplate. He hadn't had the patience to get naked. He'd needed to have her. Needed to take what he wanted at last. He wasn't sorry, except for the not-naked part. To feel her rough dark hair sliding over his chest, her mouth on his skin . . .

He tugged her elbow, forcing her to face him. His deep

purple glow flowed over her, a dark caress. He could already taste her kiss, her sighs, her luscious mouth . . .

"Look at me," he repeated softly. "It's done. I can't go back. I don't *want* to go back."

"Yes, you do!" Tears fired her eyes. "It's all you care about. Don't let me ruin that! I'm not worth it."

"You *are* worth it." He grabbed her hand, kissed it. It felt cold under his lips. She was shaking. "I drank a demon's blood, Rose. Begged him to curse me, and got off on it when it happened. It felt fucking fantastic. That's a wicked, evil, perverted thing to do and they'll never, ever forgive me so long as eternity lasts."

Rose trembled. "Let me go, Japheth. Please . . ."

He pulled her closer, tilted her chin up with his thumb. "I don't care what they think anymore. I care what you think. I've cared about nothing else since the moment we met."

"Stop it."

"No. I won't." Violet rage spilled over him, howling against everything that had ever kept them apart. But it wasn't frigid anger. It was hot, burning, scarlet and gold with hellfire.

Evil delight licked in his blood. He didn't hesitate. He just let the truth spill out, wild and unfettered and so damn beautiful he wanted to die. *The truth will make you free . . .*

"I crave you, Rose Harley. I think about you every moment of every day—"

"Japheth—"

"Shh." He touched his finger to her lips. "I'm not finished. Your every word mesmerizes me. I get dizzy just thinking about your eyes. I walk around drenched in your scent and the memory of your touch, and I've nearly gotten myself killed a dozen times because I'm too busy thinking about how I can persuade you to touch me again. And now that I've loved you—"

His throat parched, a driving thirst that nearly undid him. He wanted to tilt her head back, bare that delicate throat . . . "Now that I've been inside you, and taken you inside me? You are fucking *insane* if you think I'll let you just walk away."

* * *

Rose stared, and her heart ripped raw.

So beautiful, this hell-cursed angel. His wings glowed violet, his hair rippling azure and scarlet like sunset sky. Indigo lightning crackled between his fingers, and he stared at her with fiery eyes, bleeding out with rage and desire . . .

"No," she stammered. "This isn't happening. You can't just . . ."

"I can. I will. Be with me, Rose, and let's watch the world burn."

"Stop it!" Her voice split raw. "Stop pretending you don't believe."

"Why?" He stroked her cheek, warm. "They don't believe in me. I should've realized that a long time ago."

"But . . . you said we could all be forgiven. It has to be true! Or . . ." Her voice choked. *Or Bridie's in hell forever. And I left her there.*

"I lied." Japheth's gaze burned black. "I'm sorry. I didn't mean to. But I couldn't see the truth. It's all just a game. There is no forgiveness, Rose. Damnation is forever." He leaned closer, his gaze drifting down to her mouth. "So let's be damned together, if that's what they want."

She flailed, fighting him off. "Stop it. I won't listen . . ."

He dropped to one knee, and captured one of her hands. His eyes blazed so bright, so candid. She couldn't look away. "I've never been in love, Rose. I thought, once . . . but that was just . . ." His face colored. "Well, it doesn't matter. But I think . . ." He swallowed. "I think I'm—"

"Don't you dare!" She hit him. "Don't you *dare* put this onto me, you bastard. You think you're in love with me? After one fuck? That is so damn pathetic, I don't have the words."

The flame in his eyes drained silver. He touched his bleeding mouth, and in an ugly sparkle of bitter-stinking ash, it healed over. "Is that what you call everything we've been through together?"

Guilt tore her to shreds. The sight of his hellmagic made her cringe. He'd been so pure. Now, she'd spoiled him.

"Barely," she spat. "Over kind of quickly, wasn't it? I hope for your sake you're just out of practice."

"Rose—"

"Shut up. Just shut up." She choked on acid sobs. *You betrayed me, angel!* she wanted to howl. *You said we could be forgiven and I believed you. And now we're both damned forever* . . .

Her heart screamed, and shrank away. She couldn't look at him anymore. Not at the cursed monster she'd made of him. It was too much for her broken soul to bear.

"You think you love me?" she demanded, shaking. "You're so goddamn stupid it's funny. I win, don't you see? Fluvium and me? This was all part of our plan."

"That's not true." But his knuckles whitened.

"You think? We wanted your soul, and you gave it to us. Hell, you *begged* us to take it. Watching you drink that blood? Better than sex. Certainly a whole lot better than fucking *you*."

He didn't speak. Just stared, his beautiful mouth trembling.

Her courage wilted. She wanted to hold him, kiss him, say she was sorry. Lie down with him and make breathless, tearful love until the world died.

But it was too late. "Hope you had fun, angel," she jeered. "Time to go back to my master. I'll see you in hell."

And she whirled, tears spraying hot, and fled.

CHAPTER 40

Japheth howled, and flashed out.

Hellfire darkness drowned him. He hadn't flashed, of course, no, this was hellmagic, he'd dissolved to stinking black ash, swirling on the breeze in a caustic cloud, and he flexed and snapped back into corporeal form in mid-air.

High over Babylon, stars glaring impossibly bright. City lights spun and whirled, insane. He thrashed his wings, spilling angry purple fire, and he flung himself skywards and screamed.

It's not true. She didn't. She just . . .

Just what?

If it isn't true, why did she say it, Jae? She's a vampire. Why would she come to your bed and then . . .

Stars wheeled in his eyes, and he laughed, black and bitter like corpseflesh.

He was so fucking stupid.

To think she'd love him. To think that being with Rose would make this horrid, wicked, glorious damnation worthwhile.

He'd shown her his heart. And she'd seen him for what he really was, and given him what he deserved.

"You let me do this!" Hot wind ripped the shrieking words from his lips. Something wet hit him in the face. His own tears, hot and bloody. "I begged you for help and you gave me nothing. You *made* me what I am!"

But only ugly laughter resounded in his heart.

You don't get to blame heaven for your weakness.

Leaden truth dragged him under, and he choked, drowning. He'd done this. He'd drunk that demon's soul-burning blood to save a woman. And she'd turned on him.

Michael would laugh his shiny blue ass off.

His boots thudded into hot gravel. Dust stung his nose, clumped in his sweaty hair. He opened his eyes. A crater, gray and desolate. Charcoal coated the ruined skeletons of buildings. A broken subway entrance teemed with a pile of rats. Overhead, a helicopter thumped, searchlights slicing left and right. Harlem, aprés firebomb. Charming.

A stray dog cowered against a broken brick wall. Its starving ribs poked out like fingers. It limped on the stump of one chewed-off foreleg, and snarled at him, white foam dripping. Japheth hissed back, and the dog burst into flame.

That was new.

He laughed, hollow, and the ground cracked and trembled beneath him. He knelt, rubbed his hands in the dirt. The dog—or some other animal—had left its droppings there. The grit stung his palms, invigorating. He dug it under his nails. Wiped it in his hair. It felt real. Earthly.

Not some sugar-coated illusion, forever out of his reach.

A corpse sprawled in the crater beside him, half-decomposed. From its grinning teeth hung shreds of dried flesh. He stared, ugly fascination warming his blood. He wanted to lie down beside it. Embrace it. Kiss its cracked cheek, feel the cold caress of its dead bones . . .

His phone shrilled.

He dug it out, stared dully at the screen. Dashiel was calling. That was nice. He swiped Reject, and the ringtone echoed to silence.

A rabid chuckle infected the emptiness. "Good move. Wouldn't wanna talk to him either, if I were you."

Japheth whirled on all fours, snarling.

Zuul sat on the broken brick wall, swinging his skinny legs. He whistled, appreciative. "Well, look at you, Blondie. Love the new color! Maybe I get what Michael sees in you, after all. Will you be my girlfriend?"

He'd cleaned himself up since Bethesda, put on fresh leather armor, washed the blood from his long crimson hair. Pity. Japheth would have enjoyed licking it from his twitching corpse.

He growled, vicious at the interruption. "Let me be, demon. I'll go to hell my own way."

Zuul jumped down, dusting his long hands clean. His pointy nose twitched, amused. "All of us do, my friend. Ha ha! You mean you only just figured that out?"

"Is there a point, or are you just here to piss me off?"

A sly shrug. "Well, I *had* planned to wind you up about your vampire slut, see? Until you tried to tear my head off with your bare hands, and I could stab you through the heart?" Zuul conjured a long curved sword in a rain of silver-black ash, and demonstrated on empty air, finishing with a giggling dance step. "But I believe I've changed my mind! See, I'm moving up in the world, angel . . ." He scratched his head, frowning. "Or demon. Or whatever the hell you are. Ha ha! Anyway . . . where was I? Oh, yeah. Azaroth has promised me some sweet fucking rewards, Blondie, and I was wondering . . ." Zuul giggled, covering his mouth like a schoolgirl. "I was wondering if, y'know, like, you wanted to be in on it?"

"Not a chance." Japheth flared his wings, violet sparks threatening.

But inside, his heart twisted. *Why the hell not, Jae? What else is there to do?*

"If you say so, hero." Zuul grinned knowingly. "But I'm gonna be the new demon prince, after all! I'll need a sidekick once I get my hands on vial five. You'd make a good sidekick, Blondie. You could call me 'kemosabe.' "

"Aren't you forgetting something?" Japheth crossed his arms, reason battling dark treachery in his heart. "Vial five's no damn good without vial four. You want to fight Michael for it? Good luck with that."

"Ah, yes." Zuul shoved his hands in his pockets, kicking

idly at the dust. "Michael. I guess his little ruse finally paid off, eh?"

"What?" Japheth scowled, and the air shimmered with ash. The little bastard was up to something. He shouldn't take the bait. But . . .

"After he waited fourteen hundred years? Bleeding Christ, I wish I was that patient . . ." Zuul frowned. "Actually, no. I'd have just sliced your arrogant head off right there. But Michael always did things the elegant way—eh!"

Japheth slammed him back into the charred bricks. He conjured his dagger, a spray of purple sparks, and jammed the edge up under the demon's chin. "You weren't there," he growled. "What do you know about it?"

Don't ask, Jae. Don't. Demons lie . . .

But Zuul's skin didn't burn him. It just . . . simmered, warm and fleshy and desperately familiar.

Zuul grinned, crafty. "More than you, it seems. I know your archangel pretty well, Blondie. You learn a lot about a guy when you're wired to his dungeon wall with half your skin flayed off. Did you never think to ask why he Tainted you?"

"I know why!" Japheth dug the blade deeper. Blood steamed out, a thin scarlet line. But his heart skittered, dancing like a dervish to avoid the issue. *Don't ask, Jae. Don't . . .* "Look at me!" he snarled. "Look into my heart, demon, if you're so clever. Michael did. And he saw *this*!"

Zuul erupted into laughter.

Enraged, Japheth kicked for his balls. Zuul snickered, and vanished to ash. But Japheth was ready. He followed, their ashclouds fighting like rabid ghosts, and with a powerful fiery fist, he tore Zuul's writhing body from the hell-dark ether and slammed it backwards into the ground.

The demon choked, winded, his eyes streaming. And Japheth landed atop him, and pinned his skinny wrists to the dirt. "Talk, hellshit," he growled, "or I chew the filthy flesh from your bones strip by strip and eat it for breakfast."

Zuul groaned in ghastly delight, his black eyes rolling in ecstasy. His broken skull bones knitted with an unholy squelch. "You're dumber than I thought," he wheezed. "You really think that Michael looked into your heart and saw an evil blue-burning bastard with a hard-on for blood?"

"What else is there to see?"

"Oh, you sorry son of a whore." Zuul gasped laughter. "Is this what people call *guilt*? This disease you've got? Because you can totally have that shit, I swear on Satan's balls . . ."

Japheth slammed his head harder.

Zuul spat blood into the dust. "Think, dumbass. You'd just won a battle. Slaughtered thousands of my kind. You got accolades from Gabriel and the host and the fucking Lord himself that day, so I heard."

"So what?" Japheth's guts squirmed. He didn't like this. Didn't like the memories. "I refused them. Passed them to Michael, like I should've done."

"Yeah." A giggle. "I bet that went down a treat. Tell me, did Michael actually screw your brains out, or were you always this damn stupid?"

"That's none of your—"

"Do I have to spell it out for you?" Zuul fixed him in a gleeful stare. "You were his finest warrior. You killed a zillion demons. That, he could almost cope with. But you're also young. Beautiful. Dedicated. Honorable, Christ, I'm working up a spew over here. How long since Michael had honor, Blondie?"

"What are you saying?" Japheth's throat withered to a crisp.

"But that isn't enough for you, is it? You're also humble, curse your oily hide. Gabriel's nice to you—which he hasn't been to Michael since who the hell knows when, in case you hadn't noticed—and you shrug it off. The Lord himself pats you on the back and you say, oh, it was nothing, all Michael's doing. But Michael knew the truth." Zuul grinned. "I bet he gritted his fucking teeth so hard they snapped. And what did you do then?"

"I went home . . ." But images of Esther smothered his mind in mud. The beach, that dazzling starry sky . . . "I kissed a girl. So what? It was innocent!"

"You stupid baby." Zuul shook his head sadly. "Kissed a

girl, my ass. You found a friend who *loved* you! What did you expect would happen? Never hear of the tenth commandment?"

Disbelief struck Japheth blind.

Thou shalt not . . .

"You had everything Michael ever wanted." Zuul's hiss smoked cruelly in his ear. "He tried every way he knew to corrupt you, and none of it worked. *You're better than he is!* Why the hell do you think he slammed your face into the dirt?"

Thou shalt not covet!

Black flame roared in his ears. His stomach reeled sick. Dimly, he was aware that Zuul kicked him, flung him away. That he hit the ground, bones rattling. His wings crunched into gravel and bled. And a boot slammed down onto his neck.

His blood raged wild, scattering his senses to the wind. Wrath was a lethal sin. So was lust. Of those, he was guilty as any ugly-souled demon.

But so was envy.

His blackened heart howled. Michael had deceived him. Ruined him. Dragged him into the filth and let him condemn himself. And now, Japheth's soul was lost for good.

Nothing to hold him back.

He fought to see, parting the choking black smoke of his rage. Zuul stood over him, a triumphant smile twisting his lips. The point of his demon blade tickled the vein in Japheth's throat.

"Go on, then," Japheth snarled. "Kill me. I've been dead fourteen hundred years anyway."

But Zuul just dropped Japheth's fiery dagger onto his chest. It clanged on his armor, and bounced into the dust. Zuul crouched, leaning close. "If someone did that to me, Blondie?" Red flames flickered sweet seduction on the demon's tongue. "I'd hunt the lying asshole down and chew his fucking heart out." A dark chuckle. "But maybe that's just me."

And before Japheth could react, Zuul dissolved to ash.

For a black, silent moment, he lay in the dirt, still as death. Then, with an ugly crack, his heart shattered.

Fourteen centuries of bloody anger erupted like a volcano.

Black-light fire engulfed his wings, and a ragged scream
slashed his chest apart.

The sound crackled around the crater, echoing up into the
pre-dawn sky on a fiery shockwave. Flames leaped afresh
from the charred ruins. Jagged lightning knifed the air, and
the ground quaked and split with a crack like thunder. And he
howled, and shrieked, and laughed, until tears ran bloody
down his face, and his nails gouged his skin raw, and no more
sound remained in his exhausted body.

And then he coiled like a serpent into a black ball of stinging ash, and exploded into the dark ether, with vengeance
gnashing hungry fangs in his heart.

Rose scrabbled at the door locks, frantic. No
angelspells had survived. But still they wouldn't open. The
mirrored walls of Japheth's apartment mocked her, throwing
misshapen reflections like cruel monsters. Desperate, she
fumbled, until at last the springs snapped back and she
plunged out into the dim-lit lobby.

The stark walls threatened her. Cold sweat beaded inside
her clothes. She ran to the elevator and slammed her palm on
the button, over and again. *Don't follow me. Don't see me. Just
let me be . . .*

Four or five eternities passed, but the elevator wouldn't
come. You needed a key, or a pass card. *Captain fucking Paranoid!* She stumbled for the fire stairs. The door creaked
open, and clanged shut behind her. An alarm screeched. She
didn't care. The concrete steps thudded dully under her bare
feet. *Must reach the bottom. Must get away . . .* but before
she'd made it two floors down, her legs gave out.

She slumped against the steel railing, gulping for breath.
The sick air strangled her. Her legs ached. Her body still sang
from the delight of his caress, but the memory swamped bitter
like bile.

The look in his eyes as she'd lied to him still tore her heart, a
poisoned curseblade. So lost. So . . . broken. She had the feeling
that image would haunt her dreams for endless nights to come.

She screamed, a vile eruption of rage and guilt that tore her ears and bloodied her throat raw.

It echoed once, and died.

Cold dry sobs wracked her chest. No one could hear her. Nothing to prove she existed, that anyone cared if she lived or died.

"Please." A croak, painful. Barely audible. But it didn't matter, right? "Help me."

Silence, heavy and deafening.

You have to believe you'll be forgiven . . .

"I did it, okay?" She banged her head on the railing, once, again, gritting her teeth until her gums bled. "I broke your angel. I let myself be seduced. Bridie's a monster because of me. It's all my fault!"

Her throat swelled. "Your angel said I'd be forgiven. Japheth, that is. Do you remember him? I believed him, God, or heaven, or whoever you are. But that doesn't matter now. Send me to hell forever, if that's what you want." Hot tears slid down her face, into her mouth. "I deserve it for what I've done. I won't try to escape anymore. Just . . ." The tears filled her nose. She spluttered. "Just put things back the way they were! Make him whole again. He's so beautiful inside, Lord. Just let him have his life. I'm . . . I'm begging you. Please. If you love him at all . . ."

But her pleas faded into empty silence.

No warmth. No light on her heart.

Nothing.

Her body shook, uncontrollable. They'd abandoned her. Left her alone to suffer for her wrongs.

Everything she'd feared was true.

God didn't care. Heaven hated her. And they'd let her precious angel suffer, just to prove a point.

Well, screw that.

Rose sucked a stifling breath, and swallowed explosive tears. It hurt. She just swallowed harder. If God had left her to rot? Fine. But she wouldn't abandon Bridie.

No, she most certainly would not.

Determination fired like molten steel in her blood. Might as well go down fighting. She could still feel the curse, coiling deep inside her, whispering evil compulsions she longed to obey . . . but it meant she knew what Fluvium felt like, what he tasted like, how he smelled when he was exultant. And in just an hour or two, the demon moon would be full. Her powers would be at their bloody, wicked heights. She'd hunt down her vile demon prince, if it took her last breath. And Bridie with him.

Bridie wouldn't live another night as a monster. Not if Rose had anything to say about it. Bridie was just a little girl. Surely, a little girl wouldn't end in hell.

She had to believe that.

Rose licked bleeding lips, and crawled to her aching feet. *If I were Fluvium, and I'd just turned the whole of Babylon into a vampire coven . . . where would I go?*

Inspiration flashed her nerves wild. Somewhere she could see, that's where. Somewhere high. Like . . .

Warm laughter caressed her throat like a demon's kiss. Yes, she'd find Fluvium, and Bridie, and she'd make the demon prince sorry for what he'd done. Oh, yes, she surely would.

And then, she'd kill him. And herself. And Bridie, too.

She leapt down the stairs, two at a time, her pulse racing, urgent and alive. Bridie was better off dead. And as for Fluvium . . . well, he was one dirty motherfucker who'd be sorry he'd ever laid his slippery fingers on her.

An evil grin slicked her lips as she ran. *Eternity in hell is a long time, demon.*

And I'm gonna spend it making you miserable.

CHAPTER 41

Jadzia screamed, her pale hair alight, and stabbed the fire demon through its blazing heart.

Her sword electrified. Her muscles spasmed, jerking in fits. Her body whiplashed, excruciating, the white-hot agony stretching on and on . . . and she slammed face-first into the scorched bricks, smoke hissing from her hair.

She retched, spitting up burned blood, and dragged herself to her knees. Fumbled for her sword. Strained her ragged feathers for one more ounce of strength . . .

But the roar in her ears fell silent. The hellish red light was gone. And twelve stinking heaps of ash smoked like fat cow-pats, motionless.

She'd killed four of Luuceat's flame bodies. Michael had killed eight. They were all gone. Luuceat was dead.

She forced her exhausted body to its feet, elation surging in her blood. The vial was theirs. The world was saved. *Not bad, for a girl.*

Michael helped her up, his big hand closing around hers. Surprised, she stumbled. Her burned wings were already heal-ing, and she righted herself, her heart thudding now for a dif-ferent reason. *He'll smell Shax on me. He'll know . . .*

But Michael just grinned, deadly. "Good job. Now go find the others. I'll clean up this mess."

Dimly, she realized the Guardian—Salome—still sprawled on the floor, crucified with hell-spelled steel. Her whimpers jabbed Jadzia's teeth with cold needles. "Shouldn't we—?"

"I'll take care of it." Michael's cold eyes mesmerized her. "Go and get the others." And he shoved her gently towards the stairs.

Dumbly, she obeyed. Her boots crunched on ash-strewn stones. The stairwell was dim, the air blessedly cool after the fire-scorched battle. God, she was tired, filthy, stained with disgusting demonslime. She wanted to go outside and roll in the pristine snow, let it cool her feathers, clean her hair, wipe those horrible sights from her mind . . .

But a tiny, eager fist yanked at her thoughts, tugging her to a halt.

She'd always wanted to see a vial of holy wrath.

She'd only ever come across an empty one, at Quuzaat's sabbat. This one was still full. Was it already corrupted, by Luuceat's evil magic? Or was it clean and fresh, the unsullied power of heaven? What would that look like? What would it feel like, zinging in the air? How would it smell?

She turned, a silent breath of wings, and edged back down the stairs.

Michael dropped to one knee, and cupped the vial in his hands.

Inhaled its shimmering golden glow.

Bathed in its magical shadows and light.

Fuck, yeah. The heady flavor dizzied him, sparkled fresh strength through his limbs, imbued his ancient soul with power he'd rarely felt before in his five thousand years. Better than sex. Richer than the spurt of demon blood on his blade. More enticing than betraying a friend.

He laughed, and diamonds rained. *Yes. It's mine.*

And now I can use it for what it was made for.

Beside him, bleeding on the stones, wingless Salome groaned, whispering a few broken words.

"What?" he murmured, without interest. "Did you say something, darling?"

Her broken body shuddered. Blood oozed from her pores with the effort of the horrible wheezing noise she was making. "Set me . . . free . . ."

Michael flicked his wings, landing beside her in a crouch. She didn't smell too good, but hell, he wouldn't either if he was lying in his own piss. Her teeth were broken. She wasn't pretty anymore. "Why the hell should I do that?"

"Free . . ." It was all she could manage. Her breath exhaled, rasping. Exhaustion and pain clouded her pale blue eyes.

He leaned closer. "Do you think I don't know what you are?" He laughed, and frost crusted her bleeding lashes. "Gabriel's feathered fuck-buddy? Oh, yes, Salome, I know exactly what the two of you are up to. Did he tell you to keep this away from me? At all costs?" He dangled the vial between his fingers, taunting her.

She tried to shrink back. But she had nowhere to go. No muscles she could move.

Michael liked it when they were tied down.

He set the vial down carefully. Folded his hand around her neck, and squeezed.

Her eyes bulged. He tasted her scarred cheek with his tongue. Salty, unfresh with terror and torture. "Well, this is what 'all costs' means," he hissed. "Do you swallow for him? Do you? Well, suck up your ugly pride and swallow *that*, Salome. And tell Gabriel I'll see him on the other side."

She writhed, her face purpling. Her swelling flesh excited him. Michael squeezed harder. It made him think of doing the same to Gabriel . . .

Mmm. All in good time, brother. Satan first. Then you and I will have words. Oh, yes, we will.

Salome's eyes drained to empty gray. Pleading. Imploring him for mercy, to let her free, let her heal.

Mercy.

Now *that* was a fucking laugh.

He let go, and punched his fist through her chest, and tore out her heart.

* * *

At the bottom of the stairs, Jadzia clutched the wall in one numb hand. Her heart pounded. Her limbs screamed to flee, but she stood, frozen to that spot. *Oh shit oh shit oh shit . . .*

He killed her. So Gabriel wouldn't know. And now he's got the vial . . .

Her chest constricted, treacherous, and she gasped for air.

Michael jumped up, Salome's beating heart dripping in his hand . . . and his homicidal blue stare homed in on Jadzia.

She backed off, stumbling. "I'm sorry, I didn't mean . . ."

Michael's feathers burned, rich with glory and rage. He dropped the bleeding heart. It squelched on the stones. And he sprang, and crashed to the floor in front of her.

The shockwave staggered her. Effortlessly, Michael grabbed a fistful of her hair. Salome's still-warm blood dripped onto her armor. "I warned you, Jadzia. You weren't supposed to see that."

Panic leapt wild in her veins. She fought, kicking, clawing for his face, his fingers, anything . . .

Michael just shoved her backwards. White fire flashed from his palm, insufferably bright. She screamed, blinded, and something hard and impossibly strong punched her in the chest . . .

She fell to her knees, choking on hot liquid. Blood. She gasped for breath, but only more blood.

He'd stabbed her. Right through her silver-plated chest, into her heart.

Jadzia gasped a prayer. Her lips moved, but no sound came out. Her heartbeat stumbled, and stopped.

And oblivion drowned her.

CHAPTER 42

Hurtling on hell-whipped breeze, Japheth homed in on Michael's sugar-ice scent. He knew it well. It clogged his mouth, ran like blood in his feathers. Snow stung his face, and he plunged to earth with a hungry howl.

His body coalesced from glittering black ash, and in an explosion of feathers and clawing hands, he crashed into Michael and knocked him flat.

Lightning crackled, violet and blue, archangel on demon. Gravel grated Japheth's cheek. Dead flesh and fire stunk the air rabid. Squishy warmth coated his palms. A dead angel. Crucified, flayed, her heart torn out.

Inches from his nose, the holy vial gleamed golden.

For a moment, the sight stung him useless. *And the fourth angel poured out his vial over the sun, and power was given to him to scorch men with fire . . .*

Michael kicked him in the guts, flinging him across the room. He somersaulted, crashing into the wall. Michael sprang aloft on icy wings. Japheth fell and stumbled into a fighting crouch. And the archangel landed with a juddering crunch on the scorched stone floor of the monastery hall.

He laughed, and crystalline shards sliced the air, a sweet-sharp dissonance. "What the hell happened to you?"

Japheth spat gritty vomit. Ultraviolet flame rippled over his wings, the eerie dark light of hatred. In the corner by the stairs, another dead angel slumped, blood flowing in her pale blond hair.

Jadzia.

His heart stung, swift and poisonous. "You did," he growled. It tasted of rage and sour injustice. He liked it.

"Now, that's not fair." Michael circled, ice-blue wings glittering like knives. "I didn't shove demon's blood down your throat. Is that what happened, Jae?"

"No. *You* happened." Japheth advanced, his demon-spelled senses sharp. His vision zoomed, his ears pricked at the tiniest noise. Michael's heartbeat, his feathers as they rustled together, his tongue as he licked his beautiful lips. He could taste the archangel's deceitful breath from across the room, and rage stabbed him wild.

He clutched his sword, so tight his fingers cramped and bled. "You cast me out for nothing. You lied to me!"

"Poor you." Michael flashed a sarcastic smile. "I lie to everyone. It's my job. Doesn't make you special."

"I trusted you!" Tears burned his eyes, and he sizzled them away. "You wanted what I had, and when you couldn't have it, you got rid of me." He snarled, blood spitting, and waited for Michael to deny it. It wasn't true. Zuul lied. All demons lied . . .

But the archangel just laughed, razor-bright, and his bitterness showered like acid rain, smoking holes into the stone. "You got above yourself. You belong to *me*, Japheth. I *own* you."

Scarlet mist blinded him. The ground shook, and he struggled to see, to clear his rage before it exploded. "I never fought that! You know I didn't—"

"Then you should have pulled your fucking ego in. I gave you every chance. But you just wanted the glory." Michael's eyes flashed with starlit hatred. "Well, the glory's mine, angel. Not yours. *Mine*."

Finality slammed hard into Japheth's guts, a cruel sucker-punch. Zuul was right. All these years, he'd been so sure there was a reason. Grimly, he'd fought against the silent, creeping evil in his heart . . . and there wasn't any.

Michael had Tainted him for nothing.

Insanity gripped him, the hungry claws of hell, and he thrashed, and screamed, and surrendered.

His fangs sprang out, sharp and bleeding, and his mouth watered. A hungry smile spread over his lips. "Well, you got what you wanted. You told me I was lower than demonscum, and I believed you. And now I'm damned. Does that make you happy?"

"It makes me retch," Michael growled. "You flaunted all that fucking honor, and now you're just a demon's whore like the rest. Your stink fouls the air I breathe. Get out of my sight, hellshit. Crawl on your knees back to Babylon and suck your new master's cock. It's what you're good at."

Japheth laughed, and the walls spat fire. "I'll be in hell soon enough, don't worry about that. But I've got a job to do first."

A sarcastic grin. "Sorry. All done. The vial's mine. You can tell your demon prince his Apocalypse is over—"

"Shut up." Black lightning crackled in his fingers. He advanced, in a glitter of scarlet ash, and steel shimmered alive in his hand. He flexed hot fingers around the sword grip. Light, perfectly balanced. The burning iron felt good. "You feasted your filthy soul on my misery," he hissed. "You cut my heart out and let me bleed for fourteen hundred empty, excruciating years and I will make you pay for it, Misha, if it damns my soul for a thousand eternities. I'll have my vengeance. Tonight."

Michael's eyes glittered. He flashed his sword, and crouched, leveling it one-handed, a blinding slash of bitter blue flame. "Okay, lover," he whispered, and smiled that magnificent killer's smile. "If that's the way you want it? Come get me."

Japheth howled, and hurled hellfire.

Michael hurtled aloft, and conjured thunder. Head splitting, ripping the air asunder, the curling stink of ozone.

Japheth staggered, blood gushing from his ears, and Michael dived, a supersonic blue arrow edged in lethal heavensteel.

Japheth twisted, dizzy. Michael's sword pierced his shoulder. Blood spurted, hissing. He grabbed Michael's shimmering hair and smashed his forehead into the archangel's nose. Bone crackled. Fire mingled, blue on scarlet, and exploded, flinging them in opposite directions.

Japheth slammed backwards into the wall. Bones crunched, pain shooting through his veins like the sweetest drug. He healed his broken bones, a spritz of ashen spellwork, and they shuddered and knitted, a dark ache that invigorated him. He scrambled up. Michael was already aloft. He shook his head, dizzy. He knew Michael's moves. The archangel knew his. With his hellspells, they were evenly matched.

This could take all night.

Michael speared straight at him, wings streamlined back, shrieking electric blue hatred. Japheth met him head on. Sword blades clashed. Lightning struck and sizzled. His arm jarred with the force of the blow, and they hit the ground together. He whipped his wings taut, and rolled, just in time to avoid Michael's stabbing sword point . . . but the archangel's fist slammed into Japheth's trailing wrist, and his hell-spelled blade shrieked and shattered.

Shit! He dissolved, and sprang from the ether a foot away. But the sword didn't come back. Michael had destroyed it.

Japheth cursed, foul words souring the air. He flexed his healing wrist, fresh flame licking his skin. But his mind raced. *No sword. Should've seen that coming . . .*

From the corner of his hell-spelled vision, he spied the golden vial. Sitting on the stone floor, muttering, spitting angry orange flame like lava.

He didn't think. He just dived.

Beneath Michael's slashing diamond-blue wings, an inch aside from the archangel's lethal scything blade. He rolled, and came up with the vial in his fist.

It burned, sweet fucking hell it hurt, the glory raking under his skin and chewing at his cursed bones. He screamed, shuddering, but held on.

Lightning split the stone ceiling, cracking it apart with the force of holy wrath. The earth quaked, and split in two with a sepulchral groan. Flames leapt from the crack, hissing scarlet and blue.

Stormy wind howled, and freezing rain hammered down, deafening. He staggered, but stayed upright. "You want this?" he screamed over the roar. "Then come and get it!"

Michael growled at bay on the other side of the crack. "Give me that. You're not fit to touch it."

"And you are? Don't make me laugh."

"Let's see, then," Michael snarled, and advanced. "Why don't we ask God?"

"Because He doesn't talk to me! You made sure of that." Japheth shook the burning vial in his fist. The golden liquid sloshed dangerously, licking the vial's narrow lip. He gripped it tighter, and his blood sang with strange pleasure-pain.

Voices slithered in his veins, fighting, shouting, whispering, a cacophony he couldn't understand. *You shall know the truth . . . Avenge yourselves not . . . My name is Legion, for we are many . . . Give them blood to drink, for they deserve it . . . The power to scorch men with fire . . . You shall know the truth . . .*

He shook it off. *Let me be! I'm sorry. It's over.*

Avenge yourselves not . . . The glory pulsed harder, bleeding into his brain like long-lost memory, flooding warm sunlight over his heart . . . and a single, ineffable whisper sliced the dissonance like a crystal blade.

You shall know the truth, and the truth shall make you free.

Light stabbed deep inside him, piercing the empty blackness where his Tainted soul once lived. *Avenge not, beloved,* it whispered.

Avenge not, but give place to my wrath, for vengeance . . .

He gasped, drinking in the hallowed sunshine, and for the first time in fourteen hundred years, the Voice thundered in his brain.

. . . for vengeance is mine.

CHAPTER 43

He reeled, stunned. And Michael reared on flashing ice-blue wings, and dived through the leaping flames.

Japheth hurled himself backwards. Their bodies collided. The archangel's feathers razored his skin bloody. He crushed the vial tightly in his fist, flexed his head back, bared bleeding fangs to strike . . .

. . . conjured his rippled dagger from glittering ash, and stabbed.

The point struck flesh, and sank deep. The hell-spelled steel flashed, ugly purple flame. And Michael somersaulted backwards, rich scarlet blood spraying from his throat.

The knife ripped from Japheth's fingers. Michael crashed on his back into the stones. His sword cartwheeled from his hand, and fell into the burning chasm.

Michael screeched, and tore the burning knife from his flesh.

Japheth hurled a spell, and the knife dissolved to ash and reappeared in his own hand. And he jumped, and landed with a thud astride the archangel's chest.

Breath squeezed from Michael's lungs. Blood splurted. His flesh was already healing. It didn't matter. Japheth jammed a sharp knee into each of the archangel's massive shoulders, pinning him down, and jabbed the bloody knifepoint under Michael's chin.

With the other hand, he forced the burning golden vial to Michael's lips.

Michael fought, powerful wings and muscles straining. His lethal glare scorched Japheth's skin raw. But he didn't care. Didn't shift. The heady light invigorated him, fired his strength to impossible heights. He slammed Michael's body back into the quaking stones. "You want to drink this? Do you?"

He thrust his knife harder, drawing blood and fire. He shuddered and sweated with evil lust for revenge. *The power to scorch men with fire . . .* His flesh swelled, aroused. Christ, he wanted to pour this shit down Michael's throat and watch him burn in agony. "Hell, I'll swallow some if you will. Let's see who the Lord favors. I'm up for it."

The archangel snarled, his own bloody vengeance frosting the air white. "Try it. You're the one who's cursed."

Japheth laughed, rich and awful in his chest like thunder. "Don't be too sure. Heaven sees into my heart, Michael. Something you never did."

Light erupted behind his eyes. The Voice and the demon's curse howled in his veins as one, and he exulted, his blood glittering with energy like a million stars. Hellflame. Heavenlight. Glory, damnation. He didn't know.

It didn't matter.

What's done is done. Heaven sees into my heart. And I believe I'll be forgiven.

I believe.

Trembling, he leaned closer. Brushed a flaming kiss over Michael's cheek. He inhaled, that sweet ice-fire scent. Tasted that brilliant, terrifying beauty.

And for the first and last time, he let it go.

"I could have killed you," he whispered against Michael's bleeding lips. "But you just don't matter enough to me. Live with that."

And he flung a sweet prayer to the darkness, and it swallowed him.

* * *

The elevator doors hissed apart, and Rose Harley stole out onto the 103rd floor of One World Trade Center.

Into the midst of a shrieking, balls-to-the-wall party.

Music thumped, electric melody and thudding bass. Wild laughter and screams drifted above the din. The glass-walled room stank of alcohol and sugar, sweat and expensive perfume. Waiflike women danced stoned in tiny, ten-thousand-dollar cocktail dresses, chugged opium-laced shots of tequila or absinthe, had those dresses peeled off by drooling men old enough to be their fathers. Their bared limbs and nipples shone, sweat and spit and other body fluids.

Rose crept in further, sickened. On a red velvet sofa, a skinny girl with supermodel cheekbones gave a blowjob to some groaning old white guy in a suit. A pair of underage girls kissed and fondled each other's breasts on a heap of crumpled cash, cheered on by a drooling audience. Three guys gang-banged a redhead on the bar, leaving no cleft unfilled. A girl in a tight rubber suit licked white powder from a naked twink's chest and did nasty things to his straining private parts with her spike-ringed hand. Blood oozed. The dude was so out of his mind, he just whimpered.

Freedom Tower. The old name still made Rose shudder. Precious little freedom in Babylon since this glass-and-iron monstrosity was built. The one percent who owned had ruthlessly crushed the ninety-nine percent who didn't, and this was the result. A glittering, degrading, disgusting porn film. Snorting hellcry and fucking on the coffee table. Classy.

No one paid her any mind as she sidled through.

Neither had the terrified passengers on her nightmare subway ride from Madison Avenue, where she'd seen two knife fights and a gunshot murder. The rent-a-cops at the base of Freedom Tower certainly hadn't noticed her. Too busy screaming, and running, and dying.

Vampires, even fledglings, ran a lot faster than humans.

The lobby had been splashed in blood, littered with bodies.

Fluvium's curse was spreading. And it would only spread further.

Rose stalked towards the glass door to the observation deck. Outside, storm clouds rolled in the black pre-dawn. The doors eased open. Hot stormy wind buffeted her face. Blood and excrement, the telltale stink of curse.

She strode onto the metal platform. They nearly hadn't built this part, she remembered—too unsafe—but the mega-rich demanded an outdoor deck, and an outdoor deck they got. Gave 'em somewhere to jump from when Wall Street dropped a few thousand points.

Thunder rumbled. Raindrops stung her face. The height dizzied her. She peered cautiously over the waist-high railing, light-headed. City lights glittered like bloody jewels. Four hundred meters above ground level and then some.

But her keen vampire eyes still saw the carnage. Her ears still rang with horrible screams. She still smelled death.

With a flex of powerful thighs, she vaulted up over the parapet onto the floor above.

Her bare feet slammed into a metal catwalk that hugged the side of the building, railed in steel and six feet wide. Powerful floodlights stabbed upwards into boiling storm clouds. Bats flapped and whistled. Above, three hundred feet of glimmering knife-edge steel pierced the roiling sky . . .

Fluvium leaned over the parapet, laughing like a madman. His eyes blazed with crimson glee as he watched the screaming city, and he capered and clapped. He'd changed his clothes, again, and now he wore a red top hat and a long red tailcoat like a fucked-up circus ringmaster. He threw his head back and howled at the boiling black sky, and it answered with a deafening roll of thunder.

He swept his hat off, and his devilish grin crackled his purple hair electric. "Good evening, my pretty slut. Have you come to beg forgiveness?"

Vitriol burned her mouth. She itched to run at him, claw his evil eyes out and swallow them whole. Tip him over the edge, watch him fall . . .

Bridie poked her little head from under Fluvium's elbow, clutching his long coat. He'd dressed her in a little clown suit, and the white frill around her neck was blotted with blood. She spat out the bone she was gnawing on. "Hello, Auntie Rosie."

Rose clenched her fists. Forced her voice strong over the rolling thunder. "Hello, Bridie. Everything's going to be okay, sweetie. I promise."

Fluvium swept Bridie up, and sat her on the parapet railing. She giggled, legs swinging. He pointed down, and kissed her plump cheek affectionately. "Look, darling. Aren't the dying humans funny?"

Bridie squealed in delight, teetering wildly on the edge. *Oh, Jesus.* Panicked, Rose stumbled for her, reaching . . .

"Stop there," Fluvium ordered carelessly, and her leg muscles froze solid.

She strained, but his spell glued her feet to the catwalk. Shit. She needed to stay calm. Get close to him, and strike . . . "Let me go," she said, coolly, though her heart sprinted at the sight of Bridie on that precipice. "I don't mean any harm."

Fluvium grinned. "You didn't answer me. Have you come to ask my forgiveness?"

Bitterness stung her mouth. Forgiveness. What a sadistic lie. "Yes. I want you to love me." Just saying it made her sweat cold. "I want it to be like it was before."

"Then get on your knees, whore," he snarled, "and beg."

Fresh compulsion made her stomach crawl. Her skin dripped, clammy with sweat. But she obeyed, falling to her knees on the slick catwalk.

"Better. Come here." His gloating tone licked her skin. Lightning flashed eerily over his face, and his fingertips crackled with dark static. The tiny hairs on her arms prickled tight. The storm loved him.

Woodenly, she shuffled over to him. His ashen scent choked her. But the fat cursed slug in her guts writhed in contentment . . . Bile forced up into her mouth, and she swallowed it. *Just a moment more. Hold it together . . .*

His red eyes glinted, jubilant. "Now say it. And you'd better make it good."

She clasped shaking hands behind her back. "Please. I'm sorry I defied you, master. Can you forgive me?"

"Hmm. Not sure I should. Your angel did a much better job of humiliating himself." He prodded her chin up with one sharp finger. "But that's okay. I'll help you along. Tell me what you are to me, minion."

"I'm . . . nothing, master."

His mouth twisted. "C'mon, you can do better."

"I'm less than nothing," she forced out. "I'm . . . meat. Food. Like an animal."

"Good! Now tell me what can I do with this meat of yours."

"You can . . . drink me. Touch me. Use me however you want."

"Mmm. And you'd like that, would you?"

"Yes." Her voice dissolved, and she coughed. "Yes, I'd like that."

"So you'll obey me in everything." Lightning forked, reflecting like cracked red glass in Fluvium's eyes. "I can fuck you. Eat your flesh. Crucify you and watch you scream. Anything I feel like."

Closer, asshole. Just one more step . . . "I'll obey you in everything."

"That's nice. I like that." Thunder rolled again, a brilliant flash, almost close enough to touch. "Now show me you mean it."

She stared, dumb with shock. *Oh, Jesus . . .*

He gave a gloating smile. "I know, it's sad we don't have time for any proper fun. But all this love talk has made my dick hard. Take care of it. No need to get up."

She licked dry lips. Leaned forwards. He stepped closer, triumphant.

And Rose ripped her demon-spelled knife from the back of her jeans, and stabbed Fluvium in the heart.

Thick demon blood erupted over her hands. The storm thundered in fury. The demon's eyes flared black, pain and shock. He yelled, ash raining from his lips, and stumbled backwards.

Rose leapt up, and plunged the knife deeper into his chest. It pierced bone, flesh, soft organs. An exultant scream tore her lips raw. *Die, you evil motherfucker. Just die . . .*

Fluvium dissolved, a glittering black ashcloud that stank of blood and fire. And a deep, hellish chuckle clanged like evil bells, vibrating through her body until her guts bubbled wet. "Oh, Rose. Did you really think you could kill me?"

CHAPTER 44

Rose stumbled into the space where the demon had stood. Her mind splintered, bleeding confusion. Her knife clanged on the catwalk and bounced away.

And Fluvium coiled himself into a tight black rope of hells-lime, and dived down her throat.

Her guts cramped, and she dry heaved. Her eyes watered, her face burning. Nothing came up.

Horror throttled her blind. Frantic, she scrabbled at his thrashing black tail. He wiggled and squirmed, like a snake caught halfway down her throat. He gnashed at her insides with his razor teeth, dragging himself down, deeper . . .

She pulled, straining, stretching the demon's vile body like chewing gum, but she couldn't yank him out.

And with a final thrash of supple black-slimed muscle, Fluvium snaked from her grip and coiled himself deep inside her body.

Rose gurgled. Choked. Gasped. Her lungs wouldn't fill. Savage teeth munched in her guts. Her soft flesh tore, and she felt the awful thing *swallow*, and stinking blackness howled and dragged her gibbering soul under.

She fought, terror swamping her wits. No escape, down and

darker into a hot blood-stinking prison with no light. The snake squeezed, constricting, coiling around her, forcing her smaller, and smaller, until the trap slammed shut.

Without her, her body moved. Laughed. Howled at the shuddering black sky.

And all Rose could do was watch, and scream.

A spearing cloud of ash and fiery black sparks, Japheth zoomed in on Fluvium's foul scent.

Stormy sky, ozone's dizzy tang, the crash of forked lightning. He dived, and coalesced. His feathers hit storm-boiled air, and he glided. Below, the lights of midtown Babylon glittered like a million tiny campfires, the crisscrossing streets flowing with flaming rivers of light. Human auras pulsed like neon. But the city stank of blood and fear. Even from two thousand feet, he could hear ragged screams.

Fluvium's vampire apocalypse.

Above him, invisible beyond rolling storm clouds, the demon moon burned full and heavy, thirsty for death. He could feel it, a rich lick of pleasure and pain in his blood, dragging him in like an ugly undertow.

Japheth exulted, the storm rushing over him, sparkling with life and power. The Demon King's plan was done. The precious vial was tucked safely away, from Azaroth or Michael or anyone else who plotted to claim it.

The End of Days was over.

But fear and thirst still ruled Babylon tonight. And Japheth meant to save it, if he could.

The demon moon wasn't yet visible. The city wasn't yet bathed in its hungry light. If he could get rid of Fluvium before the storm clouds parted . . .

He wheeled on the crackling wind, climbing, hunting for the demon's sour aura. Stormwind sprang alive in his feathers, licking them with static that tingled his bones. His stomach growled, ravenous. The curse still whispered inside, tempting, leading him on . . . but now he was its master.

He licked sharp teeth, and smiled. Now, he used his hunger for blood to trace the demon's power.

And his hunger would be Fluvium's undoing. He'd already feasted on the demon's dark life force once. This time, he'd finish the job.

The thought made him shudder. But he was a soldier. He did what was necessary. Even if it meant his own destruction.

So he'd drain the demon dry. The demon moon would fail. And then, he'd hand the precious vial back to Gabriel, and he'd never see Rose Harley again.

Longing slashed at his heart, and he fought it off grimly. She'd betrayed him. Exposed his weaknesses. He'd forgotten what was important. He'd failed, screwed up, hesitated. Let Fluvium curse the city. All because he couldn't control his emotions around her.

Wanting her was stupid, selfish, a multitude of ugly sins. Better to forget she'd ever existed.

So why couldn't he carve her from his heart?

He gritted his teeth, spearing over the flashing chaos of Times Square. It was true. He longed for her dark blossom fragrance, her silken hair on his skin, her lithe body in his arms. He wanted to hold her, laugh with her, take her away from her nightmare . . .

But Japheth had no future. Not in the Tainted Host. Not anywhere. Michael had shown his true colors. Redemption was a vanished dream.

Only the demon mattered now.

Fluvium's fire-gore scent stung his nose. Yeah. He flew higher, faster, skyscrapers streaming by. Bats squeaked, flapping from his path . . . and *clang!* he landed on a narrow metal catwalk that rattled and shook with thunder.

Wind blew his hair wild. Above, the skyscraper's spire knifed skywards, shining in vast spotlights, current crackling blue and scarlet along its length. Storm clouds rumbled, shadows moving like hissing creatures along the rippled steel floor. Heat haze shimmered, pregnant with latent power. Ozone and demonstink sliced the air sharp.

Lightning forked, and struck the spire with an unearthly crack. Metal melted. Fire erupted. Voltage jolted his body, and his feathers crackled on end. The power was invigorating, sparkling through every cell. He felt invincible. Godlike. Unstoppable, answerable to nothing and no one.

Crazy laughter split his lungs. He knew now what the demon craved. To be his own master. An end to accountability. No rules, no penance, no forgiveness. A place where he was beholden to no one.

Ultimate power.

"Fluvium!" he screamed. Lightning crackled through his feathers, arcing to the floor. "Show yourself!"

Clanging footsteps. A flash of curly hair, dark seductive eyes.

For an instant, Japheth's heart stopped.

Rose sauntered along the catwalk, swaying her hips. Her bare feet crackled sparks on the metal. She wore a long red tailcoat that flapped in the breeze. Her hair blew around her face, wild and beautiful, and her sultry dark eyes blazed with power and desire and everything he'd ever longed for.

She halted before him, just inches away. "Hello, angel," she purred.

CHAPTER 45

Her beauty dizzied him. Thunder roared in his ears, pounding his senses blind, leaving only hunger.

He buried his hands in her glorious hair, and swept her cherry-sweet mouth to his.

Hot, alive, so delicious he groaned. Her tongue fought his, bruising. Her teeth grazed his lips, and blood sparkled in his throat like coppery sunshine.

She arched against him, sliding hot hands over his ass, sweet breasts swelling against his silver. "Mmm. You make me hot."

Desire swallowed him like scarlet fog. He was meant to be . . . doing something . . . ? But her mouth demanded his attention, her body insisting he caress her. He crushed her tighter, wrapped her in burning wings. She murmured into their kiss, a feminine moan of need.

Damn, she felt amazing. Fighting this was useless. His cock ached for her. He wanted her naked. He slid hungry hands under her t-shirt, hunting for fragrant skin, her luscious ripe breasts. So soft.

He fell to his knees, pulling her with him. Her wicked smile inflamed him. He tasted her throat, tongued her pulse, grazed her with his teeth and drank up her shiver. He inhaled the scent of her breasts, bared them inside her coat, tasted them. Her nipples were so sweet and hard. He sucked one, and she moaned in delight. Her flavor drowned his reason, obliterating everything except the taste and smell and feel of her. "Rose . . ."

She climbed onto his lap, and straddled him, pushing him down so his feathers zinged on the charged catwalk. "Let's fuck. Right here."

Sooner rather than later, or he'd finish it in his trousers. He yanked her down onto his chest, another bruising kiss that tore his breath ragged. "Damn, you're beautiful."

She laughed, sultry, and tore at the buckles on his armor. He helped her, fumbling, shucking the breastplate off. It clanged away, and she ripped his bloodied shirt open, raked her nails over his bare chest. The sting felt so good he couldn't breathe.

Lightning flashed, illuminating her silhouette. Flame crackled over her long red coat. Her hair glimmered. Her body glowed. She was a dark goddess, her eyes aflame with excitement. She threw back her head, stretching her long pale throat, and laughed.

Sick, gloating, hungry laughter.

Reality rocked him like thunder.

This wasn't Rose.

His muscles shocked rigid, painful . . . but the thing held him down, impossibly, devilishly strong. Her long fangs drooled, filling her smile with evil delight.

"You stupid fuck," Fluvium hissed through Rose's lips. "Did you actually think she'd want you now?"

Japheth fought broken wits. Desperately, he grasped for ash, flame, a spell, anything . . . but his fingers met empty air. No weapon. No armor. No defense.

And Fluvium arched Rose's beautiful half-naked body, and dived for Japheth's throat.

Deep in steaming darkness, Rose fought and screamed.

She could feel Japheth's kiss, his urgent caress, the hardness of his muscles beneath her. It stole her breath, made her naked breasts ache, rippled sweet desire through her body . . .

But it wasn't her body anymore. It moved without her, spoke without her. Stretched, yearned, exulted with the demon's evil lust.

Fluvium was going to kill her angel.

Chew his throat out, feast on his flesh, bathe in the fountaining blood.

She yelled, and hammered on her black prison walls. The demon just squeezed her tighter and smaller, and struck with *her* teeth for Japheth's throat.

Her sharp fangs grazed the angel's skin. Blood spurted, and Fluvium grunted with rich lust. Rose felt it, God, how she felt it, the pleasure gripping her like evil iron bands, squeezing tighter and tighter until she gasped and writhed, overcome. It felt so good. She wanted more . . .

No.

In the dark, Rose wailed and thrashed. *Not like this. He's mine, demon. Not yours. Mine. And I'll save him, if it's the last sorry thing I accomplish on this earth.*

Fresh power flooded her like sunshine, distant light in the hollow darkness. And she gathered her every muscle, and flexed with all her demon-spelled strength.

Mindless, numb with shock, Japheth fought the demon who'd stolen his lover's body.

Fluvium's teeth grazed his throat, and the demon groaned, his stolen muscles swelling. Japheth's eyes watered. Rose's hair tangled on his face, drenching his nose with her scent. Her body strained upon his. Her thighs crushed him, her breasts pressed against his naked chest, her sweet lips tore at his throat . . .

Desire and hatred screamed burning discord in his blood. He knew it was Fluvium. He wanted it to be her. He wanted to surrender. Tear the rest of her clothes off, and drown himself in her. Suck her nipples into his mouth, let her sink those beautiful teeth into his throat and suck him hard. Thrust his straining cock inside her and make her come screaming, while the sky split apart and died.

Fluvium banged his head into the catwalk, dizzying. The demon laughed, spitting fiery sparks. And he threw back his head and howled to hell.

The roiling storm clouds shuddered, and cracked asunder, and the fat blood-soaked moon grinned down, gloating like hellfire.

The sky shimmered in evil triumph. Japheth's bones burned. Already, from a hundred floors below, he could hear the howling, the fighting, thousands of dying screams.

He yelled, and blue flames erupted from his fingers. But Fluvium batted them aside effortlessly. "Don't fight me, angel," he snarled with Rose's bloody lips. "It's over. You're mine."

His strength was failing. Desperately, he flexed his wings, trying to lever the demon away . . . and his feathers brushed cold silver.

His armor. The vial. *The power to scorch men with fire* . . .

His mind raced. They'd all die. Him. Rose. The vampires. The vial would be spilled. The End would begin again. For that, he'd never be forgiven.

But millions of humans might still be saved. He had no place. His life was over. Rose would never be his.

And he was sick to his fucking heart of all this death.

He flung out one weakened arm, scrabbling desperately for the vial.

Fluvium's eyes—Rose's eyes—fired scarlet in thirsty moonlight. "You'll never do it, angel," he taunted. "You'll never end the world to stop me. You're too damn scared of hell."

And he curled back like a serpent, impossibly flexible. Rose's naked body gleamed, and she bared her beautiful fangs to strike.

And then her eyes flashed black, the human spark blazing alive. "Do it!" she screamed, and the voice was hers.

Japheth's fingers closed over the smooth vial. Golden flame burned him to the bone. He screamed, wings alight, and flung the vial skywards.

It cartwheeled, a flashing golden star. The demon moon shrieked. The storm clouds howled, and exploded in thunder. Light erupted, sweet and hot and impossibly bright . . . and the bleeding heavens rained fire.

CHAPTER 46

Rose groaned, and forced her eyes open.

The catwalk, coated in black charcoal. Ash drifted on swirling breeze, and she smelled wildfire. Radiant heat threatened her skin. The sky glowed orange, a crimson-fired sunrise. Below her, downtown Babylon burned.

Fuck, she ached all over. Wincing, she pushed to her knees. The edges of half-burned skyscrapers glowed red, flames twinkling like bloody stars. Debris littered the streets, twisted steel girders, the blackened shells of vehicles. Smoke rasped in her throat. She coughed, and whirled, fear spiking her nerves. . . .

But Fluvium wasn't there. Only a smoking heap of ash on the catwalk, black and stinking with corruption.

She wiped her hands on the demon's coat that she still wore. It felt warm, sickly like skin under her palms. Beneath it, her clothes were torn and blackened, her naked skin exposed. But she wanted to tear the coat off, fling it over the edge, get the demon off her forever . . .

Her mouth firmed, and she buttoned the coat and stumbled to her feet, dizzy. Her eyes stung, blurry and dull. Something was wrong with her ears. She couldn't hear properly.

She shook her head, trying to clear her ears. No heartbeats. No sighs, no screams, no slithering demon breath . . .

Oh, shit. Her hand flew to her mouth, and found teeth, short and blunt. She stretched her jaw. No fangs popped out. She flexed her thighs, experimental. Still strong. Still flexible. But the evil preternatural strength was gone. Fluvium was dead. He had no power over her anymore.

She was free.

Holy motherfucker. It worked . . . but what about Japheth? Is he . . . ?

"Auntie Rosie?"

Her heart leapt into her throat like a hot frog. She turned, breathless. Bridie tottered along the catwalk in her clown suit, screwing one little fist into her eye. She hiccupped. "Auntie Rosie, I'm tired."

Stunned, Rose folded the little girl into her arms. No cruel heat. No sharp teeth. Even the blood in Bridie's hair was gone.

Rose's eyes misted, burning. Did this mean the innocent were all spared? She didn't know. She didn't care.

Thank you, she whispered silently. She didn't expect a response. She didn't get one.

"Oh, honey. You okay?" Rose crushed Bridie tighter, tears flooding her cheeks. She never wanted to let go. But her heart ached, fearful. After what Bridie had been through, no telling what damage had been done . . .

But Bridie just sniffled, and wriggled. "You're squeezing me," she said indignantly. Her eyes shone clear. Untroubled. Like she'd forgotten everything.

I hope so. Oh, God, I hope so. "I'm so sorry, honey. Everything's going to be fine."

Bridie pointed. "Is that man okay?"

Rose turned, fearful, holding Bridie's hand.

Japheth lay on the scorched catwalk. Flat on his back, wings flung wide. His feathers were gone, only charred golden stumps remaining. His shirt was torn, burned to rags, and his beautiful hair had singed away, his skin burned to raw flesh.

In one blackened hand, he clutched a dirty, empty golden vial.

Sick, Rose dived to her knees at his side. Cradled his head on her lap. His ruined flesh felt hot in her hands. Her throat lumped. "Wake up, angel. C'mon. It's done. You won."

He didn't. Not moving. Not breathing.

Fresh tears spilled, acidic with injustice. *Why keep me, and let him die? So he spilled your stupid vial. He's just one man. He can't save everyone.*

Anger poured heat into her veins . . . but it was weary, defeated anger. Not the violent rage of denial. *You're all-powerful, aren't you? So you go ahead and stop the end of the world, if that's what you want. Just leave us be.*

She pressed her face to Japheth's scorched cheek. Kissed his burned lips. They still tasted of him, fire and rage and sweet sorrow. Tears slipped into her mouth, and she forced them back.

Maybe he didn't save the world. But he saved us.

He saved me.

"You did good, baby," she whispered, stroking his charred face. "Them and their stupid rules? Fuck 'em. I see you. And you did real good."

Warmth coalesced, and surrounded her with light.

She gasped, energized. A golden aura rippled over Japheth's body, shimmering, healing his ravaged skin. His feathers glimmered, and sparkled, renewed. His hair gleamed fresh and golden, alight with gentle flame.

And he heaved in a choking breath, and opened his eyes.

Rose stared, speechless. So green, her angel's gaze. No violet-dark flame to spoil his glory. He was healed. Un-cursed.

Forgiven.

Japheth stared up at her. Pushed up on his elbows, arms bulging, and scratched his hair with the edge of one bewildered wing. "What the hell just happened?"

Tears and laughter choked her at the same time. Her chest ached inside. But it was a good pain. "You happened, angel." She played her fingers through his magnificent hair. Damn, he looked fine shirtless. "God fucking help us."

Beside her, Bridie giggled, and covered her mouth. "Auntie said a naughty word."

Japheth looked at Bridie. Glanced at Rose, a hint of an enchanted smile. And he hopped up onto his haunches, elbows on knees and wings swept back. "And who are you?"

"I'm Bridie. I'm six."

"Hello, Bridie-who's-six." He offered his hand. "I'm Japheth."

She shook it gravely. "Are you an angel?"

He touched her chin softly, and Rose felt an irrational urge to burst into tears. "I am that. How would you like to fly with me? If it's okay with your auntie, of course."

"Awesome!" Bridie tugged Rose's arm. "Can I?"

Rose laughed, delirious. Right now, she'd agree to anything . . .

But cold spidery legs scuttled down her spine. What now? Surely, he was just being kind to her. She had no home. No job. Nowhere to go. If he left her alone, she'd have . . .

Nothing.

The stray thought fired her anger. No, that wasn't true. She had Bridie. They'd manage, just the two of them, like before . . .

Japheth scooped up his armor. The silver gleamed, newly spotless. His wings shimmered, and disappeared, and swiftly he buckled the armor over his bare chest. He flashed his wings back, and golden feathers sparkled, catching the glorious light of dawn.

Rose's breath caught. Beautiful devil, this angel. Too beautiful to be real, and alive, and hers.

She forced a smile, shivering both cold and warm. "Sure you can, honey. Where are we going?"

Japheth picked up the empty golden vial. Hesitated, his gaze shadowed. And then he tightened resolute fingers around it, and held out his arm to embrace her. "Home."

Deep in endless black oblivion, light poured into Jadzia's eyes.

She screamed, reaching for it, clawing through the darkness. Light. Sensation. Feeling. Not this awful nothingness. Anything but that . . .

"Jadzia." Shax's dark velvety voice pierced the silence. "Come back, Jadzia."

She grasped for the sound, frantic. *Yes. I'm alive. Something's out there. Someone . . . I'm not alone.*

Not alone!

"Jadzia, come to me." Commanding, remorseless. Dragging her from the emptiness.

Air slammed into her lungs, and her lifeless heart started beating.

The world exploded around her, relighting her consciousness like fireworks. Broken rock scraped her face. Dirt crumbled under her nails. Her skin warmed, brightened, glistening with glory. Her feathers sprang taut. She exulted. Sensation. Feeling. Life.

She gasped in shuddering release, and her eyes flickered open.

CHAPTER 47

Fatigued, Rose hefted herself up from Japheth's sofa, blinking in mid-morning sun.

She sighed, stretching the small of her back over linked hands. Stiff vertebrae popped. Being a vampire had sucked, sure. But now she was weary.

"Is she sleeping?" Japheth drifted up behind her, a waft of latte-scented breeze.

Bridie curled beneath a blanket on the sofa, cheek resting on one little fist. She murmured, some sugar-sweet dream.

"Yep." Rose's smile faded. They'd ventured out to get food, after she discovered that Japheth had only fruit juice and iced water in his fridge, and the place had been like a war zone. The city stank of ash and burned flesh, and the air howled with sirens. Near Japheth's place, the city still buzzed, frantic, but downtown Babylon from SoHo to Battery Park was scorched earth, and still burning. People looted, fought, killed each other for food or weapons. The polluted water mains were clogged with bloody sludge, and the mess had gurgled up into the subway. The fire department had no power, no water. Debris blocked most of the roads. The charred corpses of vampires clogged the streets and gutters, with not enough vehicles to clear them away.

It was going to be a long day.

"Good." Japheth eased his arm around Rose's waist and kissed her, just below her ear.

"Mmm." His hair drifted on her shoulder, damp from the shower. He'd changed out of his armor, too, naked to the waist. Hoo boy. His big body fit seductively against hers, and gently he eased her stained red coat from her shoulders and dropped it. Ran his thumbs along her tense shoulder muscles, rubbing, caressing . . .

God, that felt good. Rose shivered, and tried to pull away. "Don't you have someplace to be?"

"Uh-huh." He swept her up in one arm. A golden flurry of breeze, and he dropped her on her back onto his bed. "Here."

His sizzling gaze undressed her. She swallowed, her heart thumping. "I mean . . . don't you have cities to save? People to rescue? Angel stuff to take care of?"

Softly, he clicked the door shut. Drifted onto the quilt beside her. Curled one glowing golden wing over her, a secret place just for them. "I'm taking care of you, Rose Harley," he whispered. "For once, the world can wait. Besides"—he stroked hair from her eyes—"I believe I'm out of a job."

He brushed warm lips over hers. Gentle, at first, exploring, like they'd never kissed before. His fingers played softly in her hair. She reeled, undone by his tenderness, already dizzy. Opened her mouth, kissed him deeper, hungry for this hour, this minute, whatever it was.

Because it wouldn't last. It couldn't. Nothing ever did.

His sigh of longing sparkled over her skin. A hot ache twisted deep inside her, and she groaned. She needed to have him. Now. Before this moment passed forever.

She sat up, murmuring in protest when his lips left hers. Peeled off her torn t-shirt. Beneath it, her breasts were bare. His eyes burned dark. He pulled her close, kissing hot tingles over her throat, her collarbone, between her breasts. *Oh, damn.* She squirmed, flushing. She'd forgotten how she stank, blood and sweat and God knew what else. "Um. I'll take a shower. Just let me . . ."

"Don't you dare." His mouth burned her, insistent. "You taste like you." And he slid a slow, hot kiss over one nipple.

She groaned and arched, helpless. She hadn't realized how much pleasure her breasts could feel. He suckled her, his tongue pulling until she was so hard there it ached. Desire burned through her. She fumbled her jeans undone. He helped her, pulling them over her hips and off, kissing hot urgency down over her belly, her hip, the crease at the top of her thigh. He unfolded her legs, and she strained into him, desperate for his touch, and when he eased his tongue into her folds she thought she'd die of bliss.

He explored her, fingertips and tongue, so gentle it broke her heart. She was already so wet, so sensitive. She fisted his hair in both hands, trying to pull him closer. "Harder. Please. I need you."

But he laughed, a tiny vibration that thrilled deep. "Peace, Rose Harley," he whispered, "let me love you," and he glided his tongue softly over her clit and licked her until she melted into a puddle of pure pleasure.

She'd never felt it like that, never had a man take such exquisite care, like she was the most precious thing in the world, and then effortlessly he quickened her, brought her on, harder and faster and tighter until he suckled her deep into his hot delicious mouth and she broke apart, exploding from her clit to her deepest insides to her fingertips and toes.

She panted, dizzy with release. He swept her up in his arms. "*Now* we shower," he whispered, and fluttered to his feet. In moments, he'd stripped naked. His magnificent warrior's body gleamed, hard, tough. Big lean thighs, smooth hips, tight butt, perfect cock. Just the way she liked it.

And soon, he'd be gone. Sorrow licked her exquisitely, sharpening her desire.

She grabbed his hand, yanked him back onto the bed. He tumbled, laughing, and she jumped astride him, fighting him still. "My turn," she said, and fell on him.

She'd wanted to taste that magnificent chest since she'd laid eyes on it. He started to push her off him but groaned at the touch of her lips. She licked him, bit his flat nipples to make them peak, traced her tongue over his steel-hard abdomen. Mmm. Her mouth watered. She dipped and took his cock in her mouth. God, he tasted so good, smooth hot male skin. She took more, running her tongue over him, sucking lightly.

His breath quickened. "Don't. I can't . . . it's, uh, been a long time."

"Good," she whispered, and teased him with her tongue, watching his thighs jerk as he tried not to push deeper into her mouth. The power freshened her desire. "That makes you all mine."

He growled, and with a taut snap of wings, he flipped her onto her back. Fought for her wrists, pinned them over her head. His green eyes burned, intense, and he whispered against her lips. "You want to fight me?"

Her breasts pressed against his chest, her hard nipples slipping on his damp skin. She'd never feel that again. She wrapped her thigh around his hips, and tilted up invitingly. "I want to *fuck* you. Now."

He caught her bottom lip in his teeth, and fucked her. A long, hot, slow, possessive thrust that blurred her vision, it felt so damned good. "Oh, yes." He was big, hot, talented, gorgeous. It didn't matter. He was just him. And she opened her legs and folded them higher and gave herself up to his loving. Slow yet demanding, insistent yet achingly gentle. He took her, let her take him, drowned her in kisses and sensation and sweet, excruciating pleasure that swelled and sparkled and ignited in her flesh like liquid starlight. She shuddered, cried out, surrendered, and it melted her, impossibly perfect.

He rode it with her, crushing her in his embrace, enfolding her in warmth and sighs and sparkling golden heat. "Rose." His whisper glittered in her mouth. "Rose." Just that one word. As if it was the only word he'd ever need.

Dizzy, sated, she buried her face in his warm crisp feathers. Jesus, she was crying again. She tried to smile, to swallow her sorrow, but her throat ached so hard she couldn't breathe. Couldn't think past the swift stabbing pain in her heart.

He didn't ask. Didn't challenge her. Just held her, soothed her with the steady thudding of his heart. And at last she slept,

curled in her angel's embrace. No dreams. No nightmare. Just
soft, blessed silence.

Japheth's feathers prickled, the scent of summer rain.

The quilt, warm and Rose scented beneath him. He hadn't
really been sleeping. Just drifting, breathless with delight, his
amazing woman in his arms. She was . . . Well, he was speechless. Her scent still made him dizzy, her long smooth body
against him a honey-sweet revelation that faded everything he'd
endured for fourteen hundred years into pale glassy memory.

She was totally worth waiting for.

But danger prickled his spine. That scent of rain persisted,
and . . . well, he was pretty sure it wasn't raining.

He kissed her, a light brush of lips. She tasted of warm
female flesh and pleasure. He stifled a groan, his body reacting
with longing that nearly made him forget . . . "Rose, wake up.
We've got company."

She murmured, lashes fluttering. Her lovely dark hair spilled
over naked shoulders. So beautiful, his heart ached afresh.

Worth losing everything for?

He fluttered up, retrieved his trousers, and walked out to
face his fate.

Rose's little girl still lay napping on the sofa, one arm
thrown above her head. He whispered a sparkling charm, and
she sighed, falling into deeper, dreamless sleep. She didn't
need to see this.

Afternoon sunlight poured in, licking the floorboards with
gold. But it was easily outshone by silvery glory. Soft feathery
wings, the color of storm clouds. Black suit, neat iron hair,
steely eyes.

Japheth coughed. "I guess I should thank you for not coming sooner."

Gabriel leaned his elbow on the dark granite bench, lifting
the empty vial to the sun. Sunlight glinted on the golden
curves. "'The power to scorch men with fire,'" he quoted
blandly. "In case you're not keeping up—" He cast a mocking
glance over Japheth's half-undressed state. "The vampires are

all dead. Or their curse dissolved, thanks to your little accident. The city's on fire. The Apocalypse, however . . ." He
smiled, a flash of chilly sun. "Well, it doesn't matter who spills
the wrath, does it? But not how I'd expected this one would
turn out."

"Me neither." Japheth shrugged, square. "I did what I had
to, Seraph. I don't expect pardon."

"Japheth?" Rose emerged from the bedroom, blinking and
tucking the sheet around her lithe body. "What are you—?
Oh." She halted, awkward. "Sorry. I didn't realize . . ."

Gabriel swept her with a rain-dark glare. "Silence, human."

Rose stalked up to stand beside Japheth, eyes flashing.
" 'Silence, human'?" She mocked Gabriel's deep smooth
voice. "How about, 'screw you, angel'? Are all your lot this
stuck-up, Japheth? Because y'all could really use an attitude
adjustment."

Crazy laughter tempted Japheth, and he swallowed it. She
was amazing. He wanted to kiss her, strip her naked, take her
right there in front of Gabriel.

The archangel swept back stormy wings, a glittering ozone
breeze. "Such charming company you keep," he remarked
acidly. "Forgive me if I don't stay. But there's the matter of a
debt to be paid, soldier."

Japheth swallowed, cold. He'd thought he was ready for
hell. His courage had never failed him before.

But now the time had come . . . He wanted to fall on his
knees, scream, *No, please. Just give me a few moments longer.*

A few more moments with her.

But too late. What's done was done. And hell awaited him.

He squared his shoulders, taking a last breath of sweet
earthly air, and let his gaze rest on Rose's face.

She stared back, confusion glimmering in her eyes. His
heart ached, sweet and bitter. She was perfect. She was everything. She'd made him whole. For a few glorious hours, his
empty heart had filled . . . and that was worth any eternity of
torment.

Triumph glowed in his blood. *I win. You know it.*

I win.

His vision blurred, warm. He blinked, impatient, waiting for the fire.

Gabriel tucked the vial away in his inside pocket, and flickered his feathers. "Don't have all day. Are you coming?"

Japheth's numb wits refused him. "Huh?"

The archangel's thin lips pressed even thinner. "The demon prince is dead, isn't he?"

"Well, yeah, but—"

"Michael made you a promise," said Gabriel impatiently. "He can't be here right now. But I see no reason to renege. You wanted back into heaven? You got it."

Japheth reeled, and light exploded behind his eyes. Heaven. Redemption. An end to all his earthly suffering. No more ugliness. No more unspeakable emotion, fear, yearning.

Everything he'd ever thought he wanted.

He steadied himself. Blinked away the dizziness. Caught Rose's hand in his, and squeezed.

Gabriel sighed. "Well?"

Japheth swallowed. "No, thanks. I'll stay. If it's all the same to you. I, uh . . ." He smiled, as he realized it was true. "I like it here."

Rose's eyes shimmered wide. She gripped his hand, damp. "Japheth, you can't—"

"I can," he whispered. "I am. Peace, Rose Harley."

And strange, wonderful, heady warmth flooded his heart. Peace.

Gabriel's wing and eyebrow lifted in unison, displeasure or surprise or faint disgust. "I won't ask again."

"I know." Japheth's voice was steady. He squeezed Rose's hand tighter. "If you see Michael, tell him I said we're even."

Gabriel sniffed, haughty, and vanished in a pop of thunder.

Silence clamored . . . and Japheth's wings prickled, a faint shimmer of Tainted glory. He flexed his left hand, palm upturned. The twin-lightning sigil glowed, azure bright and true.

Japheth of the Tainted.

Rose stared at him, aghast. "Who was that? What did you do?"

"That was Gabriel." He grinned, and drew her close. "And I told him no."

"*Gabriel* was going to let you back into heaven, and you said *no*?" She shook her head, bewildered. "You crazy son of a bitch. Did you do this for me? Because I'm gonna kick your feathered golden ass—"

He cut her off with a kiss. She gasped, and kissed him back, and by the time they parted, his pulse hammered, his body afire with her rich velvet scent. "My heart's here," he whispered, crushing her close. "I don't want to leave."

"For a frosty-ass angel of death, you are *such* a fucking romantic." Rose tilted her head back, tugging at his hair, and sighed. "Bridie's watching us."

"She won't wake up." He kissed her throat, inhaling her. God, he felt drunk, high, up to his eyeballs in wonderful. He hadn't been drunk in fourteen hundred years.

About time.

She purred, nestling closer, and when he swept her onto her back on the warm granite bench, she yelped, laughing. "What about your precious rules, angel?"

"Let me think." He yanked the sheet away, baring her gorgeous body. He kissed her, wallowing in her skin's fragrant delight. She sighed in bliss, folding herself around and against him, and it only took him a few seconds to strip naked. She was already wet, longing for him. She eased him inside her, and he shuddered, so delicious and warm and right . . .

But the pleasure was matched by the delightful sunshine in his heart. Nothing so perfect could ever be evil.

You shall know the truth, and the truth shall make you free.

"Forget them and their rules," he breathed as he moved inside her. "You see me, Rose Harley. And I see you."

CHAPTER 48

On the catwalk atop Freedom Tower, Gabriel stood in hot summer wind, sniffing the stink of burned flesh. Below, downtown Babylon burned and rioted. He swept his gaze over the smoky horizon, unsettled. It had been . . . a strange day.

Behind him, the air stung with diamantine chill.

Gabriel didn't turn. "You took your time."

Michael strode up beside him. Their auras clashed, a painful frisson. "I was busy."

"So I hear." Gabriel tossed the empty vial. It tumbled, spun, catching the sun. "I think this is yours."

Michael plucked it from the breeze. He studied it, his icy eyes narrowing. "What do you want, Gabriel?"

"You killed Salome." A fact, not a question.

Michael shrugged. Snowflakes melted on the hot catwalk. "Luuceat killed Salome. I was just there when it happened."

"Don't lie—"

"What did you expect?" Michael laughed, grating. "You shouldn't have made her a Guardian if you didn't want her dead."

Gabriel swallowed angry thunder. "I know what you're doing. You want Lucifer."

"I want what I should've had the first time," corrected Michael smoothly. "You know him. You know what he's capable of. You just don't have the balls to finish him off."

"Last chance, Michael. I have my orders—"

"Fuck your orders!" The steel railing shattered in Michael's grip, and he flung the shards away with an electric curse that set the air alight. "When's the last time He said anything new? The Plan is obsolete, brother. A bunch of cryptic stone-age riddles. It doesn't make sense anymore."

"That's blasphemy."

"Blasphemy, hell. He gave the world to the monkeys and look what they've done with it. They spew their filth into the sky and shit in the water and scuttle about like rats, slaughtering each other in His name. He gave them everything and they pissed it away. That's what I call fucking *blasphemy*."

"Michael—"

"Enough, Gabriel!" Ice crackled along the catwalk under Michael's glare. "They had their chance. They wasted it. This world is ours now. And I don't want Lucifer in it. Stop me if you can."

Lightning forked, striking the catwalk. Frost blasted Gabriel's face. And Michael vanished.

Gabriel cursed, thunderous. *Lord, give me a sign. Tell me what you want. Did I make a mistake, all those years ago?*

Is it over, Lord? Do I let this run its course?

The sun glared, hot and silent.

And the archangel sighed, and flashed back to his empty heaven.

Across the city, high in another shining glass tower, the Demon King stood on a different balcony, watching Babylon burn.

Satisfaction warmed his cold flesh. All according to plan. The vials were emptying, one by one, their perverted wrath spilling out. Michael was corrupting himself, surely as hell was afire.

And the demon princes? Azaroth wrinkled his nose in distaste. Vile, carnal creatures. Expendable. Fluvium in particular.

A petty psychopath, better off burned. Likewise Luuceat. He'd used them. They'd done their jobs. Now, they were out of his way.

And he was only three vials from his goal. Satan, Lord of Torment, erupting from the pit. The final battle.

He sighed, triumphant. His side would win. The creature once named Lucifer was a fierce warrior, his unspeakable rage stabbed wild by millennia locked in a fiery black prison. And with Michael teetering on damnation's brink . . . well, he'd deal with Michael when the time came. And then no one would remain to defeat the beast.

Not Gabriel, that gray-feathered weakling. Not that crawling scum Dashiel, or his pitiful Tainted Host. No one.

No one except Azaroth. Lord of Emptiness and Despair. Second to Satan for thousands of years. Loyal caretaker in the boss's absence . . . and he'd been busy. His power now swelled unimaginably vast, strengthened by untold thousands of captured souls. He'd just proved that . . . unexpectedly, to be sure. But nonetheless.

The Demon King smiled, and cold wind swirled. Oh, yes. Hell would reign on this dismal earth and its wretched, wormlike creatures. Holocaust, unnamable torment and destruction . . . and when the stinking ashes settled? He and Satan—that aged, bleeding, exhausted warrior—would have a little chat about who should be in charge.

Oh yes, they most definitely would.

Azaroth turned his face to the restless sun, and allowed himself a moment to gloat. Yes, everything was certainly going according to plan . . .

Behind him, feathers rustled, a soft contented female sigh. His icy heart quickened, and warmed.

And his smile faded.

Everything except this.

He turned, and slid the tinted glass door aside with a spell-charged finger. Let the preferred illusion settle around him, soft black hair, pale skin, wiry limbs.

In his bed, Jadzia smiled sleepily. Pale blond feathers spread around her, a glittering halo. She stretched out one slender arm. "Shax," she murmured. "Come back to bed."

His chest contracted. She was so delicate and strong. So lovely.

So doomed.

It had happened by accident. A chance meeting, an opportunity to wreak amusing havoc. She was Dashiel's protégée, and Dashiel was his vilest enemy. He'd thought to use her. But she'd enchanted him. Impressed him with her courage. Bewitched him with her deep blue eyes.

And today, as she lay lifeless on those charred monastery stones, something deeply, strangely wonderful had happened.

Resurrection. The forbidden power still haunted his blood, a mocking echo of that bleeding, crucified trickster at Golgotha. He'd dragged Jadzia back from oblivion like a perverted savior. Used his deepest, darkest urges to restore her to life . . . and then . . . well, here she was.

Get rid of her. Wrap your hands around that pretty throat and take back the gift you gave her. Before she ruins everything . . .

Compelled, Azaroth slid into bed beside her. Her warm body molded to his, her lips parting under his kiss. Instantly, his ancient, cold body responded to her, aching hard. He stroked her, coaxed her open for him, drove himself inside her with a dangerous rush of delight, and the dizzying heat that tortured him was no illusion.

*An angel finds passion and danger in the arms
of an unexpected lover...*

FROM *NEW YORK TIMES* BESTSELLING AUTHOR

NALINI SINGH

ANGELS' DANCE

A Guild Hunter Special Novella

A gentle teacher and historian, Jessamy is respected
and admired by everyone who knows her. Yet, unable
to fly, she has spent thousands of years trapped in the
mountain stronghold of the Refuge, her heart encased
in painful loneliness ... until the arrival of Galen, warrior angel from a martial court.

Rough-edged and blunt, Galen is a weapons-master at
home with violence, a stranger to sweet words—but he is
also a man determined to claim Jessamy for his own ...
even if their exhilarating passion proves as dangerous as
the landscape of war and unrest that lies before them.

nalinisingh.com
facebook.com/AuthorNaliniSingh
facebook.com/ProjectParanormalBooks
penguin.com

M1190T0912